# HOW NOT TO DISAPPEAR

'[Clare Furniss is] a brilliantly talented writer…
moving, while also managing to be funny'
MAXIMUM POP

'Amazing… If you're into your kickass female characters
then you're going to NEED to stick your nose into
How Not To Disappear…SO GOOD'
SUGARSCAPE

'I loved this story'
THE BOOK BAG

'A beautiful, bittersweet story about family bonds, the
cycle of life and love in all its forms'
LOVEREADING4KIDS.CO.UK

'Talks of love, family and the defining nature of memories
in a way that is completely pitch-perfect'
SO MANY BOOKS. SO LITTLE TIME

Also by Clare Furniss

*The Year of The Rat*

# Clare Furniss

# HOW NOT TO DISAPPEAR

SIMON & SCHUSTER

First published in Great Britain in 2016 by Simon and Schuster UK Ltd
A CBS COMPANY
This paperback edition published 2016

3 5 7 9 10 8 6 4

Simon & Schuster UK Ltd
1st Floor, 222 Gray's Inn Road
London
WC1X 8HB

www.simonandschuster.co.uk

Simon & Schuster Australia, Sydney
Simon & Schuster India, New Delhi

A CIP catalogue record for this book is available from the British Library.

PB ISBN 978-1-4711-2031-2
eBook ISBN 978-1-4711-2032-9

Typeset in the UK by Hewer Text UK Ltd, Edinburgh
Printed and bound by CPI Group (UK) Ltd, Croydon, CR0 4YY

Simon & Schuster UK Ltd are committed to sourcing paper that is made
from wood grown in sustainable forests and supports the Forest Stewardship
Council, the leading international forest certification organisation. Our
books displaying the FSC logo are printed on FSC certified paper.

For my mum and dad, with love and thanks

I'm spinning, round and round, my arms held out, head thrown back towards the pale spring sun.

'Stop!' Mum calls out. 'Gloria, really! You're not a child. Seventeen is too old to be dancing in the middle of the Common.' Half laughing, but anxious, always anxious.

'I can't stop,' I call out to the blur that I know is her, the grey of her good Sunday coat and the fading blonde of her hair under her neat, blue hat, disappearing and reappearing, disappearing and reappearing, against the green of the Common as I turn.

'Please, Gloria. We'll be late. I've got to get the roast in the oven in time for Gwen and Vinnie. You know Vinnie is ever so particular about punctuality.'

'Vinnie,' I sneer. 'Who gives a damn about Vinnie and his punctuality?'

'Watch your language, Gloria, really.'

'Damn, damn, damn. Damn Vinnie. *Bloody* Vinnie.'

'Gloria!'

'I don't like him and I'm not going to pretend I do,' I say, laughing. 'Everyone's always telling me not to tell lies. You, Gwen, Sister Mary Francis. I'm telling the truth. I wish Gwen had never married him.'

1

'He just likes people to be punctual. It's because of him being a businessman, I expect.'

'It's because of him being an idiot.'

'Gloria!'

'He's rude. Even to Gwen. And he thinks he's better than everyone else. Just because he's rich. And anyway, who says he's a "businessman", apart from him? Everyone else says he's not much better than a crook.'

'Everyone who?'

'Just people.'

'Jealous, I expect.'

'Oh! Let's not talk about him,' I say. 'It's too beautiful a day to spoil with Vinnie. Let's just pretend he doesn't exist.'

'Gloria—'

'Go on! I'm pretending; are you? You see? Doesn't the sun seem to shine a bit brighter in a world with no Vinnie in it?'

Mum shakes her head. 'I don't know what gets into you sometimes.'

'It's Sundays,' I say, stopping spinning and trying to stand still but swaying a bit. My hair has come unpinned on one side and the wind blows strands of it across my face. 'Church. All that being quiet and looking like you're thinking holy thoughts. It's as if all the noise and unholiness builds up and builds up inside me and eventually I just have to let it out or I'd explode. You don't want me to explode do you, Mum? I'd make an awful mess.'

'You always make an awful mess.' She laughs her nervous laugh and shakes her head. 'You don't need to explode to do that. Now come on. Your father will be wondering where we are.'

She turns to walk on. But I can't follow. I can't bear the thought of lunch and Father drinking until he's all pink and sweaty and staring unfocused at nothing, half smiling, but angry in a secret way that you can only recognize if you know him. And Vinnie sitting there, his face as shiny as the Brylcreem in his hair, puffed

2

up and smirking, droning on about how well his business is doing and looking down his nose at us, making little comments to make Mum and Gwen feel stupid. And all the time knowing it's a beautiful day and I could be outside, I could be with Sam . . . Even thinking his name makes my heart skip a little.

I start spinning again, in the opposite direction and the feeling of it makes my stomach lurch gloriously and I can't help giggling.

'*Stop* that, Gloria,' Mum calls, sharp now.

'I can't,' I call out to her. 'I'd forgotten it could be sunny and warm. Isn't it funny how by the end of every winter we forget what it feels like to have the sun shining and not have to wear a coat? Doesn't it make your feet want to dance? Doesn't it make you feel light and free and as if you could just float off into the sky?'

I stop spinning and stagger, giggling, towards where Mum's waiting for me with her hands on her hips, grabbing hold of her so as not to fall over.

'No,' she says, her voice quiet. 'It doesn't make me feel like that.' I don't like to think of it, of how another spring might make her feel. She seems weighed down by it, the fresh pale sunshine and the thought of another year exhausting, not full of hope and promise. I feel a familiar flash of impatience with her, followed by the familiar pang of guilt that goes with it.

'That's because you're not dancing!' Holding both her hands I start to try and spin her round with me, like Louise and I used to do in the school playground. She smiles and for a moment I think she's going to let me. Then her face tightens and she forces her hands free of mine.

'What would Father think if he could see you?' she says. I look up at her and wonder if she was ever young and full of life like me, and I think how pretty she must have been once, before he broke her nose and her jawbone. He broke something else, too. Something I cannot name, that didn't crack or bleed or

3

bruise, but broke quietly and slowly over many years, and won't heal itself like bones can. She looks older than she is, faded. I feel as though one day I'll look at her and I'll be able to see right through her, as though she's slowly vanishing.

I let go of her arms.

'He'd think what he always thinks,' I say, turning away. 'That I'm going to hell and the sooner I get there the better.'

'That's not true, Gloria, you know it's not.' She tries to laugh, like she does when she's trying to placate him. It's a reflex, a defence; there's no humour in it, just a plea: *don't be angry*.

I turn back to her. 'I don't care what he thinks!' I shout, ignoring her plea, just as he does. 'And—' My voice fails, looking at her, thin and slightly hunched under her Sunday coat. It's as though she's always trying to make herself look smaller than she is. 'And nor should you.'

'Come on, love,' she says. 'You know he doesn't mean what he says when he's angry. He's not a bad man.'

'Really?' I mutter. 'Well, he's certainly not a good man.'

'He was a different person before the war.'

She always says this, as if it makes everything all right, as if it lets him off the hook for the drinking and the rages. I have no idea if it's true, or whether she believes it to be true even if it's not. When I was little, I thought perhaps she really meant it; that the person she married, the father I should have had, disappeared on a beach in France and never came back from the war. Maybe, in a way, that is what happened. I don't care. I know what he is now. It's all I've ever known.

Mum bends to pick up one of my gloves, which has fallen out of my pocket without me noticing. She hands it to me but I turn away. I can't bear her fear, her quiet desperation to prevent confrontation. It hurts to see it.

'I'm not afraid of him,' I say. 'I'm not scared of anything.'

I say it as clearly and firmly as I can, because if I say it often enough, perhaps I can make it true.

# Chapter one

From: hattiedlockwood@starmail.com
To: wilde_one666@starmail.com
Subject: On The Road

So, Reuben, I'm assuming you're still alive despite the fact
that I haven't heard a SINGLE BLOODY THING from you
since you got off the Eurostar THREE WEEKS AGO!?! I guess
you're just too busy leading the life of an international
playboy to worry about your oldest and dearest friends. By
which I mean ME, despite the fact that I am NOT old and
dear at all, but young and relatively cheap considering.

How is St Tropez? (Assuming you got to your dad's as
planned and aren't still under a table somewhere in St
Germain in an absinthe-fuelled coma like on the school
Paris trip?) UNBEARABLE, I expect. Far too hot. All those
beautiful people with their tans and their toned abs. The
clear blue sea and sandy beaches. The endless sunshine
and cocktails. I bet you find your thoughts often turn
mournfully to the drizzly London suburbs and all you've
left behind . . . Your dear co-workers in the Men's

Casualwear department at Debenhams who I feel certain are still lamenting the loss of your unique approach to customer service. Warm snakebite at The Lion. Chips with curry sauce and fights and vomit-dodging on the night bus. Didn't think about the gaping hole all of THAT would leave in your soul when you decided to go off travelling and Finding Yourself and all that, did you, Jack bloody Kerouac?

So anyway, things can TOTALLY be exciting here too because GUESS WHAT???? I passed my driving test!!!! I KNOW!!!! As miracles go, this is right up there with Lazarus and water into wine and you not failing GCSE Maths. Who'd've thought I'd ever be legally sanctioned to be in control of a moving vehicle? It's madness, I tell you. Celebrated by reversing mum's car into a pillar in the multi-storey. Oops. Haven't told her yet.

Anyway, motoring-related marvels aside, the summer holidays are turning out to be a Disaster Of Epic Proportions. Carl's being such a pain in the arse about the wedding I almost hope mum calls it off. He's booked a castle for the reception. Seriously. And he wants me to be a bridesmaid. In a PEACH DRESS. I'M NOT EVEN JOKING, REUBEN. Meanwhile the twins are madder than ever. Mum's working all hours, so when I'm not at the Happy Diner in my brown nylon air-stewardess-from-the-1970s uniform, my days are spent being tortured by Alice in the name of 'Science' (she's SO going to grow up to be a serial killer) or reading Watership Down to Ollie AGAIN. I know it off by heart, Reuben. Literally, I could go on Mastermind and answer EVERY BLOODY QUESTION ANYONE COULD EVER THINK OF about Fiver and Hazel and flipping Bigwig. And the worst thing is that no matter how many times we read it, it always makes both of us cry. Not saying I don't like a good cry but seriously, my life is depressing enough at the moment without any help from **SPOILER ALERT** dying bunnies.

And the Happy Diner is pushing me beyond the edge of sanity. I actually DREAM about the All-Day Breakfast of Champions. My hair smells of hash browns. It really does. I fantasize about ways of murdering Melanie the Manager. It's the only thing that gets me through the shifts. I can't work out whether her cleavage is constantly expanding like the universe or her tops are shrinking, but either way it's verging on pornography. She's always calling the boys into her office for a coffee and a Little Chat. Mack had to spend a good five minutes in the walk-in freezer after the last one. Needless to say she never calls me in for a Little Chat. She just gives me evils and makes me clean the toilets. She told me yesterday I'd actually look quite pretty if I did something with my hair. She suggested a perm. A PERM!!! Said it would help with the lankness, although it might be prone to frizz. I tell you she's evil. EVIL I tell you.

Kat's spent the whole summer so far off with all her art college friends pretending to be a tree as part of some kind of guerrilla eco pop-up something or other. I've only seen her once, at the pub with the other trees. She's irritatingly happy, although to be honest the trees seem like pretentious tossers to me, and I spent the whole evening trying not to notice that their faces were streaked with some kind of indelible green. She's still going out with Zoe-from-Kettering (remember Kat brought her to the pub that time – the condescending one with the nose) and totally loved

7

up. They've gone off to Edinburgh now because Zoe-from-Kettering's ex is in a fringe show up there or something. I can't keep up.

I stop typing and look out of the bedroom window for a while, wishing I'd had a chance to talk properly to Kat before she went. I watch the wind gently wafting the leaves of the trees that line the road. Actual ones, I mean, not just students painted green. The movement of the leaves is slow and soothing. Then I type:

Oh and by the way, you know how we accidentally had sex a month ago? Turns out I'm pregnant.

I stare at the screen. It makes my stomach flip, seeing it there in black and white. Worse even than the line on the pregnancy test somehow. I delete the words quickly. Once they're gone I feel a bit better. In their place I type:

So ALL my friends have abandoned me!! (Can you hear that violin playing in the background?) Mum and Carl and the twins are off to Mallorca soon and instead of the 'shenanigans' Carl thinks I'll be getting up to, I'll be here on my own with a ready-meal for one and a mug of cocoa. No danger of even a single shenanigan.

Meanwhile, no doubt, you're bathing in champagne with beautiful French heiresses or doing obscene things with cocktail waitresses. Again.

I feel tears pricking my eyes and I rub them away before they can fall and carry on typing.

8

Anyway, if you have 5 minutes to spare between your many assignations, send me an email, will you? Vicarious hedonism is better than none at all. And I miss you.

Yours a teeny bit resentfully if I'm honest,
Hattie xxx

I read it through a billion times, trying to see it as he will, editing it, hoping it sounds clever and funny and like I just wrote it in five seconds without even thinking about it, and not at all needy or desperate or like someone who might be pregnant.

I click Send and then I hug my arms round my middle and lean forward until my forehead is flat against the desk. The wood is cool and hard and I press my head against it until it hurts a bit. And I find that I'm crying, horrible, big, silent crying that feels like it's coming from a space inside me that's bigger than I am, bigger than the room, than the house, bigger than the whole city. I haven't cried like this in years. Not since Mum threw out all of Dad's old clothes. It must have been a few months after he died. She stuffed them in a bin bag and took them to the charity shop along with a load of baby clothes the twins had grown out of. When she'd gone, I went and looked at the empty wardrobe, the bare hangers swaying a little as I opened the door, and I cried more than I'd ever cried before. I don't know why. It wasn't like I missed Dad really.

I try not to think about that, or about Reuben, or what's going on inside me and what's going to happen next. I switch it all off and just let myself cry.

When the crying stops I look in the mirror. My face is puffy and sad and streaked with grey. I sort out my mascara and dab a bit of concealer under my eyes to make them look less red and blotchy. Bit of lippy. I smile at myself. Almost convincing.

All the time I'm doing it, I realize I'm half waiting for a reply from Reuben, waiting for my laptop to ping or my phone to buzz. As if. I should know him by now.

When I finally get a a reply, several days of denial and fried food and *Watership Down* later, it says this:

From: wilde_one666@starmail.com
To: hattiedlockwood@starmail.com
Subject: Re: On The Road

your hair smells of hashbrowns you say? thats actually quite alluring to a certain kind of man. so i've heard.

i'll write more soon. phenomenally hungover.

oh and i am never ever ever getting in a car with you. ever. can only assume you bribed the instructor. was it money drugs or sexual favours? all three? i'm guessing all three.

and who the hell is Jack keroauk>? dcos he play for Chelsea?

xR

PS can you think what I might have done with my left shoe? and er trousers? they don't seem to be where I am. was quite a night! least i think itwas

PPS also you have an over-punctuation disorder. all those
CAPITALS and exclamation marks make me dizzy!!!!!!!!!!!
or that could be the hangover

A whole week and that's it? I've been sitting here, pregnant
and miserable, waiting for hungover abuse and a lame football gag?

I type a reply saying:

FUCK OFF REUBEN AND NEVER CONTACT ME AGAIN.

But of course I don't send it.

## Chapter two

I'm sitting on the closed lid of the downstairs loo with the phone in one hand and yet another pregnancy test in the other, trying to get my head straight. I'm not being helped by the fact that on the other side of the locked door, Alice is pretending to be an FBI SWAT team.

'IT'S NO USE, PETROVICH!' she bellows in a terrible attempt at an American accent. 'WE GOT THE PLACE SURROUNDED. YOU BETTER COME ON OUT WITH YOUR HANDS IN THE AIR OR WE'RE COMIN' IN THERE.'

Anyone using the downstairs loo instantly becomes a criminal overlord, Nazi, orc, Dalek, elephant poacher or other variety of baddie in Alice's mind. She waits outside with an arsenal of guns, swords, bows and arrows and sonic screwdrivers, and lays elaborate traps for the unfortunate victim. We're used to it, but it can be unnerving for visitors.

'Jesus, Alice,' I yell back. 'Can I not go to the loo in peace? Just once?'

'No!' She's angry with me because I wouldn't let her watch a documentary on psychopaths, making her settle instead for one on shark attacks.

*'Please.'*

'IT'S OVER, PETROVICH. WE KNOW WHAT YOU'VE DONE. WE KNOW WHAT YOU ARE, YOU COLD-BLOODED, TWO-FACED, MURDERING MONSTER.'

I stare at the pregnancy test in my slightly shaking hand. There's no way I can bring myself to wee on it with Alice only metres away. Carl was supposed to take them out today but he's been called in as emergency cover for Senior Zumba at the gym because one of the other trainers called in sick. I'd hoped the sharks would keep Alice occupied for a while, but clearly they hadn't been gruesome enough to hold her attention.

'Mum hid two packs of Jaffa Cakes at the back of the food cupboard last night,' I say in desperation.

The shouting stops and as I hear Alice's feet thumping down the hall to the kitchen, I focus again on the little white stick of doom. It's the fourth test I've done. As soon as I was late I started to worry. After a week I bought a test, but somehow even though I was fearing the worst, when it was positive I didn't believe it could be right. So I got another kit, a different brand this time, just in case. And then, panicking, I bought another, just to be sure. I know it's stupid. The leaflet that came with it makes it all too clear that you can't get a false positive: if there are two lines you've got a bun in the oven and that's all there is to it. And the test kits are bloody expensive. Plus there's the whole embarrassment of buying them – I've had to go to different shops each time to avoid being served by the same person, and every time I imagine what they're thinking as they take my money: wondering if it'll be positive, and how old I am, and thinking how glad they are they're not me. And then there's the bother of secretly getting rid of them afterwards so that no one will find them. I'm so paranoid about Mum or Carl finding them I can't risk putting them in the kitchen bin. But to get to the wheelie bin at the side of the house I have to go through the kitchen to get to the back door and there's always someone in there cooking or doing homework or watching TV, waiting to pounce on anyone who might be wandering through clutching a stash of positive pregnancy tests. So I've got them all hidden in several layers of carrier bags under the bed so I can sneak them out of the house and get rid of them anonymously.

But after I got Reuben's email I was so desperate not to be pregnant that I decided I had to check just one last time. It still seems so completely impossible that I keep thinking it must be a mistake. First off, the whole concept of pregnancy suddenly seems absurd. I've known the facts of life since I was six and Kai O'Leary explained the process of baby-making in detail to the whole of Squirrel Class during Circle Time, in spite of Mrs Bean's best efforts to distract us. We all took it pretty well, I think, although some of the parents weren't best pleased. And then at secondary school it was all condoms on bananas and diagrams labelled with unlikely words like 'epididymis' that made me and Kat giggle.

So *obviously* I've known where babies come from for pretty much as long as I can remember. And yet now, suddenly, it seems so improbable. You have sex, and then a *whole new person* grows inside you and eventually emerges, painfully, out of what Kat refers to as your lady-regions? It's bizarre, when you really stop and think about it. And deeply disturbing. Kind of like a horror movie.

And on top of all that, I'm just not the sort of person that gets pregnant. At the end of Year Eleven in our yearbook I was Most Likely To: Become An Accountant. I'd been pretty upset at the time. 'But I don't want to be an accountant,' I'd said to Reuben. 'Why would they think that? I want to be a film director. Or an archaeologist. Or an internationally acclaimed tap dancer.' 'Don't worry,' Reuben had said. He'd been judged Most Likely To: Be Divorced By Somebody Famous. 'I don't suppose they even know what an accountant is. It's just code for "we think you're clever and boring".' '*Great,*' I said. 'That makes me feel much better.' But looking back, even accountancy seems better than pregnancy. Anyway, how stupid do you have to be to think you won't get pregnant because you're not that sort of person? Not really a very reliable method of contraception, Hattie, actually.

Anyway, I decided I'll just give it one more try, take one more test, just in case I was some kind of scientific anomaly or I'd just happened to buy a rogue batch of faulty tests or . . . something. Anything.

And if it's still positive I'll have to phone the doctor's and make an appointment. That's the deal I've made with myself. I've been trying to psych myself up to call the surgery all week. But each time I panicked and bottled it at the last minute. Making an appointment would mean it was real. There would be no going back. I'd have to tell someone else; I'd have to sit face to face with someone and say the words out loud: *I'm pregnant.* And then I'd have to answer humiliating questions. *Yes, I did have unprotected sex.* (I pictured the doctor looking at me, wondering how I could have been so stupid. How could I explain that it didn't seem like that at the time? It just seemed right.) *How long ago? Four weeks. And five days, actually. I know it was stupid. But I thought it was the wrong time of the month and—*

15

And what? I try to think of reasons, to explain it to myself.

*And I was a bit drunk and emotional and . . .*

And?

*And it was Reuben.*

I imagine the doctor staring over her glasses at me, stifling a sigh, trying not to look judgemental but inside thinking, *You silly, silly girl.* And me sitting there, knowing she's thinking it and knowing she's right. Why hadn't I done anything about it afterwards? I could have got the morning-after pill. But the truth is I was too confused, too busy trying to pretend it hadn't happened, that nothing had changed.

And then there would be more questions to answer. *Symptoms? A missed period. I'm a bit tired. The smell of congealing saturated fat at the Happy Diner's been making me feel even queasier than usual. Alcohol makes me want to vomit. Other than that, nothing really.*

And then . . .

Then she'd ask me more questions. Difficult questions that I don't know the answer to.

Yes. Then I'd have to make decisions.

I stare at the inevitable new line that has appeared in the little window of the pregnancy test. The fact that I knew it would be there doesn't help. I'm overwhelmed by the reality of it suddenly. I feel so tiny, sitting here in my little locked room and the world outside seems so big and loud and difficult and dangerous. I lean my head into my hands, press my fingers against my eyelids and watch the bright flashes of light flicker and pulse. Maybe I'll just stay here for a while. Maybe for ever.

'Oi! Hattie!' Alice hammers loudly on the door. 'They were *HOBNOBS*, you liar! I hate bloody Hobnobs.'

'Wrong cupboard,' I lie, not opening my eyes. 'Check the other one. And don't swear.'

'Piss off.'

She thunders away to the kitchen again and I open my eyes. Right. This is it. I have to make the phone call.

I get the scrap of paper with the doctor's surgery number scribbled on it out of my jeans pocket and take a deep breath. My finger is poised, shakily, over the button. There is no escape.

And then the phone rings.

'Is that Mrs Lockwood?' It's a woman's voice. She's elderly, I'd say, with an accent, Irish, I think. 'Mrs Ruth Lockwood?'

'No,' I say, my mind still on the call to the doctors I'd been about to make, relief flooding through me at this excuse to avoid it. 'She's at work. Can I give her a message?'

'Well,' the voice says, doubtfully. 'Could you tell her it's . . . it's about her husband.'

'She hasn't got a husband. Do you mean Carl?' A thought occurs to me. 'Wait, you're not one of his clients, are you?' Carl is very popular among the older ladies at the gym, and Mum's always joking that he's going to end up with a stalker. Perhaps that day has come.

'No, I mean her husband,' the voice says. 'Dominic.'

*Dad?*

I'm so surprised I don't know what to say. Someone wants to talk about Dad? No one ever talks about Dad. Mum certainly doesn't. Ollie asks me about him sometimes; he and Alice were just babies when Dad died. I don't like to admit I don't remember much either.

'But he's dead. He died eight years ago.'

'I know. Are you . . . Harriet?'

'Hattie,' I say, surprised. 'Who did you say you are again? What's this all about? Did you know Dad?'

'No, I didn't know him, dear. My name's Mrs Cleary. You can call me Peggy. But I'd really rather speak to your mother about it, Harriet, if you don't mind.'

'*Hattie*. Look, Dominic was my dad so if you've got anything to say about him you can say it to me. I'll let Mum know.'

'Well,' she says, hesitating. 'It's not really about him, as such. It's about a relative of his.'

'A relative?' I thought hard. I didn't think Dad had any relatives apart from Nan, and she died when I was a kid. He was an only child and Nan had brought him up on her own; his dad had died in an accident when he was a baby and no one was ever allowed to talk about him.

'Yes, his aunt. Gloria. Your grandmother Gwen's younger sister. She's my upstairs neighbour. And my—' she pauses a little doubtfully— 'my friend. In a manner of speaking.'

Nan had a sister? But that can't be right. I'd have known.

'I'm sorry, I think you've made a mistake. I've never met her. No one's ever even mentioned her. Nan didn't have a sister.'

'She hasn't been in contact with her family for many years, Harriet,' Peggy says. 'Well, you know how families can be. And, well, Gloria is . . . well, she's what you might call "a bit of character".'

'YOU LIED!' Alice is yelling. 'You totally and utterly lied about the Jaffa Cakes, you . . . LIAR! Bloody, bloody liar!' She starts hammering on the door again.

18

'Pack it in, Alice,' I hiss, putting my hand over the receiver.

'Are you still there?' Peggy says.

'Yes,' I say loudly. 'But could you speak up a bit? My sister is also what you might call "a bit of a character" and is being *extremely noisy and annoying and immature*.'

'I was saying she hasn't been in contact with her family for a very long time.'

'Why not?'

'Well . . . that's not really . . .' The voice on the other end of the phone pauses uncertainly.

The voice outside the door doesn't.

'*COWBAG. FIEND. STRUMPET. IGNORAMUS. BUMFACE.*' Alice's fires her varied repertoire of high-decibel insults at me through the door.

'And why has she decided to get in contact now?'

'Well, now you come to ask—' there's an awkward pause— 'she hasn't as such. Not *as such*.'

'What do you mean?'

'The thing is, she's not very well, Gloria. She's really not very well at all. That's why I wanted to speak to your mother, you see? You're her only living relatives, as far as I know. And I just thought, with her being the way she is and with her not having anyone else . . . well, I thought you might want to know. About her being poorly. I thought perhaps you might want to see her.'

'Right.' My mind is flitting around from the pregnancy test to Dad to mysterious aunts and then to whether Alice is going to manage to break the door down, and this whole conversation is so weird that it's hard to focus on what she's saying.

'She's been ever so low, you see, Harriet. I think it would give her a real lift to have some visitors. To know that somebody cares. We all need our family, don't we?'

'Hmm,' I say, unconvinced, as Alice's stream of abuse continues. '*HAG. MONSTROSITY. WEIRDO. LOSERRR.*'

'Could you pass the message on to your mother and ask her to call me? Tell her it's very important.'

'Yep, sure . . . hang on, I need to get a pen.'

I frantically wrap the pregnancy test in loo roll and the carrier bag it came in and stuff it as deep into my jeans pocket as it will go, pulling my top down over it to try to disguise the bulge. I've been wearing long tops anyway because my jeans are a bit tight and the button keeps popping undone at unfortunate moments. I've been wondering whether this is because of being pregnant but, to be honest, they've always been a bit tight and the industrial quantities of pancakes I've been eating are more likely to be the cause. Still though, the thought makes me a bit panicky. How soon will I start to show? Are there any other telltale signs that might give me away to someone who's been pregnant themselves (i.e. Mum)? Beyond the obvious I know nothing much about pregnancy.

I open the door and am hit in the face by a stream of water being fired by Alice from a water pistol.

'For Christ's sake, Al!'

'Are you all right there, Harriet?' comes Peggy's voice from the dripping phone.

'You shouldn't have lied about the Jaffa Cakes!' Alice yells.

I run past her to the living room where Ollie is sitting, oblivious to the great white shark rearing up behind him on the TV screen, humming 'Somewhere Over the Rainbow' and drawing an elaborate picture of our family in rabbit form. I'm pleased to see that I'm the next biggest after the Ollie and Alice rabbits. Mum and Carl are minor rabbits, and I smirk at the fact that the Carl rabbit is wearing a figure-hugging peach-coloured jumper that does him no favours.

'Give us a pen will you, Ols?'

He looks up, smiles his faraway smile, and hands me a silver glitter pen that I use to scribble down Peggy's number and her address, which is in London. I read it back to her while Alice tries to rugby-tackle me from behind.

'You won't forget to pass the message on, will you?' Peggy says, doubtfully. 'I'm . . . concerned.'

'No, I'm fine,' I say. 'Just a misunderstanding about Jaffa Cakes.'

'I meant about Gloria, dear.'

'Oh yes,' I say. 'Of course.'

'I want to help her but . . . She's not exactly what you might call an easy person. And now, with the way she is . . . You will make sure your mother understands it's serious?'

'Don't worry,' I say from where I'm lying, Alice sitting triumphant on my chest, whacking my head with a cushion. 'I'll let Mum know.'

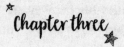

It's late and pouring with rain by the time Mum gets in, so she's soaked through as well as tired.

'Sorry I'm so late again, love.' She grimaces as she folds down her umbrella and it sprays water over her and the floor. 'Honestly, I've had the day from hell. Had a load of work dumped on me that's got to be done before we go to Mallorca. And then Bernard collared me and that was another hour of listening to him waffle on about budget cuts and belt-tightening. And then . . .'

I tune out. How boring it must be to do a job like Mum's. I mean, she seems okay with it, but is this how she thought her life would turn out? What would she be doing if she hadn't had me and the twins? I think again about the pregnancy test. I never did call the doctor. Maybe I'll just leave it a few more days. I want to get my head straight first. If only I could talk it through with Kat . . .

'Hattie?'

'Sorry, what?'

'Is Carl getting the twins to bed?'

'No, he's already gone out.'

She gets a bottle of wine out of the fridge and pours herself a glass as she sits down at the table and eases her feet out of her work shoes.

'Sorry, Hats, you've been left in charge again. You're too reliable, that's your problem. We take you for granted.'

'It's all right,' I say. 'It's not like I've got anything better to do.'

'Poor Hattie,' Mum says. 'Are you missing Kat?'

I am. I haven't even spoken to her since she went to Edinburgh so she doesn't know I'm pregnant yet. I arranged to meet up with her at the pub before she left so that I could tell her I was worried. It was before I'd done the first test and I suppose I just wanted her to be reassuring and tell me I was being silly and I'd probably just got my dates wrong. I hadn't even told her about me and Reuben (partly because she was never around and partly because I knew she'd give me a hard time about it) but I decided it was time to fess up and talk it all through. Kat always makes me feel better, despite her brutal honesty. She always makes everything seem simple somehow. And then Zoe-from-Kettering and the trees turned up too, so I couldn't tell her. And now she's hundreds of miles away. I sent her a text yesterday morning saying: **Hope you're having an amazing time. Call me when you can. I've got something important to tell you xxx.** I got a reply saying: **Love u Hats, speak soon xxxxxxxx** but I haven't heard any more from her. I'm sure it's Zoe's fault. She's quite a lot older than us and very possessive and doesn't like Kat having other friends.

'Yeah,' I say to Mum. 'She's not going to be back for ages. It's not the same without her and Reuben around. And for all I know, Reuben might never come back.'

'Hmmm.'

Mum avoids talking about Reuben if she can help it. I don't think she even realizes she's doing it; she just sort of edits him out whenever she's talking about my friends. I asked her once why she doesn't like him and she'd looked at me, surprised. 'I don't *not* like him,' she said. 'I like him very much. He's charming. And he's always very sweet with the twins. It's just ... Reuben always makes me think of that Chinese curse: *May you live in interesting times*. Reuben is "interesting times" in teenage boy form. Which is why you like him, of course. I get that.' She'd smiled and cupped my face in her hand for a moment. Thinking about that moment now, I'm overwhelmed by the urge to tell her I'm pregnant, to share the burden of it.

'Mum,' I say, not looking at her, 'I've got something to tell you.' My heart pounds at the thought of just saying the words to her. Just two words ...

'Oww!' she yelps. 'Dammit!' I look up to see that she's stepped barefoot on a Lego space ship that Alice has left abandoned in the middle of the floor.

'You okay?'

'No,' she says, sitting down and rubbing her foot. 'Why does Carl never get them to tidy up? Where is he anyway? It's not Hips, Bums 'n' Tums at the Leisure Centre is it? Or has he got a session at the new place?'

I grin. 'You mean "Pecs Appeal"?'

Mum grimaces. 'No,' I say. 'Some wedding thing. He was meeting with the florist. Or was it the caterers? I dunno. He said you knew about it. Think he was hoping you'd be there, whatever it was.'

'Oh God, I completely forgot,' she says, sighing. 'Honestly, this wretched wedding is turning into a full-time job.'

'You do want to get married, don't you? I mean, you're not having second thoughts?'

'No,' Mum says, a bit too quickly, not meeting my eye. 'No, of course not! Why would I?'

'I dunno,' I say. 'You don't exactly seem enthusiastic about the whole choosing the flowers and dress and stuff.'

There's a tiny, guilty bit of me that almost hopes she might call it off, just so I can get out of the peach-brides-maid-dress horror. But I don't really want her to. Poor Carl. He and Mum have been together four years now, and he's wanted to marry her all that time. Mum finally gave in last Christmas after his billionth proposal. He'd be devastated if she called it off and I don't want that. I enjoy winding Carl up, and he may be a bit of an idiot, but he's all right really, and he adores Mum.

'I'm just snowed under at work that's all,' Mum says. 'And the whole big *Hello!* magazine wedding thing . . . I don't know. It's not really me. But it's what Carl wants.' She smiles. 'I'm tired, that's all. And hungry.'

'We saved you some pizza,' I say. 'Might be a bit cold, though.'

She pads across the kitchen and nukes the leftover pizza in the microwave.

'How have things been here?' she says. 'You look tired too. Pale. Not coming down with something, are you?'

'No,' I say. 'I'm fine.'

'What were you going to say before? You said you had something to tell me?' My heart thuds. Perhaps I should tell her . . . But I can't. She's just got in. She's tired. The twins are charging about like rocket-fuelled maniacs upstairs. I can't just blurt it out. And I need to work out how I feel about it, what I want to do. It's my problem, my mess. I have to sort it out.

'A woman phoned earlier,' I say instead.

'Hmmm?' Mum sits back down and looks at the unappetizing blob of soggy dough and rubbery cheese on her plate.

'It was kind of weird, actually.'

'Was it?' she says vaguely, as she chews her pizza and flicks through the post, sifting out the bills and junk mail and takeaway leaflets.

'Her name was Peggy.'

There's a loud shout of 'GERONIMO!' from upstairs (Alice) and then 'Watch out!' (Ollie) followed by a very loud crash. Mum sighs. 'Have the twins had a bath?'

'No.'

'This week?'

'Yes. Ish. Probably.'

'Are you two going to be ready for bed when I come up?' Mum calls upstairs.

'Mummyyyyyyy! You're back!'

'Did you bring Jaffa Cakes?'

'Pyjamas on,' she calls up to them. 'Or no bedtime story.'

'Did you ever meet any of Dad's family apart from Nan? Or did he ever talk about them?'

She looks up sharply at the mention of Dad. We never really talk about him. It's not that we can't. We just don't. There's no reason to. Even when he first died we didn't talk about him that much. He'd been away so much when he was alive that he hadn't really been part of the day-to-day, so things didn't really change when he died. Not in a way I could explain anyway. And I knew somehow, like you do when you're a kid even though no one tells you stuff, that although Mum would have talked about him if I'd wanted to, she didn't really want to.

'Why do you ask?' she says.

'The phone call.' Mum looks blank. 'The one I just told you about?' She hasn't heard a word I've said. 'The woman I spoke to – Peggy – was the neighbour of someone called Gloria. Dad's aunt, supposedly.'

'His *aunt*?' Mum pulls a face. 'I don't remember him ever mentioning anything about an aunt. Or about any family other than his mother. He didn't really talk about that kind of stuff. I always got the impression they were a bit . . . dysfunctional. But who knows?' She shrugs. 'Family wasn't really his thing.'

It's an innocent-sounding comment but there's an edge to her voice as she says it. I know she's not just talking about long-lost relatives.

'Well,' I say, defensive, 'maybe he didn't get on with them. Anyway, he was hardly ever here, was he? He could hardly be popping round to see his aunty every weekend if he was in Iraq or Bosnia or wherever, could he?'

Even we didn't see much of him, except on TV, reporting from faraway places I knew nothing about except that there were wars going on there. I didn't mind. I was used to it. I loved it when he was on the news, looking all brave and blond, sometimes in a flak jacket. My dad on telly. When I was little, Mum would call me in to see when he was on. But then, when I was a bit older, she wouldn't watch. Sometimes you'd hear explosions in the background or gunfire, but I knew it couldn't hurt him. He'd told me it couldn't and I'd believed him. He was invincible.

'What on earth did she want anyway? This aunt?'

'It wasn't her, it was her neighbour. Apparently the aunt – Gloria – she's not very well. Sounded serious. She was worried. Peggy, the neighbour, I mean. She thought maybe you'd want to know.'

'Why would I want to know? Given that I've never heard of her before today?'

I stare at her. 'She doesn't have any other family.'

'Sorry,' she says, rubbing her head as though it's aching. 'That came out wrong. Of course I'm very sorry that she's ill, but we're hardly family, are we?'

'Well, Dad was,' I say. 'So I am, even if you're not.'

'They can't exactly have been close, Hats. I don't remember her sending us any Christmas cards or inviting us round for Sunday lunch, do you? And now she's ill she wants to play happy families? It's a bit weird, isn't it?'

'I really don't think—'

'I mean, as far as I know she wasn't even at Nan's funeral. Her own sister. Perhaps they didn't get on. How did she know how to get hold of us anyway? How did she have our phone number?'

'I don't know.' I hadn't thought of this. 'I didn't ask. Phone book? Internet. I dunno. It's not hard to find people, is it? She knew about us, though. She knew my name.'

'Did it sound as though she wanted money? Do you think that was it?'

'No! I'm sure that's not what she meant. Peggy's just worried about this woman. Gloria. I think she just thought maybe we'd like to see her. And maybe it would help her to have some family around. She's an old lady and she hasn't got anyone else. Peggy didn't ask for anything. She just made it sound as though she was lonely.' I edit out the bit about Gloria being 'a bit of a character'.

Mum sits down and sighs, topping up her glass of wine.

'I don't mean to be unkind, Hats. It's just I've got enough on my plate what with work and the twins and Carl's wedding-planning frenzy without long-lost relatives who aren't even *my* relatives turning up and needing my help. There must be someone else who can help. Some real family.' She shakes her head and picks the pepperoni off her pizza. 'Typical of Dominic that he can still manage to cause me problems even now,' she mutters.

Which really winds me up. How dare she criticize Dad?

'Well, she's *my* real family even if she's not yours. And Alice and Ollie's too. If you can't be bothered to go and see her I'll go on my own.'

'Fine,' Mum says. 'You do that, if it's what you want to do.'

'Good. I will.'

Mum sighs again and puts her hands over her eyes. Then she pushes her hair back and looks at me. 'I'm not going to argue about this, Hattie. I haven't got the energy. If you want to go and see this woman, I'm not going to stop you. But I don't think it's a good idea. Perhaps there's a reason your dad never talked about her.You've got to admit it's pretty strange, isn't it? That she's never been mentioned or turned up before now? I mean, even Nan didn't talk about her. There must have been some kind of family feud. Best not to get mixed up in it, love. You don't know anything about her.'

'I know she's a sick, lonely old lady. What else do I need to know?' I say, piously.

At which point a fishing net is plunged over my head from behind.

'Gotcha!' shouts Alice, who STILL hasn't forgiven me for the Hobnobs thing.

'Ow!' I snap. 'Alice that really hurt.'

'*And* you're not in your pyjamas,' Mum says. 'Horrors.' Alice is still in her 'spy outfit' of wetsuit and night goggles.

Ollie is behind her in the Sleeping Beauty dress Alice was given for her birthday and tried to set fire to.

'Don't be cross with her, Hattie,' he says. 'She was just practising stealth. You need it to be a spy.' It's true that stealth isn't Alice's usual tactic and it could certainly do with a bit of practice.

'Okay,' I say, still annoyed with Alice, but knowing that Ollie hates her being told off.

'Come on,' Mum says, shepherding Alice upstairs. 'If you're really quick, there might still be time for a story.'

When I look up Ollie's hovering, watching me.

'Are you okay, Hattie?'

'I'm fine, Ols. Never better.'

'You don't seem like it. You seem a bit sad.'

'Do I?' Ollie notices everything about everyone. He'd make a much better spy than Alice, for all her night-vision goggles and invisible ink pens.

'Is it because Reuben's not here?'

'No!'

'I'd be very sad if Alice was in another country.'

'Yes, but Ollie, Reuben isn't my twin, is he? He's just my friend.'

'He's your best friend. Alice is my best friend.'

'It's different, Ols.' I look at my little brother, his serious face frowning as he thinks, completely at odds with the garish pink dress. 'But yeah, I do miss him. He'd only be getting on my nerves if he was here, though. Now go and get your jammies on.'

Ollie comes over and gives me hug.

'Night,' I say, kissing him on his freckly nose. 'Love you.'

'Night, Hattie,' he says.

I sit for a minute after he's gone, trying to imagine how it would feel to have your own kids. How much you'd love them. The thought of it terrifies me. But then what if you didn't? What if you had a baby and you didn't love it? What if it just got on your nerves all the time and you were stuck with it for life? People with kids always say you can't hate your own, but do they just say that because they have to? And anyway, if you never wanted the baby in the first place, wouldn't it be different?

I wish I could talk to someone about it all. I wish Kat was here. I don't want to tell her on the phone. And she's never exactly been Reuben's biggest fan. I send her a text. **Hey HellKat, you ok? Call me? xx**

But she doesn't.

## Chapter four

From: hattiedlockwood@starmail.com
To: wilde_one666@starmail.com
Subject: NOT BEHAVING LIKE A KNOB: A BEGINNER'S GUIDE

I've been ignoring you, Reuben, but a) I don't suppose you've noticed and b) even if you had, I'm resigned to the fact that you wouldn't even know why. So let me help you out.

I know you're *terribly* busy lounging around on beaches and everything but you're supposed to be my friend and part of what that entails, dearest Reub, is NOT FORGETTING ABOUT ME JUST BECAUSE I'M NOT WHERE YOU ARE.

So, here is a short guide to not being COMPLETELY CRAP: (YES I KNOW I'M USING TOO MANY CAPITALS BUT I DON'T CARE.)

1) Open laptop or take phone from pocket*
2) Write friendly, informative message, featuring amusing

anecdotes and asking after the wellbeing of your dearest friend (me)

3) Send

4) Go back to whatever more interesting thing you were doing

*Ideally when sober enough to type

Not difficult really, is it?

ANYWAY because I am a generous and forgiving person I am writing to you anyway.

So, I know you're probably still getting over the driving test excitement but I have more thrilling news . . . I have discovered a mystery long-lost relative. A great-aunt to be precise. Her neighbour phoned earlier in the week and told me about her. Gloria. She's my dad's aunt and she's not very well so she wants us to go and visit. But the weird thing is, none of us knew anything about her till now. No one ever mentioned her before. Do you think there was some massive family feud? Or maybe she's got a criminal past or she was locked up in one of those awful lunatic asylums or something? I hope it wasn't something boring like someone being left out of someone else's will or not turning up to someone else's wedding. Mum's being funny about it. She says it's because she's so stressy about work and Carl's wedding madness. But also I reckon it's because this old lady is related to Dad. I don't know. It's like she wants to pretend she was never married to him. Anyway, I've decided I'm going to go and see the great-aunt – Gloria – on my own. Everyone else is off having an adventure.

You're in France (I assume) being an international playboy. Kat's in Edinburgh being a drama queen. Admittedly, going to see my great-aunt isn't quite as glamorous as partying in Biarritz or wherever you are but still, it's better than another day at the Happy Diner. I was having a totally rubbish day at work and I just told Mel that's it. I'm going. There's nothing you can do about it.

Other than that everything's the same. Of course.

Hattie x

PS Please tell me you know really that Jack Kerouac is an American novelist, poet and literary iconoclast and NEVER, under ANY CIRCUMSTANCES, played for Chelsea.

In fact, my conversation with Melanie hadn't happened quite like that. I'd been on my break and Mack had said, 'Coming outside? Or have you still "given up"?', waving a pack of Marlboro Lights at me. And I'd gone, because it was a lovely sunny day and the staff room in the Happy Diner where we have our lunch was hot and airless and full of angry wasps, which are my all-time nemesis. And also because I really, really wanted a cigarette, and because I just wanted everything to be like it always is, and I thought what harm can it do, really? But then outside had been just as hot and everything smelt of traffic fumes and the cigarette had just made me feel sick and dizzy and a bit sad.

Mack looked at me.

'You all right?' You seem a bit down.'

I shrugged, because I didn't quite trust myself to speak, and Mack said, 'Hey, what's up, Hats?'

He's a good bloke, Mack. Not the sharpest knife in the drawer, if you know what I mean, but kind. I managed to say, 'Oh, you know,' but I knew I was going to cry and I think he did too, so I just legged it to the loos and locked myself in a cubicle and cried in there. And I was just thinking how wrong it was that I'd become the sort of person who's forever crying in toilets, when I heard the door go and someone came in. I sat and waited for whoever it was to go to the loo and then go away but they didn't, they just made lots of clattering and hissing noises, so eventually I had to wipe my eyes and go out. And when I did it was only Evil Melanie, spraying her non-lank hair until it was this kind of rock-hard halo, surrounded by a hanging cloud of Elnett fumes that made my mouth taste of chemicals. She stared at my face, which I thought I'd done an okay job of cleaning up in the toilet cubicle, but could now see in the mirror was all smeary and puffy, and said, 'You've been crying, haven't you?' Queen of Empathy, she is, our Mel. I mumbled something about hay fever, as she got out a bottle of perfume, dabbing some on her neck and then, horrifically, into her monumental cleavage. And then she fixed me with this deeply unnerving look and said, 'I've thought you've been looking a bit peaky recently. And don't think I haven't noticed Mack sneaking you extra pancakes when you've been on your breaks.'

And I panicked big time, because Melanie has this amazing instinct for gossip and sussing out people's darkest secrets. According to Mack, she worked out Big Jim's dad was gay before Big Jim did. So I said, 'Yeah, my great-aunt's really ill actually. I didn't want to say anything but it's really getting to me.' And then without planning it, I said, 'I was wondering if I could swap my shifts so I can go and visit her.'

She gave me a hard stare. Asking to swap shifts is a worse offence than poisoning the customers, in Mel's book.

'We think she may not have long,' I said, and I sort of did a bit more crying, for effect.

'Yeah okay,' she said. 'You'll have to make it up next week, though.'

'Thanks Melanie,' I said. 'Really appreciate it.' And she said, 'Here, borrow my mascara. You look a right state.' When I'd finished sorting my face out she said, 'You sure that's all it is? Nothing else going on? You can tell me if there is, you know.' And I said, 'No, that's all,' and practically ran out of the loos before she could say anything else.

When I got back to the staff room, Mack had left some pancakes for me, covered with a plate to stop the wasps getting them, which set me off crying again, but luckily no one was around to see.

From: wilde_one666@starmail.com
To: hattiedlockwood@starmail.com
Subject: Re: NOT BEHAVING LIKE A KNOB: A BEGINNER'S GUIDE

What? NO! Are you out of your tiny mind? You're going to meet someone you've never heard of who claims to be your mysterioius great-aunt? This is a terrible idea Hats. Really. Possibly your worst ever. And there's some pretty stiff competiton for that particular accolade.

It's like paying money into the bank account of whoever sends the emails saying they're the son of the deposed king of Nigeria. Did they ask you for your pin number/date of birth/mother's maiden name/inside leg measurement? Your 'great-aunt' is probably some evil fraudster type with a terrible beard and a yacht full of Bollinger and glamour models all funded by gullible fools like you, and you'll end up on Watchdog sounding like a right bloody mug and all the viewers will laugh at your idiocy. Or even worse the aunt will turn out to be a serial-killer pervert with a penchant for short buxom know-it-all redheads. And when you get there you'll be led down to a dungeon filled with such people, all chained up, wearing metal bikinis like Princess Leia when she's Jabba the Hut's slave, and you'll all be forced to submit to his every twisted desire (ok we may possibly be wandering into the world of mty own private fantasies here) But anyway the point is that as you are led down to your doom all your fellow stunted flame-haired know-it-alls will all be wailing HOW COULD WE HAVE BEEN SO STUPID AS TO FALL FOR THE GREAT-AUNT STORY? HOW?! WE, WHO ALWAYS THOUGHT WE WERE SO BLOODY CLEVER.

And in twenty-seven years time, when I come and rescue you, (because obviously I will have been on the case, Sherlock-Holmes-like, for all those years, following up leads the slow witted police miss, never giving up on you) you will be wizened and grey and broken while I will have retained my youthful good looks and possibly even become sexier with age in a sadder worldly kind of a way. And the frist thing you will do is to put your aged, bony hand on my surprisingly muscular upper arm and say REUBEN I TOTALLY SHOULD HAVE LISTENED TO YOU. IF ONLY I HAD HEEDED YOUR WISE WORDS ABOUT NOT FALLING FOR THIS NONSENSICAL DRIVEL ABOUT GREAT-AUNTS NONE OF THIS WOULD HAVE HAPPENED.

But on the plus side there will probably be a film of it and Johnny Depp will play the older me.

So don't say I didn't warn you. And anyway even in the highly unlikely event that she does turn out to be your actual great-aunt, do you really want to spend all that time and money going to visit an ill pensioner you don't know? You'll probably just spend the whole day looking at old photos of her long-dead cats and changing incontinence pads. Although I suppose she might be really ill and secretly a millionaire and put you in her will.

I'm JOking. Obviously.

DON'T GO.

xR

PS I am fine, thnks for asking. Oh no, you didn't did you – Is that part of the sulking thing? Well I am tickety-boo actually (just to annoy you) apart from my liver which is um not. Anyway must go. These cocktails won't drink themselves you know. xx

From: hattiedlockwood@starmail.com
To: wilde_one666@starmail.com
Subject: Re: NOT BEHAVING LIKE A KNOB: A BEGINNER'S GUIDE

Reuben,

I am not completely stupid. I have not given anyone my pin number. And while you may think it's a waste of time to

show some concern for an elderly relative, I don't.
Anyway, you just enjoy your cocktails.


PS BUXOM? You make me sound like a medieval serving
wench. And I'm not a Know-It-All. I'm just cleverer than
you.


I press Send. But the truth is I'm smiling as I do it. It's the
first proper email I've had from Reuben since he left. It's
funny. It's Reuben funny. It's everything I've been missing
about him. And he's been thinking about me.

'Emailing Reuben by any chance?'

Carl comes into the kitchen as I'm typing and I shut my
laptop quickly.

'No.'

'Yes you were.' He grins. 'I know you were. You were
smiling as you were typing.'

'No, I wasn't. Anyway, I was . . . researching something,
actually. For college. About . . . Shakespeare.'

He laughs and nods in a *Yeah, right* kind of a way. Bloody
Carl.

'So have you heard from him?'

'Who? Shakespeare?'

'*Reuben*,' he says, pretending to cuff me round the head.
'Smart arse.'

'Oh, him. Yes, as it happens, I have.'

'Nice of him to get in touch. Still living the high life is
he?'

I shrug. 'No need to make it sound like a crime, Carl. If
your dad was loaded and lived in the south of France
wouldn't you go and stay with him instead of staying here
being a personal trainer to the aged?'

'How long's he going to be out there for then? Has he said?'

'Dunno. He's staying with his dad for a while and then maybe going travelling a bit. Maybe a few months. Maybe a year. I don't think he knows.' I try to sound bored, as if it's no big deal to me what he does.

'So he's definitely dropped out of college? Not coming back?'

'Nope.'

'Shame,' he says. 'For you, I mean.'

'Why for me?' I say. 'I'm the one who's going to get my A-levels and go to university and have a brilliant time and then get an amazing job and earn loads of money and change the world.'

*Unless I have a baby.*

'Course you are, Hats,' Carl says. 'That's my girl. I just meant you'll miss him.'

I shrug.

'Well, fair play to him, I suppose,' Carl says. 'You can learn a lot by seeing the world. Wish I'd done more of it myself when I was younger. Travel and adventure is in some people's nature you know. Restless souls. Itchy feet.'

'Oh what? Like *yours*, you mean?'

He nods, completely missing my sarcasm.

'That'll be your athlete's foot. You should really see someone about that.'

Carl's always going on about how he's got Irish and Guianese grandparents and how he's got Traveller roots back in the distant past; he's trying to make himself sound a bit exotic and interesting. He grew up in Surrey. It's like how he always says he wants *Wild Thing* played at his funeral. As Kat said, he doth protest *way* too much. Although

40

Kat did once say she thought he was quite sexy in an obvious, toothpaste-ad kind of way, for a dad. I pointed out that he's not a dad and that, what with Kat being gay and all, she may not be the best judge of Carl's sexiness, obvious or otherwise. She rolled her eyes and said, 'Just because people fancy girls it doesn't mean they can't fancy boys too.' And I said, 'Yes, I'm perfectly well aware of that, thank you, but have you ever actually once in your life fancied a boy?' And she said, 'Not yet.' So I said, 'And if you ever do fancy a bloke, is it really likely to be Carl?' And she said, 'Ew, no, not in a billion years. But he's the kind of bloke my gran would describe as "dishy",' and I said, 'EXACTLY, THANK YOU, I REST MY CASE.'

Mum doesn't seem to notice that Carl isn't in fact exotic *or* interesting. Maybe that's what love is: the failure to notice your beloved's inherent ordinariness. She once said Carl was her Heathcliff, by which I think she meant all rugged and good-looking and in love with her, rather than a sadistic, damaged and obsessive madman. And I laughed and said if someone made *Wuthering Heights* into a musical and there was a TV show to choose who would play Heathcliff, they'd want someone who looks exactly like Carl to win. He's like Heathcliff Lite. Heathcliff ÷ ageing boyband singer + catalogue model = Carl. When I told him this he thought it was a compliment. Mum knew it wasn't.

'Oh, you're soooo clever aren't you, Hattie? So bloody *clever*.'

'What, so now being clever's a bad thing?' I said innocently. 'That wasn't what you said when I was doing my exams.'

Mum gave me her Someone-*Please*-Remind-Me-Why-I-Ever-Had-Kids look.

I smiled at her sweetly but I knew really I was being a bit mean so I offered to make Carl a cup of tea and he was pathetically grateful, which made me feel bad but also completely right about the Heathcliff thing.

The most annoying thing about Carl, apart from his tendency to wear tight-fitting pastel-coloured clothing and the fact that he can never quite manage to walk past any kind of reflective surface without checking himself out, AND the fact that he can refer to himself in the third person as The Bingo Wings Buster, is that he never quite knows whether he's supposed to be my parent or my friend. When he moved in four years ago he was full of how he's not trying to replace anyone and it's not his role to give me a hard time blah-de-blah. But he can't help himself. It'll be evening, and Mum'll be upstairs working or out at one of her things – yoga or Italian or Mindfulness – and he'll be all 'Hey, Hats, how you doing?' or 'D'you wanna bottle of beer?' and I'll know he's about to start on one of his 'I Know I'm Not Your Dad But . . .' conversations about how important it is to knuckle down and get my grades, or drugs, or positive body image or whatever. Or about Reuben.

The last one was about Reuben, back before he went away. Looking back, it makes me think maybe Carl's not as stupid as he looks because it was way before what happened with me and Reuben, that weekend in Norfolk. I didn't know it was going to happen then. Didn't even want it to. Not really. Not *exactly*.

'I hope you know what you're doing with Reuben,' Carl had said.

'I'm not doing anything with Reuben.'

He raised an eyebrow.

'Not like that,' I said. 'I've told you. He's my *friend*.'

Carl just stared at me.

'What?' I folded my arms and stared back. 'Are you seriously telling me you think it's impossible for men and women to just be friends?'

He shook his head. 'I *know* men and women can just be friends, Hattie.' He looked at me. 'But I don't think you and Reuben can.'

I didn't know what to say for a second. I felt myself blush, as though he'd caught me doing something embarrassing.

'I'm going out with William, in case you'd forgotten.' (Which I was at the time. More or less. It was just before he dumped me because he felt our relationship had begun to 'lose its spark'. I was furious that lethargy and not wanting Reuben to be right meant I hadn't got round to dumping him first.)

Carl laughed.

'What?' I said, folding my arms and trying to look him in the eye but not quite managing it.

He shook his head. 'William.'

'What about him?'

'Well, exactly.'

I tried to think of an indignant reply, but somehow nothing came out so I just sat there with my mouth open, knowing I looked stupid.

'Don't think I haven't noticed you ignoring his phone calls,' Carl said. 'Making excuses not to meet up with him.'

'No I don't. I really did have a headache.'

'I thought you were dyeing your hair.'

'I was going to. But then I . . . forgot.'

Carl smiled and shook his head. 'Hattie, I can always tell whether it's Reuben or William calling by your face when you look at the caller ID on your phone. When it's William, your face looks a little bit like it did that time when you put your boot on and Alice had filled it with jelly. Whereas when it's Reuben—'

'Yeah, all right, Carl,' I cut in quickly. 'I know you're just trying to wind me up and you're not going to. So you might as well give up now.'

He laughed and then carried on looking at me in his sad-eyed way that would probably get his Senior Zumba ladies a bit over-excited but I think just makes him look slightly vacant. 'I'm only trying to help, Hats. I just don't want you to get hurt. I like Reuben, I really do. He's funny. He's fun to be around. But he's—'

'He's what?'

'He's . . .' Carl paused. I could tell he was choosing his words carefully. 'He's not a person you want someone you care about to fall in love with.' He looked away from me as he said it.

'Well,' I said lightly, 'if anyone I care about looks like falling in love with him, I'll be sure to pass on the warning.'

We haven't really talked about Reuben since then, until now. I've avoided Carl's 'I Know I'm Not Your Dad But . . .' chats since what happened between me and Reuben in Norfolk, in case he could tell somehow. And, since I missed my period and started to suspect, I've tried to avoid conversations with Carl completely. Somehow he seems to have a knack for getting under my skin. Perhaps he really does understand me better than I want him to. I can't risk him working out that something's not right. Sure enough, he now gives me one of his concerned and understanding looks.

'You sure everything's okay, Hats?'

'Course.' I smile brightly. 'My days are spent serving deep-fried lard to the ungrateful and the morbidly obese. My evenings are spent being tortured by my deranged siblings. I'm totally living the dream.'

I know Carl likes my sarcasm. Sure enough he laughs.

'You know Al and Ollie think the world of you. And your mum and I really appreciate you doing your bit looking after them over the holidays while we're both so busy.'

'I couldn't take you away from your work, Carl. I'd feel personally responsible if the Hips, Bums and Tums of south London started to sag because of me. I couldn't have that on my conscience.'

As I'm speaking, an email from Reuben appears. I'm probably happier than I should be that he's got in touch again so soon. I try not to let it show but of course Carl clocks it.

'Oh,' Carl says with a smirk. 'Who's that from then? Shakespeare?'

I open it, already grinning as I read:

From: wilde_one666@starmail.com
To: hattiedlockwood@starmail.com
Subject: Re: NOT BEHAVING LIKE A KNOB: A BEGINNER'S GUIDE

Oh by the way Hats I'm going travelling for a while. with Camille. french girl ive met. she's very . . . well french if you know what i mean. tres hot Hattie. tres tres hot. you'd like her.

anything going on in your lovelife or shouldn't i ask? please dont tell me youve got back with William. life's too short for Williams Hats. Find a male Camille thats my advice. that sounds wrong. find yourself a hot enigmatic frenchman is what I mean. doesn't even have to be french. could be i dunno italian. german even if necessary. basically someone you don't really speak the same language as. thats my advice to you Hattie. you can have that for nothing. Much better idea than going round bothering elderly relatives who might really be psychopaths, don't you think?

xR

'You sure you're all right, Hats?' Carl says. Not bad news is it?'

'I said I'm fine, Carl,' I snap. 'Anyway, shouldn't you be at octogenarian boxercise or tasting gluten-free wedding cakes or something?'

From: hattiedlockwood@starmail.com
To: wilde_one666@starmail.com
Subject: Re: NOT BEHAVING LIKE A KNOB: A BEGINNER'S GUIDE

Reuben.

a) No. There is nothing going on in what I laughingly refer to as 'my love life'.
b) Why oh why must you keep bringing up William? I stopped going out with him FIVE MONTHS ago Reuben. I think maybe you have some kind of weird William fixation. Please never mention him again. He was SO INCREDIBLY DULL that if you didn't keep going on about him I'd have completely forgotten him by now. Let's all MOVE THE HELL

ON, shall we? We all make mistakes – you more than most.

c) How am I supposed to find a smouldering non-English-speaking sex god in the Happy Diner hmmmm? Tell me that.

d) Is your recipe for a happy and satisfying relationship *really* to find someone you can't talk to? Ever considered a career as an agony aunt, Reuben? Relationship counsellor? No? Good. DON'T.

e) I'm not sure why Camille being hot and French should mean I like her, though I can certainly see why it means you would.

Hattie

But Reuben's last email has made my mind up completely about visiting Gloria. If I don't go Reuben will think it's because he told me not to and he'll think he was right. And he's not. He's an idiot. I'm going to prove him and Mum wrong, and I'm going to prove to myself what a good person I am, thoughtful and responsible and caring, not feckless and stupid, which is how I feel.

Yes. I don't care what everyone else says. I'm going to visit Gloria.

## Chapter five

It's a Tube ride and a bus journey to Gloria's flat in north London. Even though Peggy gave me detailed instructions when I phoned her to say I'd be coming, I get off the bus too early and have to walk the rest of the way, past newsagents and cab offices and bookies and Turkish cafés and food stores with shelves filled with crates of fruit, kebab shops and bakers selling piles of baklava. It's a bustling, busy place, the noise of traffic and music floating down from the windows of the flats above the shops and thumping out of passing cars and sirens blaring somewhere further along the road. I turn off the main road into more peaceful, tree-lined roads of tall, bay-windowed houses, past a school, deserted for the summer. It's a sunny day and I enjoy the walk through this part of my city I've never been to. Okay, it's not foreign or exotic, but it's new to me, and it feels almost like a small adventure. On the Tube, pressed up against other people's sweaty armpits, I'd been asking myself whether I'd done the right thing travelling across London to see an old lady I know nothing about when I could have spent my day off sunbathing in the garden but now, as I get closer, the sun reflecting in the windows of the

48

houses, the buzz of a lawnmower and the smell of grass being cut somewhere nearby, I'm sure I have. After all, if I'd been at home I wouldn't have relaxed. I'd have worried. I still haven't phoned the doctors. It's more than five weeks now, time's ticking by. There never seems to be a time when the surgery's open and no one else is around. Even as I think it, I know it's a lame excuse. I've got to stop putting it off . . . I push the thought away. Today is about Gloria. I'm relieved to have something else to think about.

All the houses along the road I scribbled down with Ollie's glitter pen are the same design, old with big bay windows, but they all look quite different. Some are dark, dirty yellow brick with peeling paintwork and grey net curtains at the windows, others have been cleaned up and are painted dazzling white with window boxes and hanging baskets. Some are still houses, but many have been divided into flats with multiple buzzers and bells.

As I reach the house I see that a person who must be Peggy is looking out for me from the window of the downstairs flat, overlooking a neat square of front garden. She waves energetically as she catches sight of me, and then disappears behind net curtains, reaching the front door before I get there.

'Harriet?' She smiles and the smile seems to take up most of her face. 'Come in, dear, come in. I'm Peggy, of course, and Malcolm's just – MALCOLM,' she bellows down the hall. 'Harriet's here.' She's a tiny woman, with skin that's a web of wrinkles, and very dark, bright eyes. Her hair is an unconvincing black. It's hard to guess how old she is. Very, I'd guess, but she's so lively and alert and quick-moving that she seems younger. She hurries in front of me through the dark communal hallway to the open front door of her flat, talking all the way, not pausing for breath. 'Lovely to see you, dear, lovely, such a shame your mother wasn't able to come. How was the journey? Did you get the train? And the bus? And did you eat? Awful food they give you on the trains now. There's some cake here in case you want it. Lemon drizzle? Malcolm does like his lemon drizzle, although the doctor says he shouldn't really, what with his heart. Or I can make you a sandwich if you'd like that? I can do ham? Or cheese? You're sure? Well, you'll have a cup of tea won't you? *Malcolm!*' she calls again as we step through the door into the flat. 'Put the kettle on will you? Harriet needs a cup of tea and some cake. You do like lemon drizzle don't you, Harriet? Or biscuits? We've biscuits if you'd rather have biscuits? Malcolm likes a fig roll. But I prefer Bourbons myself. Do you care for a Bourbon biscuit yourself, dear?'

She pauses for breath at last.

'Oh, well, yes, please. But please don't go to any trouble. I can always just go up and see Gloria and have a cup of tea with her?'

'Well now,' Peggy says in a significant-sounding tone. 'The thing is, it might be best if we have a little chat before you go up to see Gloria. Just about ... Certain Things. *Malcolm*! Hurry up with that tea, will you? Poor Harriet's parched, aren't you, Harriet? Sit down, dear, sit down, rest those feet of yours.' She gestures to a large, floral armchair and I sink down into it, tired from the journey. Malcolm, an elderly man with thick, white hair, brings in the tea and pours it for us.

'So, now. I was just going to tell Harriet here a bit about Gloria, Malcolm. Before she goes up to see her.'

'Ah,' says Malcolm. 'Well, don't tell her too much or she might not go and see her at all.'

'*Malcolm*!' says Peggy. 'He's only joking, dear.'

Malcolm does a sort of cough.

'She's quite a character.' Peggy smiles and takes a sip of her tea. 'As I may have mentioned. Ever so well spoken. "The Duchess", we call her.'

'That's one of the things we call her,' Malcolm says. 'When she goes putting her records on at top volume in the middle of the night we call her some other things.'

'*You* do, Malcolm,' Peggy says forcefully, giving him a look that clearly means 'shut up'. From his expression, I'm guessing it's a look he's used to. 'And shame on you for it. Anyway, Harriet doesn't want to hear all about you and your coarse language, do you, Harriet, dear?'

'She plays records in the middle of the night?' This wasn't what I'd been expecting.

'Oh yes,' says Malcolm, nodding. 'Opera. Edith Piaf. Janis Joplin. And musicals of course. *Cabaret*, that's her favourite. You name it—'

'The thing is,' Peggy interrupts, 'as I mentioned on the telephone, dear, she hasn't been very well. She's a little . . . unpredictable.'

'And she likes a drink,' Malcolm adds.

'A drink?' I chew on my lemon drizzle cake. The Gloria I'd imagined, who looked a bit like the grandmother in Alice and Ollie's *Little Red Riding Hood* book, and who probably had one of those shopping trolleys and possibly some kind of a paisley shawl, disappears.

'Well, yes, there's that. She's always liked a drop, that's true enough. But recently, well . . . you'll see when you meet her. She's always been a bit – what's the word, Malcolm?'

'I can think of several words, but I couldn't possibly say them in front of Harriet here.' Malcolm winks at me.

'Eccentric,' Peggy says firmly. '*That's* the word. She's always been a bit eccentric, Harriet. And I don't mean that as a criticism. She's a very clever lady, very interesting when you get talking to her. But you should be prepared for the fact that she's not exactly what you'd call house-proud.'

'You can say that again.' Malcolm snorts.

'Things are a little . . . chaotic in her flat. But then again they always were. Gloria was never a great one for tidying up. It's the artistic temperament I expect. She was an actress, you know.'

'No,' I say. 'I don't know anything about her. And I'm surprised she knows anything about me. How did she know my name? And our phone number for that matter?'

'I think Gwen must have given them to her. Your granny.'

'But I thought you said they weren't in contact?'

'Well,' Peggy says, looking a bit flustered. 'I'm not sure, dear. Perhaps they patched things up before your granny passed away. It often happens when people are near the end, doesn't it? But you'd have to ask her about that. The thing is, Gloria's getting a bit forgetful, Harriet. I mean, we all are, aren't we, Malcolm? And what with her liking a drop . . . well, it's hard to know, isn't it? Some days she's absolutely fine and she can remember things from forty years ago, no problem. But it's getting her down, you see, and she's got it into her head . . . I mean she's not getting any younger and what with the gin and whatnot . . . perhaps that's all it is. But she's convinced herself . . . She can be a bit dramatic.'

I feel like I ought to say something but I'm not sure what, so I just nod.

'Well, anyway.' Peggy says, 'You'll see.'

Once I've eaten what Peggy considers to be an acceptable amount of cake and assured her that I really don't need a sandwich, she decides that Malcolm should take me up. 'Gloria likes you, Malcolm,' she says when he protests, and then to me, under her breath, 'She flirts with him something terrible, Harriet.'

My heart's beating fast as we walk up the stairs and I realize I'm nervous. Why have I really come here? Because I want to help an old lady? Because I'm curious? Because everyone told me not to? Because it's a good excuse not to think about my own problems for a while? None of these seem like very convincing reasons at this precise moment.

As we get towards the top of the stairs I hear a man's voice coming from inside the flat.

'Has she got someone in there with her?' I call up to Malcolm, who's a few steps ahead of me. 'Perhaps I should come back another time.'

I feel quite relieved that I might have an excuse. He turns and smiles.

'That's Richard Burton.'

'Richard Burton?'

'You know, the actor.' Malcolm stops and leans against the bannister, out of breath. 'Married Elizabeth Taylor. Twice. Lucky so-and-so.'

'I know who he was,' I say. 'But what's he doing in my great-aunt's flat?'

Malcolm laughs.

'Reading *Under Milk Wood*. It's one of her records. One of her favourites. We hear it a lot. Richard's a lovely speaking voice, but at one o'clock in the morning you could do without it.'

We reach the front door and Malcolm knocks on it. There's no response, just the boom of *Under Milk Wood* vibrating through the door. Malcolm knocks again.

'Gloria! It's Malcolm. I've Harriet here with me, Gloria. You remember we talked about young Harriet coming round? Your nephew Dominic's girl?'

Still nothing.

'Do you think she's okay?' I say.

'She'll be fine. Maybe just dozed off.' Malcolm rummages in his jacket pocket and brings out a key. 'Like I said, she likes a wee drink, does Gloria,' he says, conspiratorially. I look at my watch. It's just gone eleven thirty.

'Oh,' I say, trying to sound totally okay about the whole thing.

'We had spare keys cut because she kept losing them,' Malcolm carries on. 'And a couple of times she's gone out and left a pan of something boiling on the hob. We've only known about it when the smoke alarm's gone off. Just as well I fitted that alarm for her.'

I stare at him. 'But that's really dangerous.'

'I know. But you try telling her that. We're coming in, Gloria!' he calls cheerily through the door. 'Hope you're decent!' He winks at me and smiles, then turns the key in the lock.

I follow him into the flat and am hit by a rancid smell – something rotting, combined with smoke and general staleness, with an underlying whiff of public toilets. I try not to react but for a second I think I'm going to be sick and I clamp my hand over my mouth.

'Oh,' Malcolm says, apologetically, pulling shut the door to the kitchen, which seems to be the source of the worst of the smell. 'I should have warned you about the, er . . .' He waves his hand in front of his nose to indicate 'foul stench'. 'She does sometimes forget about things in the fridge. Peggy pops up every now and then when she's out or asleep and tries to give the place a quick once-over,' he stage-whispers. 'But Her Ladyship doesn't like it.'

I follow him through the dark, poky hall into a light, high-ceilinged room at the front of the house, and stop in the doorway, looking around in wonder. It's like one of those old bric-a-brac shops. Every surface is full of unlikely objects. On the mantelpiece there are china shepherdesses, a lurid figurine of the Virgin Mary, ships in bottles, dried flowers, Christmas cards, a scattering of what look like old theatre tickets. There are ashtrays of every variety on shelves and tables, some nicked from pubs by the look of it, others made of crystal or plastic or ceramic, and one on its own chrome stand. Most of them are full of dog-ends. There are teetering piles of newspapers and magazines, some of which look quite recent, others curled and yellowing. There are shelves and shelves of books. On the wall there are three flying ducks soaring above what looks like an expensive painting. There's an old-fashioned desk in the corner of the room, covered with fountain pens and piles of notebooks next to an incongruous-looking sleek silver laptop. Beside that there's an ancient-looking portable TV. A few empty gin and champagne bottles are among the ornaments, and a selection of full ones sit on a table next to the bureau. A motorcycle helmet rests on a footstool next to the fireplace, a ukelele casually leaned up against it. In one corner a stuffed ginger cat stares glassy-eyed at me from the shadows. The whole place is both unsettling and incredible. I wish Reuben could see it.

Gloria herself is reclined on a rather battered, moth-eaten chaise longue in the bay window at the far end of the room, with the sun shining in on her. Her thick hair is dyed a startling, glamorous red. She is wearing a flowing, purple velvet dressing gown that even from here I can tell has seen better days, and oversized sunglasses. Next to her on the wooden floor are two bottles of champagne, one empty and toppled onto its side, the other newly open. Standing next to it is a full glass.

She doesn't acknowledge us in any way, just lies so still that I wonder for a moment if she's asleep. Then without turning her head she says, 'Decent, darling? I should hope not,' and reaches down for her glass of champagne.

Malcolm laughs a bit nervously. 'So, Gloria, this is Harriet—'

'Hattie,' I correct automatically.

'Hattie, yes, of course. You remember Peggy saying she was coming to see you?'

Gloria doesn't respond.

'She's Dominic's daughter,' Malcolm persists. 'Remember you and Peggy had that chat about Dominic, your sister Gwen's boy, God rest his soul? And her soul too, of course.'

Gloria sits up, slowly, and pushes the sunglasses back on her head to reveal vivid blue eyes: eyes that, even through the heavy layer of make-up, I can see are like mine, and like Dad's. Nan's too. It's a shock, somehow, seeing someone I almost recognize in this unexpected person, but reassuring too. Proof that there is a link between us. She seems so alien, so unlike what I was expecting, so unlike what I remember of Nan, who was always so neat and brisk, so unforgiving of unbrushed hair or unpolished shoes or smeary fingerprints left on her patio doors, so impatient of daydreaming and dawdling – can this woman really be Nan's sister? But yes, her eyes tell me that she can, that she is. She stares at me for a while, still not speaking, and I don't know what to do, so in the end I pick my way across the jumbled room and I'm unsure whether to hold out my hand to her or give her a kiss so I just stand there awkwardly in front of her.

'It's so lovely to meet you at last,' I say, blushing at how formal I sound.

She carries on staring at me and eventually she takes my hand.

'Peggy made you come, I suppose?' she says. Her voice is deep and theatrical.

'Well, she phoned, yes. But she didn't force me or anything. I mean, she didn't threaten me with violence or blackmail.' I smile, sensing hostility, trying to diffuse it with a lame attempt at humour like I always do.

'I wanted to come,' I persevere. 'I'd have come before but I didn't know anything about you until Peggy told me. I mean, I didn't even know you existed.'

'No,' Gloria says, and she smiles a humourless little smile that makes me wonder. 'I don't suppose you did.'

There's a silence, and I want to fill it but I can't think of anything to say that won't come out wrong. I want to ask her what's the matter with her and whether she knew Dad well and why she wasn't at Nan's funeral, and why they lost touch. But none of those feel like things you can ask someone you've just met, even if they are a bit drunk on champagne at eleven thirty in the morning, so the silence just grows more awkward. And all the while Gloria is staring intently at me, her eyes scanning my face as though she's looking for something specific that might be hiding there, and I feel so self-conscious that eventually I have to pretend I'm looking for a tissue in my bag.

'Well now,' Malcolm says eventually, slapping his hands together, full of fake cheeriness. 'You ladies have a lot to catch up on, and you don't want an old fella like me getting in the way now do you? So I'll leave you to it.'

I want to yell 'NO, YOU CAN'T GO' but instead I smile and say, 'Thanks Malcolm.' Gloria blows him a kiss. 'Adieu, dear heart.'

'Pop in and say goodbye before you go, won't you, Harriet?' he says.

'They'll be asking for a full report,' Gloria says. 'Him and that busybody wife of his.'

Malcolm laughs. 'You've a vivid imagination, Gloria.'

'You don't know the half of it, darling,' she says, raising an eyebrow, and Malcolm hurries out before she can elaborate.

She lies back on the chaise longue and pulls the sunglasses back down to cover her eyes. Behind the enormous, enigmatic lenses I can't tell whether she's got her eyes open or not. Is she looking at me? Is she waiting for me to speak? Or has she decided to go back to sleep? What with the smell and the weirdness of everything and being pregnant I'm starting to feel a bit wobbly, so although Gloria doesn't offer me a seat, I try to clear a small space among the ancient copies of *Private Eye* and *The London Review of Books* that are piled on the sofa and squeeze myself into the gap. I sit awkwardly in silence, smiling in case she's looking me. Eventually I clear my throat, just in case she really has dozed off.

'So . . .' I say, trying to sound positive, but realizing as I say it that I don't really have anything to add.

'Hmmm?' Gloria says, turning her head to me as if she'd forgotten I was there. 'Oh, yes.' She sounds mildly disappointed.

'Drink?' she says, waving in the direction of the champagne bottle.

'No thanks,' I say. Pregnancy is turning out to be a bit like a very long hangover. My head is fuzzy and aches and even the smell of alcohol makes me want to puke. I'd kill for a glass of water but I can't really face venturing into the putrid-smelling kitchen.

'Suit yourself,' Gloria says, sounding offended. 'So, what story did they concoct to make you come here? That I'm some poor little old lady? Or that I'm mad and need locking up? Or perhaps you thought I might be at death's door with a large fortune?'

I assume she's joking, but if she is there's no sign of it, no flicker of a smile or any suggestion that behind the sunglasses there's a twinkle in her eye. 'Peggy just phoned and said you were dad's aunt and that you weren't very well and that she thought you might appreciate a visit. That's all.'

'Hmmm.' She makes no attempt to hide the fact that she doesn't believe me.

'And why did you come?'

To be honest, I've been asking myself this same question since I arrived here. What was I thinking? Reuben had been right for once, not that I'd tell him that of course. It was a crazy idea.

'I'd have thought you'd have better things to do, a girl of your age. You're not one of those saintly, do-gooding types are you?' she says, suspicious suddenly, and raises her sunglasses to look me in the eye. 'Because I can't be doing with any of that. If you're hoping to convert me on my deathbed, I can tell you now you're wasting your time. I'm a lost cause.'

'No!' I say brightly. 'Nothing like that. I just wanted to meet you. It's not every day you find out you've got a long-lost relative, is it?'

'And?'

'And what?'

'Oh, come on,' she says. 'There must be more to it than that.'

'My mum didn't want me to,' I admit. 'I suppose that was part of it.'

She looks pleased, though whether because she was right or because she'd been disapproved of I can't tell. 'That's more like it. And?'

'And my friend, Reuben. He said you'd be a mad psychopath and that it was a stupid idea to come and visit you.'

'Did he, indeed?'

'Yes. I wanted to prove him wrong.'

'Perhaps he wasn't,' she says.

*Exactly*, I think.

'So you came here because everyone told you not to?' She half smiles. 'That rather runs in the family I'm afraid.'

'And the other reason . . .' I hesitate. 'Well, Dad died a few years ago and I don't really remember that much about him.' The words come out in a jumble. I hadn't planned to say this. To be honest I hadn't even realized till now that this is part of the reason I'm here. 'There were questions I never got to ask him.'

Gloria looks at me blankly.

'Nothing big,' I say hurriedly. 'I mean, just stupid stuff about him growing up. What he was like when he was my age. I don't know. I just thought you might have some photos or, you know, maybe you'd remember his birthday parties or seen him in a school play or something. Anything really.'

Gloria pulls a small tin of long, thin cigars and a lighter out from under a faded patchwork cushion on the chaise longue, and takes one out.

'Well, I'm afraid I can't help you there.' She says it with a finality that makes me afraid to ask anything else, about why she hadn't been at Nan's funeral and why none of us really knew anything about her. 'You've had a wasted journey.'

'Oh, no, I didn't mean it like that,' I say quickly, trying not to feel disappointed. 'Like I said, I wanted to see *you*. And Peggy thought a visitor might cheer you up.'

Gloria doesn't say anything. The notion of my visit cheering her up now seems about as ridiculous as Reuben's dungeon full of Princess Leias. This isn't how it was supposed to be. The Gloria I'd vaguely expected to find here – the little old lady who looked a bit like what I remember of Nan with white hair set in a perm and soft blue cardigans and rose-embroidered handkerchiefs and a faint scent of lavender – she'd definitely have been cheered up by my visit. We'd have watched *Countdown* together and listened to *The Archers* and she'd probably have taught me how to knit or darn socks or something useful like that. We'd have gone for a little walk if she'd been up to it, perhaps to the park, and she'd have laughed at me for ordering a decaf skinny vanilla latte with soya at the café. 'You young people,' she'd have said, fondly. 'Everything's so complicated these days. I can't keep up. Just a plain old cup of tea for me.' And then when we got back she'd have got out a cake she'd made specially for my visit and said, 'Oh, it's lovely to have someone to bake for again!' and then we'd have talked about Dad and all the hilarious scrapes he got into as a kid. She'd say stuff like, 'Oh yes, he was a real live wire, that one. Always knew he'd go far.' And when she got tired I'd have made her go and have a little lie-down and I'd have sat and read to her. Probably a Miss Marple or a short story about a holiday romance from a magazine. I look at Gloria with her red hair and glass of champagne and expression of utter disdain and wonder how many expletives she'd manage to fit into a sentence if I asked her to teach me to knit or bake me a cake.

The smell of the smoke is making me feel really nauseous now and my mouth is dry. Gloria is still saying nothing. Before, she just seemed uninterested in me, perhaps a little inconvenienced by my presence. Now the silence feels almost hostile. Or am I imagining it? I don't know, but I do know I have to have something to drink that isn't champagne. There's nothing for it. I'm going to have to brave the kitchen.

'Do you mind if I make myself a cup of tea?'

She shrugs. 'Suit yourself. Though why you'd want tea when there's perfectly good Bollinger on offer, I don't know.'

I pick my way through to the kitchen, almost tripping over a pair of discarded platform shoes (can they really be Louboutins?) and crashing into a garden gnome that's being used as doorstop. Gloria's kitchen smells of death, with faint overtones of something that might possibly be slightly worse than death. I gag and clamp my hand over my mouth. Maybe I'll hatch a plan with Peggy and come back sometime with some heavy-duty cleaning products and a load of bin bags and clear up, but for now I can't face investigating the cause of the smell, which seems to be emanating from the fridge. I fill the kettle up and search for mugs and teabags. Judging by the contents of the cupboards Gloria's diet seems to consist largely of violet creams. There are boxes of them everywhere, some full, some empty. Other than this there are a few tins of soup, mostly dramatically out of date (one, oxtail, reads: *Best Before: Oct 1999*) a couple of jars of marmalade and – thankfully – several different kinds of tea. I choose peppermint to settle my stomach and because it means I won't have to risk delving into the fridge to find milk. In the absence of a mug I rinse out a bone-china teacup. The kitchen isn't filthy – due to Peggy, I bet, not Gloria – it's just chaotic. There's stuff on all the surfaces and I try to tidy up a bit but it's all so random – pens, a tube of toothpaste, a pair of socks, a bulb of garlic – it's hard to know where to begin. And there are notes everywhere, written on Post-it notes, envelopes, pages torn out of books. They're on the table, on cupboard doors, on the fridge. Sometimes they just say one word: *Sugar* or *Coffee* or *Gin*. Some are longer: *Tesco – no. 13 bus, 3 stops*, or Gloria's own address or lists of names. Others are more cryptic: *optimism, tricycle, hydrangea*. Another one says: *Ophelia Act 1, Scene 3*. Some are in different handwriting, again I'm assuming it's Peggy's. These say things like: *Don't forget your tablets at breakfast time (in the right-hand drawer of the dresser)*. One says: *HARRIET (Dominic's daughter) is coming on TUESDAY*.

Does she really need reminding about all this stuff? I know Peggy said she'd been forgetting things but I didn't realize she meant like this. Could it really be because she drinks? Perhaps she's an alcoholic and it's got to the point where Peggy thinks she can't cope any more. Maybe that's what this is all about. But then maybe she's drinking because she's worried about the fact that she's forgetting stuff . . .

When I've made my tea I go back in to see Gloria. She's still lying on the chaise longue but she doesn't stir when I say her name and I realize from her steady breathing that she's fallen asleep. I think about waking her but I can't think of a way to do it that won't annoy her, and anyway, to be honest, it's quite a relief not to have to make conversation. Even better, it gives me a chance to explore the flat a bit more.

I stick my head round the door of a room that turns out to be Gloria's bedroom. It has a four-poster bed in it, far too big and grand for the room. There's a dressing table along the wall, covered in jars and bottles of make-up. On the far side of the room is a wardrobe with a door hanging open, bursting with exotic-looking clothes – evening gowns and hats, several fur coats and shoes piled high. It's tidier than the rest of the house and smells better too, of perfume and moisturizing creams and face powder. Next door to it there's a spare room with a double bed but every inch of the room, including the bed, is piled high with boxes and stacks of paper. I have a quick look, telling myself I'm just being concerned, not nosy. There are bills, quite a few of them red, receipts and letters – official-looking ones from banks or the council. There's one lying on the floor. As I pick it up I can't help noticing it's an appointment letter from the hospital and I take a glance as I put it with all the others on the bed. Neurologist ... PET scan ... The date is in a month's time. I stop myself reading more. *It's none of my business*, I tell myself. *If Gloria wants to tell me about it she will*. Not that it seems very likely.

There's a photo on the mantelpiece, not framed, black and white and curling at the edges, tucked up behind an old carriage clock, against the wall. It's of a girl about my age and another much younger girl standing together outside a house. Is it Nan and Gloria? I look closely. It could be but I can't be sure. I bet there are loads of other photos in these boxes. Maybe even some of Dad.

I take the picture through to Gloria, thinking I'll ask her about them when she wakes up. Perhaps I'll be able to get her talking; she might be in a better mood if I let her have a bit of a rest and sleep off the effects of the champagne. But when I go into the room she sits up sharply.

'Yes?' she says. 'What do you want?'

I stare at her, alarmed, wondering if she's half asleep, or more drunk than I realized. 'I'm Hattie, remember? We were talking and then you fell asleep.'

She stares at me.

'I'm your great-niece. Your nephew Dominic's daughter?'

'Dominic?'

But then I think about the notes in the kitchen and some of the things Peggy said before.

'Wait,' I say, and I go and get the note that Peggy wrote saying I was coming.

'See?' I say, holding the note out.

She wafts it away dismissively. 'Yes, all right, all right,' she says. 'Of course I know who you are. You just took me by surprise, that's all, sneaking up on me while I was asleep.'

'Sorry. Can I get you anything? Tea? Or lunch? I could go to the shops? Or we could go to a café?'

She leans down to pour herself another drink.

'This is just fine for me, thank you.' She raises her glass to me.

'Gloria,' I say, tentative. 'You can't live on violet creams and champagne and the occasional cigar.'

'Cigarillo.'

'Whatever.'

'Actually I think you'll find I can, my dear, if I so choose.'

'No,' I say. 'You'll get . . . I dunno. Scurvy. Thingy of the liver.' I rummage around in my brain for any other medical conditions that sound like they might result from malnutrition. We did it in biology, I'm sure of it. 'Rickets!' I pluck out triumphantly.

Gloria snorts dismissively.

'And cancer, obviously,' I add. 'That goes without saying.'

'Well, don't say it then,' she snaps. 'Why is everyone so bossy nowadays? You can't step out of the front door without someone ramming good sense and vegetables and low-fat, smoke-free tedium down everybody's throat all the bloody time. You can't even sit in your own living room without some neighbour or—' she gestures at me—'do-gooder preaching at you.'

'I'm not a do-gooder—'

'Even on the wireless they're at it. There's always some know-it-all doctor or politician wittering on about . . . saturated whatevers. Morbid obesity. Well, I like violet creams and I like champagne. And if I want them for breakfast I shall damn well have them.'

She glares at me.

'Look,' I say. 'You're right. It's none of my business. If I live to be as old as you, I'll eat whatever I want too. Chip butties and pancakes for every meal.' The thought of it makes me realize how hungry I am.

'I'm not *old*, thank you very much.'

66

I wonder how old she is. It's hard to tell with the make-up. Old, but not ancient. Younger than Peggy, I'd guess. She must be at least seventy, though.

'I was only trying to help. I'm more than happy to go away and leave you in peace to do whatever you like. I could have been doing a million other much more interesting things than clearing up your kitchen . . .' It's not strictly true, obviously. In fact it's a blatant lie; I'd have been reading *Watership* bloody *Down* to Ollie again while being tied to a chair by Alice, wouldn't I? But Gloria doesn't know that.

She looks at me haughtily. 'I didn't ask you to clean my kitchen.' Then she pauses and looks at me suddenly, uncertain. 'Did I?'

I can see the panic behind her eyes, and I remember what Peggy said, about Gloria being worried about her memory. I wonder how often she feels it, that panic. Is it there all the time, underneath all her stroppiness? The uncertainty, the disorientation? Feeling that she's not quite sure whether she knows what's going on? Hard to tell. She'd hide it well, stubborn old boot that she is.

'No,' I say. 'You're right. You didn't.'

She looks at me for a moment and then picks up a very old newspaper that's lying on the floor next to her.

'Anyway,' she says. 'It's been lovely meeting you but I'd like you to leave now, and please don't come back.'

I stare at her, but she doesn't show any awareness of the fact that I haven't done what she asked and left. She turns a page of the newspaper.

'I've come all this way to see you,' I say, feeling tears pricking my eyes. 'I thought—'

'What did you think?'

'I don't know. I thought we could at least get to know each other a bit.'

Gloria sighs.

'But there's no point, is there?'

'What do you mean?'

She lowers her newspaper.

'I assume Peggy told you about my . . . condition.'

'Not exactly. She just said you hadn't been well. She seemed quite worried,' I say. 'I hope it's nothing too serious?'

She smiles and turns her head to look out of the window, pulling the sunglasses back down over her eyes. 'It's fairly serious.'

'Oh?'

'Do you want the good news or the bad news?'

'Um.' I smile nervously. 'The good news?'

She blows smoke out through her nose. Then she says: 'The good news is I'm dying. That serious enough for you?'

I nearly laugh; I don't know whether it's because I'm shocked, or because I think she's making some kind of dark joke, or maybe it's just like that awful urge to giggle that people get at funerals. She watches my reaction, even behind the glasses I know she's not taken her eyes off me. It's like she's challenging me. Trying to shock me.

But I know she's telling the truth too.

'How is that the good news?' I say eventually.

She smiles, and her smile makes me shiver. 'How young you are,' she says, in a way that reminds me how Peggy said she used to be an actress, and takes another sip from her glass. 'There are things worse than death you know.'

I think about this. 'Like what? Pain?'

68

She snorts. 'Pain?' she says, derisively. 'No, not pain.'

'What then?'

She looks at me for so long I think she's not going to answer. Then she gets up and walks to where the bottles and glasses are and picks up another champagne flute.

'Go on,' she says. 'Join me for just one little drink. Just to humour me. I've just told you I'm dying. It's the least you can do.'

'Okay,' I say. Even thinking about it makes me feel queasy again, like the thought of drinking with a hangover, but I'm half scared of Gloria and half sorry for her, so I let her pour me out a glass and take it from her.

'Cheers,' she says and clinks her glass against mine, as she settles herself back on the chaise longue.

'Cheers,' I echo, taking a small sip and attempting to smile.

'What makes us who we are?' she says, suddenly.

I stare at her, feeling a bit like Alice at the Mad Hatter's Tea Party. 'Sorry,' I say. 'I don't think I understand.'

'It's simple enough. What makes us who we are?'

It's not simple, I want to say. A million different things make us who we are, but I know that's not the answer she wants. 'Well, I suppose, genes and environment. Nature and nurture.' I look at her hopefully.

'*Memories*,' she says, as if I'm very, very stupid. 'Our memories are what make us who we are. Some are real. Some are made up. But they are the stories that tell us who we are. Without them we are nobody.' She turns to look out of the window again.

I wait for her to say more, but she doesn't.

'You have dementia?' I say.

'Yes. The terminal illness where you get to die twice. Two for the price of one. Lucky me, eh?'

69

'You might find you're worrying about nothing. Everyone forgets stuff when they get old. I mean *slightly older*,' I amend hastily as Gloria huffs. 'Even Mum does it. She's always walking into a room and saying, "What did I come in here for?" It's normal. And worrying about it probably makes you notice it more so you think it's more serious than it is. If you just try to be positive—'

She shakes her head and looks at me through the smoke. 'Don't patronize me, dear. You have absolutely no idea what you're talking about. Young people think everything can be solved with a bit of positive thinking and an inspirational quote about believing or being you or dancing in the rain.'

In spite of myself I can't help silently agreeing with her. Carl's big on inspirational quotes and stuck one up in the downstairs loo that says LIVE EVERY MOMENT! LOVE LIKE YOU'VE NEVER BEEN HURT! LAUGH OUT LOUD! which makes me feel harangued when all I want to do is go for a wee in peace.

'But Peggy said—'

'Oh yes?' Gloria interrupts. 'What did Peggy say exactly?'

I try to work out how to say '*that you're a bit mad and untidy and drink too much*' diplomatically. 'She said she thought you might be worrying yourself unnecessarily. And you seem okay,' I say, not sure whether I'm being honest or not. It's hard to judge what's 'okay' when I've never met her before. 'I mean, we're sitting here having a conversation, aren't we?'

She shakes her head.

'Mostly everything's fine. I can talk to you. I can remember who I am and where I am and why.'

'Well then. What's the problem?'

'And then suddenly I reach for a word, not a difficult word, not "*onomatopoeia*" or "*discombobulated*". Something simple, something that should just be there, like "hand" or "bottle"—' she holds up the one she's about to pour another drink from as if it somehow proves her point—'and the word's not there. There's just empty space. It's like when you think you've got to the bottom of a flight of stairs and you put your foot down and you're waiting for your foot to connect with the solid surface you know should be there. But instead of the floor there's just air and you realize you're falling . . .'

'But everyone forgets words. And, well . . .'

She sees me looking at her half-empty glass, which I can't help feeling might be at least part of the problem, and tuts.

'It's nothing to do with that. It's not just words. Sometimes I'll forget where I am. One time I couldn't for the life of me remember where I lived. The only address I could remember was the house I grew up in. That's the thing with this disease, you see. As the present fades the past becomes clearer. I know what it does to you. I saw it with my mum.'

'You mum had dementia?'

'I remember her calling out for dead people, thinking they were in the next room.'

I think about this, about how frightened Gloria must feel.

'Was this the house you grew up in?' I say, holding out the photo I found in the bedroom, wanting to change the subject and also hoping to move her on to the subject of Nan, to see if I can find out what happened between them, whether they'd fallen out and what about.

'We were very close when we were growing up,' Gloria says. There's something about the way she says it that makes me decide it's best not to ask any more. She takes the photo from me. 'Yes,' she says. 'That's me and Gwen outside the house in Clapham. She must have been eighteen in that picture. Which means I'd have been, what, ten?'

'Clapham?' I say, surprised. 'That's not all that far from where I live. Same side of the river anyway.' For some reason I'd assumed Gloria must have grown up around here.

'I dream about it so often, that house,' she says. The house I grew up in. It's never exactly how it was; places never are in dreams, are they? Why is that? I wonder. But I remember it so clearly. Tiny details only children notice. If I close my eyes I can see the pattern on the wallpaper in my bedroom. The way the shadow of the laburnum tree in the garden fell across my bedcovers in the morning. The smell of soap flakes in the kitchen.' She closes her eyes and breathes it in. 'Strange how clear it all is. Things from decades ago. I can see them. Smell them. I feel I could almost reach out and touch them. But all the time the present and future are disappearing, until one day all I'll have is fragments of the past. So many places that formed my life and they'll be wiped from my mind. I won't even know they existed. People too. I can see that house in my dreams, and yet I'll never see it again in real life.'

I stare at her and I have an idea.

'Let's go,' I say.

'What do you mean?'

'I could take you,' I say. 'I've got Mum's car while they're away. We could go there.'

She looks confused.

'Where?'

'To your old house, if you want to. So you can see it one last time.'

'Go there?' She looks doubtful.

I nod, excited by the idea. 'Why not?'

'There are lots of reasons why not,' she says.

'But if you're right, if you really are losing your memory—'

'I am right.'

'Well then, wouldn't you like to see it again while it still means something to you?'

For a moment something flickers across her face and I think she's going to say yes but it vanishes. She looks away from me, through the window to the street outside.

'What's the point?' she says. 'It'll all be gone soon. Everything I've ever done. Everyone I've ever known.'

I want to argue with her, to persuade her, but I don't want to make her angry again, and anyway, I can't force her to do it if she doesn't want to. I can't imagine how it must feel to face a future like hers.

'I'm sorry,' I say.

She turns back to me, her face fierce. 'I don't want pity,' she says. 'Not from you. Not from those interfering halfwits from social services. Not from them downstairs.'

'Peggy and Malcolm seem really kind. They're only trying to help—'

'I don't want help. That's *exactly* what I'm trying to explain, if you people would only listen. I want to be left alone to live and die at a time and in a manner of my own choosing. So please, if you really want to help, go away and leave me in peace.'

I try to understand what she's saying to me.

'In a time and manner of your own choosing . . . ?'

'Yes,' she says. 'It's my business how and when I die. No one else's.'

She looks at me defiantly.

'You want to . . . end your own life?'

She shrugs. 'Perhaps.'

'I don't believe you,' I say, shaking my head.

'Believe what you like.'

'Even if that's true—'

'It is.'

'Why not make the most of the time you *do* have? Why push people away when they care about you?'

'People all think they know what's best for you. But they can't.'

'So you're just going to lock yourself away? Cut yourself off from everyone?'

'Yes.'

I look around at the chaos, the mess, the empty bottles, the room full of the leftover pieces of a life, left behind like driftwood as the tide goes out. Gloria's acting as though her life is already over.

'But you can't.'

She turns to me, fierce. 'I've always done as I choose. I'm not going to stop now.'

'I'm trying to help.'

'Why?'

'I'm your family.'

She turns away. 'Well, I've never been one for family. It became clear fairly early on in my life that I was better off without my family and they were better off without me.'

Her voice sounds a little choked and I can't work out whether she's upset or angry. Again I wonder what the story is behind her disappearance from the family tree. Why hadn't we known about her?

'You don't even know me.'

'But I want to. I could if you'd let me.'

She turns away.

'There's no point. I've already told you. There's no point. I'm going to die.'

'We're all going to die,' I say, impatiently. 'Why not live while you've still got the chance?' I realize I sound like one of Carl's posters and try again. 'I could die before you. I could walk out of here and get run over by a bus. Does that mean I should just give up on everything and sit around feeling sorry for myself and getting drunk?'

Her mouth twists into a smirk.

'It's easy for young people to talk about death. You don't really believe it'll ever happen to you.'

'I think you're just wallowing in self-pity.'

She looks at me, her face tight with fury. 'You can't understand any of this. I don't want you here, in my home. I don't want to know you. You don't interest me. You're just a silly child.' Then she twists herself round on the chaise longue so her back is turned towards me. 'Go home.'

And now I'm not only knackered and very low blood-sugar (which, as Reuben has pointed out, does tend to turn me into something resembling the Incredible Hulk) not to mention pregnant and anxious and angry, but also insulted AND humiliated. And I lose it.

'Fine,' I say. 'I'm going. I've done my best. I'm not going to stick around to be insulted. I've got enough to worry about—'

'Oh, really?' She spits the words at me. 'What have you got to worry about? You young people and your cosseted

75

lives and your sense of entitlement. What's the problem? Mummy won't buy you the car you want? Not enough channels on the widescreen TV in your bedroom?'

Her words sting. I've come all this way to see her and she's treating me like a spoilt, naive kid. Tears spring to my eyes. I hope she doesn't see them.

'Actually I'm pregnant,' I say, the words out of my mouth before I knew I was going to say them. They sound strange and unreal, hanging in the smoky air. It's a relief somehow. For a fleeting, crazy second it feels as though I've come here just to say it, just to tell Gloria this fact, just to share it with her.

She stops and stares at me, absolutely still. 'What?' she says, and her voice is different, soft. 'What did you say?'

'Goodbye,' I say, and I walk out of the room, fumbling for the front door through the dark of the hallway and the blur of my tears.

'Hattie!' Gloria calls. 'Wait!'

I slam the door hard behind me and I run down the stairs. I don't stop to say goodbye to Peggy and Malcolm. I can't. I just run out of the front door and down the front path, trying to remember the way to the Tube station.

The tears are still coming as I walk down the road, turning back to see Gloria's face, pale at the window, watching me go.

I watch as she walks down the road, turning back once to look up at the window, then turning away. Is she still crying? I can't tell. *I don't care*, I tell myself. I have always been good at telling myself lies, always found that if you say a thing enough times you can make yourself believe it, if you ignore a thing long enough it will go away. But it seems I am losing my knack for it.

I close my eyes. When I open them she will have disappeared from view she will be gone and I will forget her; I will forget her name, and then that she ever came, and then that she ever existed in the first place, and that will be that.

But when I close my eyes she does not go away. She is there, still, looking at me with my mother's eyes. I curse my brain. Why must it remember the things I want it to forget?

'No,' I say to the girl, even though she is only in my head. 'Go away. Shoo.' I say it because I have drunk a little too much on an empty stomach, and because no one can hear me, and because even if they could I have never much cared whether people think I am crazy or not. Which I suppose I am, talking to an imaginary girl as though she were a stray cat who had sneaked into my flat. But mainly I say it because there is panic beating in my chest. She brings other things with her, this girl, other things that I would rather forget. She doesn't know it, of course, this (I look at her name, scrawled on the back of my hand) *Hattie.* I had written it hurriedly when she was out of the room, busybodying about in the kitchen.

Why did I write it, though, if I want to forget?

I sit down on the chaise and light a cigarette. It is entirely the wrong thing to do if you have dementia, as St Peggy is forever telling me, as is drinking large quantities of gin, and this pleases me immensely. It becomes harder to rebel as you get old, largely because no one takes any notice of you no matter what you do. But ignoring good advice is a luxury that shouldn't be monopolized by the young, in my not particularly humble opinion.

I lie back and close my eyes and allow myself to drift. I am spinning in the sunshine in the middle of the Common. I see a jam jar of pale-pink roses, I can smell them. *Be careful, Gloria,* my mother is saying, but there is blood dripping on her yellow-flowered dress . . . I feel the ache of cold feet in too-pointed shoes, the soft, thrilling warmth of a kiss in the snow. I am lying in the heat of summer thinking of Sam. I hear feet on the stairs and I freeze. I see a dropped mirror, shattered on the floor. *That's seven years' bad luck—*

No. I try to make it stop but the images keep coming, clear but disjointed, like those old home movies people used to make. I smell the green leather and smoky tea and antiseptic cleanness and somewhere babies are crying as the afternoon sun slants in through large, draughty windows and I cannot make them stop. I don't know how and panic numbs me—

I am closing my fingers round the cool metal of a locket that I will keep safe but never open.

I am standing on the edge of a cliff—

*NO.* I will not go back there.

And yet—

It is my story. It is a story no one left alive knows except for me. And soon, unless I tell it, it will be gone, washed away like words written in the sand as the tide comes in . . .

It is a liberating thought. It will be as if none of it happened. It will be unwritten.

Except that it won't. Except that it can't be. I cannot pretend that it can. Not now. That is what she has done by coming here today. Hattie.

And perhaps I don't want it to be. Perhaps the only way to release yourself from a secret, from the past, is to share it. Perhaps it is like confession, the act of admitting the sin is the way to release yourself from it . . . *Bless me, Father, for I have sinned* . . . I see the shape of Sister Mary Francis dark against the sun.

It is so clear, all of it. So vivid. I can smell it, I can *feel* it. It is the curse of this disease; it erases the present and the future so that all you are left with is the past.

I am scared.

Am I brave enough to tell my story to her, to the girl? To – what was her name again?

Hattie. Yes. The girl carrying a secret.

Perhaps I can. If I go back there I can't do it alone. Perhaps I can take her with me.

After all, it is her story too.

## Chapter six

From: hattiedlockwood@starmail.com
To: wilde_one666@starmail.com
Subject:

Well, Reuben, even a stopped clock gives the right time twice a day as the saying goes. And on this occasion you were – well, not right exactly, but not as wrong as you usually are. My great-aunt was completely mad. And rude. I shouldn't have gone to visit her.

But looking on the bright side she wasn't a serial killer. And I didn't have to wear a Slave Leia bikini.

Hope you're ok. Would be good to hear from you. Are you getting on ok with your dad? Is it weird after so long? What's his new girlfriend like?

Hxx

I don't tell anyone at home about what happened at Gloria's. When Mum asks me about it I avoid telling her much. I tell her she was tired so I couldn't stay long.

'What was she like?'

'Okay. I mean, you know. She was old. She's got Alzheimer's or something. Dementia.'

'That's sad,' Mum says, as she folds shorts and T-shirts for the twins. 'Look, I'll give her a call when we're back from Spain, see what we can do for her.'

'I wouldn't bother,' I say. 'I don't think she really wants any help.'

'It can be hard for people to accept they need help,' Mum says.

'Hmmm.'

Mum watches me closely.

'Are you okay?'

'I'm fine,' I say.

Luckily she and Carl are too busy rushing around getting ready to go on holiday to pay too much attention to me. Even so, Mum is fussing around me like she senses something isn't quite right.

'I wish you were coming with us,' she says for the ten-billionth time.

'We could always look into last-minute flights if you like, Hats,' Carl says. Bless him.

'No,' I say. 'I've got all my shifts at the Happy Diner.'

I'd decided not to go with them before I knew Reuben and Kat weren't going to be around. I'd thought we'd have the house to ourselves for two and a half weeks while they were away in Spain and then staying with Carl's annoying sister Becky and her family for a few days on the way back. Now I'll be stuck here on my own. Half of me wishes I was going but I know Mum would work out something was wrong if we spent nearly three weeks together and I can't face telling her yet. I want to get everything straight in my own head. A bit of time to myself will give me the space to work it all out. I'm hoping everything will suddenly seem clear. At the moment I can't even think about it without my head going fuzzy with panic.

'Well, you could always come and stay when we go to Becky's?' Carl says. 'I know she'd love to see you.' Which is a blatant lie. Becky never looks particularly pleased to see any of us. She clearly thinks Carl could do a lot better for himself than Mum and her odd collection of offspring.

'No thanks,' I say quickly. 'Like I say, I've got my shifts all lined up.'

'How come Hattie doesn't have to go? That's not fair!' Alice whines. She hates Becky's son, Bertie.

'Are you sure you're okay, love?' Mum says to me. 'You don't seem yourself at the moment.'

'I told you, I'm fine. Just tired.'

Peggy phones a few days later, sounding flustered and anxious.

'You left in such a hurry,' she says. 'We were hoping to have a chance to say goodbye.'

I don't reply. I know she means well but to be honest I wish I'd never spoken to Peggy, never gone to see Gloria. Why did she have to drag me into it?

'We heard a bit of shouting, Harriet,' she says, hesitantly. 'Was she in one of her moods?'

'I don't think you can really call it a mood, can you? More of a catastrophic character defect. And it's *Hattie*.'

'She's been very low since you left, dear. Won't talk to me or Malcolm. Just ignores us or tells us to—' she coughs delicately—'well, "Go Away" is the general gist of it.'

'If I were you I'd do exactly that. Leave her to it.'

'Malcolm tried to let himself in yesterday to make sure she was okay, but she'd put the chain on the door. He thought he heard her crying.'

'I've got to go,' I say. 'I'm late for work.'

'Of course. I'm sorry if she upset you. We were just trying to help.'

'I know,' I say. 'But she doesn't want to be helped.'

I wake up most nights worrying about the baby – NO, it's not a baby – the positive pregnancy tests, that's better. I wake up worrying about the positive pregnancy tests and what I'm going to do and Reuben and why, why, WHY did this have to happen, my mind leaping feverishly in the darkness from abortion clinic to labour ward.

And then when I've exhausted myself and I'm trying to switch my brain off and coax myself back to sleep I find I'm thinking about Gloria. At first I felt angry, and stupid for having gone to see her, for thinking she'd be pleased to see me. But now, lying wide awake in the dark, I keep thinking about the photo of her when she was young and of how her eyes looked like mine. And after a while I just feel sad. I see her face at the window as I left . . .

*He thought he heard her crying . . .*

*There was something underneath all that act*, I think, drifting towards sleep. *Something vulnerable.*

But maybe I just want that to be true.

It's so early when the taxi arrives to take the others to the airport it's still dark. I make my way blearily downstairs to say goodbye.

'I hate leaving you, Hattie,' Mum says at the front door, pulling me to her and hugging me. 'Are you sure you'll be okay?'

'Mum, for God's sake. I'm not a kid.' But stupidly my eyes prick with tears and I'm glad she can't see my face. 'I'll be glad to get you lot out of my hair for a while. Might actually get some peace and quiet for a change.'

'You'll be sorry when we're gone,' Alice says. She's angry with me for not going with them. 'And if you die no one will probably find you for a week and they'll have to work out how long your corpse has been rotting from the life cycle of a maggot.'

'Alice!' Carl gives her a look.

'It's true,' she says. 'I saw it on a programme about forensics.'

'Cheers, Al,' I say.

'She won't die,' says Ollie, anxious. 'You won't, will you, Hattie?'

'No, she won't,' says Mum firmly. 'I expressly forbid it. Now go and get in the taxi.' When they've gone she holds me back from her so she can see my face and examines me closely. I smile a bright smile.

'You seem . . . I don't know,' she says. 'I know something's the matter—'

'*Nothing's* the matter, Mum. You're being neurotic. I'm totally fine.'

'We'll talk properly when I get back.'

'About what? There's nothing to talk about. Just have a great time.'

'Okay,' she says, doubtful. 'Well. Okay. If you use the oven, just make sure you've switched the gas off afterwards. And if there's a fat fire, remember don't throw water on it—'

'Mum,' I say. 'Honestly. Yes. And I'll do my best not to drown or fall down the stairs or spontaneously combust. I

84

won't accept sweets from strangers or run with my shoelaces undone. Happy?'

But she's not. 'Promise me you'll drive carefully if you borrow the car. No overtaking on bends or—'

'GO.' I turn her round and push her out of the door.

'Anyway, you're a fine one to give driving advice,' Carl says to her, carrying out the last suitcase, making a big show of how heavy it is. 'Jeez, what have you got in here, woman?'

Mum laughs, turns back and gives me a last kiss.

'Love you,' she says.

'You too,' I call after her.

'Take it easy, Hats,' Carl calls over his shoulder. 'Don't do anything I wouldn't do. If you have any wild parties just make sure you clear up afterwards, yeah?' He winks at me and then gets into the taxi.

'I wish,' I say. After I've waved them off I turn back into the empty house and feel the weight of silence all around me. I'm almost glad when it's time to leave for my shift at the Happy Diner.


I check the display on my alarm clock. It's 12.52 a.m. I can't sleep. The house is oppressively quiet and my thoughts are loud and panicky. I spent the evening hoping Kat would phone. I'm missing her. And now I can't bear it any longer. I pick up my phone and text her.

**I'm pregnant. By Reuben.**

I send it, my heart pounding. That's it. I've told Kat. Will she pick up the message now or in the morning? And when she does what will she say? She's never really liked Reuben. Ever since he started at our school three years ago she's been wary of him. I lie back down in the dark. She probably

85

won't see it tonight. I close my eyes and then start awake as my phone starts ringing.

'Jesus, Hattie!' Kat says as I answer.

'I know,' I say.

'I mean . . .'

'I know.' I switch my bedside lamp on.

'*Reuben.*'

'I know.'

'Why didn't you—'

'I KNOW.' I start to cry.

'Oh, no,' she says. 'No, Hattie, don't cry. You can't cry. It's okay. Look, it's all going to be fine. Please don't cry. I didn't mean . . . I just wish you'd told me.'

'I tried,' I say. 'I kept texting you to call me and you didn't.'

I'm wailing now.

'Oh, Hats, I'm so sorry. It's just . . . hang on a minute—'

There's rustling and banging and the music in the background gets quieter until eventually I can hardly hear it.

'I've come outside so I can hear you properly,' she says. 'Look, I'm really sorry I didn't call. It's Zoe. She sort of wants it to be just me and her while we're up here. I was going to phone you and she got a bit funny about it.'

Typical. She's such a cow.

'Her ex really messed her around,' Kat says. 'So, you know. She's kind of a bit . . . She gets a bit jealous. But obviously if I'd known I'd have called straight away.'

'I know,' I say. 'I didn't mean to make you feel bad.'

There's some shouting in the background wherever Kat is. I imagine her standing in a cobbled street in Edinburgh having a great night out and the house seems even lonelier and emptier, and my life seems even more of a mess.

'So what are you going to do?' Kat says.

'I don't know.'

'Have you been to the doctor's?'

'Not yet.'

'Have you told Reuben?'

'No.'

'Are you going to?'

'I don't know. He's in France. Or he was. I think he's heading for Italy or Greece or somewhere. With a girl he's met out there.'

'Oh, Hattie.' We're silent for a while, and I can tell Kat's thinking of all the painful and unpleasant things she'd do to Reuben if she could.

'What about your mum?' she says at last. 'Have you told her?'

'Not yet. I will. They're all off in Mallorca at the moment.'

'How many weeks are you?' she says at last.

'Six, I think. Well, between six and seven.'

'Okay. Well, you know if you're going to have an abortion the sooner the better. I think you're supposed to have it by twelve weeks? I mean that's when my sister had her scan pictures and everything.'

'I know.' I remember going to the hospital with Mum when she had her scan for the twins. Mum was in shock afterwards; she hadn't been expecting two babies. I was so excited. For a split second I'm annoyed that Kat's just assuming I'm going to have an abortion. She's making it sound easier than it is. I do have to make a decision. But she's right. It doesn't feel like much of a choice. I don't want a baby and Reuben sure as hell doesn't.

'So, not being funny, Hats, but if that's what you're going to do, you need to get on and make an appointment.'

87

I don't say anything.

There's a pause.

'You aren't thinking about actually having the baby, are you?'

'I don't know. I don't think so. I can't, can I?'

'You mean you're not sure?'

'I don't know. I don't want to be pregnant. But . . . I just want to be sure.'

'Okay. Well, there are pregnancy books, aren't there? I remember my sister had a whole library of them when she was pregnant. Maybe you should have a look. Might help you get your head around it all.'

'I can't face it, Kat. I looked on a website and it was all adverts for nappies and baby milk and advice on breastfeeding.'

I start crying again.

'Oh, Hattie, I wish I could give you a hug,' she says.

'Me too,' I sniff.

'Listen to me,' Kat says. 'It's going to be okay. You just need to work out what you're going to do and then do it. It's all fine. And whatever you decide, I'll be with you if you need me, okay?'

I can hear that she's shivering.

'Are you cold?'

'Of course I'm cold. I'm in Scotland, aren't I?'

'You should go back in,' I say. 'I'll be fine.'

'Look,' she says. 'I'm going to buy a book or find a website or something, and I'll look up everything you need to know.'

'You won't tell Zoe, though, will you? I don't want anyone to know except you.'

'No, course not. I'll do it when she's not around. Anything you want to know, just text me and ask. Or email.'

'Okay,' I say. 'I won't phone, though. I don't want to mess things up with you and Zoe. Is it still going well between you two?'

I try very hard not to hope that it isn't.

'I really like her, Hattie,' she says. 'I think I might love her.'

'Wow,' I say. Kat's not generally the falling-in-love type. It must be really serious.

'I just wish I could make her understand that she can trust me.'

'She will,' I say. 'There's no one more trustworthy in the whole world than you.'

'That's what I keep telling her.' She sighs. 'I miss you.'

'Me too.' My voice sounds small in the dark.

'It'll be okay, you know.'

I try to hold on to her words after she's gone. Eventually I sleep.

The next day, when I finish my shift, limp, hot and exuding a stale aroma of burnt bacon fat, there's a pile of post lying on the doormat. It's mainly bills and catalogues and some fitness magazine for Carl, but as I pick it up I see that underneath it all is a white envelope with the address handwritten neatly in blue ink. It's addressed to me.

13b Iona Road

12 August

Dear Hattie,
On reflection, I may have been a little hasty when you came to see me last week. I use 'hasty' as a euphemism for rude, obviously. Also possibly a bit

drunk. Staring death and oncoming oblivion in the face makes one rather tetchy, I find.

Anyway, I have been thinking about what you said and I would like you to visit again. Your visit stirred up a lot of memories and I have decided that perhaps you are right. I have avoided thinking about the past for many years. I thought it was better that way, that I was being strong by leaving it behind. But perhaps it was fear. There are things in my past that no one else living knows, and soon I will have forgotten them. Perhaps I may share them with you. If you are still willing to take me, I should like to visit my childhood home. I should warn you, though, my past is not a particularly happy place.

I understand if you choose not to visit again. If I were you I'd probably tell me to bugger off. But I suspect you are a nicer person than me so I hope you will consider it.

Yours,
Gloria

The girl. I wake thinking of her, dreaming of her maybe. Gwen. No, not Gwen.

'I'm pregnant,' she says.

Hattie. Yes. That is her name.

She will have received the letter by now. Will she read it? It took a long time to write it. Words take a long time to make the journey from my head to my hand these days, they get tangled and go missing and pop up in the wrong places if I'm not careful. Perhaps she won't even open it, she will guess it is from me and she will throw it away without opening it.

I don't care if she does. Perhaps it would be for the best. Perhaps it would be a relief for the days to pass and realize that she is not coming, that she never will, that my secrets are safe.

And yet—

I do care. I try not to. It has always been my way, to try not to care. I don't think I'm being immodest when I say that I've done very well at it over the years, perfected it. Almost . . .

The past visits me so often now, clearer than the present. Ghosts, some more welcome than others. Gwen and Vinnie and Sam and Edie . . . I want to share it. I want to share it with *her*. I want her to know.

91

*I'm pregnant.* She was crying. I know about secrets, about the burden of them. I would like to help her if I can . . . But how can I? Can sharing my burden help her?

Is it fair? It is not a happy story, that's for sure. Young people think the past was gentler than the present, innocent. My past was never like that, not even my earliest memories . . .

Is she ready for these things, the girl, Hattie? The violence and worse that came later? Is it right to share it with her, to reawaken it? Or should it be left where it is?

Perhaps she will make the decision for me. Perhaps she will not come.

## Chapter seven

'Ah,' Gloria says as she opens the door. She's wearing an elegant trouser suit, a fedora and extremely red lipstick. 'There you are. Gin sling?'

'What?'

'Would you like a gin sling? Malcolm did a supermarket run and got all the ingredients. He is a treasure.'

I've been reading up on dementia since the last time I was here, and I know that mood swings are common, so I try not to look surprised by this total change of attitude. She ushers me into the hall, which I can't help noticing smells a little less rancid than last time I was there.

'No!' I say. 'And nor should you. It's too early.'

'Sun's over the yard arm, isn't it?'

'It's half past ten in the morning,' I say, frowning.

'Well.' She smiles. 'As Russell, my first husband, used to say, the sun's always over the yard arm somewhere in the world. Mind you, of all my husbands he was by far the stupidest. And they were none of them exactly Einstein, if you know what I mean.'

I wonder how I can tactfully check that she knows who I am and why I'm there. Perhaps she's mistaking me for someone else, or has forgotten that she asked me. My research has told me that people with dementia can be very good at covering it up. I also know that people have good days and bad days, that it can progress quite slowly in some people, that symptoms differ a lot between people. I'd been hoping for a nice checklist that I could measure Gloria against but apparently it doesn't work like that.

In the end I can't think of a subtle way of dropping my name into the conversation so I just come out with it.

'You do know who I am, don't you? And why I'm here?'

She looks irritated.

'Yes. I asked you here because I want you to take me back to the house I grew up in. You're Hattie Lockwood,' she says. 'You are Dominic's daughter. You are seventeen years old, your birthday is in January, you have a brother, Ollie, and a sister, Alice. You are studying for your A-levels, you are pregnant. Did I miss anything?'

I stare at her.

'Blimey,' I say. 'Vital statistics?'

'Hmmm,' she says, looking me up and down. 'No, I don't know those, but I could guess if you like?'

'I'd really rather you didn't,' I say hastily. 'How did you know about my birthday?'

'I know about a lot of things,' she says grandly. 'I've got it all written down in my book.' She picks up a red, hardback notebook from the kitchen table and waves it at me. 'Everyone and everything I need to remember goes in there. It was whatsername's idea.' She leafs through the book. 'Peggy!' she says, evidently reaching Peggy and Malcolm's page in the notebook. 'She may be an interfering do-gooder but she's not as stupid as she looks.'

'She doesn't look stupid at all.'

But she ignores me, and starts measuring gin and cherry brandy into a glass.

'How many husbands have you had then? All together?'

'Husbands?' She thinks. 'Three. And one fiancé. All ended in acrimonious divorce,' she says. 'Except for the engagement of course. That just ended in acrimony.'

'How come it didn't work out with any of them?'

She looks up at me as she opens a carton of pineapple juice.

'If you'd met them you wouldn't need to ask that question. And, to be honest, I'm not sure I'm really cut out for marriage. Always found the thought of it rather horrifying, actually.'

She's in such a different mood today, jokey, playful almost. I'd been expecting it to be awkward, even thought she might have changed her mind completely about seeing me, about our day trip together. I'd wondered whether I might actually be a little bit relieved if she had. Still, at the very least she's not being rude to me. It's a chance to get to know her better, which was all I really wanted in the first place.

'So why did you get married to them at all?'

'Oh, I don't know now. Why does one do anything? Boredom. Intoxication. Lack of willpower. Because they asked. Because, despite their many and varied failings, they were either rich or handsome. Perhaps I'm just a girl who can't say no.'

'I find that hard to believe,' I say. I imagine Gloria's very good at saying no.

She smiles.

'You're quite right, of course,' she says.

'What's this?' I say, pointing to the note on the fridge with 'Ophelia Act 1 Scene 3' written on it. I've been looking at it as Gloria's been talking, wondering about it.

'Oh,' she says. 'It's a memory test. I write down parts I've played and see if I can remember any of them.'

I smile. It's not hard to imagine Gloria as an actress.

'And can you? Remember them?'

'Yes, of course. Bits of them anyway. Long-term memory isn't a problem, you see. Not yet anyway. Things from long ago are safely stored away. They haven't gone yet. Though I suppose they will soon enough. It's the short term that gets muddled.'

'Is it Alzheimer's?' I ask.

'Probably,' she says. 'But I need a doctor to tell me what exact brand of dementia it is.'

I remember the letter from the hospital I found last time. 'So have you got an appointment?' I ask, not wanting her to think I've been snooping.

'Delicious,' Gloria declares, taking a sip from her glass, not looking at me.

'I didn't realize that there were so many different kinds of dementia,' I say.

'You've been investigating?' she says, looking amused.

'Yes,' I say, blushing. 'I just wanted to understand it better.'

'And what did you find out?'

I think it over. That it affects everyone differently, especially in the early stages, that no one knows how fast it will develop, that it is terminal – none of these are things I really want to say out loud. It's not as though Gloria doesn't already know this stuff.

'Just everything you've already told me really. I think

you put the gin in already,' I say as she attempts to pour in a second measure.

'Oh,' she says. 'Oh, well. A little more won't hurt. Shall we sit out on the balcony? Bring that, will you? The book thing.'

She gestures to a leather-bound photo album and I pick it up and bring it outside.

We sit in the sunshine at a little wrought-iron table, Gloria with her gin sling, me with my glass of water. ('Are you *quite* sure you won't have a cocktail?' Gloria has now asked three times and I'm not quite sure whether it's because she's determined I should have one or because she forgets she's already asked.) She picks up the album and starts to flick through it. There aren't any of Dad, as I'd hoped. The pictures are all much older, of Gloria and Nan as babies, of her dad in his army uniform.

'Is that your mum?' I say, pointing to one of the photos.

I show her a faded black-and-white picture of a young woman, a girl really, my age perhaps. She's petite and fair, dressed rather formally, looking wide-eyed into the camera with half a smile.

'My mother,' Gloria says, and her voice is unexpectedly soft, almost surprised. I look up at her and see that her face is different too, gentler, sad, more real somehow, as if she's taken off a mask of herself.

She sits in silence for a moment, staring intently at the picture, tracing the woman's face with her finger, the nail of which is painted an unexpected iridescent blue like a peacock feather. She's deep in thought, staring at the photo, and it's such an intimate moment I feel as though I shouldn't be watching. I just sit there as quietly as I can and examine my own unmanicured nails, trying not to intrude, thinking about how precious this moment is for Gloria, remembering the mother she might not be able to remember for much longer.

'I don't remember her like this,' she says at last. 'She's like another person from the one I knew.' Her voice is tight and contained, trying not to let out whatever emotion is inside.

'She does look very young,' I say.

She shakes her head. 'It's not just that. She looks so . . . unguarded. She's looking straight into the camera. She could never meet anyone's eyes by the time I can remember her. She'd look at the floor or at her hands. If you caught her gaze, her eyes would slide away to somewhere to the side of your head.'

I look over her shoulder at the girl in the photo.

'Why?' I ask. 'What changed her?'

'By the time I knew her, my real mother had hidden, leaving behind a person who looked just like her but was completely empty. So that no one noticed she was gone, you see? The empty person did all the basic things that were necessary so that people wouldn't notice she was gone, smiling and saying what terrible weather we'd been having to the neighbours and cooking liver and onions for tea. And all the while she just kept quiet in her hiding place and hoped she wouldn't be noticed. Like leaving pillows under the bedclothes when you sneak off at night. If you don't look too closely, if you don't shine a light on it, it's really quite convincing.'

She snaps the album shut.

'What's the matter?' I say.

'Like I said in my letter, my past is not a very happy place,' she says. 'You must know that.'

'I do.'

She looks unsure.

'Perhaps this isn't such a good idea after all.'

'What?' I say. 'I've come all this way. Come on. It'll be great.'

'I don't know,' she says.

'Look, if nothing else, we can go and sit on the Common and eat ice creams.'

She looks at me, uncertain. Scared almost.

'Or perhaps a pub,' I say, certain she won't be able to resist. 'Maybe we can find somewhere with a nice beer garden.'

She nods. 'Right then,' she says, draining her glass of the last drops of her gin sling. 'Let's hit the road.'

The address Gloria has given me is in south London. The journey there isn't too difficult, and I only get lost a couple of times. Gloria is quiet and I can't tell whether she's nervous or lost in thought.

'This is it,' she says at last. 'I used to walk along this road every day on the way back from school.' We're driving along a busy road lined with tapas and sushi bars, organic cafés, little boutiques, toyshops and billions of estate agents. She is looking out of the window intently, at the shops, at groups of well-dressed women pushing complicated-looking buggies, at joggers, and men with beards and trendy glasses clutching takeaway coffees.

'Posh, isn't it?' I say. 'Lots of fancy shops. Loads of four-by-fours. I bet the houses round here cost a bomb, don't you?'

Gloria is quiet, and just keeps watching out of the window as we stop at the lights.

'It's so different,' she says. 'The same but at the same time so different. It's like a picture that's been painted on top of an old painting. The ghost of the old one is still there under-neath, and that's the one I know. But all this—' she gestures at an All Bar One—'It's all so different. That's where the greengrocer's was. And the haberdasher's was just there – or was it the sweet shop?' She sounds disconcerted.

'Well, it's bound to have changed, isn't it?' I say. 'I mean, it is more than half a century since you lived here.'

'Yes, thank you,' Gloria snaps. 'I'm quite aware of that.'

'Sorry,' I say. 'I didn't mean . . .' I try and fail to think of something that sounds diplomatic and not like I'm saying she's unbelievably old. 'It must be really weird seeing all the changes. Especially when it's somewhere you've got so many memories of.'

I park near the Common, which is stressful. I get hooted at by two Land Rovers going in opposite directions (*bloody yummy mummies*, I mutter under my breath, as I accidentally switch the rear windscreen wiper on and reverse into the bumper of the mint-green convertible behind us, and I catch Gloria looking at me approvingly).

Once I've finally managed to get the car somewhere near the kerb and fed the meter, I help Gloria out of the car.

'Where do you want to go? Straight to your old house? Is it near here?' I ask, but she's not listening to me. I watch her face as she looks out over the wide expanse of grass in front of us, criss-crossed with paths, cyclists zooming along them, more joggers and buggies too, and people lying out in the sun, children kicking balls about and scooting.

'Yes,' she says, though not to me. 'This is right. This is how I remember it.'

And then she just walks off as though I'm not there.

'All right, wait for me,' I call after her, double-checking I've locked the car, then checking again one last time, imagining Mum's face if I had to phone Spain to tell her the car had been stolen.

She keeps walking across the grass, looking around at the trees, and the houses that fringe the Common, taking it all in.

When I catch up with her and see her face, I can see Gloria's not really here with me. She puts her arms out and her head back and slowly starts to spin.

'What are you doing?' I say, looking around to check whether anyone's watching. 'Gloria, steady. You'll get dizzy.'

But she can't hear me, because she isn't here with me. She's back there on a long-ago Sunday morning, twirling, round and round, her arms held out, head tilted back in the sunshine.

She tells me about walking across the Common with her mum – my great-grandmother – on a Sunday after Mass, about her drunk father and her smug, irritating brother-in-law. She tells me about Sam, the boy she wished she'd been meeting instead, and how she couldn't stop herself from dancing in the sunlight in the middle of the Common. And as she tells it, she is transformed. I can see the girl she used to be standing in front of me.

# Chapter eight

'Just a large gin and tonic for me, please,' Gloria says to the very handsome, very camp waiter. We've settled on a gastropub near the Common for lunch before going to Gloria's old house. Now we're here she seems to want to put it off.

'Gloria,' I say.

'What?'

'I thought we were going to have lunch.'

She looks at me. 'I'm not hungry.'

'Perhaps I can interest you in one of our Lighter Bites, madam?' says the waiter. 'The goat's cheese and quinoa salad with the honey and orange dressing is to die for.'

She ignores him.

'It does sound *delicious* ...' I say, trying to sound enthusiastic. Gloria is pretending she can't hear either of us. 'I think I'll go for the burger and chips.'

She's been quiet since our walk on the Common, and so have I, my head full of everything she described. It was so vivid, so real for her, so present. I was thrown off balance by it somehow, the realization that she had been young once, that inside she still felt young when she remembered it. I could almost see the girl she had been, still there inside, and it made me feel sad, the thought that she had grown old, and that soon she wouldn't be able to remember the girl she had been.

My head is buzzing with her story, there's so much more I want to know, about her violent father, her poor mum, about Nan and annoying Vinnie – my grandad. And most of all I want to know about – what was his name? – Sam. Her face when she'd spoken about him, her voice ... My food and Gloria's drink arrive. I try to prompt her into telling me more as I devour my burger, offering Gloria the occasional chip, which she declines with a wave of her turquoise-nailed hand. She drains her first gin and tonic and asks for another. 'With a little more lime this time, if you please,' she says accusingly.

'Your wish is my command, madam,' says the waiter, winking at me, and I smile at him apologetically.

After she's finished the second gin I try again.

'So,' I say. 'Sam. Was he your boyfriend?'

She looks at me.

'Yes.'

I wait for her to tell me more, but she doesn't.

She snaps her bag shut and goes off to the loo.

As I'm waiting I can't help noticing the group of women at the next table who all have tiny babies. They're talking about breastfeeding and how many times their babies wake in the night and whether you should give them formula milk or was that bad for them and should you sleep with them in your bed or in a crib next to your bed or in a different room and which was most likely to cause cot death, whether you should feed them at particular times or just whenever they felt like it and whether you should let them cry or was that practically child abuse and then what about colic, what a nightmare that was, babies crying non-stop for five hours every night and—

I try to think about something else because their conversation is making me feel sick and panicky. It's nothing to do with me. I'm not going to have a baby. But I can't stop listening. How can looking after a baby be so difficult? And from nowhere I have a sudden memory of Mum after the twins were born. Dad was off reporting from somewhere – where was it? Gaza maybe. I used to stick drawing pins in a map on the kitchen wall to show where he was. Wherever it was, it was a long way away from us. The twins were growing bigger every day and Mum was looking thinner and paler all the time, as if the twins were tiny vampires, sucking the life from her with their perfect, hungry little mouths. I remember something waking me in the night and going downstairs and finding Mum feeding them, one baby tucked under each arm, and tears were streaming down her cheeks. 'Does it hurt?' I'd asked. She'd nodded and for a while I almost wished the twins hadn't been born.

I look back at the women and think how weird tiny babies look, some of them with bald, scaly scalps, some with too much hair, some scrawny, some with rolls of fat. The mums all seem transfixed by them. The baskets of their buggies are full of cloth books and toys for their tiny babies. Do babies really need all that stuff? And how do you find out? How do you know if you're doing it right?

I look away again. I don't know why I'm even thinking about it. This has nothing to do with me. I'm not having a baby. I'm going to university. I'm going to book the doctor's appointment and then the doctor will send me off to the abortion clinic and it'll be as if it never happened. Perhaps I don't even have to tell Reuben.

It can all be exactly as it was before.

After lunch we walk to Gloria's old house. She doesn't speak as we walk down her street but I can see that she's taking in every detail. At last, about three quarters of the way down, she stops in front of the house. I can see from the buzzer at the front door that it's divided into flats. The front garden is paved, with a few half-hearted shrubs growing in tubs. It's hardly changed from the house in the black-and-white photo in Gloria's album; it's still an ordinary-looking terraced house in a street of identical houses.

'Is this it?' I say, pointlessly. She doesn't answer.

'It must bring back a lot of memories,' I try. I'm hoping that seeing the house will prompt another outpouring of memories, a continuation of her story.

But her face is set and she doesn't speak. Whatever she's remembering, she's not sharing it with me.

At last she turns away.

'There used to be roses growing in the front garden,' she says at last. 'You could smell them as you walked down the street.'

And she walks away from the house and away from me.

'It must bring back a lot of memories,' she says, the girl at my elbow. Hattie.

This house that I have only seen in my dreams for so many years. It is hard to believe it really exists, that the memories in my head are things that really happened once, to someone who was me, long ago. I wonder what she thinks I feel as I look at the house, its blank windows staring back at me. She cannot imagine the darkness of the things I remember in this house.

The wood of the table is cold under my chin. I examine the stems of the roses in the jam jar of water in front of me. They are cloaked in tiny bubbles, each bubble perfectly round, like the Earth. Gwen told me the world is round. She learned it at school. I imagine that each bubble is a world with millions of tiny people living on it, a tiny me and a tiny Gwen, a tiny Mum and Father. Perhaps in one of the worlds I am more like Gwen, prettier and less naughty. I don't mean to be bad, but the things that seem to me to be the right things to do don't seem to be the things that everyone else thinks are right. *Think before you act,* Mum says, but my thoughts don't work like that. They come afterwards. *You're too soft on her,* Father says. Perhaps in one of the worlds, Father is less angry.

I like looking at the room through the jam jar. It bends and stretches like the Hall of Mirrors at the circus that pitches up on the Common every year. They are talking, Mum and Father, but I'm only half listening. It's boring things like mutton for dinner again and paying the milkman, and then she makes a joke about his tie not being straight and reaches a hand out to straighten it for him. There is a crack and her head whips back. She has her back to me and the flowers – pale-pink roses, they were, that Mum and I had cut from the bush by the back gate the day before, taking care the thorns didn't prick us – block my view of Father. Then I hear the back door slam and I know he has gone. Perhaps I have misunderstood what has happened. I must have. But when she turns to me there is blood trickling from her nose. She tries to cover the look of dazed hurt on her face with a smile.

'Just a little accident,' she says to me. 'Up to your room now, Gloria, time for a nap,' which is all wrong because I've only just had breakfast.

'I don't want to,' I say.

'Go on now,' she says, sharply. She is never sharp. This and the blood make me scared and being scared makes me obstinate.

'No.'

'Gloria, *please*.'

The blood drips down onto her dress. It's my favourite one with the yellow flowers and I cry because the stain won't come out in the wash.

'Course it will,' she says, 'A bit of bicarb will do it.'

I tell Gwen about it when she comes home from school that afternoon. I think she will be shocked, but she turns away as I say it, pretending to be concentrating on something else.

'It was an accident,' she says.

107

'No, Gwen,' I say, trying to think how I can make her understand. He had hit Mum and then he had left her standing there in the kitchen, with an empty milk bottle in her hand and blood dripping onto her prettiest dress. 'It wasn't.'

'*Yes*,' she says. 'It was.'

'But you weren't there!' I feel angry tears in my eyes.

She bites her lip and says nothing. Then she comes and sits next to me on the bed. She picks up Ursula, my teddy, and looks at her rather sombre face and glassy eyes as she speaks, as if she is talking to Ursula, not me.

'Father loves Mum,' she says in a silly, growly voice, pretending it is Ursula who is speaking. 'That's what matters, isn't it? And she loves him.'

I look at Gwen and I think that there are other things that matter, and that being in love doesn't sound like a very good idea at all.

She hands the teddy to me. 'Here. Give Ursula a cuddle. She'll make you feel better.' She puts on the growly Ursula voice again. 'Cheer up, Gloria. You're too young to understand. 'When you're older and you fall in love and get married you'll see.'

I lie down on my bed with my back to Gwen and don't say anything. When she goes downstairs I hide Ursula in the back of the wardrobe behind our old shoes and boots, along with the Snow White book with the scary picture of the witch that gives me nightmares. But I know she is there and in time, in my mind, she becomes bigger and grows claws, hiding in the shadows at the back of the wardrobe and at night she comes to replace the witch in my nightmares.

The windows of the house where all this happened stare back blankly at me now, but I see inside them. I see the pink roses in a jam jar on the table. I see a stiff, rather ugly teddy bear hidden at the back of a cupboard. I see a girl sneaking out of the back door and running out of the back gate and down the alley to the Common to meet the boy she loves. I hear the tread of feet that shouldn't be there coming down the stairs. I see a mirror, shattered, on a tiled floor. I see a place where the pattern of the wallpaper does not align and I must not take my eyes off it—

Perhaps it was wrong to come back.

I look at her – Hattie – and see concern in her eyes.

'Are you okay?' she says. 'Do you want to go now?'

I am not scared. The words recite themselves in my head. If I say it often enough perhaps I can make it true.

## Chapter nine

On the way back to Gloria's flat I can't stop thinking about everything she told me, about what she had been like when she was my age and about Nan and Vinnie – my grandfather. Dad's father. If Gloria couldn't tell me anything about Dad, the next best thing was finding out about his family, the father who died when he was a just a kid.

'Why didn't you like Vinnie?' I ask, hoping to prompt her into more stories, but she doesn't answer.

She invites me in when we get to the flat and pours herself a large gin. After investigating the fridge I discover that Malcolm's supermarket run included a couple of frozen pizzas so I stick these in the oven.

'Was your father really different before the war?' I try again as we sit in Gloria's cluttered sitting room waiting for the pizzas to cook.

'How would I know?' she says, drinking the gin and tonic she'd poured for me, even though I told her twice I didn't want one. 'I was born during the war. When he came back, he wasn't the man my mother thought she'd married but that may not have had anything to do with the war. I can't say.'

'Was Sam your boyfriend?'

She hesitates. 'Yes.'

I watch her closely. Her voice had changed when she'd talked about him. Her face too. I could almost see a glimpse of the girl she'd been.

'Was it serious?' I say. 'Between you and Sam? I mean, were you in love with him?'

She hesitates again, for longer this time.

'Yes,' she says at last. 'I was. I thought I was anyway. I was young.'

I think again about how she had been when she talked about the past. It was so clear to her, as if she could see it, touch it. She seemed so certain, so animated. In the present she is different, more distant. From my hasty research into dementia I know that old memories are often clear, while more recent ones can be confused. Perhaps she feels less confident in the present and the distance is her protection.

'What was he like?' I say. 'How did you meet him?'

She pauses, as though she's considering answering.

'You're asking an awful lot of questions,' she says at last. 'Isn't it my turn now?'

I shrug. 'Ask away. But I haven't got anything interesting to tell you. I'm really very boring.'

'Are you going to keep your baby?' she says.

I wasn't expecting that. I feel myself go red, and my heart thuds. I'd almost hoped she might have forgotten that I'm pregnant. But I suppose even if she does it's all written down in that notebook of hers. Why did I tell her? I was angry, I suppose. Maybe I wanted to tell someone, someone who wouldn't care one way or the other. It felt like such a big secret to be keeping. And after all I'd thought I'd never see her again, and that she'd forget.

111

'No,' I say. 'I mean . . . well, I can't.'

She watches me and I wonder what she's thinking.

'I want to go to university,' I say. 'And Reuben – well, he's not really . . .'

I can't even begin to find all the words for the things Reuben isn't really.

'Reuben?' she says, her eyes lighting up. 'Is he the father?'

'Yes,' I say and as she takes out her book and starts scribbling it strikes me how preposterous it is, how laughable and yet at the same time not very funny. Reuben, a father. He can't even look after himself. 'He's not my boyfriend or anything. He's just a friend.'

She looks sceptical.

'Really,' I say. 'It was just the once that we . . .' I blush again. 'You know.'

She smiles. 'I certainly do.'

'It was stupid really.'

'Tell me about him,' she says.

'Oh, God,' I say. 'I don't know where to begin.'

'At the beginning?' she suggests.


Reuben Wilde.

The first time I heard his name was three years ago. And two months. And five days. Give or take.

A few of Mum's mates had come round, supposedly for 'Book Group', but when I ventured into the kitchen to get a glass of juice there was only one lonely copy of *Wolf Hall* on the table and it had a bowl of Twiglets on top of it. By contrast, there were quite a few empty wine bottles.

I tried to sneak in and out without being noticed but Mum's friend Sally spotted me.

'Ooh, now, Hattie,' she said. 'You've got a treat in store ,my dear, if the rumours are true.'

'What rumours?'

Sally smiled. 'He's Trouble. You'll like him. But he's definitely Trouble.'

I had no idea what she was on about, but what with all the empty bottles and the fact that Sally was a bit flushed I just smiled back. 'Who is?'

'Reuben Wilde.'

Even his name sent a little thrill through me. Did it? Or do I just think that now, looking back on it?

'What are you on about, Sal?' Mum said. 'Pass the crisps down here will you?'

'We're sending you lot at Mayfield a present. A St Augustine's cast-off. Rather an interesting one too.' Sally's an art teacher at St Augustine's, a super-posh private school where loads of celebs and Russian oligarchs send their kids.

'He's been to more expensive schools than you've had hot dinners. Started at Harrow and worked his way down from there. Been kicked out of all of them for assorted and inventive misdemeanours. Anyway, the rumour in the staff room is that now his old man's run out of patience or money or schools that will take him, depending on who you believe. So now he's off to Mayfield. Because whatever he does they'll never kick him out.'

'What did he get kicked out of all the schools for? Is he a psychopath? Sociopath? Habitual drug user? Anarchist?' I asked.

'Oh.' Sally stifled a hiccup. 'I couldn't possibly say. It would be *completely unprofessional*.'

'Like this whole conversation hasn't been *completely unprofessional*,' Mum said.

'Well, you'll have to ask him,' Sally said. 'He hasn't had an easy time of it really. He's a good kid underneath it all. Well, maybe not good exactly. Likeable?' She thinks about it. 'Interesting. Not like some of them. Just . . . well, like I say, Trouble.'

'Hmm,' I said, trying not to sound too interested, 'I'll look out for him.'

'Oh, you won't need to,' Sally said. 'He'll make himself noticed.'

So when Reuben strolled into my history lesson two weeks later, all tall and stylishly bedraggled, hair hanging down over his left eye, a cigarette behind one ear and several earrings in the other, and only the most token of gestures towards school uniform, I'd been waiting for him, *anticipating* him. He smiled dazzlingly at Ms Horace (who he'd caught mid bubonic plague symptoms and was none too happy about being interrupted) and said in his poshest voice, 'So sorry I'm late. Got a little held up. Have I missed all the fun?', like he was attending a soiree in 1920s Belgravia, probably with Jay Gatsby and/or Noel Coward. And I actually had to stop myself from smiling a big, embarrassing smile. Ever since Sally had told me about him I'd been building him up to be something exciting and dangerous and complicated and magnificent.

And he was.

Ms Horace didn't seem to share my opinion. She gave him her best and most contemptuous death stare, whipped the cigarette from behind his ear and snapped, 'Sit down, will you?', gesturing towards the only empty chair in the room – which was *next to me* – before moving seamlessly back to pustules. I half smiled at him as he slid into his seat, trying to look conspiratorial rather than adoring, and he

114

winked at me before turning to survey the rest of the room. His gaze settled quickly on Soraya Jones (everyone's gaze always does – she's eye-hurtingly beautiful) and he leaned over to me and whispered, 'Hey, babe, what's her name? With the long black hair?'

Ms Horace fixed Reuben with a look that left us in no doubt that she fervently wished it was within her power to inflict the Black Death upon him, and continued with her graphic descriptions of buboes in the underarm and nether regions and the vomiting of blood, without once taking her eyes off him. And I remember thinking that really I should have found him quite ridiculous, not to mention annoying. But instead I just felt happy that he was sitting next to me.

So when Ms Horace told us to write a paragraph from the perspective of a plague-ridden villager, I scribbled him a note that said:

Soraya. But her boyfriend Paddy is a boxer. Just so you know. Also never call me 'babe' again. EVER. I'm Hattie ☺

He sent me back a note that said:

Thanks Babe ☺ Do you think Ms H is fantasizing about me dying in agony of exploding armpits and groin? I do.

So I sent back a note that said:

Yes Babe, I suspect she really is ☺

Which was when Ms Horace spotted me and gave me a half-hour detention on Friday afternoon. And that was where I was, in a stuffy classroom that smelt of stale sweat and hormones and cheese-and-onion crisps, when I spotted Reuben through the window, walking arm in arm in the sunshine with Soraya Jones.

\*   \*   \*

Next time I saw Reuben, a couple of days later, he had a black eye and a really nasty cut across his cheekbone, and a split lip just for good measure.

I caught up with him as we pushed our way out of the classroom and down the stairs and grimaced in a way that could have been sympathetic or repulsed. 'Warned you about Paddy.'

He put his hand up to the cut and pressed it gently, wincing a bit.

'Sore?' I said.

He nodded and smiled. 'Kind of attractive, though, right?' he said hopefully, heading through the door out to the lower-school playground and then holding it open for me with his foot. 'It'll make girls want to look after me?'

'*No*,' I said, walking next to him down the steps. 'You just look . . . misshapen. And thuggish. A misshapen thug. That's not attractive in any possible way.'

'You say the sweetest things, babe,' he said.

'*Don't*—'

'I'm kidding,' he said, elbowing me in the ribs. 'Holly.'

'Hattie.'

He laughed, flinching because it made his lip hurt. 'I *know*,' he said. And I couldn't tell whether he was lying or not.

It's all been pretty much like that ever since.

Gloria takes out her notebook and writes a few notes as I'm talking. I try to read upside down but she spots me and holds the book at an angle so I can't.

'It's nothing interesting,' she says. 'Just the key facts so I don't forget. He doesn't know you're pregnant?'

'No.'

'Are you going to tell him?'

'NO. I mean, yes. I don't know. Does he really have to know?'

She doesn't say anything, just watches me intently.

'He's in France at the moment anyway,' I say. 'I can't tell him in an email or on the phone, can I?'

'What's he doing in France?'

'I dunno. Travelling. Finding Himself. Getting drunk and stoned a lot, I expect. Having sex with lots of people. That kind of thing.'

'Well, yes,' she says, putting her notebook away. 'They do go in for all that in France, don't they? Always liked the French.'

'Have you been? To France, I mean?'

'Yes, lots of times. I don't suppose I'll ever see Paris again now.'

I look at her, trying to imagine how it would feel to know you didn't have long.

'Well, instead of sitting here feeling sorry for yourself why don't you go? I told you, I'll take you wherever you want to go. What's on your bucket list?'

'My what?'

'It's a list people make of things they want to do before they . . . well, you know.'

She looks at me.

'Kick the bucket. You know, like – I dunno. Go up the Eiffel Tower. Or run a marathon. Bungee-jumping. Threesomes. Go to the Maldives. I mean, I'm not saying that's what you'd have on yours obviously—'

'Threesomes?'

'Yes,' I say, wishing I hadn't mentioned it now. She looks at me questioningly.

'It's when, um, people – three of them – have . . . you know . . .' I try to work out whether 'sex' or 'intercourse' would be better and I realize that neither would.

'I know perfectly well what a threesome is, thank you very much. But I thought you said this bucket list was supposed to be things I'd never tried before.'

'You mean you've . . .'

She looks at me and raises an eyebrow.

'Well,' I say, coughing and feeling myself go red. 'Anyway. The point is, it's up to you what goes on it. It could be anything. Stuff you've always wanted to do. Or maybe going to more places you care about like we did today, or people you want to see while . . . while you can still remember. I could take you. Just like today. Just tell me where you want to go. They call it a trip down memory lane, don't they? Well, we can *literally* do it.'

Gloria looks uncertain.

'"Tis in my memory lock'd and you yourself shall keep the key of it,"' she says thoughtfully, more to herself than me.

'What?' I ask.

'Ophelia,' she says. 'Act one, scene three.'

'Does that mean yes?' I say hopefully.

'Let me think about it.'

It's starting to get dark by the time I leave. When I get to the door I turn to her.

'What made you change your mind?' I say.

'About what?'

'About me. About all of it.'

She stops and there's a long pause. I wonder whether I've offended her in some way, or whether she's forgotten we were having a conversation.

118

'It was because of something you said.'

I look at her.

'What?'

She doesn't answer me.

'Do you remember what I said about memories?' she says at last. 'Without them we are nobody.'

I nod.

'Well, I don't want to be nobody,' she says quietly, to herself more than me, I think.

I'm starting to understand. If Gloria tells me her memories, they can't be lost. *She* can't be lost.

# Chapter ten

'*There* you are,' I say, as Gloria saunters elegantly into the Savoy bar as if she own the place. She's an hour and ten minutes late, and I've been sitting feeling unbelievably self-conscious, because I feel horribly out of place, not to mention broke, as the drinks are a bit beyond my price bracket. I've made my glass of sparkling mineral water last as long as possible, watching the barman mix incredibly beautiful jewel-coloured cocktails for well-dressed tourists, and checking my phone, trying to look calm and sophisti-cated. My fake-serenity hasn't been helped by the fact that a text arrived about fifteen minutes ago from Kat saying: **You're 8 weeks now, right? Embryo is size of a raspberry according to book. Have u seen doc yet? I'll try and call u soon xxxxxxx**. So, all in all, I'm in a pretty bad mood, but even in my annoyance I can't help admiring Gloria's poise as she walks in.

She looks round as I speak and there's a tiny hint of relief in her face as she sees me that makes me guess that under that poise she's not as certain of herself as she seems.

'Yes,' she says. 'Here I am. Could you go and order me a Martini, dear, I just need to sort myself out.'

'I've been sitting here for more than an hour!'

120

She looks at me blankly. 'Why?'

'You're late,' I say.

'No, I'm not. I'm a little early. See!' She waves her hand at me jubilantly and on it is written: *HATTIE 5 p.m. Savoy.*

'But it's six fifteen.'

'No, dear. You've obviously got confused.'

'Look!'

I show her my watch.

'Well, it's clearly wrong.'

She goes to look at her own watch but it's not there.

'Oh, yes,' she says vaguely. 'I couldn't find my—' She stops and tuts. 'Clock thing, you know.' She points at her wrist.

'Watch.'

'Anyway,' she says firmly. 'I didn't come all this way to talk about what time it is. Order me a Martini, will you, and then I can tell you the plan.'

I think about arguing but it strikes me that there's not a lot of point. I'd actually wondered whether Gloria would remember that we'd arranged to meet at all. And Gloria's mention of 'the plan' has got me interested. She was very mysterious when we'd spoken on the phone. All she'd told me was that she wanted me to meet her at the Savoy the next day.

'So,' she says, once I've handed over her Martini. 'I thought about what you said, about places I'd like to go and people I wanted to see and bucket lists and whatnot and there is somewhere I'd like us to go.'

'Oh, yes?' I'm only half paying attention to be honest. I can't help thinking about Kat's text. I'm not eight weeks yet, not quite, but still. The fact that there really is something growing inside me is unnerving. 'Where's that?'

She pauses for dramatic effect.

'Whitby,' she announces, triumphant.

121

I stare at her.

'*Whitby?*'

'Yes.'

I stare at her blankly.

'It's in North Yorkshire,' she says. 'By the sea.'

'Right.' I don't know what exactly I was expecting to be on Gloria's bucket list, but it certainly wasn't this. 'So, not the Maldives then?'

'No.'

'Not Paris, even?'

'No.'

'Because we could go to Paris, you know. I was thinking about it. It's really easy now, with the Eurostar. Have you got a passport?'

'I want to go to Whitby,' she says.

'So, your bucket list is to go to the seaside in Yorkshire?

'I thought we could make a proper trip of it. There are some other places I'd like to stop off at on the way.'

I try not to look too disappointed. 'Okay,' I say. 'So where are we going?'

'Cambridge first. I went there with Sam.'

'Oh,' I say, brightening. 'My dad went to university there. I've never been.' It's not exactly exotic but it'll be a chance to see somewhere that was part of Dad's life. And taking Gloria back to somewhere she went with Sam seems very romantic.

'And then the Lake District,' she says.

I attempt enthusiasm.

'We did go on holiday to the Lake District once, when I was really little.' I try, unsuccessfully, to dredge up a happy memory from that holiday. 'It rained pretty much non-stop.'

'Oh, well,' she snaps. 'If you don't want to—'

'I didn't say that. It's just . . . Why do you want to go there?'

122

'*You* were the one who pointed out that this is my last opportunity to go to these places and remember them. *You* were the one who wanted to get to know each other. But if you've changed your mind . . .'

'No,' I say. 'I'm definitely up for it. It'll be a laugh. But how long for? I'm supposed to be working.'

'I don't know. A week? Maybe more.'

I think it all through. Is it really possible? Could we actually do it? I know I suggested it, but to be honest I never thought Gloria would go through with it.

But as I take a moment to think about it, the idea becomes more and more appealing. The thought of getting away even for a few days, of having an adventure, of doing something for Gloria, of finding out more about her and about Dad's family, not to mention having some space to think about my own problems . . . Why not?

'We'd have to go soon,' I say. 'Like really soon. In the next few days, so that we can be home before Mum gets back from Mallorca. And we could only go for a week at most. She'd kill me if she got back and I'd gone off with her car. Could we do it in a week?'

Gloria rolls her eyes theatrically. 'I once went to New York for a party and was back onstage in the West End the following night. Well, more or less. Mind you that was in the days of Concorde.'

'We'd be in Mum's Ford Fiesta. Not quite the same.' I think it through. Judging by what Peggy said and what I vaguely know about dementia, I don't think organization will be a strong point for Gloria. 'Where would we stay? I can't really afford hotels or anything like that.'

Gloria waves her hand airily.

'I'll be paying, of course,' she says. 'My husbands may

have been stupid but they were rich. Apart from Gianni, of course, who was just beautiful and so didn't need to be rich.'

'It's a bit late to be booking. Especially during the summer holidays.'

'I've spoken to Peggy already. She's going to sort out all the boring details,' Gloria says, as if it's decided we're going. 'Peggy's good at that sort of thing. She just talks people into submission. She's always trying to stick her nose in, *organize me*. She's delighted that I'm finally going to let her.'

I realize as she's speaking that Gloria hasn't invited me here to ask me if I'll take her. She's come here to *tell* me. And, perhaps, if Peggy's agreed to sort everything out . . . perhaps we can do it. Why not? So, despite my panic about Kat's text and the fact that we're going to Whitby not the Maldives and the general insanity of the whole idea, I feel myself smiling.

We're really going to do this.

'We'll be like Thelma and Louise,' I say. 'Kind of.'

'Who?'

'Thelma and Louise. It's a film. Mum has it on DVD; it's about two women who go on a road trip.'

'Does either of them have dementia?'

'No.'

'Is either of them pregnant?'

'No.'

'Well, then our road trip should be much more exciting than theirs.'

'Hmm,' I say, unconvinced. It strikes me that there are quite a few things that could go wrong with this plan. 'They meet Brad Pitt on their journey.'

'Who?'

I get out my phone and search the internet for a picture of Brad Pitt and show it to Gloria.

'Oh, I say,' she exclaims.

'Do they go to Whitby?'

'Not really,' I say. 'It's more the Arizona desert, from memory. The Grand Canyon. They end up—'

'Well,' she says firmly. 'They should have gone to Whitby. It's very nice. Good fish and chips.'

'Whitby,' I say, trying to dredge up everything I know about it, which is that it's something to do with Dracula. 'Won't it be a bit . . . chilly?'

'I'm not going for the weather.'

I'd kind of worked that out.

'What are you going for then?'

'That's where the end of the story is.'

I try not to feel impatient about the fact that she's talking in riddles.

'What story?'

'My story. There's a story that no one else knows. About me.'

'A secret?'

She shrugs. 'If you like. It feels suddenly very strange to think that if I don't tell it now, then no one will ever know. Part of me feels that would be a blessing.' She takes a sip from her glass. 'It's not a happy story. I made myself forget it for a long, long time.'

'But now you don't want to?'

She hesitates.

'Let's go for a walk,' she says, draining her glass. 'You were asking me about Sam last time, if I remember right? I'll show you where we met.'

We walk along the Strand in the early-evening sun, with tourists and people in suits leaving their offices, trooping towards the station or the pub. As we walk Gloria remembers.

Aching cold fingers. Feet pinched into points, kitten heels sliding on snow that has melted and refrozen.

'You'll catch your death, you two,' Louise's mum calls after us as we totter down the road. 'Don't be late back, now. Midnight, remember, girls?'

'We'll see,' Louise says to me under her breath, smiling. Louise is the same age as me, but she looks much older than seventeen. She left school last year to go to secretarial college and has a sort of woman-of-the-world air about her, but we still go out together on a Friday night.

'There's the bus, run, Gloria!' Louise screeches.

'Run? I can't even walk in these shoes!'

We hang on to one another, squealing and laughing as we slip on the ice, nearly ending up on our arses. The bus conductor sees us and makes the bus wait until we jump on, breathless, and I give him a peck on the cheek before we climb noisily up the stairs, collapsing in giggles as we reach a free seat.

It's warm and smoky on the bus. Outside the night is dark and clear.

'What's he like then, this friend of Johnny's?' I ask Louise when I've got my breath back.

'Never met him,' Louise says. 'Johnny says he's nice, though.'

'Good-looking?'

'Well, my Johnny's not going to be much of a judge of that, is he? Least, I hope not.' She laughs and lights a cigarette, her pink lipstick staining the filter. 'Your nose is bright red, you know.'

'It's not, is it?' I get my compact out and dab powder on my frozen nose. I'm not nervous. I don't really care about this Sam; Louise has set me up before with Johnny's friends and none of them has been what you might call memorable, at least not in a good way. But still, I don't want to turn up looking like a circus clown.

I'm just looking forward to a night out. Father tried to stop me coming. Nothing new there. Knowing I've made him angry only makes it sweeter. Unless he takes it out on Mum, of course . . . I push the thought away and concentrate on reapplying my lipstick.

As we pull up at the traffic lights near the Lyceum, Louise is looking out of the window.

'There they are,' she says, pointing.

I lean over her shoulder to look out of the steamed-up window. I rub it with my sleeve and peer through the gap. There's Johnny, almost as wide as he is tall, rubbing his hands together in the cold and blowing on them. Next to him is a tall, skinny chap with his hands in his pockets, wearing a trilby hat. I turn to stare at Louise.

'But he's coloured, Lou!' I say. 'You never told me!'

'Didn't I?' she says, leaning over to ring the bell. 'Well, what difference does it make?'

'None, I suppose,' I say, imagining Father's face if he knew, and smiling.

'Johnny says some of the fellas they work with are a bit funny about it. Call him names, some of them do. But they're idiots.

Not like this Sam. He's dead clever, apparently.' She stands up as the bus starts to slow down. 'So what he's doing hanging around with my Johnny, God only knows. He keeps his brains in his You-Know-What.'

'*Lou!*' I giggle. 'What would Sister Mary Francis say if she heard you talking like that?'

'She'd say she was right about me all along.' Louise laughs, putting out her cigarette end with an impossibly pointed red-satin toe.

We clatter down the stairs of the bus and off onto the icy pavement. I hold on to Louise's arm, walking self-consciously, taking care not to slip, now I know Johnny and Sam have seen us.

'He *is* good-looking, too,' Louise whispers in my ear, as we get closer to them. 'You lucky devil, Gloria. I'll swap you, if you like!'

'No thanks,' I say, laughing. 'Johnny's all yours, Lou.'

As we get close I can feel my heart thudding but I don't let my nerves show.

'Gloria?' he says, holding out his hand for me to shake and smiling wide. 'I'm Sam.'

I look up at him and I find I'm suddenly very aware that my nose might still be red, and hoping I haven't got lipstick on my teeth, and glad I wore the new patent winklepickers Gwen got me for Christmas even though they're killing my feet already and I know there's no way I'll still be wearing them by the end of the night.

I smile my most dazzling smile.

'Pleased to meet you, Sam,' I say, taking his hand and feeling a little thrill where our cold skin touches. Next to us Louise and Johnny are greeting each other in a rather more intimate way, his tongue halfway down her throat. We both look at them and then I look at Sam and we laugh, awkward but nice, like we're sharing a joke.

'Well,' he says. 'Shall we go in? I don't think they're going to miss us somehow.' He's hardly got an accent, I reckon he must have lived in London most of his life, but still his voice sounds exotic to me. I've never been further than Eastbourne in my life. 'I hope you like dancing, Gloria,' he says, smiling, and I think how much I like it that when he smiles his whole face smiles, not just his mouth. And then I think how much I like his mouth too. And then I think *Shut up, Gloria*, because I'm used to being bored by the boys I go out with, and it's a bit unnerving to find that I'm not bored by Sam. Not at all.

I look up at him from under my false eyelashes. 'I do, as it happens, Sam,' I say. 'Hope you can keep up.'

He laughs and holds out his arm. 'Sounds like a challenge to me.'

I take his arm and I walk as slowly as I can towards the doors of the Lyceum because I don't want to have to let go of him.

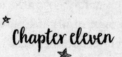
## Chapter eleven

From: hattiedlockwood@starmail.com
To: wilde_one666@starmail.com
Subject:

Ok so this is a bit weird but I've agreed to go on a road
trip with Gloria. Don't look at me like that, Reuben (I can
tell you are). It'll be fine. Like that film Thelma and
Louise but without the shooting (I hope) and with a
70-year-old in the early stages of dementia. And going to
the Seaview Hotel, Whitby (three and half stars, all
rooms with hot beverage facilities and free wifi, 'terrific
value for money!' – TripAdvisor) not the Grand Canyon.
And ideally not ending up by ***SPOILER ALERT*** driving off a cliff. Hmmm. Perhaps the Thelma and Louise
analogy wasn't a good one after all. I only really said it
because I'm hoping we might meet a young Brad Pitt on
the way . . .

Anyway, it seemed like a good idea when I suggested it
(not the Seaview Hotel, obviously, just the idea of going
back to places that meant something to her). I just feel so

sorry for her, Reuben. Imagine knowing that everything and everyone and everywhere you ever cared about is going to be wiped from your mind. Wouldn't you want to relive some of it while you still had the chance? I think perhaps there's someone she wants to meet in Whitby. There's some kind of mystery in her past. She's going to tell me more about it on the way. Although I do kind of worry about that. What if she forgets why we're going? I don't think she will, though. It's weird how clearly she remembers everything from the past.

It'll only be for a week. It'll be fine. Won't it? Most of the time her memory seems fine. Except when it doesn't. Or when she's very drunk.

OH GOD, WHAT HAVE I DONE, REUBEN????

No. I'm being silly. It'll be fine. A little break for us both. Might as well, given that everyone else has ABANDONED ME. Had a text from Kat earlier. She's still all loved up in Edinburgh, but Zoe is a cow. I can tell. Also a message from Carl saying please can I check the wedding caterers got his messages about gluten-free options on the menus. It's good to know they're all missing me so much.

Hope you and la belle Camille are having a great time on your travels. Tell me where you are so I can live vicariously through you. And if you're lucky I will reciprocate by telling you heartwarming and hilarious anecdotes about the motorway services on the M1.

Hattie xxx

131

Peggy calls me the day before we're due to leave.

'Of course Gloria wants to be in charge of the arrangements, Harriet, but I thought I'd better give you a quick call and talk it through with you, just in case. I've booked you into a lovely bed and breakfast in Cambridge, and then in the Lake District you'll be in a cottage, it belongs to the nephew of a friend of a friend from church – Edwin, his name is – and they usually rent it out over the summer, you see, Harriet, but then—'

She goes into a long, complicated story about some medical emergency that meant the cottage was unexpectedly vacant and my mind wanders. I know I ought to call Mum and tell her that I'm going away, or at least email her. I missed a call from her yesterday, and she left a voicemail saying they were missing me and how sorry they were that I was working all hours. As it happened, the reason I missed the call was because I'd been in the middle of a massive row with Melanie the Manager.

'You can't just take a week off whenever you feel like it,' she said. 'And not at this late notice. It's totally unprofessional. You're letting the team down.'

'It's because of my great-aunt,' I said. 'She wants me to take her away to Yorkshire.'

'I thought she was dying?' Mel said, trying to catch me out.

'She is! That's why it's so important. It's her dying wish.'

'To go to Yorkshire?' Mel looked sceptical. I nodded. 'Why?'

'I don't know.'

'You must think I was born yesterday,' she said. 'Sorry, Hetty—' she always gets my name wrong on purpose to wind me up—'but no can do.'

'Fine, I quit,' I shouted, mainly because I've fantasized about doing it every day since I started work there. It didn't feel as good as I thought it would. A fat customer with a toupee who'd had his eyes fixed on Mel's cleavage the whole time he'd been messily eating his double egg and sausage special said, 'No work ethic, youngsters, that's the problem. Country's going to the dogs.'

Mel said, 'You'll be back.'

'No, I won't,' I said, storming out, and then I remembered I'd left my bag and jacket in the staffroom and had to sneak in to retrieve them, so Mel was right.

'. . . And then the Seaview Hotel in Whitby for two nights,' Peggy's saying. 'It looks tremendous, dear, it really does. Malcolm and I are tempted to take a visit there ourselves. Now.' she pauses for breath. 'Are you quite sure about this, Harriet, dear? I think it'll do Gloria the power of good to get away but I don't want you going if you don't feel you can cope. I know she can be very . . . forceful.' I hear Malcolm muttering something in the background. 'She hasn't talked you into it against your will now, has she, Harriet?'

'No,' I say. 'I want to go.'

And as I say it, I realize it's actually true.

*Chapter twelve*

It's light when I wake in Gloria's spare room (miraculously de-cluttered and cleaned, by Peggy, I assume), but it feels early. It takes me a few seconds to remember where I am. And then I remember. I check my watch: not even six yet, but I know I won't get back to sleep, even though I have that weariness that comes from a bad night's sleep. I spent most of the night dreaming about driving out-of-control cars, my foot not quite able to reach the brake pedal, my eyes unable to focus on the road ahead, the steering wheel failing to respond to anything I do, pitching me into the middle of oncoming traffic. Now the day of the road trip is here I find myself wishing I'd never agreed to it. There are so many things that could go wrong . . .

No. I force myself to think of Carl and his irritating positivity. He swears by thinking three positive things every day before he gets up. *I am feeling strong, calm and healthy. Today I will be a force for good.* That kind of thing. ('He doesn't say them out loud, does he?' I said to Mum once. 'God no,' she said, 'or he wouldn't be feeling healthy for long.') I'm not one to ever admit Carl might be right about something, and usually I mock him mercilessly for this kind of stuff, but today I think maybe he's got a point so I try to think of three good things.

*I am feeling healthy.* Well, I suppose I am, even if I am pregnant. There are worse things than being pregnant after all, like bubonic plague (as graphically outlined by Ms Horace) or Ebola or flesh-eating diseases. I don't have any of those, so I'm going to count that as a positive thing.

*Today is full of new opportunity.* Well, I'm doing something that doesn't involve hash browns, aren't I? I'm going somewhere I've never been before. It's an adventure of sorts. It's getting away. And it *is* an opportunity to find out more about Gloria, to get to know her, before she starts to disappear. I know from what I've read that, as a new acquaintance, I'm likely to be erased from her mind fairly early on. Memories that have been laid down longest are the most enduring, so the website said. Like Gloria said herself, those memories almost become clearer. The new ones don't really ever get saved properly. And perhaps she will be able to tell me a bit about Dad, about what he was like when he was growing up. Just some little insight. Nothing big. It could be an opportunity to get to understand him better.

*I will be a force for good . . .* Well, I don't know about that. But I'm trying to help Gloria do something she wants to while she still can. I think of her face again when she remembered spinning on the Common, and imagine what it would be like to be in her situation, looking ahead to blankness and a future you won't even be aware of. She wants to share her memories, her story, while she still can. That has to be a good thing. Doesn't it? Or am I just opening up old wounds? She's already told me her story isn't a happy one and I still have no real idea how serious her dementia is. Sometimes she seems absolutely fine, sharp, funny and seems to remember everything about everything. But is it an act? She *is* an actress after all, so playing the part of someone who knows exactly what's going on would be easy for her. Just occasionally, when we're talking, something will change ever so slightly in her expression and I'll wonder if she really knows who I am or what we're talking about. Could I be putting her in danger by taking her somewhere she doesn't know?

Tea. I need tea. That'll make everything better. And sugar. Lots of sugar.

Before I get up I text Kat.

**I'm going away for a few days with my great-aunt – long story! Hope you and Zoe are ok xx**

I don't expect to get a reply. It's early, and anyway, I've hardly heard from Kat at all since she went away, apart from that first conversation when I told her was pregnant. I blame Zoe-from-Kettering. I know she doesn't like me and there was something about her. Manipulative, that's what she is. I watched her doing whatever it took to keep Kat focused entirely on her: flirting with other people, turning on the tears, pretending she was ill. She wanted Kat all to herself. I didn't like her. As I'm thinking all this, my phone chimes with a message.

**We are ok. Have a great time! The books says you should be needing to wee all the time and your boobs should hurt. Have u been to docs????! xxxxx**

My heart sinks at the mention of the doctor's. I'll be more than nine weeks pregnant when we get back. I finally booked a doctor's appointment a couple days after we get back. Even thinking about it makes me feel jittery. While we're away I just want to forget about it. And maybe when I get back things will be different somehow. Maybe I'll feel different, and the panic will subside. Maybe it will all be clear, what I need to do. Maybe I'll feel brave enough to tell Mum. Maybe Reuben will come back and . . .

And what?

**No not yet** I text Kat. **When I get back xxx**

**Make sure you do! Take care Hats. Love u xxxxxxxx**

Her message makes my eyes prickle with tears.

'Today is full of new opportunity,' I mutter to myself. Then I go into the kitchen and make myself a cup of tea, using so much sugar from a paper packet I find lurking in one of Gloria's cupboards that the spoon practically stands up in it. I look in the fridge for milk but only find some lemons and a ball of string. Then, in the absence of bread, cereal, eggs or anything else that might pass for breakfast, I help myself to the pineapple juice left over from the gin slings, some lemon shortbread and a couple of violet creams. Not exactly nutritious but I'm starving so it'll have to do. There's no sign of Gloria yet and the nerves are still there in my stomach, for all Carl's positive affirmations. Will she even remember who I am when she gets up? Will she have changed her mind about the trip or forgotten it completely? I still don't really have a grip on how bad Gloria's memory is. What I really want to know is what the trip's about. Does she really want to see a few places while she can still remember them? Is it about sharing her story, this secret from her past? Or is it something else, something she's not telling me?

I think of what she said the first time about dying *at a time and in a manner of my own choosing* . . . What if that's it? What if it's a genuine bucket list, and she's doing all these things because at the end of it she plans to top herself?

*Jesus, Hattie,* I can hear Reuben's voice in my head. *Melodramatic much?*

*I know*, I reply silently. But think about it. Could that be what she means by Whitby being *'where the story ends'*? Perhaps she had a really happy time there as a kid or something, and she wants to go back there to . . . you know. End it all.

*You are such a catastrophist*, says the Reuben voice. *Remember that time you couldn't find Alice and you thought there was blood on the kitchen floor and she'd been abducted but it turned out it was ketchup and Alice had just gone off on some spying expedition in the garden? You've got a vivid imagination, that's your problem. I'm telling you, you read too many books. It's bad for your health. Scientific FACT.*

It's true. Not the book thing, but the tendency to envisage worst-case scenarios. And I do get a teeny bit paranoid when I haven't had enough sleep. Yes, I'm overreacting. The tea and the sugar buzz is starting to kick in and everything seems a bit better. The road trip will be fine. It will be more than fine. It will be an adventure. Gloria just wants to remember things from her past – to mark them, pass them on. I'm going to help her do it. And what about the secret? What could it be? I feel a thrill of excitement. Something no one else knows, and Gloria has chosen to tell me.

I make another cup of tea and psyche myself up to get washed in Gloria's dank bathroom.

When I come out, Gloria is up and sitting at her computer, wearing an emerald-green kimono and smoking a cigarillo.

'Morning,' I say, trying not to sound nervous. 'I'm Hattie—'

'Yes, yes,' she says briskly. 'I *know*.'

'Okay,' I say. 'Are you packed?'

'More or less.' She hesitates. 'I do sometimes get a little muddled with packing.'

'Would you like me to take a look?' I say.

I try to persuade Gloria that she probably doesn't need eight pairs of shoes. 'But I like them all,' she says.

'Don't you have something a little more comfortable?' I ask, looking at the array of pointed toes and heels of varying heights. 'Some trainers or something?'

She looks at me as if I've said something incredibly insulting. 'Comfortable shoes?' she says. 'No, I certainly do not. The day I wear "comfortable shoes" is the day it's all over, that every last bit of me has gone. I hope I die before that day ever comes.'

Which seems a tiny bit extreme.

While Gloria's having a shower I remove a couple of the more random items that have sneaked in, a fork and an onion. At first I can't help smiling to myself, but then I think how unnerving it must be to know your brain is playing tricks on you all the time. She's folded a necklace into one of her dresses, a heavy silver thing. I pull it out to look at it as she comes into the room.

'Did you mean to pack this?' I say. It's a locket, I realize.

'Yes, I did. Give it to me.' She snatches it from me and puts it round her neck. 'What were you doing nosing through my stuff anyway?'

'You asked me to help you pack,' I say.

'Did I?'

'*Yes*.' She looks at me, suspicious. 'Look, Gloria, if we're going to do this you have to trust me.'

'Yes,' she says. She pauses. 'I know. I'll try.'

Peggy makes us take a packed lunch, which looks as though it would probably last us the entire week, and waves us goodbye.

139

'You've got the folder with all the information?'

'Yes.'

'It's got all the dates and the addresses—'

'I know,' Gloria snaps. 'You've already told me a hundred times. I know my memory's bad but it's not that bad yet.'

'And you've got my number, in case of emergencies?' Peggy says, ignoring Gloria's outburst.

'Yes,' says Gloria, 'Although I'm not sure what you think you'll do if we phone you in an emergency.'

Gloria sits next to me, checking her make-up in the passenger-seat mirror.

'Are you sure about this?' I say to her before I start the car.

She turns her face to me, and underneath the make-up I can see that she's scared.

'No,' she says. 'Are you?'

I smile at her. 'God, no,' I say, smiling.

'Well, we'd better get going then,' she says irritably. 'Before we change our minds.'

## Chapter thirteen

The drive to Cambridge is a nightmare. My terror at driving unsupervised on a motorway proves unfounded since almost as soon as we're on the motorway we grind to a complete halt. The car is stifling; there's something wrong with the air conditioning so I have to open the windows and breathe in the heavy, warm, fume-filled air. I'd hoped to interrogate Gloria a bit more, about what she's told me, about her plans for where we're going and why. But Gloria is asleep.

I play about with the radio, trying in vain to find something I want to listen to. I keep replaying the things Gloria told me in my head. If that is the beginning of her story, what is the end? And why is it in Whitby? What is the secret? Why are we going to Cambridge? Too many questions. My head feels thick and is starting to throb. In the end I text Reuben.

**Sitting on the M25 with snoring great-aunt. Is like a never-ending car park. Like a dystopian vision of the future, Reuben. One massive bloody car park. Bet u r on beach. I hate u.**

To my surprise, he replies.

**Oh god pleas dont tell me u have turned into 1 of those people who talks about roads now u have passed driving test. oh i always take the A624 not the M7 or the H40. NO ONE CARES**

I know he's joking but I'm not in the mood. I take a swig from the bottle of horribly warm water and grimace. There is something so very wrong about drinking water that is at body temperature.

**I don't think the H40 is an actual road Reuben. ANd anyway I was only saying hi because I'm in a traffic jam and VERY VERY bored. I don't think roads are interesting. THAT'S MY POINT. I thought you might make it more interesting but you're making it MORE BORING so GOODBYE**

I'm so annoyed with him that I throw the phone down into the footwell. Bloody Reuben. No wonder his relationships work better when the other person can't understand what he's saying. After a second it chimes again with another message. I pretend not to hear it and turn the radio up. But after a while I can't resist taking a look, groping around by my feet to find the phone.

**WHATEVER PETROLHEAD ☺ Hope the thelma & louise thing is going ok xx**

I relent.

**Yeah Thelma and Louise would have been a v different film if they'd have had to contend with the M25 clockwise. less freedom & sisterhood, more swearing at caravans & traffic cones & wondering if you can hold on for a wee till birchanger green. don't fancy my chances of bumping into young brad pitt at the birchanger green services much either. next time i take an aged relative on a bucket list road trip remind me to do it in arizona will you? x**

I look out of my window at the car next to me, piled high with camping stuff, bikes on the roof. A small child in the back sees me watching, presses its face to the window and rolls its eyes up into its head at me.

Eventually we turn off the motorway onto clearer roads. Gloria stirs in the seat next to me.

'Are we nearly there yet?' she says.

142

'No,' I say.

'Who are you, anyway?' she says. 'I mean, I know who you are but I've forgotten your name.'

'It's Hattie,' I say, grateful to her for admitting it. Perhaps this is progress. Perhaps she is starting to trust me after all.

'Is it?'

She looks genuinely surprised.

'You don't look like a Hattie.'

'Don't I?' I say, pleased. 'No. I don't think so either. I had exactly this conversation with Reuben . . .'

I stop. That had been the weekend in Norfolk. The last time I saw him. The time—

No, I don't want to think about it. But the conversation comes back to me. I feel a pang thinking about it. God, I miss Reuben.

'I was saying that it would all have been different if I'd been called Bathsheba or Demelza. I'd have had a life of being beautiful and spirited and adventurous. No one called Bathsheba could ever have ended up working in the Happy Diner. Demelza would never have been Most Likely To: Become An Accountant. It's just not possible. I'd have had countless exotic lovers and not a single one of them would have been called William.'

'William?' says Gloria, getting out her notebook. 'Who's William? Should I make a note of him? Is he relevant?'

'NO,' I say. 'He is entirely irrelevant.'

Gloria seems satisfied with this.

'Harriet Lockwood is at best a minor player in a Jane Austen novel. You know, she'd be one of the annoying ones who marries the stupid vicar, or makes snarky comments about the heroine's needlework. If I'd even been a Raphaella or a—'

'Susan,' Gloria says firmly. 'You look like a Susan.'

'*Susan?*' I say. 'I do not look like a Susan.'

'Yes, you do.'

'No!'

'What's wrong with that?'

'There's nothing *wrong* with it. In fact, there are some very impressive Susans. It's just . . .'

'What?'

'Well, it's just you can't help feeling they've done it *in spite* of being called Susan. I mean it's not very exciting, is it? Susans are the sensible ones in books who boss everyone else around and tell them to buck up and get to bed on time and oh *do* stop snivelling or it will upset poor Mother dreadfully.'

I stare at her so challengingly that we end up going round the roundabout three times and get beeped at again, thankfully by a different driver from the last time.

When Gloria's finished giving them the two-fingered salute she turns her attention back to me.

'Yes, I suppose they are,' she says. 'What of it?'

'But that's not me,' I say.

'Isn't it?'

'NO.'

'Oh, well, if you say so.'

We drive on in silence for a while.

'Well, I think you look like a Myrtle,' I snap.

Gloria sniffs. 'Myrtle,' she mutters.

'Or an Edwina perhaps.'

'I draw the line at Edwina,' she says.

I look at her and we both start to laugh.

'Not far to Cambridge now,' I say. 'Tell me about the time you went there before.'

'We used to go for days out, Sam and I, to the museums or to Kew or Hampstead. He always wanted to see new

144

places. He worked extra hours and saved up the money for the train fare. He said his mum didn't like it because doing extra work interfered with his school studies. She was determined he was going to make something of himself.'

'And did he?' I say. She ignores me.

'He told me that his Auntie Esther in Jamaica always listened to the *Carols from King's* on the World Service at Christmas. He wanted to send her a postcard. Not that I know why I can remember that Sam's Auntie was called Esther, when this morning I couldn't remember what my toothbrush was for. Anyway. Esther. That was her name. So we went for a day trip. Breakfast on the Cambridge Buffet Express. I can't remember much about the day itself, but maybe going back there will bring it back. Perhaps not. All I really remember about that day is that it was the day I knew for sure I was in love with Sam.'

Was that true? Was it really when I fell in love with him? Or was it just the day I admitted it to myself? I'd liked him right from the start. He wasn't like other boys I'd gone out with. I never gave them a second thought. Sam was different. I couldn't get him out of my mind. I look at the girl next to me as she drives. I'm just old to her. It's unimaginable to her that I should ever have felt love or desire as she does. But I did. Oh yes, I did.

I'm lying down on the grass, and the warmth makes me pleasantly lethargic, and I lie completely still on the grass, pinned down by the heavy heat, hoping no one will spot me. The bell has rung and everyone else has filed slowly in for afternoon lessons, but I can't resist lying here a while longer. The thought of Latin in a dark, poky classroom is hardly enticing. Miss Lytton is a good sort but so very thin and she reeks of mothballs and melancholy, it comes off her in waves, filling the classroom with a kind of grey fog and the thought of it on a day like this, golden and green and full of life, is unbearable. It is not a day for dead languages. It is a day of life and being alive. All around things are growing and unfurling and bursting forth and all that sort of thing. The smell of the warm grass hangs in the air around me, sweet and fresh, and the breeze touches my skin gently, lifting the tiny hairs on my arms, caressing my face and the skin where I've undone the top buttons of my school dress. I think of Sam, of his fingers on my skin, of where they have touched and where I would like them to touch and my body shivers with the thrill of it. Most of the boys I've been out with I've grown bored with after a few weeks. But it's different with Sam. It's months since we met and the more I know about him, the more I want to know. I imagine him lying next to me on the grass, reaching out to touch me, pulling me to him. I imagine his hands under my blouse, our bodies intertwining and hot. I imagine the feel of his skin against mine, the taste of him, his finger tracing the shape of my breast. My breath comes a little faster.

'Gloria Harper!' A shadow falls across me. 'What are you doing here?' I squint up and see that what's blocking out the sunlight is the sizable form of Sister Mary Francis. I can only see her silhouette, black and ominous to my unfocused eyes, but I can imagine the look on her face. I have always been a source of annoyance to Sister Mary Francis, just by existing. I ask too many questions. I'm untidy. I don't listen. The sun is directly behind her head so it looks like she's got a halo, and I want to tell her because I think in her own mind that's what she looks like all the time. I sit up quickly and smile.

'Oh,' I say. 'Sorry, Sister, I lost track of time.'

She draws herself up and folds her arms, so that what Louise always refers to as 'her ample bosom' juts further out under her habit. I remember Louise speculating on the feat of engineering that Sister Mary Francis' undergarments must be and I find myself wondering if ever a finger has traced the shape of either of Sister Mary Francis' impressive breasts. I don't mean to think it. The thought just pops into my head. The owner of the hand would have to have been a very daring sort, that's for sure. Her

147

face is set in an expression that makes me think perhaps she can read my thoughts. 'God can see into our hearts and our minds. He knows our true intentions,' she is fond of saying, rather threateningly, in assembly, when considering the nature of sin and repentance. I can't help wondering whether years of devoting herself to God mean that some of that omniscience has rubbed off. I blush a little, thinking of what I'd been imagining Sam doing. But only a little. Why would God have given us bodies that enjoy the touch of another person or minds that fall in love if He hadn't wanted us to use them? Aren't we saying He got it wrong by imagining that these things are sinful? I don't imagine this line of argument would cut much ice with Sister Mary Francis, though.

'Get to class, Gloria. And if I see you down here again when you should be in lessons, it'll be detention for you. *Again*. And do your buttons up, for goodness' sake.'

'Yes, Sister.' I try to look penitent and demure because I really don't want a detention; after school is the only time I can see Sam, but it's not a look I'm very good at. Sister Mary Francis knows what's in my heart and mind all right.

'You know,' she says. 'If you're serious about wanting to go to university you'd better pull your socks up. You're clever, Gloria. That should not be a source of pride. It is a gift from God and you have a duty to use it. But you won't get anywhere by being too clever for your own good.'

I look up at her.

'And who decides what's too clever?' I ask. 'You or God?'

'Your arrogance will get you into trouble, Gloria,' she says. 'You see if it doesn't. So unlike your sister.'

I've had this all my life. Baby Gwen was such a good sleeper – slept through everything. I slept for an hour at a time and screamed the moment I woke up. *It was the Blitz*, I pointed out.

*Wasn't it quite noisy?* Mum just laughed and said she was so exhausted she half wished a bomb would land on our house, just to give her some peace. Gwen's smooth blonde hair never seemed to be out of place while my curls always fought their way out of pigtails, falling untidily into my eyes. At school it got worse. She was eight years older than me so we were never at school together, but I felt her presence all the time, as perfect and serene and good and impossible to emulate as the Virgin Mary herself. Her writing and her sewing and her uniform had always been neat. She never answered back or asked unnecessary questions. She was never too clever for her own good. She was just the right amount of clever.

'I always felt she probably took after your mother,' Sister Mary Francis says. 'Whereas you, I think, are more like your father.'

I turn on her.

'You don't know anything about it,' I shout. 'I'm nothing like my father.'

## Chapter fourteen

It's late morning by the time we arrive in Cambridge. Irene, who runs the bed and breakfast, greets us with strong tea, which I gulp down. Gloria picks at hers. She's pale and tired, and says she'd like to go and sit in the garden for a while.

'Are you sure?' I say. 'I fancied a walk around.'

'I'm not stopping you,' she says. So I go and wander through the streets, watching people wobble along on their bikes and tourists drinking outside pubs, listening to the chime of bells, looking up at the spires and towers and peering through archways into perfectly manicured court-yards, thinking how Dad must have walked along here or got drunk in these pubs in his student days.

As I'm walking my phone rings. It's Kat.

'Hey,' I say, smiling. 'How's it going?'

'Hats,' she says quickly. 'I can't talk for long. Look, just tell me, when you said you were six weeks pregnant, how were you working it out?'

'What do you mean?'

'The thing is, Hats, the book says you don't work out the date from conception. You work it out from the start of your last period.'

I'm silent for a moment. 'What do you mean?' I say again, feeling panic grow inside me.

'I mean you're not eight weeks pregnant. You're probably more like ten.'

'But I can't be! That doesn't make any sense.'

'That's what it says, Hats. Sorry. Look, I've got to go, Zoe's going to be back in a minute. But you need to decide what you're going to do soon. I'll text you later.'

When I get back to the bed and breakfast, Irene has decided that Gloria and I should go punting and has packed us a picnic to take with us. I'm grateful. Anything to take my mind off Kat's panic-inducing message. Ten weeks pregnant! That means by the time of my appointment I'll be eleven weeks.

'You all right, dear?' Irene says. 'You look a bit pasty, if you don't mind me saying. Not sickening for something I hope? Don't want to be poorly on your holidays.'

'No,' I say. 'Just the drive. Bit of a headache.'

'Oh, well,' she says. 'Punting's just what you need. Bit of fresh air. Nice and relaxing.'

Punting turns out not to be nice and relaxing at all but extremely hard work. For me, that is. For Gloria it turns out to be very nice and relaxing indeed, sitting back in a rather stylish floppy sunhat, waving regally at people leaning over the bridges above us, laughing appreciatively at silly tourists getting stuck on their punting poles and ending up in the Cam for her amusement, and sipping chilled cans of *Pimm's* that I'd spotted were on special offer in the off licence and picked up for her on the walk down from the bed and breakfast.

'Not the same in a can, of course,' she says, but as I've

151

punted what feels like halfway to Grantchester (though in fact isn't very far at all) and am drenched in sweat and aching all over, I'm not all that sympathetic.

'*Sorry,*' I say. 'Bit tricky manoeuvring a punt and mixing drinks at the same time.'

She smiles up at me. She likes it when I'm sarcastic.

'So hard to find decent staff these days,' she says.

Eventually I get fed up of punting and we stop (which isn't as easy as you'd think) and clamber out. We eat Irene's picnic of crusty bread and cheese and ham, and slices of banana loaf and cherries.

I try to imagine what it would be like to be a student living in one of the colleges along the river.

'It's weird to think that Dad was at university here.'

I try to picture Dad as a teenager, on a bicycle wearing one of those college scarves, or maybe striding through a courtyard – quad, isn't that what they call them? – in one of those black academic gowns that make you look like Batman. But I can barely even remember him as he was when I was a kid. The images I have of him are from photos.

'Clever, was he?' Gloria says.

'Must have been, I suppose. Although I think he nearly failed his degree. He spent all his time writing for the student newspaper.'

All of this I know from an obituary that was printed in one of the newspapers he used to write for. I wonder how much Gloria actually knows about Dad.

'Did you know he became a journalist?'

'Who?'

'Dad.' She doesn't respond. 'Dominic. Gwen's son,' I add, not sure if she's forgotten or just isn't interested. 'He was a war correspondent.' I add. 'That's how he died. In Afghanistan. His vehicle was hit by a roadside bomb.'

'Oh,' she says.

'He'd been warned not to go. But he went anyway.'

'Sounds about right,' Gloria mutters to herself.

I look at her.

'What do you mean? I thought you didn't know him?'

Gloria looks at me.

'Who?'

'My dad.'

'I didn't,' she says.

'But you said—'

'I just meant,' she says, 'he reminds me of someone.'

'Who?'

She hesitates. 'You,' she says at last.

'Me?'

'You were warned not to come and visit me, weren't you? By your mum and that boyfriend of yours.'

'He's not my boyfriend.'

'I bet everyone was always warning you about him, weren't they?' I think of Carl and Kat.

'I suppose,' I say. I like the idea that I might be a bit like dad, that there's a real connection between us. He always felt distant, even when he was alive. He spent so much of his life away from us, in a world I couldn't even imagine. And as time passes he becomes more distant, a dwindling collection of memories that I've stuck together to try and create a person.

'What was our dad like?' Ollie had asked me once.

I didn't really know what to tell him. The things I remember about Dad – that he used to bring me a *Toblerone* and Mum *Chanel No. 5* that she never wore, that he was blond and tall, that he used to throw me up in the air even when Mum told him not to, that he let me drive the car once in a car park early on a Sunday morning when no one was around, that he smelt of whisky and aftershave, that I'd cry after he left to go abroad – none of them seemed substantial enough.

'He was brave,' I said to Ollie. 'He travelled to all sorts of dangerous places where there were wars going on.'

'I know,' Ollie said. 'But what was he actually like?'

The truth is, I don't know what sort of person he was, really. I was nine when he died and he was away far more than he was at home even when he was alive. So I found the photo of me and Dad that I kept on my phone and showed it to Ollie. I told him about the holiday it was taken on, and about what a great time we had, and how proud Dad had been of the twins in their double buggy, showing them off to everyone we met. I told him about all the amazing things people said about Dad at his funeral, about how he was a hero, how he'd always put the story before his own safety, how he'd believed it was vital for people to know the truth, about how he'd seen terrible things. I didn't tell Ollie what, though. Dead children and their dead mothers, busy marketplaces where bombs had gone off . . . What would it have felt like, I wondered, to see all those things and then come back home? Back to suburbia, to mowing the lawn, to weekly supermarket shops and taking the twins to Crazy Dayz soft play on a Sunday morning so Mum could have a break. Maybe that was why Dad had always seemed a bit distant, even when he was at home. I don't miss him, not really. That makes me sad in a way. I just wish I'd had the chance to know him.

'Did you really not have anything to do with my dad when he was growing up?'

I keep trying to steer the conversation round to talking about Nan and Dad. I know Gloria said she didn't remember anything about Dad but that was when she didn't want anything to do with me. Perhaps it was just her way of trying to get rid of me. I hand her another can of *Pimm's*.

She takes a drink from her can but doesn't say anything. In the end I decide it's not worth trying to be subtle. After all, she was the one who wanted to come on this trip, share her memories and her secrets.

'Why weren't you at Nan's funeral?' I blurt out.

I half expect her to snap that it's none of my business, but she doesn't.

'It's a long story.'

I wait but she doesn't say any more.

'What was she like?' I persevere. It's so strange to think of her ever having been anything other than an old lady.

Gloria smiles.

'Oh, Gwen was perfect.'

Is it my imagination or is there an edge to her voice?

'Didn't you get on?'

'I loved her with all my heart,' Gloria says. 'I adored Gwen. And she loved me. But I think she made me rebellious. From as early as I can remember I was failing to live up to my perfect sister. At home, at school. Especially at school. And then once she married Vinnie . . .'

'You didn't like him?'

She laughs. 'I despised him. Vinnie had money and he thought that made him better than us. He liked to make a point of the fact that we didn't have much. He acted as though Gwen was lucky he'd condescended to marry her. That was rubbish. She was beautiful, Gwen. She could have done much better than Vinnie. He was charming, a smooth talker and that's why she fell for him. Once they were married I hardly saw her. They moved out to the suburbs, to a modern house with a fitted kitchen and a garage and a big garden and they only came round to us for Sunday lunch occasionally so that Vinnie could show off about his new car or the holiday he and Gwen were about to go on and make jokes about our outdated furniture. I always felt he was laughing at us.'

I wonder whether that was true, or whether Gloria just resented him for taking away the big sister who had always looked out for her. Especially given how unhappy things were at home.

'You must have really missed her after she'd gone?'

'Yes,' she says. 'I was lonely. I felt that Gwen had abandoned me. I suppose that was selfish really. She had her own life to live. But she'd always made things easier at home. She was the only one Father would listen to when he was drunk. She could persuade him to stop drinking. She could spot the signs that he was heading for a rage and divert it. Me and Mum always made it worse. Mum would annoy him by being too timid and weak, by trying too hard to please him and placate him. I'd stand up to him, get angry. Gwen could stay calm. She seemed to understand his dark days too. When he couldn't speak to anyone or even get up out of his chair – sometimes he couldn't even get out of bed – Gwen would sit with him and hold his hand. She'd have made a brilliant nurse. That's what she wanted to do.'

'And she never did?'

'No. Vinnie wouldn't let her. His wife going out to work? He wouldn't have stood for it. Mind you, that wasn't unusual then. Once you were married you were expected to stay at home and devote yourself to looking after your husband.'

I shake my head. 'But that's so unfair.'

'I was only twelve when they got married. I felt abandoned and angry with her. How could she leave me, knowing what it would be like for me at home? Then I realized it wasn't really her fault. It was Vinnie's.'

So I was right. Gloria blamed Vinnie for taking her sister away. No wonder she didn't like him. And perhaps that was why she and Nan hadn't been close, why she wasn't at Nan's funeral and why she hadn't kept in touch with Dad. Maybe she'd never really forgiven her sister for leaving.

'After she married Vinnie, Gwen was distant,' Gloria says. 'Cut off. I thought then it was because she thought she was too good for us, now she had her big house and her fancy clothes. I thought she didn't want to see us any more.'

The way she says it makes me wonder.

'You don't think that now?'

She pauses. 'There was a lot I didn't understand back then.'

Was it that same day, the Sunday Mum and I walked back from church and I spun round and round on the Common? Perhaps it was. I think it was.

*Stop! Gloria, really! You're not a child—*

*Damn, damn, damn. Damn Vinnie. Bloody Vinnie—*

Yes. I think it was the same day.

I can tell Father's been drinking when Mum and I get back from church, and by the time we sit down for Sunday lunch with Gwen and Vinnie he's drunk. He never really looks properly drunk, like Uncle Bert at cousin Betsy's wedding. Bert was laughing and dancing, crying and then back to laughing till his face was wet with tears again. 'No fool like an old fool,' Aunty Alice said.

But Father doesn't laugh or dance when he's drunk.

As I sit down across the table from him, I take in the pink flush in his cheeks, and the knowing smirk that flickers round his mouth, like the gin tells him secrets the rest of us are too stupid to understand. Yes, he's drunk plenty. You'd never notice the tiny telltale signs if you didn't know him. But I notice them. My stomach flips with – what is it? Not fear exactly. It's the nervous feeling you get when someone's blowing up a balloon and it's getting bigger and bigger and bigger. You try to brace yourself for the BANG so you won't flinch. But there's no way you can do it.

'There we go,' Mum says, too brightly, placing the roast beef on the table.

Father stares at me across the glistening meat, his pale-blue eyes not quite focused. I look away, down at my plate, because I know it's a challenge, just like it always is. He wants a fight and he knows he won't get one from Mum. So he'll prod me and goad me and toy with me until I crack, until I lose my temper, until I scream or cry. We've played this game, his game, for as long as I can remember. But today I won't do it. I don't want to accept his challenge. I think of the sunshine, that *joy* I felt on the Common. I want to hold on to it. It feels precious.

'Well, this is nice, isn't it?' Vinnie says, and Mum laughs nervously.

Gwen smiles. Father pours another drink. I say nothing.

They talk and talk, about business and how well Vinnie's doing, about how he and Gwen have had a new bathroom suite fitted.

'It's blue,' Gwen says.

'Lovely,' I say, thinking about Sam and how soon I can get away to meet him. I check my watch. I'm later than I thought I'd be already, but I know he'll wait for me.

'Got somewhere to be, have you, Gloria?' Vinnie smiles at me in his knowing way.

'No.'

'Not keeping secrets, are you, Gloria?'

The atmosphere in the room thickens.

'Not off to see your fella, are you?'

'What?' I say, palms prickling. He can't know about Sam. I haven't told anyone.

'Must say it's very open-minded of you, Des, letting Gloria go out with a darkie. I'd hit the roof if she was my daughter.'

159

I stare at Vinnie. How does he know about Sam? He always seems to know about everything. I bet it was stupid Brenda Onions who told him. She saw me and Sam together at the pictures a couple of weeks ago. I knew she wouldn't keep her mouth shut.

At first I'd wanted to tell Father about Sam because I knew how angry it would make him. He hates everyone, Father, and any difference between him and another person gives him an excuse. Having different coloured skin from his own is blatant provocation in his view.

He turns to me, quiet.

'Tell me that's not true.'

I don't say anything.

'Tell me it's not true.'

'No,' I say. 'I won't tell you anything. It's none of your business.'

'What did you say?'

'I said it's none of your damn business.'

'Gloria!' said Mum.

'That's no way to talk to your father, Gloria.' It's Vinnie. Bloody Vinnie, looking all pleased with himself. He's goading me. I try to stay calm. I concentrate on eating. I chew my meat, chew it and chew it, but it seems to be growing in my mouth. 'You want to take her in hand, Des. You're too soft on her.'

'What would you know about it?' I snap. 'It's none of your business.'

'You really shouldn't talk to me like that, Gloria.' Vinnie's smiling but his voice isn't. 'Of course it's my business. You're family. I've got your best interests at heart, you know. And anyway, your . . . behaviour, it reflects badly on Gwen. And I can't have that. I'd like you to apologize, please.'

I can't swallow the meat without gagging. Panicking I reach out for my glass of water and knock over the gravy boat. Dark reddish brown spreads across the white tablecloth.

Mum jumps up.

'Oh dear.' She laughs nervously, 'Not to worry, Gloria, I'll get a cloth.'

'No, I'll go,' I say, out of the door before anyone can stop me.

In the kitchen I lean against the wall, gulping in air as though I've come up from underwater.

'You get back in here, Gloria!'

It's Father.

My eyes fix on the picture of Jesus hanging on the wall next to the sink, his Sacred Heart so red and hot and fiery that it has burst right out of his chest. I always hated that picture as a child; it seemed grotesque. But now I press my hand against my own heart, feel it beating and beating, and inside me I feel the red heat of it.

I look at Jesus, at his eyes, so sad and still and calm. And all the while his heart is on fire.

'Help me,' I mutter to him and I squeeze my eyes shut.

'GLORIA!'

It's Father again.

I take a cloth, run it under the cold tap, splash a little of the water onto my face. The ghost of my reflection looks back at me from the window above the sink. Beyond it, out in the garden, the sun is still shining.

I clench my teeth and brush away the tears that are on my cheeks.

'Sorry,' I whisper to Jesus as I open the back door. I haven't believed in him since I was seven, but I still can't help feeling it's partly my fault he looks so sad. 'Sorry,' I whisper to Mum too, although I know she can't hear me.

I step out into the warmth and the light.

'Gloria!'

'I am going to see him. You can't stop me.'

'Really? We'll see about that,' Vinnie says.

But I'm already running out of the back gate.

## Chapter fifteen

I wake in the middle of the night, from a dream where Ollie and I had been standing on a balcony outside a house that was ours but wasn't. It was by the sea and as we stood there the sea kept rising higher and higher. 'It'll reach us in a minute,' a boy who was Ollie but also wasn't him was saying, and I'd said, 'Hold my hand tight,' but his hand was wet and kept slipping from mine, and I'd shouted at him and he'd started to cry, not because he was scared of the sea but because I was angry, and then he'd disappeared under the water . . .

I stare blindly into the dark, completely unable to remember where I am. I can feel it's not home, the wall isn't where it should be next to my bed, and I have a moment of sheer panic as my mind gropes for where I am and why. Then it comes to me: the bed and breakfast. Cambridge. Gloria is in the adjoining room.

I have a sudden understanding of what it must be like for her. That's what dementia must be like. I feel the hollow fear that must be with Gloria all the time. It must be terrifying, the reality of it and the fear of it getting worse, of it getting more frequent, until that's all there is . . .

My heart is still pounding from the dream, but at least it wasn't about driving or pancakes. I lie there trying to fall asleep again but I can't switch my brain off. There's too much to think about. Eventually I give in and get up to go to the shared bathroom down the corridor. As I go past Gloria's room I hear movement and I notice that there's light shining through the gap at the bottom of the door.

I hesitate, unsure whether to knock. What if Gloria doesn't recognize me? The last thing I want to do is give her a fright in the middle of the night. And she had made it very clear last night that she didn't want me fussing. 'Will you be all right?' I'd said, remembering the bit in my book that said people with dementia can find it difficult to be in new surroundings. 'Well, I've managed to struggle on without your help for the last seventy-two years,' she said. 'I dare say I'll survive another night, don't you think?'

But what if she's ill or needs help? I knock gently on the door.

'Gloria,' I call softly. 'Are you awake?'

There's a pause, then footsteps. The door opens a crack. Gloria's face behind it looks tired, and older without her make-up.

'What is it?' she says.

I pause, not sure whether she knows who I am, and unsure how to ask without annoying her.

'I know who you are, Hattie,' she says. 'If at any point I don't recognize you I'll say, okay, so we can avoid this ridiculous charade every time we see each other.'

'Okay,' I say, even though I don't believe for a moment that she would admit it if she didn't recognize me. She's too proud. And too clever. She'd talk to me until she worked it out. But I'm not going to argue about it. 'I saw your light was on,' I say. 'Couldn't you sleep?'

'No,' she says. 'Too much to think about.'

'I know,' I say. 'Me too.'

She hesitates. 'Do you want to come in?'

It's not just the lack of make-up that makes her face look different. She's less guarded somehow. Funny how the small hours of the morning have that effect.

'Yes, please,' I say.

I go in and sit on the bed. The room is lamplit and Gloria has obviously been sitting at the desk writing in her notebook.

'Are you okay?'

'Yes,' she says. 'I just can't sleep. Usually when I wake up in the middle of the night I'm terrified. It's easy to pretend you're not scared during the day. But in the middle of the night somehow that rational-sounding voice that tells you everything's going to be okay seems to stay asleep.'

'Yes,' I say. 'I know.'

'But tonight it hasn't been like that. I woke up with my head full of memories.'

'Happy memories? Or sad ones?'

'Both,' she replies. 'I was remembering Sam.'

'Tell me,' I say.

As we walk down the street we see a couple wrestling a pram up some steps into one of the houses.

'Maybe that'll be us one day,' Sam says. 'What will we call them?'

'Who?'

'Our children, of course!'

'Who said anything about children?' I say, laughing. 'No thanks! I want to travel. I want to be a famous actress or go to university or . . . *something.*'

He laughs. 'Well, you can do all that. And then we'll have our children. And we'll call them . . . Danny, that's a good name. And I always thought Vivienne for a girl. What do you say? Danny and Vivienne?'

I stare at him, unsure whether he's serious.

'I'll be a great dad. I will. I'll change nappies and everything. I'll teach them how to play guitar. I'm good with kids. I've spent enough time looking after the little ones at home. I tell you what, I'll stay at home with Danny and Vivienne and you can go out and be a famous actress-professor-explorer. Okay?'

I laugh. 'You're not right in the head,' I say.

I look at the house, with its window boxes and its lamps lit inside and the couple smiling, besotted with their baby. The

165

thought of it has always horrified me. Gwen's the one for settling down and having babies. The thought of domesticity and responsibility, it's always made me panic. It's not what I want. I've never wanted it. I want to run as far away from it as I can. But maybe I could one day. Maybe. Sam makes anything seem possible. Or maybe it's not Sam. Maybe that's what love does.

'Family doesn't have to be a bad thing,' he says, seriously now, putting his hand up to my face. 'It doesn't have to make you sad. There's nothing to be afraid of.'

Sometimes he seems to understand what I'm feeling better than I understand it myself.

I look at him, and I can't think of anything to say, so I just kiss him.

'Filthy nigger!'

I spin round to see a kid going past on his bike. He spits at me.

'Filthy nigger's whore.'

'Hey!' I shout after him. 'You come back here, you little bastard, I'll kill you—'

Sam puts his arm round me and turns me back to him.

'It's just a kid,' he says. 'He's just some little kid who doesn't know any better.'

'That doesn't make it all right,' I say, fighting to hold back tears.

'No,' he says and although his voice is calm there's an intensity behind it that I haven't seen before. 'I know it's not all right. I'm used to this; I get it all the time. And not just from kids.'

I know he's right. I'm used to the looks he gets when we're out together, the looks I get for being with him, too. Sometimes it's just curiosity, people gawping like idiots. *What d'you think you're looking at?* I'd snapped at a woman on the bus last week. Sometimes people mutter things that I'm glad I can't hear. But I've never seen such outright hostility.

'Aren't you ever afraid?'

'Yes, of course. I know all about being afraid,' he says, looking me in the eye. 'My brother Jimmy was in Notting Hill when the riots broke out. He was attacked by teddy boys who told him he should go back to his own country. They cut him with razor blades. He's still got the scars. They kicked him and punched him till they thought he was dead. We didn't even recognize him when we went to see him in hospital.'

I want to say something but I can't.

'The worst thing was my dad's face when he saw Jimmy. Dad fought for this country in the war, just like yours did. He thought we'd be welcomed with open arms by the mother country. He thought we'd be treated like heroes. And instead, there he was looking at his son, nearly dead in a hospital bed. He just couldn't understand why.'

'Why aren't you angry?' I say. 'How can you talk about it so calmly?'

'Oh, I'm angry all right,' he says. 'Don't ever think I'm not angry. But there are good people too, people who have welcomed my family, helped us, treated us no differently from anyone else. And some of the people who do treat us differently, I know they're just scared. They can't understand we're just people, same as them.'

'That's no excuse,' I say.

'No,' Sam says. 'It's not. But I can't let those people change me. If I let my anger take over, if I fight fire with fire, I'll become someone else. I'll have let them stop me being the person I am. The way to fight is to prove them wrong.'

'But don't you worry about your family? Aren't you frightened of what might happen to you if you're out one night and you run into the wrong people?'

As I say the words, I realize that I'm frightened *for him*. More frightened for him than for myself. I've never felt like that about anyone before. If anything happened to him . . .

'Of course,' he says.

'I've never admitted that I'm afraid of anything,' I say. 'Not to anyone. Not to Mum or Gwen.'

He holds my face in his hands. 'People think being brave means not being scared of anything. But that's wrong, Gloria. How can you be brave if you're not scared? Feeling afraid and not letting it stop you. That's really being brave.'

It's right then, in that moment standing in the street in Cambridge with the horrible boy cycling off down the road, that I realize I love Sam.

'It's amazing to think people were so hostile,' I say. 'So openly racist. Thank God things have changed.'

Gloria looks at me and raises an eyebrow. 'Really?' she says. 'Everyone's welcomed with open arms now, are they?'

She's got a point.

'He sounds pretty amazing, your Sam,' I say. 'How come things didn't work out with you two?'

She ignores me. 'Tell me more about whatsisname.' She flicks through the notebook. 'Reuben.'

I sigh. I don't really want to. Thinking about him just reminds me of my conversation with Kat earlier and the fact that the clock is ticking down way faster than I'd thought.

But fair's fair. Gloria has told me about Sam, so I tell her about Reuben.

Reuben and I became friends for two reasons. First, because within an impressively short time he'd managed to alienate, sleep with, split up with, insult (either intentionally or by omission), start a fight with or otherwise piss off pretty much everyone else in our year or their best friend/

boyfriend/girlfriend. Most of the boys hated him because most of the girls fancied him, and because he swaggered about the place like he owned it from the first day he arrived, paying no attention to all those long-established hierarchies that everyone else just accepted. Reuben didn't care about in-crowds or geeks or bullies or being bullied. It would have been refreshing if he hadn't managed to unite all these groups in universal dislike of him.

Of course, not everyone hated him. The ones who didn't adored him. He had a little cluster of acolytes and admirers around him most of the time, an odd assortment of fellow rebels, outcasts, misfits whether by choice or misfortune, and just those who felt they needed a bit more excitement and glamour in their lives. The exact members of his crowd changed regularly, but they were mainly clever, thin girls from the year above us with a lot of black eyeliner and dyed hair. Hard kids who liked trouble and disruption and recognized that Reuben was trouble and disruption made flesh.

There's a power in not appearing to care what anyone thinks of you. Not many people can pull it off. Reuben did it with style. He seemed not to even notice he was doing it. And of course, the fact that he was tall and had long dark eyelashes and cheekbones so sharp they were almost painful to look at and a general air that teetered (in my mind anyway) somewhere between rock star and Lord Byron probably helped.

Loads of girls fancied him. Some boys too. But I didn't want to be one of them.

'You like him, don't you?' Kat had said to me one day, about a month after Reuben had started at school. We were huddled in a corner of the playground. Reuben had been sent to the Head – again – by his arch-nemesis, Mr Monroe, and was now holding court in the playground, surrounded by admirers who were asking him about it.

'Yes,' I said.

'Like every other girl in the school, apparently.' She sighed. 'And a few of the boys. Well, I'm sure he'll get round to you one of these days; he seems to be working his way through the very long list of anyone who's up for it. Why does everyone always fancy the people I think are utter knobs?'

'I didn't say I fancied him,' I said quickly.

'Don't you?' Kat said, curious.

I shrugged. 'Nah, not really.'

'In other words, yes you do. You want to go out with him. Hattie and Reuben sitting in a tree, K-I-S-S-I-N-G—'

'Shut up. He's not my type,' I said, casually chewing on an apple. 'I just think he's – interesting.'

Kat raised an eyebrow. 'He's a knob,' she said.

'Well,' I said. 'Knobs can be interesting.'

Kat snorted.

'I didn't mean it like that,' I said.

'Well, I'll have to take your word for it, Hats,' she said. 'Not really my area of expertise.'

And we both laughed so much I inhaled my apple and Kat had to thump me on the back, just as Reuben and his gaggle of groupies were walking past.

'You all right, babe?' He was clearly amused, presumably by my red face, tears and general inability to speak or breathe.

'Fine,' I tried to say, but couldn't, thanks to the piece of apple firmly lodged in my trachea.

A groupie giggled and they all trailed off after him.

'Knob,' said Kat, emphasizing her point by whacking me so hard on the back that the piece of apple flew out and landed on the spot where Reuben had just been standing.

I can't exactly say in all absolute, total, swear-on-your-mum's-life honesty that I didn't fancy Reuben even one little bit. But I didn't want to go out with him. Well, not exactly. Okay, so maybe *in a way* I sort of did want to. But I knew if I had it would have made me just like everyone else. And I didn't want to be like everyone else was to Reuben. I wanted to be special.

I wasn't special to Reuben for a long time. He'd smile at me if he saw me in the corridor and say, 'All right, Holly, how's it going?' and I'd say, 'Fine thank you, Rupert'. He always sat next to me in History (when he bothered to turn up) because Ms Horace always made him – presumably in case my ability to listen and write essays that did not suggest sausages as one of the causes of the Second World War rubbed off. (It didn't.) But he was always too busy trying to annoy Ms Horace, or impress Soraya or some other girl who wasn't me, to pay me much attention other than when he needed to copy my notes.

The only time we ever really talked to each other was on the bus home from school. Loads of people would pile on the bus outside the school gates, but most people lived pretty nearby. We both lived further out, so after all his groupies had got off the bus Reuben would come and sit next to me and we'd talk. He was different, I noticed, when other people weren't around. He was still rude and funny and full of himself but less swaggering, more willing to have an actual conversation about something that wasn't him. We never had that long, just five or ten minutes before it was my stop but I found myself looking forward to it every day. On the days he wasn't there because he was skiving or in detention (which wasn't unusual) I missed him.

'Why are you such an arsehole at school?' I asked him one day when he'd been particularly awful, reducing a supply teacher to tears.

He smiled. 'It's just the way I'm made.'

'But it's not. You're not like it now. When it's just us you're nice. Why can't you be like that all the time?'

He shrugged.

'No, don't just shrug.'

He stopped smiling. 'Okay. Well, if you really want to know, it's because it would be so unbelievably boring.'

I stared at him, my heart pounding with anger. 'Are you saying *this* is boring? Are you saying *I'm* boring?'

'Yeah, maybe I am.'

'Fine. Well, I'll put you out of your misery then. This is my stop,' I said. I got up and pressed the bell.

I went home via the convenience store on the high street to buy a magazine and some sweets and to give myself a chance to calm down. I tried not to think about Reuben, told myself I couldn't care less what he thought. But when I came out of the shop, there was Reuben, leaning against the wall smoking a cigarette.

He smiled when he saw me.

My stomach may or may not have done a little flippety thing. Let's just assume for now that it didn't. 'Are you stalking me?' I said, trying not to sound pleased.

'I just came to say, no. You're not boring.'

'You needn't have bothered,' I said, unwrapping the chewing gum I'd just bought and popping it in my mouth. 'I knew that already. I don't need you to tell me, thanks very much.'

'What I mean is, I'm sorry,' he said.

We walked along the road back towards my house.

'Good,' I said.

'Anyway, I was thinking about what the real answer to your question is, and I suppose it's that I've got a reputation to uphold.'

I rolled my eyes.

'And anyway,' he said, kicking up dried leaves that were scattered along the pavement and avoiding eye contact. 'What if no one liked the real me?'

'I do,' I said.

After that Reuben and I hung out together more. He'd quite often get off the bus at my stop and come round to my house and hang out for a while. Sometimes I'd force him to do homework. Sometimes, if Mum was working late, we'd cook (he was surprisingly good at it). Usually he'd just sit and watch cartoons with the twins or go and smoke in the garden with Mum giving him 'I wish you wouldn't' looks through the kitchen window.

'It's nice here,' he'd say.

'Is it?' That wasn't the word I'd use. 'Nice' sounds like matching curtains and cushions and everything tidy and calm and painted cream like in magazines. Our house is noisy and there's always Lego on the floor waiting to spring at you when you walk barefoot. It usually smells a bit of burning, either because of forgotten toast or Alice's 'science'. There are yellow stains on the hall wall from when Alice filled her water pistol with custard and fired it at Carl because he'd upset her in some way.

'Yeah,' Reuben said. 'It's . . . normal.'

'Jesus, Reuben.' I laughed. 'If you think this is normal, what the hell is it like at yours?'

When I finally went round to his, I found out. It did have matching curtains and cushions, and everything was very tidy. It had security gates and lights that came on as we walked up the drive on a dark November evening. It had a gleaming marble and chrome kitchen, which opened out onto a glass box that overlooked the garden. But it wasn't 'nice'. Reuben's home life was like an unexploded bomb. Everything everyone said was laced with frustration or resentment or undisguised dislike. His dad was still living there then. He had a tan, even in November, and very white teeth. When he spoke to Reuben (which was just to ask him who I was) his tone suggested he found Reuben intensely irritating. Reuben was politer to him than I'd ever seen him be to anyone else. I thought his dad was a tosser. He gave me a nod. 'Pleased to meet you,' he said, with a brief gleaming smile that didn't look pleased at all. 'Always a delight to meet my son's friends.' He slapped Reuben on the back and Reuben flinched slightly, not in a scared way, more in response to his words, I think. There was a passive aggressive tone there. Then he turned to Reuben's mum, who was lying on the sofa and seemed completely out of it. Not drunk; hazy, removed from everything. She was beautiful but it was as if she wasn't really there, responding slowly, if at all, to anything that was said to her.

'I'm going out,' Reuben's dad told her. It's hard to imagine how you can get as much hatred into three innocuous words as he did. 'I'll be back late, if at all. Don't wait up.'

She showed no sign of having heard him.

'Don't know why I bother,' he said, flashing that smile at me again, apparently joking but his tone said otherwise.

'Is your mum okay?' I asked Reuben when we went up to his room. Even his bedroom seemed weirdly impersonal, almost like a hotel room or something.

'I never stayed here much till this year,' he explained. 'I was at boarding school from the age of eight, don't forget.'

'What was it like?'

He shrugged. 'Not great. But maybe it was better than being here. At least there people took an interest in me.'

The bomb exploded not long after that. Reuben's dad left for the south of France where they had a house and stayed there.

'You can't really blame him,' Reuben had said to me. 'I'd go if I were him.' I could blame him, quite a lot.

I could also understand why Reuben came round to ours.

'Just goes to show,' Carl said, when I was telling Mum about it. 'Money can't buy you happiness.'

Alice wasn't convinced.

'I bet their house is wicked, though,' she said. 'Did it have a helipad?'

Gloria is sleeping when I leave her. I lay her back on the pillows and pull the duvet up around her. She looks smaller now she's asleep, more fragile. I feel protective of her suddenly, although I try not to because I know she'd hate it.

I lean over and kiss her lightly on the forehead.

'Night, Gloria,' I whisper before I tiptoe out. Her eyes flicker open and she smiles.

'Night, Gwen,' she whispers.

When I get back to my room I'm restless. I try to read a book but I find I'm just reading the same page over and over again. I can't stop thinking about Gloria. She's so different when she's talking about the past, more open, everything so clear and vivid. She seems more certain somehow. It's as if she's really there, inhabiting the past. And yet it's as if she sees it in flashes. If I ask her about what happened next, or about where she was, or the order that things happened in she closes up and I can't tell whether it's because she doesn't know or because she doesn't want to be pushed. Is it because she wants to be in control or because she feels lost? It's as though she's only showing me pieces of a jigsaw; I don't know how they fit together and I can't see the whole picture. And I'm not sure if she's keeping the missing pieces back or if she's lost them completely.

I decide I'd probably better email Mum and tell her what's going on. I've been putting it off but I keep getting text messages from Carl saying things like: **Hey Hats, just to let u know the venue may call about numbers 4 the evening do, can u tell them we think about 80?** and **Has the florist got back with a quote yet? We r missing u x** Also telling her feels like sharing the responsibility somehow. I know she'll be angry.

I take a deep breath and type, trying to think of the best way to ensure that Mum doesn't go mental because I've taken her car and driven across England in it:

From: hattiedlockwood@starmail.com
To: ruthslockwood70@starmail.com
Subject: Hola!

Hi!

Hope you're all well and enjoying Spain.

Just thought I'd let you know that I'm having a holiday of my
own. You know how I went to visit Dad's aunt Gloria? Well, she
decided to take a little break and she wanted a bit of company
so I said I'd go with her. She wanted to visit some of the places
she'd been when she was young and it would have been
impossible for her to get to all of them without a car. So I knew
you wouldn't mind if I borrowed yours and drove her as it's for
such a good cause, what with her having dementia and everything and soon she will be unable to remember any of these
places. It is quite tragic and I knew you wouldn't be so cruel as
to want her to miss out on the chance to see them one last
time just because she didn't have a car.

I read it through. Have I gone too far with the guilt trip? Or
not far enough?

I'm not sure of all the places we're going but we're in
Cambridge at the moment and apparently the next stop is
the Lake District! We'll be back by the time you are back
from Mallorca, don't worry!

I will send you a postcard!
Anyway, love to all and see you soon. Don't drink too much Sangria!
Hxx

Later, as I'm going to sleep I hear an email arrive in my inbox. I think about not looking at it, as it's bound to be Mum giving me a hard time. But it's not. It's from Reuben.

From: wilde_one666@starmail.com
To: hattiedlockwood@starmail.com
Subject: you're the one that I want

HATTIE!

I'm sittng outdide a bar overlooking the sea and you'll never guess what song is playing RIGHT NOW Hats – only You're the one that I want! it's our song ,right? remember we sang it at that mad basement karaoke place – Kat made us go there and then disappeared off without singing a single song because that girlfriend of hers called and she just took off? I was John Travolta and you were Olivia Newton John remebmerer? Oh it was beautiful. A beautiful beeeaauuuutiful thing. You were a bit off key, not to mention a bit staggery and slurred what with all the double vodkas, but I didn't let that put me off because like Travolta I am a born performer and a spectacular dancer. It was a truly moving occasion until you managed to inhale your drink and spit it all over the microphone and I had to hit you on the back and then you started hitting me back you maniac and it all descended into more of a brawl than a cheesy love ballad. ah Hats. great times.

I was trying to explain to Camille why it was so funny but she didn't get it. Well I had to mime most of it and anyway I guess you had to be there really. Anyway she doesn't really understand English and you know how well i (don't)

179

speak french. for some reason the words I mainly remember are boite ouvert (tin opener) and chapeau (hat) and cochon d'Inde (guinea pig) and none of these have proved very useful in my conversations with the divine Camille. Of course we speak the international language of lurrrve but after we've finished that, it would be nice to be able to have a laugh. I miss having a laugh. Camille doesn't do all that much laughing. What is the french for laugh I wonder? You probably know don't you, bloody smart arse that you are.

Aaaaah Hats. i won't lie, a few refreshing beverages have been consumed, but I'm sitting outsied here at this bar by the sea and I'm humming Take That and I feel. i dunno. It's not really lik e i thought it wold be. travelling i mean. I misss you HAts. I do. I thinkTHat's all I wanted to say. not very profoudn i know.

xR (JT)

I try not to think about what Camille does a lot of instead of laughing; she probably smokes Gauloises, and looks effortlessly chic and sexy, and reads Sartre and is intellectual but also fantastic in bed in ways I can't even imagine. I bet Camille's hair has never been either lank or prone to frizz, let alone both.

And obviously Camille would never be stupid enough to get herself accidentally up the duff. She'd be far too much of a woman of the world for that.

But I'm better at laughing than her. Which might actually cheer me up if didn't feel so very much not like laughing.

I do remember that night. We decided to walk home afterwards – all the way from town, what were we thinking? Half-way home I was desperate for a wee, so I went behind a tree in someone's garden. I ran all the rest of the way home with my skirt tucked in my knickers something Reuben didn't tell me till the next morning. In fact, it *was* the next morning by the time we got home. It was starting to get light and the birds were singing. And Reuben joined in singing 'Endless Love' – both the Diana Ross and Lionel Ritchie parts – which made us laugh again.

I'm overwhelmed for a moment with how much I miss Reuben. We've shared so much. Not just stupid karaoke. Real stuff.

I remember one day a couple of months after Reuben's dad left. We were sitting in the garden at ours, while he had a cigarette. It was early spring, still freezing, our breath puffing out as we spoke. I was holding a cup of tea to keep me warm.

'He hasn't called me once since he left,' Reuben said. 'He sent me an email to say Happy Christmas.'

'That's pretty lame,' I say. I wanted to say more, but didn't trust myself not to offend Reuben. He has a bit of a blind spot about his dad.

'He did say I could go and stay with him if I wanted.'

'Do you think you will?'

He shrugged.

'Do you miss your dad?' he said suddenly.

I thought about it and decided to be honest in a way I'd never been with anyone else who'd asked about Dad. 'Not exactly,' I said. 'I want to, though.'

He smiled. 'Same,' he said. He reached out and squeezed my hand briefly. 'Shit, isn't it?'

181

'Yeah,' I said.

Oh, Reuben. I wish he'd just come home. I can't let him know that, though, obviously.

I nearly write:

Sing some dodgy backing vocals for me will you?

But then I realize that the song will have finished ages ago. Reuben will have forgotten all about it and me and the karaoke and how I make him laugh and that he sort of sometimes misses me a bit. He'll be back in the club now, or back at his apartment speaking the language of lurve with Camille.

So instead I type:

The French for laugh is 'rire'. Je ris. I laugh. Xxx

But I don't. *Je pleure*. I cry.

## Chapter seventeen

I wake to the sound of someone knocking on my door. I check my watch: it's not even seven a.m. yet. I stagger out of bed expecting to see Gloria there, but it's Irene the bed and breakfast owner.

'Has something happened to Gloria?' I say, panic rising. Images of Gloria wandering off in the night, not knowing where she is, getting lost or injured or—

'No,' Irene says, looking awkward. 'Not exactly. It's just that she's sitting downstairs in the hall saying you're going home. And I didn't have you down as leaving till later in the week. I wondered if she might have got . . . confused.'

I pull on some clothes and make my way downstairs. Sure enough, Gloria's sitting in the hall with her big, heavy (totally unnecessary) coat on and her suitcase all packed.

'What's going on, Gloria?'

'We've got to go,' she says. 'I want to go home.'

'What do you mean?' I say. 'We're going to the Lake District, and Whitby. And wherever else it is you want to take me. Remember? You and Peggy booked it all. Look in your notebook. It's all in there.'

'I haven't forgotten,' she says. 'I've just changed my mind. I don't want to go. It was a bad idea.'

'No!' I say. 'It was a great idea.'

I'm surprised how upset I feel. I really felt like we were just getting started, like she was getting started. And I'm dying to know more of Gloria's story. What happened with Sam. Finding out about Nan and Vinnie. What Gloria's secret was. She can't change her mind.

'No.' She's firm. 'It was a mistake.'

I look at Irene helplessly and she shrugs.

'Okay,' I say. 'Let's go for a walk.'

'No,' says Gloria. 'I just want to go home now.'

'Well, I don't,' I say. 'And I'm driving. I want to go for a walk. You can either come with me or wait for me here.'

She looks at me.

'Or you can call a cab if you want to pay the fare back to London. Be my guest.'

And I open the front door and walk off down the steps of the bed and breakfast. My heart is thudding. I'm taking a risk.

'Wait!' Gloria calls after me. I turn round. 'Well,' she says. 'If you're going to be difficult about it, I suppose I may as well walk with you.'

It's quiet in the centre of town, just a few people around compared to the throngs there will be later, the still-early morning broken by occasional bells ringing. Along the backs of the colleges the grass is still dewy. Gloria and I walk in silence.

'So, go on,' I say at last. 'Why do you want to go home?'

'I just do,' she says.

'I thought you wanted to tell me stuff.'

She doesn't reply.

'I think you still do.'

She still doesn't reply.

'So why the sudden change of plan?' I try to think it through. 'What is it that's made you want to give up?'

'It was a mistake,' she says at last. 'I shouldn't have started delving back into the past. It's best left there.'

'What is?' I say. 'Your secret, the one no one else knows. Is that why you want to go home? Are you scared to tell me?'

'I'm not scared,' she says, too fiercely. I know I'm right.

'Tell me,' I say. 'Look. You know you can trust me. I know you want to tell me. What harm can it do now, all these years later?'

She doesn't answer and we follow the path slowly round, back towards the bed and breakfast.

As we get close she stops.

'I had a baby,' she says, quiet but clear.

I stop and turn to her.

'What?'

I'm so shocked it takes a while to sink in. That was her secret. But of course. It all makes sense. The way she reacted when I told her I was pregnant. That was why she changed her mind. That's why she's so interested in me. She went through the same thing. Except for her it must have been a million times worse than for me. Unmarried and pregnant in the 1950s – and with Sam being the father, the racism she would have suffered. I can't even begin to think what that must have been like.

'When I was seventeen,' she says. 'I had a baby.'

Dr Gilbert's surgery. It has a particular smell, though I'm not really sure what it is. In my mind it is the smell of cleanness and healing: antiseptic, soap, cod liver oil and bandages, and books and the green leather of his desk. It's always been comforting somehow, the smell of being looked after, of knowing you would be made better. But this time I will not be made better.

Dr Gilbert is old. He's been my doctor all my life and he has been old all that time. When I had measles he came to visit me at home. I can glimpse memories of lying in a darkened room for an unguessable length of time, shapes looming at me from the dark, some of them familiar, some dreamlike and other-worldly, terrifying. I remember the cold press of Dr Gilbert's stethoscope on my skin, Mum's anxious voice and the fingertips as she pushed my hair back from my forehead, Gwen crying. They were very worried about me, I discovered afterwards with a thrill. There had been prayers for me at church, and talk of 'preparing for the worst', Gwen told me when I was all better. Dr Gilbert had brought me ice cream when I began to recover, telling me it was good for a sore throat. I had never had it before. Sweets were still rationed then, and he seemed impossibly powerful, magical even, for producing this miraculous gift.

He smiled and asked me how I liked it. 'Very much,' I said. 'But could you make it hotter next time?' '*Gloria!*' Gwen had hissed, but Dr Gilbert had laughed. 'You've got spirit,' he said. 'That's for sure.'

Now he does not laugh. He purses his lips, steepling his fingers and staring at the point where they meet, rather than at me.

'Yes,' he says. 'Sixteen weeks, I would estimate.'

The room seems to tilt a little, and I hold on tight to the wooden arms of my chair in case it should tip me off. Behind me I hear Mum stifle a sob. I can't bear to look round at her, wearing her good shoes and the Sunday coat as if to prove our respectability, and I can't meet Dr Gilbert's eye, so I stare at the photograph behind his left shoulder, on his bookshelf, of someone who I assume is his son in a fur-lined university gown.

When I can breathe, and when I can trust my voice to be steady I say, 'Are you sure?'

'Quite sure.' His voice is blunt.

He says nothing more, and I wonder if I should say something, if he's expecting some kind of explanation or apology, so I open my mouth but he cuts me off.

'I don't wish to know any more about this matter,' he says, dismissive. He is angry with me, I think, for not being the five-year-old girl any more. 'You will be passed to a social worker. She will deal with you.'

'How do you mean?'

He sighs, as if it is beneath him to discuss such things. 'She will find you a place in a Mother and Baby Home. You will go there six weeks before you give birth and leave six weeks after. If you're lucky, you may be able to conceal your condition from everyone until you go away.'

The word 'birth' makes me feel sick. I push it from my mind.

'And then what? I mean, what will happen to it?'

'The Home will sort out the adoption for you.'

'And I can pretend it never happened?'

'I think that's for the best.'

'Twelve weeks?' I say. 'What about school? My A-levels?'

I think of Sister Mary Francis. Will they tell her? She'll think she was right all along about me. Arrogant. Too clever for my own good.

'I rather think you should have thought about that before, don't you? In the meantime you may wish to try gin and hot baths. Don't be tempted to try knitting needles or crochet hooks, though. I had a patient die last year. Haemorrhaged. She was younger than you.'

He scribbles on a piece of paper.

'This is who you need to contact.' He hands the piece of paper to Mum rather than to me and then carries on writing.

He doesn't say goodbye.

When I get to the door I say, 'You were very kind to me when I was a little girl. When I had measles. You said I had spirit.' He had said it as if it was a good thing to have; no one else had ever said it like that before. The ice cream had been like a reward for it.

He pauses briefly but does not look up. Then he carries on writing. I wonder if he even remembers the ice cream.

## Chapter eighteen

I'm sitting opposite Gloria in an olde worlde café in the middle of Cambridge while she examines the menu. Having decided to stay, Gloria announced she wanted to spend the day sightseeing so we've traipsed around colleges and museums. It's unbelievably hot and the place is packed with tourists. I can't think about anything except Gloria's revelation that she had a baby. At first I couldn't believe it, but then it began to make sense. No wonder me turning up had reminded her of her own past. I'm dying to know more, but she's steadfastly refused to say anything more about it. I haven't wanted to push her in case she decides she wants to go home again but my mind has been full of questions. What happened to her baby? Had it been adopted? Is that what this whole trip is about? Has she found her son or daughter and that's why we're going to Whitby – to see them? I'm excited at the thought, that there might be a reunion, before it's too late for Gloria. And what did Sam say when she told him about the baby? But any time I've even hinted at these questions Gloria has ignored me and pointedly changed the subject. Now we're in the café I try again.

'So?' I say to Gloria as she looks at the menu.

'So what?'

'So . . . what happened? What did he say when you told him?'

'Told who?'

Again I find myself wondering whether she really can't remember what we were talking about or whether she's just trying to avoid the question. I look at her to see whether there's a clue in her expression, but she's holding the menu up in front of her so that I can't see her face.

'Sam,' I say. 'Remember, we were talking about when you found out you were pregnant. What did Sam say when you told him?'

'Scones might be nice,' she said. 'If they're not too dry. I can't abide a dry scone.'

'Was he happy? I mean, I know he must have been shocked but it was what he wanted, right?'

'Or carrot cake.'

'Gloria!' I try not to let my frustration show in my voice because I don't really know why I'm so desperate to know what happened, and also if there's one thing I've learned over the last week it's that the more Gloria thinks someone wants her to do something, the less likely she is to do it. 'Do you not want to tell me?'

She puts down the menu and looks at me.

'There's nothing to tell,' she says, her voice flat. 'I never saw him again after that day.'

I stare at her. I'm so shocked that for a moment I can't speak. The waitress comes and takes our order and I'm so busy thinking about what Gloria's told me that I just sit there and she orders for me.

'No,' I say, once the waitress has gone. 'I don't understand. He can't have.'

Gloria just stares out of the window as if I haven't spoken.

'He can't have abandoned you. Not Sam. He wouldn't do that.'

Gloria still doesn't say anything, just sits and hums quietly to herself. I tell myself not to push it. It's not fair. Just because it all happened a long time ago doesn't mean it doesn't still hurt to think about it. Maybe she's changed her mind. Maybe she doesn't want it all dragged up after all. Or maybe she does, but in her own time.

We sit there in silence for a while and I become aware of the family next to us, with a baby in a highchair and a screechy toddler. The baby is dribbling regurgitated chocolate cake down its chin. I'm grateful when the waitress brings our order.

'What shall we do after this? We've done a lot of walking. We could just go back to the bed and breakfast. Or a film? Do you like the cinema? Or just go and find a pub by the river before dinner?'

'Yes,' she says half-heartedly, and gives me one of those looks that makes me doubt not only whether she's listening, but whether she's completely sure who I am.

'What did he actually say?'

'Young lady,' Gloria says loudly to the waitress as she passes. 'Could you bring us another pot of tea? This one is chipped. I'm not paying good money to drink tea out of a chipped pot.'

I think about the fetid state of Gloria's kitchen and attempt to give her a stern look, which she pretends not to notice. I smile apologetically at the waitress, knowing what I'd feel like saying if a customer said this to me at the Happy Diner, what I'd say to Mack and Big Jim about them afterwards. The waitress ignores me and sullenly takes away the teapot without a word.

'Gloria,' I whisper. 'It's not her fault.'

Gloria doesn't say anything, and I suspect her of having said it just to change the subject.

'So what happened? What did you say to him? What did he say to you? You can't just have left it like that?'

'Can't I? You seem to know an awful lot about it all of a sudden. About what people should and shouldn't have said or done.'

'Sorry,' I say. 'I didn't mean it like that.'

'It was a long time ago,' she says. 'More than half a century. I can't remember who said what to whom. I'm senile, remember? I can't remember who the prime minister is.'

'Well, he's not very memorable, to be fair. But . . .' I try to work out what she's telling me. 'But he wanted to marry you. What about everything he'd imagined? Little Vivienne and Danny? This was what he wanted, wasn't it? I thought he'd be over the bloody moon. I thought he'd be marching you up the aisle before you could say "shotgun wedding".'

'You don't have a clue what it was like back then.'

'So tell me.'

'Well, for a start you couldn't get married in those days under the age of twenty-one without your parents' permission.'

'Seriously? Well, couldn't you have run away together? Eloped, or whatever?'

She concentrates on flattening crumbs on her plate with her fork.

'No.'

'Why not?'

'It wasn't like that.'

'What was it like then?'

She stares out of the window again, and is silent for so long that I think perhaps she's forgotten I'm there, or what we were talking about. It happens sometimes, this losing of the thread. I can't tell when it's the dementia, or when it's just a convenient way of changing the subject.

She turns to me. 'Could you find me an ashtray, dear? They've forgotten to put one on our table.'

I try not to roll my eyes.

'Gloria,' I say patiently, 'you can't smoke in cafés any more. I explained it all to you at the Savoy when you shouted at the poor barman for asking you not to, remember?'

'Did I?' she says vaguely. 'I'll just pop outside then.'

She picks up her bag, and as she weaves her way through the chintzy tablecloths I can't help feeling I've been had, and that she engineered it as a way to stop the conversation. The waitress plonks a fresh pot of tea down on the table in front of me.

'There,' she says, making it sound like an accusation.

'Sorry,' I say, thinking of the number of times I've smiled sweetly at a rude Happy Diner customer, while imagining tipping the contents of the tray I'm carrying into their lap. 'She doesn't mean anything by it. She's not very well.'

The waitress tuts and gives me a what-do-I-care look and I feel defensive of Gloria suddenly. The more time I spend with her, the more I think that she's most likely to be a total pain in the bum when she's feeling most vulnerable. Like an armadillo defending itself by rolling itself up into a ball so that only its hard shell shows. Well, a bit like that. I watch Gloria's back and imagine her face if she knew that in my head I was comparing her to an armadillo.

Am I right? Is it defensiveness, because she's feeling scared? Or am I just projecting onto her the characteristics I think she ought to have, like Ollie used to with his pet rat before it died? I'd explained to him that animals felt things differently to us, that we couldn't imagine how they saw the world. (He'd looked at me pityingly.) But we do it all the time with people. Give them feelings that are ours, imagine they're feeling what we would, or what we think they ought to, when really they might not be at all.

Is that what I do with Reuben? Do I give him credit for being more than he is? Let him off for being an insensitive idiot because I know there's more going on underneath? Or think I know . . .

I scoop a forkful of Gloria's untouched carrot cake into my mouth and chew it thoughtfully. Maybe that's what happened with Sam. Maybe Gloria let herself believe that he was honest and kind and in love with her because she wanted him to be. Everything she's told me about him makes me think he was in love with her, that he'd have done anything for her. But maybe she's not even remembering it right. What was it she'd said about memories? *Some are real. Some are made up. But they are the stories that tell us who we are.*

But still, I feel shocked at the thought of it, of seventeen-year-old Gloria going to tell the man she loved that she was having his baby, and then – for whatever reason – never seeing him again. In fact, I don't just feel shocked, I feel shaken. How could he have done that to her? Had they argued? Had he pretended to be pleased and then done a runner? None of it makes sense.

The carrot cake is delicious and when I look down at the plate I realize I've eaten most of it without noticing. No wonder my jeans are feeling so tight.

I don't know. I can't help feeling Gloria's not telling me everything. There are so many gaps. Why doesn't she want to talk about it?

I turn back round to the window and Gloria's gone.

'So what happened? What did he say when you told him?'

She sits there, the girl – Hattie – wide-eyed, waiting for me to tell her the next instalment. It is just a story to her. Something that happened so long ago it has no relevance now, no real meaning. It is not her fault. Perhaps it was a mistake, coming on this journey. Perhaps the past should be left where it is, buried and allowed to disappear.

'Told who?'

'Sam,' she says. 'Remember, we were talking about when you found out you were pregnant. What did Sam say when you told him?'

I can't tell her, of course. Not yet. Not ever perhaps. I don't even want to think about it myself, and yet it is there suddenly in my head. I see myself, walking up to the park gates where we had arranged to meet. I know I must tell him but I know I cannot. I am heavy with sadness and dread; I can feel it now, the weight of it inside me. Sam and I haven't seen each other for almost a month – I have invented excuses to avoid it – and he lights up as he catches sight of me. It breaks my heart.

As I get closer I see his face change. I open my mouth to speak to him but no words will come. He reaches up to my eye and I flinch away from his touch.

'Who did this to you?'

I say nothing.

'It was your dad, wasn't it?'

I take a deep breath and try to start the story about the bus and how I can never resist jumping off before it stops moving. It has the advantage of being true, and I've learned over the years of my dealings with Sister Mary Francis and others that the closer a lie is to the truth the more convincing it will be. It would make him smile if I could say it, the thought of my impatience, my inability to keep still, my clumsiness. These are all things he loves about me. He has told me so. Telling him that lie would take the anger and hurt out of his eyes.

But I can't say it. I just stand there silently.

'How can he do that to you?'

'Don't fuss,' I say. 'It was weeks ago. It's nearly healed now.'

'To his own daughter? I'm going to go round to your house right now. I'm going to go and tell him—'

'No.' I want to say more but I'm too tired. Speaking is exhausting. I feel a bit faint.

'He can't just get away with it. It's not right.'

'I can stand up for myself.'

'I've seen too many people getting treated badly and taking it. I'm not going to be one of those people, Gloria. You're not one of those people.'

'Please,' I say. 'Sam. Just leave it. It's none of your business.'

He stares at me. 'Of course it's my business,' he says. 'I love you.'

He's so open, so unafraid, so *truthful*. I can't look at him.

'This isn't like you,' he says.

'How do you know?' I say, and although I swore I wouldn't cry there are tears in my eyes. 'How do you know what I'm really like? We've only known each other a few months.'

He shakes his head and puts his arms round me. 'Gloria, I knew you the first time I met you. That time after the Lyceum. I knew you were strong, and clever, and funny, and a dreamer, full of crazy ideas, a little bit wild even. But kind too, underneath, although you try not to let it show.' He smiles at me and I know he wants me to smile back and I want to, I really do, but I can't. 'I understood more about you than I do about people I've known for years and years.'

'I've got something I have to tell you,' I say.

'She went that way,' the grumpy waitress says, seeing me panic.

'When?' I say, scrabbling to find my purse and leaving far too big a tip.

'Dunno,' says the waitress. 'Few minutes ago. If you want to go and look for her I'll keep an eye out here.'

'Thanks,' I say, running out of the shop. I look down the street, which is full of tourists milling about and groups of foreign students all dressed in matching sweatshirts. I can't see Gloria anywhere.

My head is aching. My feet too. I suppose if I wore those ugly old lady shoes people my age are supposed to they wouldn't. But it would be admitting defeat. I suppose when I don't know who I am any more someone will slide my feet into a pair of those beige monstrosities whatsername downstairs wears. St Peggy. But for now I will stick to my kitten heels. '*Il Faut souffrir pour être belle*, Gloria,' Mum used to say when I was a little girl, smiling, when I squealed as she curled my hair, pulling it at the roots. 'One must suffer to be beautiful.' Well, she suffered all right, but broken teeth and black eyes don't do much for your looks. I never fell for it, the idea that beauty and suffering were inseparable. 'It's stupid,' I said to Gwen when Mum was out of earshot. 'No, it's not,' Gwen said.

I sit down on a bench and close my eyes. Poor Mum. She

only ever dared smile when we were alone together. If Father saw he'd take it as a personal affront. How dare she be happy? Or he'd think she was laughing at him.

I hadn't been completely truthful with her. It had been the last time I spoke to him, but it wasn't the last time I saw him.

The last time I saw him I was out shopping with Gwen. Must have been just before I went into the Mother and Baby Home because we were shopping for the list of things I'd been told I had to take with me for the baby. My duffel-coat buttons wouldn't do up any more. The idea of going into the Home six weeks before was that if you were lucky no one would guess you were expecting, everyone could pretend you'd got ill and gone to some relative in the country to recuperate and then you could come back and pretend nothing had happened. 'Especially you young girls. You stay so flat no one'd ever know you were in the family way till the last few weeks,' Beattie, the Social Worker, had said the first time we met, looking a little ruefully at her own saggy midriff. But my belly hadn't got that message and had expanded at such a rate that there was no hiding it, even with the enormous duffel coat Mum insisted I wore whenever I went outside. Father thought I was doing it on purpose, to shame him. And I probably would have done too, if I'd had any control over it, just to spite him. It would have been worth enduring the looks I got from the neighbours, from strangers on the bus just to know I'd made him suffer. Mum gave me a *Woolworth*'s wedding ring to wear but it was too big and it kept falling off and I lost it after a couple of days; it rolled off along the pavement and into the gutter and I couldn't bring myself to get down on my hands and knees and scrabble about for it. Not with people watching. I was sure they all knew I wasn't really married anyway. I kept telling myself I didn't care what anyone thought of me, and that they were stupid and ignorant and knew nothing about me, that I was better than them, no matter what they

199

thought. Sometimes I believed myself. And the fact that it angered Father, that it humiliated him, was a consolation.

So I stood on Oxford Street trying to disappear and there Sam was, suddenly, walking towards us on the other side of the road. I wanted to hide but at the same time I couldn't take my eyes off him and eventually he noticed me.

At first I thought he was going to call out and run across the road. But then he stopped dead, just staring at me. I can still see him now as he stood and watched me walk past, clear as anything, still as if I'd turned him to stone.

We'd walked past him by then but I still couldn't take my eyes off him, craning my head round to see him through the crowds and he put his hands up to his face and turned away.

That was the last time I saw him. It still feels so raw and fresh that it seems impossible that I should ever forget it. But I will of course. I will sit in a chair in the day room of some nursing home, not knowing what a chair is or what sitting is. I will forget his name, and my own, and I will forget that I ever had a baby, that I ever loved.

And so yes, of course I will forget that day, when I saw him for the last time, when I thought that it wasn't possible that I could go on living without him, that my heart would break and that I would be glad of it.

I've learned over the years that they are stubborn things, though, hearts. They go on beating whether you want them to or not.

I open my eyes. Where am I? I am on a bench. I have been asleep, I think. Is that right? There is a man in front of me dressed in silver pretending to be a statue. I don't know why. I don't know where I am. What am I doing here? I look around me. There is a bridge and a river and lots of people I don't know, young people most of them, sitting on the grass, walking around arm in arm. This is not a place I know.

Is it?

How would I know, if I've forgotten it? Why can I not remember? Perhaps it is somewhere I come every day. I look around, trying not to show panic.

I am not scared. Perhaps if I say it enough I will believe it.

Oh, God, where is she? Where would she have gone? I try to get myself into her head. Did she just wander off because she felt like it, or because I was asking her about stuff she didn't want to talk about? What if she's changed her mind again and decided to go home after all? Perhaps I'm panicking about nothing. She might just turn up at the bed and breakfast later. Or has she forgotten where she is? What if she can't remember where we're staying? It's all in the red book, of course, but the book is in my bag. She gave it to me to carry when we were on the punt. There's no way of anyone knowing. I imagine for a moment how terrifying that must be, to have no point of reference, like one of those dreams that you arrive in halfway through and have no idea why anything is the way it is. I run down the street, trying to think of a clue as to where Gloria might have gone. She wanted to see the river. I hurry down the road that leads to the Cam and spy a pub on the corner. Yes! Surely that's where she'll be.

I run in and look around, out of breath. The bar is full of tourists buying *Pimm's* and pints of lager in plastic cups to take outside and drink by the river.

And sure enough, in the middle of them all, there's Gloria, giving the barman an earful.

'You make it with pineapple juice and cherry brandy,' she's saying. 'Plus *Cointreau* and lemon juice, of course. Any bartender worth his salt knows that.'

'Gloria!' I call out. She turns to me and just for a moment

201

I see a look of intense gratitude and relief cross her face. It's gone in an instant, though.

'This young man doesn't know how to make a gin sling!' she says, outraged. What an actress she is.

'Why did you go wandering off?' I say, trying not to sound angry and failing.

'So I'm not to be trusted to go for a walk on my own now? I just fancied a stroll that's all, and then I saw the pub.'

She looks at me.

'I knew you'd find me.'

I'm beginning to get tuned in to her act, the way she pretends you're overreacting, her little evasions, her generalizing or implying that you should already know so she's not going to tell you. She's bloody good at it. She could fool you into thinking she was totally on the ball if you only saw her every now and then. It's only because I'm with her all the time that I'm starting to see the gaps, the inconsistencies, the little moments of fear, the empty spaces before the act kicks in to fill them. And I realize that Gloria must have known that going away together would mean letting me in on this secret side of her, exposing her vulnerability to me. That's a pretty big deal, it strikes me, and I tell myself to remember this next time she's being a pain.

'Okay,' I say. 'I'll get the drinks. You go and sit down.'

As we sit there, a group of women all totter in together, wearing fancy dress, laughing and chatting. I'd guess most of them are in their twenties or thirties and one of them is wearing a tiara and a sash. They're laughing and chatting and Gloria looks interested.

'Hen night,' I say.

Carl had been on at me about what I was going to

organize for Mum's hen do, even though the wedding was months away. Mum had grimaced and said 'Just nothing involving fancy dress, *please*.' Carl was planning a weekend away with his mates in Barcelona.

'Looks rather fun,' Gloria says.

I go to the loo, and when I come back Gloria's not sitting at the table. I panic for a moment, thinking she's wandered off again, but then I see that she's gone to join the hen-night table, talking to a couple of the women as though they were old friends. One of them is pouring her a drink from a pitcher of lurid pink cocktail. Somehow I'm not surprised. I sigh inwardly and wave to Gloria, gesturing to her to come over to where I am so we can get going and find somewhere for dinner. Gloria sees me, I'm sure she does, but she pretends not to and carries on telling what I can tell from here is a rather rude story to her new best friends. They cackle with laughter and one of them, who's definitely had quite a lot to drink already, puts her arm round Gloria. I hurry over to extricate her, feeling shy and a bit embarrassed.

'Hattie,' Gloria calls out as I get close to the table. 'Everyone, this is Hattie, my great-niece. Hattie, this is . . .'

She stops.

'Rachel,' says the woman sitting next to her.

'Rachel,' says Gloria. 'It's her sister, Emily, who's getting married.'

'Hello,' I say. 'Um, nice to meet you. Congratulations,' I say to the woman in the tiara. 'Sorry, but we need to get going, don't we, Gloria? We need to go and get something to eat.'

'Oh, no!' Emily says. 'No, don't go! Come with us. We're just off to eat and we've got a couple of spaces at the table because a couple of people couldn't make it.'

'Oh, I don't think—' I begin.

'Marvellous!' says Gloria. 'What a splendid idea. If you're sure?'

'Of course,' they chorus.

'Gloria was just telling us about her weddings,' Rachel says to me, and she starts laughing again. 'She's quite a character, isn't she?'

'Mmm,' I say. I'm a bit annoyed that they know something about Gloria that I don't and the last thing I want to do is get embroiled in a hen night. But looking at Gloria, in her element, I know I don't stand a chance of talking her out of it.

'We're going clubbing later,' Rachel says. 'You can come along if you like.'

'Well, Gloria gets tired. We'll need an early night,' I say.

Several hours later I'm sitting in a packed, sweaty nightclub. I'm sitting with the only other sober person, Lisa, who is six-months pregnant. Gloria and the others are on the dance floor doing the Macarena. I've got a pulsing headache and all I want to do is sleep. My resentment towards Gloria is increasing every second. 'I'm really tired,' I'd said to her earlier. 'I feel quite ill.' 'Have a drink,' she'd said. 'Let your hair down.' 'I can't,' I'd said. 'I'm pregnant, remember?' 'If you're not keeping the baby, what does it matter?' I didn't have an answer for that.

Now sitting here, I'm overwhelmed suddenly by rage towards Gloria, towards Reuben, and most of all towards the baby that isn't a baby yet inside me. It feels like a parasite. I feel invaded. And I think suddenly about Gloria's Dr Gilbert and his suggestion about gin and think, *why not*?

I go to the bar and order two double gins.

I take them back to the table and down the first one. It's disgusting.

'Wow, you're going for it!' says Lisa. 'I thought you didn't drink?'

'I've changed my mind,' I say.

The gin burns inside me and seems to make my head blur a little almost immediately. I pick up the next glass and drink that one too. Then I sit back and close my eyes. Everything feels distant but not in a good way. My head is still thudding, worse than ever, and I feel so hot I'm sweating and the taste of gin is in my mouth and the smell is in my nose and it's disgusting.

'You all right?' Lisa says.

'No,' I say. 'I think I'm going to be sick.'

Gloria appears in front of me.

'Come on,' she says. 'Come and have a dance with me and the girls!'

Her cheeks are flushed and her eyes are bright.

'Gloria, I've got to go,' I say. 'I feel sick. And we're leaving in the morning remember?'

She looks blank.

'For the Lake District.'

I have no idea whether she remembers what I'm talking about or not.

'We can't go now!' she says. 'Not when everyone's having so much fun!'

'Well, I'm not,' I shout over the thumping music. 'I've got to go.'

'Okay,' she shouts. 'You go. I'll see you back there.'

'No!' I shout. 'I can't leave you!'

'Why not?'

'You might get lost,' I say.

'I have a very good sense of direction, I'll have you know,' she says.

'But can you even remember the name of where we're staying?' I say. 'Can you even remember *my* name?'

'Yes,' she says. 'SUSAN.'

And I don't know whether she's saying it to annoy me or if she really thinks that's my name.

'I'm not a child,' she says, defiant. 'I don't need baby-sitting. I've survived till now without you watching my every move.'

'*Fine*,' I say. 'Your new friends can get you home.'

As I leave, I give Lisa the name of our bed and breakfast and some money. 'Sorry to ask, but can you make sure Gloria gets back all right?' I say. 'I've got to go.'

And with that I run to the exit and down the stairs of the club because I know I'm going to be sick.

Once I'm at the bed and breakfast, my rage at Gloria subsides and I start to worry. But I think to myself that what she says was right. She's an adult; she's got by without me all this time. Still, though, I'm sure she had no idea where she was when I found her this afternoon.

I check my email as a distraction, hoping there might be something from Reuben. Instead there's a message from Mum.

From: ruthslockwood70@starmail.com
To: hattiedlockwood@starmail.com
Subject: Re: Hola!

So let me get this straight. You've taken my car – the car that you crashed into a pillar in the car park the very first time you drove it – and you're driving an old lady to Whitby in it? Hattie,

206

you and I are going to have words about this when I get home.
In the meantime, DRIVE SAFELY.
We love you lots and are missing you.

Mum xxx

I type back:

From: hattiedlockwood@starmail.com
To: ruthslockwood70@starmail.com
Subject: Re: Hola!

Would you rather I was at home having wild drug-crazed
orgies and trashing the house? I'm missing you too.

Hxxx

At some point I doze off because what seems like the next
minute I'm woken by a knock on the door.

I get up and answer it, and sure enough it's Gloria,
carrying her shoes in one hand, a bag of chips in the other
and wearing a pair of deely boppers.

'Thank God!' I say. 'You got back okay.'

'Well, of course I did. Rachel walked me back. We sang
songs.' She giggles as she slumps down in the armchair in
my room. I climb back into bed and put my glasses on to
look at her properly.

'Gloria, you're wearing deely boppers.'

'I know,' she says, shaking her head. 'Look at them go!'

'And they've got – oh, God! Are those pink glittery—'

'Penises!' exclaims Gloria, delighted. 'Aren't they splendid?'

'*No!*' I say. 'Ugh.'

And then I think about how my reaction to the bobbing glittery penises is really VERY Susan indeed. So I say grudgingly, 'Did you have a good time?'

'I had a simply splendid time,' says Gloria. 'What a hoot those girls were. Rachel invited us to join up with them tomorrow. They've got a burlesque dancing lesson and then cocktail-making and then punting.'

'You did tell her you couldn't go, didn't you? You did remember that we're going tomorrow?'

'Yes. Such a shame.' She looks so disappointed that I feel bad.

'Still, it'll be great to get to the Lake District, won't it? The next bit of our journey? The next bit of the story.'

I let the words hang there in the hope that Gloria might tell me why we're going there, but she doesn't take the hint.

'And why are we going there?' I say it casually, hoping to catch her off guard.

Her face changes.

Oh yes, she remembers that all right.

'I went there a long time ago,' she says.

'Is it part of the story?' I ask. 'Has it got something to do with what happened? To you and Sam? The baby?'

I can tell I've gone too far. The shutters come down.

'What baby?' she says, looking me in the eye. I know perfectly well she hasn't forgotten. When she's really forgotten, she does her best to cover it up; there's a tiny glimpse of panic beneath the surface. This isn't that. Stuff from the old days doesn't slip away like new memories do. Every detail of it is stored away – for now at least. She's just reminding me that she doesn't have to tell me anything if she doesn't want to. I know from the set of her jaw and the way the sparkly willies are trembling belligerently above her head that she is all ready for an argument and I think, *What's the point?* She's warning me not to push it so I don't.

After Gloria's gone I lie back and think about what she's said. I look at my watch – nearly two thirty a.m. The thought of getting up early tomorrow and getting everything packed ready to leave isn't appealing. But moving on must mean finding out what happened next in Gloria's story, and getting an answer to some of my questions. What happened after she found out she was pregnant? Did she even actually have the baby? Or did she take the risk of a backstreet abortion and get luckier than the poor girl who Dr Gilbert talked about, who died? I shiver just thinking of her. I wonder what her name was, this anonymous bit-part player in Gloria's story, used as a cautionary tale by an old grey-haired doctor. I try to imagine how scared and desperate she would have had to be to have tried such a brutal, dangerous way to end her pregnancy. If I'd been born fifty years earlier I wouldn't have to imagine it. That's the choice I'd be facing myself.

I force myself to turn my thoughts back to Gloria and the next bit of her story. Why the Lake District? Could she and Sam have run away there together? But no, she said she never saw him again. And then I open my eyes wide in the darkness because I've had a brilliant, wonderful idea. Could it be that she wants to see him now?

Could Sam be in the Lake District? My heart beats faster at the thought of it. Is that it? A reunion, after all these years?

My head swims as I try to remember everything that Gloria has told me so far. There are so many gaps and things I don't quite understand. But I will. I just have to be patient and let Gloria tell me in her own time.

## Chapter nineteen

The next morning we set off early because I'm so worried about having to drive all the way to the Lake District, and we stop at a motorway service station for breakfast. Gloria is in a very bad mood, I'm guessing because she has a hangover.

'These places,' she says, shuddering and pulling her coat around her. 'I always imagine hell as some variation on the motorway service station theme, don't you? But without the motorway, obviously.'

'Shall I get you a coffee?' I say brightly. 'Or a sandwich if you're hungry?'

'They exude a kind of pointlessness, don't they? A kind of empty desperation.'

'Perhaps a *pain au chocolat*?'

'Just look at them all,' Gloria says, gazing around at the people sitting at other tables. To be fair, the grey-faced, shiny-suited man sitting at next table, staring blankly at his mobile phone, does look a bit fed up. Gloria stares at him.

'You can almost hear the silent screams of their tormented souls.'

I cup my hand to my ear. 'I Should Be So Lucky' is playing tinnily from somewhere nearby. 'Nope,' I say. 'All I can hear is Kylie.'

'That's one good thing about this wretched disease,' she says. 'It won't be long before all memory of motorway service stations will be expunged from my memory. The sooner the better, quite frankly.'

'Don't start that again.'

'Tell me honestly it doesn't make you want to end it all.'

'No,' I say. 'It doesn't. It makes me want to buy a hazelnut latte and possibly a breakfast bap. But if you'd rather sit there being bloody miserable, be my guest. Just don't moan later that you're hungry because you were too busy staring into the abyss to eat. Anyway, you're the one who wanted to go to the Lake District and Whitby. I suggested the Maldives, if you remember. No motorway service stations there.'

In the end she relents and says I can buy her an espresso, as if she's doing me a massive favour.

In the queue I get a text from Reuben.

**How's the road trip going? Don't go driving off any cliffs now xx**

I reply: **That might be the nicest thing you've ever said to me ;) x**

I get Gloria an almond croissant too, which she says she doesn't want but eats anyway. I'm still hungry after my breakfast bap so I get a blueberry muffin. I've never felt so hungry. Eating for two, I suppose. I push the thought away. Enough time to think about that after Whitby. The appointment is only a few days from now, I realize uncomfortably.

As we sit there eating, my phone buzzes with another text from Reuben.

**Just thinking of the wellbeing of the great-aunt babe ;)**

Gloria watches me as I read it.

'What?' I say.

211

'That was him, wasn't it? The one who—' She inclines her head delicately in the direction of my womb.

'Yes.'

'Thought so.'

Something in her face makes me feel defensive.

'Come on,' I say. 'I need to get some petrol and then we'd better get back on the road.'

The closer we get to the Lake District, the more I wonder why it is we're going all this way. Is it something to do with Sam? Or the baby? I try to steer Gloria back to her story.

'I've worked it out,' I say. 'Why you never saw Sam again.'

She looks up sharply.

'Really?'

'It was your father, wasn't it? He threatened Sam, told him he'd kill him if he ever saw him with you again. Or Vinnie. God, they didn't really do it, did they? They didn't really hurt him?'

I think of the hatred on Gloria's face when she talked about Vinnie. Was that why? Had he scared off Sam? Threatened him? Beaten him up? Or worse? Vinnie sounded like a nasty piece of work but surely—

'No,' Gloria says, her voice flat, without emotion. 'They didn't.'

There's something about the way she says it that makes me think she's not telling me the whole story. I watch her, trying to find some clue about what she's hiding. Whatever it is, I've got a right to know. Vinnie was my grandfather, after all. But maybe that's it. Maybe it's because he's my grandfather that she doesn't want to tell me. If he was a violent racist, perhaps she thinks I'd rather not know. I think about it. It's a pretty uncomfortable thought. But I never knew him. It's not like he was someone I cared about, or even someone that Dad cared about, for that matter, because he died before Dad could even remember him.

'So then why—'

'I don't want to talk about it.'

I was right. There's definitely something she's not telling me.

'Okay,' I say. 'Then tell me why we're going to the Lake District.'

I half expect her to argue, to refuse, to change the subject.

Instead she says: 'It's where St Monica's was.'

I stare at her blankly.

'The Mother and Baby Home,' she says. 'It's where I had my baby.'

The woman who opens the door is a thin-lipped nun with eyebrows that want to meet in the middle, stretching towards each other across her nose. I'm too tired and nauseous to say anything much; I just stand there, taking in the gloomy hallway, dark wood, trying not to gag on the overpowering smell of wood polish and boiled cabbage, trying not to let the tears leak from my eyes.

'You've missed dinner,' the thin-lipped woman says, critically, and despite my hunger I can't help feeling relieved. 'We put some aside for you but it'll be cold by now.'

'It's fine. I'm not hungry,' I say, trying to keep my voice strong. 'Thank you.'

'You've got to eat, dear,' she says. 'You can't go skipping meals in your condition.'

But I don't eat.

It's strange being surrounded by girls in the same state as me, some younger, some older, but all with swollen bellies, or else already with babies. There is a solidarity among the girls, they sit and smoke and play cards together in the evenings or chat and knit bootees for their babies, but I can't join in. I keep myself to myself and spend as much time as I can in the dormitory I share with three other girls.

'It's a relief, you know, talking to the others. You should try it.'

I look up and see it's the tall, smiley northern girl whose bed is the one next to mine.

'D'you mind?' she says, and sits down on my bed without waiting for me to answer.

I pretend I'm not listening, concentrating hard on folding the baby clothes Mum packed. Little white matinee jackets. She couldn't have knitted them, Father wouldn't have let her and she wouldn't have done it in secret; wouldn't have risked him finding out. Must have been mine when I was a baby, maybe Gwen's, too. I press one of them to my face. It smells faintly of lavender and soap. She'd kept them all this time, folded away somewhere, safe in a drawer. I stop folding and turn my head away from the northern girl – Edie wasn't it? – so she can't see my face.

She reaches out and puts her hand on mine.

'Eh,' she says. 'Come on. It's not so bad.' She squeezes my hand but I still can't look at her. No one except Gwen has seen me cry since I was six years old. 'Don't worry,' she says. 'There's always at least two of us in tears. We joke about it. It's being in the family way does it, in't it?' She takes out a clean white hankie from her pocket and hands it to me. I take it and wipe my eyes quickly, and then I scrunch it up in my hands, uncertain whether to hand it back or not.

'Keep it,' she says and I look up at her briefly, grateful. She must be about my age, maybe a year or two older. Pretty. Dark hair. Looks like she's about to give birth any minute.

'Listen,' she says. 'Before you come in here you think you're the only one. It's the same for all of us out there.' She jerks her head towards the window. 'Everyone looking down their nose at you and shaking their heads. All the neighbours

215

pulling that face.' She sucks her cheeks in and turns her mouth down severely, tilting her head back and looking so far down her nose at me she goes cross-eyed. I know she's trying to make me smile but I can't, I just look down at the damp hankie in my hands. '*You* know the face I mean,' she says. And the funny thing is that it does look a bit like how Mrs Onions and goody-flaming-two-shoes Brenda Onions looked at me that time in the shop after Edna-next-door had overheard Father raging at me that time and blabbed it all along the street. Brenda had looked pointedly at my middle and then she'd pulled her fluffy white cardigan tight round her like she was trying to protect herself from my sinfulness and whispered something to her mother, and then they'd both stood there, giving me the look.

I'd turned and smiled sweetly.

'Six months gone, if you must know,' I said. 'And I've still got more of a waist than you'll ever have, Brenda Onions.' Well, she's always hated me, Brenda has, ever since I cut one of her pigtails off when we were four.

And then I'd marched past them, head in the air, hoping I looked just the tiniest little bit like Rita Hayworth, and not like a schoolgirl whose face was puffy with hormones and heat, who'd had to let out her skirt with elastic. Not like a girl who had woken up that morning before it was light, nauseous and panicky and alone, and cried until her eyes were sore and swollen, but quietly, *silently*, so that no one would hear her, no one would know she was scared.

'Ten Players, please,' I'd said, as Gwen's hand clamped on my arm from behind and she hissed in my ear, 'Why, Gloria, why do you have to be like this?'

And Mrs Hawkins who's known me since I was born and used to sneak me extra sweets when they were still rationed,

216

she does give me the cigarettes, but she gives me the look as well, the look that Edie's doing again now, as if you were a disappointment, and maybe even a little bit dangerous.

'You *do* know, don't you?' Edie says, watching me. 'I knew you would. We all do. That's why it's good being in here, with other people like you. They understand.'

I look at her. 'They're not like me,' I say. 'I'm not like them.'

I expect her to get annoyed but she just smiles. 'How d'you know if you never bloody talk to 'em, eh, Mrs High and Mighty?'

'*Miss* High and Mighty, you mean,' I say, half smiling. 'That's rather the problem, isn't it?'

'Out there maybe,' she says. 'Not in here. Come on. Come and have a game of cards downstairs.'

'This isn't how I remember the Lake District at all,' I say to Gloria, looking through the windscreen at the mountains ahead of us, purple and green, the late-afternoon sun lighting the peaks in gold and casting dark shadows. Throughout our family holiday mist and clouds had hidden the mountains, so that everything was a claustrophobic fog of grey. This, along with soggy sandwiches, ill-fitting wellies, and being damp right down to my underwear, are my main memories of that holiday.

Gloria doesn't reply.

'It's incredible, isn't it?' I say, trying to catch her up in my excitement. 'It's all so big. So free.' Exhilaration surges inside me as I drive. I feel so far from home in this wild, ancient, unfamiliar landscape. Maybe we are like Thelma and Louise after all, albeit in a Ford Fiesta instead of a 1966 Thunderbird, and still lacking a Brad Pitt.

'Hmmph,' says Gloria. She's been unusually quiet on the way here, looking watchfully out of the window.

'Are you okay?' I say. I think of everything she's told me, about arriving at the Home, about Edie. How must it feel for her, coming back here?

'Of course I'm okay,' she snaps. 'I just wish we'd hurry up and get there. I want a smoke.' She says this rather accusingly, as though I'm being completely unreasonable for insisting she doesn't smoke her foul-smelling cigarillos in the car.

'Well, we're not far now. Should be there in about ten minutes.'

'It's incredible, isn't it?' she says, the girl, whatshername. Hetty. Harry. Damn. I reach into my bag for my notebook. There she is: Hattie.

As she drives I watch her face, from behind my sunglasses so she can't see. Her eyes are wide. She sees mountains and sky and possibility. She wants me to see it too.

I can't. This place doesn't mean possibility to me. It means fear. I never thought I'd miss home, but I did when I was here. I wanted terraced streets, and kids playing outside, and motor cars and buses. I wanted Mum and Gwen. 'It's good you're going so far away, isn't it?' Gwen said. 'No one will ever find out.' Was she trying to protect me or was she ashamed of me? Vinnie had told her he didn't want her to see me while I was pregnant, that it was bad for their reputation. But by the time I left it was obvious I was pregnant anyway, and being sent away felt like a punishment. I was being banished. The mountains seemed threatening, looming and dark.

I didn't let my fear show, of course. I was a good actress, even then. But it was there all the time, a cold ball of terror hidden inside me. I was afraid of giving birth. I was afraid of the other girls with their swollen bellies or their tiny babies. And I was even more afraid of the babies. Even now when I hear a newborn baby crying it takes me back to St Monica's. I can hear it now, the sound of the babies in the nursery, screaming. I close my eyes, but I can't make it stop.

There's a baby crying. Screaming. That desperate, breathless cry of a newborn. Not my baby. My baby is still safe inside me. It is Edie's baby, Ted.

I'm in the nursery at St Monica's, late afternoon it must be from the low slant of the orange autumn light streaming in through the large, draughty windows. In the distance, through the window, I see the hills against the sky. I'm looking after the babies with one of the nuns, but she's had to hurry off because one of the girls has gone into labour unexpectedly.

'I'll be back soon,' she said. But she isn't.

I find it hard to tell the babies apart, although Edie says that you know your own baby without even looking, just by hearing its cry. But when I go over to the cot I recognize Ted, because he has a little dimple in his chin and very long dark eyelashes. 'Like his daddy,' Edie had told me, winking. 'That's what got me into this flaming mess in the first place.'

Ted's little face is bright red, his eyes screwed shut, his mouth wide. He is swaddled tight, like all the babies. They say it makes them feel safe but I don't like the idea of them being bound so tightly. The idea of not being able to move like that, to be constricted and held in one position, makes me panicky. I have dreams like that sometimes, where I can't move and I wake up sweating. I pick him up and cradle him in one arm and loosen the blanket bundled round his body until his arms are free. He balls his hand into little fists and holds them by his face.

'Shhhhh,' I say, rocking him. 'Come on, Ted.'

He doesn't *shhh*, though, he keeps crying. I walk around the room with him and sing to him softly as I've seen Edie do. 'I know I'm not your mummy,' I say, 'But I'll do for now, won't I?'

He looks at me with his dark eyes and I think how much they look like Edie's. I couldn't see it before. Babies just look like babies to me. But I can see it suddenly, in the shape and the colour and something of his expression somehow. Am I just imagining it? I think how strange it is that there is a person who will grow up looking like Edie and her Bobby because of one afternoon they spent together, because Edie's nan had tripped on a loose paving stone and fallen and broken her hip and her mum had gone to see her. If the paving stone hadn't been loose, if Edie's nan hadn't fallen, Ted wouldn't exist. A whole person with a life of his own to live.

And how strange it is that he will never know that he looks like her, that his eyes are hers and his chin is Bobby's. The nuns made it clear that there can be no contact with the baby once they are with their new family. Edie asked if she could write to him but they said no, it would just make things hard for him. She didn't want to make things hard for him, did she? She wanted the best for him, didn't she? The new family would mean a proper home, *two* parents, and toys and lovely clothes and all the things she couldn't give him. She could write him one letter to take with him, to open when he's older. That's all he'll ever have of her. Edie had wept so much as she told me this that I didn't know what to do except hold her.

'I want the best for him, Gloria, I do. But I want to keep him. I want to look after him. Is that selfish?'

'No,' I said. 'Course not.'

'I think I'd be a good mum,' she said.

'You would be,' I said. I meant it too. Any idiot could see it. Edie's kind and practical and devoted to Ted. 'I know you would be.'

Just as I know I wouldn't be. I can't even stop Ted crying now, he's screaming so much I can't think. I walk around the room with him, humming, as I've seen Edie do.

Eventually his cries die down and his eyelids droop. After a while I'm brave enough to put him down. He doesn't stir. I'll tell Edie how I calmed him and got him off to sleep. That'll make her pleased. She hates the fact that they won't let her spend much time with him. She'd carry him round with her all day if she could. I look at him now, so still you can't even tell that he's breathing. I think of Edie's face when she's watching him sleep, sort of fierce, it is, but soft too.

'You'll understand when yours is here,' she said to me once. 'You'll feel the same.'

I won't, though. I can't. It will be a relief, when they take it away.

The baby will be gone and I will never have to think of it again.

## Chapter twenty

My ten-minute guess turns out to be really wrong as forty minutes later we've still not reached the cottage. The Sat Nav has tried to make me drive into a field of unimpressed-looking cows and then across a river. I check my phone but there is absolutely no signal. In the end I have to get the road atlas out.

'They weren't kidding about it being secluded, were they?' I say.

'Don't suppose there's a pub for miles,' Gloria says gloomily. 'Didn't you think to check?'

'We're lucky Peggy found us anywhere at all,' I say, trying to sound calm.

But when we finally turn into the drive and see the cottage I know it's perfect. It's an old, white-painted farm-house, with huge windows that look out over the fells, hills rising up steeply behind it.

I get out of the car and stretch my legs. Peggy's cousin's nephew or whatever it was has left the key under a particular stone according to Peggy's notes, but it takes me a while to identify the right one. My head is fuzzy from focusing on the road for so long, but as I breathe in the fresh-smelling air and look around at the trees and the mountains and the big expanse of blue sky I feel that there's nowhere I'd rather be. We were right to come here, I know it. We were *meant* to come. We're away from everything, just the two of us. Even the lack of phone signal is a good thing. We're out of reach. There's space here, space for me to work out what I'm feeling and what I'm going to do next, get everything clear in my mind. And space for Gloria to tell her story.

After I've hauled the cases upstairs, Gloria gives me her cash card and then goes for a rest while I drive to the nearest town to pick up some food. I'm a bit worried about leaving her on her own in the house when we've only just arrived, but she promises me she'll be fine, and when I go to tell her I'm leaving she's already fast asleep. In fact, she's still asleep when I get back and only appears as I'm pottering about in the kitchen trying to work out how to use the Aga stove so I can cook us some pasta for dinner. She looks a bit less tired, but still seems tense.

'I got you some gin,' I say. I hadn't risked trying to buy it in the supermarket, but I'd spotted a convenience store on the way back to the car park and decided it was worth a try. The guy behind the counter had given me a very hard stare but he hadn't asked me for ID. 'And some pineapple juice. They didn't have cherry brandy, so I just got brandy. Or there's Cava in the fridge if you'd rather have that.'

'Thank you,' she says. She takes her drink and goes to sit down with it on a window seat looking out over the hills.

When the dinner's ready we eat it at the table but Gloria just picks at her food.

'Are you not hungry?' I say.

'Hmmm?'

It's clear she hasn't been listening to me. Her mind is somewhere else.

'Are you nervous about coming back here?'

'No.' She avoids looking me in the eye.

'You know, we don't have to go to St Monica's tomorrow if you don't want to. We could wait, have a sightseeing day. Go on a boat trip or something.' This was something I'd been promised on our family holiday, but it had never happened. I'd been so disappointed. We'd had to leave early. I'd forgotten that. Why was that? I try to drag it up from my memory but I can't remember. Mum wasn't happy, I remember that.

'We don't *have* to go to St Monica's at all,' she says. 'It's up to me.'

I look at her, anxious. After what happened in Cambridge I still worry that she might suddenly change her mind and call the whole thing off, and I'd have to drive her back to London without ever knowing the end of the story. I know I shouldn't be treating it like a mystery I want to solve. These are Gloria's memories and painful ones too. But I also feel certain that she does want to share the story really, that it's fear holding her back.

'Are you having doubts about going there?'

She doesn't answer.

'I thought you wanted to remember it all while you still can.'

'Well, it's my prerogative to change my mind if I choose to.'

I look at her face, trying to gauge what she's feeling, but it's blank, closed up.

'Of course it is,' I say, trying to sound soothing. 'It must be hard going back to somewhere that holds painful memories. But there are happy memories too, right? Tell me more about Edie. Did you two become friends? And what about Sam? Did you ever write to him, tell him about the baby when it was born?'

'You're very keen to ask questions, aren't you?' she says. 'Not so keen to answer them, though.'

'What do you mean?' I say, defensive. I know exactly what she means.

'Well, whenever I ask about your . . . Robin—'

'Reuben? I've told you about him.'

She picks up the red notebook and flicks through it.

'No, you haven't,' she says firmly, presumably having checked. 'Not really. I've even written "Hattie evasive"' – she frowns – 'Evasive. That is the word I mean, isn't it?'

'Yes,' I say flatly. She's right, of course.

'You've told me who he is but you haven't told me how you feel about him or how it is that if you're just good friends you're in the family way, or what he thinks about it all and why he's in France—'

'Long story,' I interrupt.

'And do *you* want to tell it?'

I don't really. I haven't even let myself think about the night that Reuben and I had sex. The night that meant everything in my life changed. But perhaps now is the time.

I'd decided to surprise Reuben. It was not long after he'd announced he wasn't coming back to college. He'd disappeared off to Norfolk, where his parents had a holiday home by the sea. It used to be his gran's. He was always going on about how much he loved it there.

I didn't know what to expect. He'd been quite un-Reuben-like over the last few weeks: quiet, not getting into fights, not even flirting really. Not by his standards. He'd split up with Melody, the beautiful American girl he'd been going out with, a few weeks before. I wondered if it was that. Perhaps he'd really loved her. Or maybe it was his parents. His mum was going through a rough patch, he said, and his dad was in the south of France and wasn't interested. He just seemed down and then one day he'd decided to jack in college and disappeared off to Norfolk.

'But you can't,' I'd said on the phone. Now Kat was at art college Reuben was my only good friend at school. And although I missed Kat, I liked the fact that Reuben and I were now an established double act.

'Course I can,' he said. 'School can't stop me. And I don't suppose they'd want to.'

'Yes, I know,' I said. 'Obviously. What I mean is, I don't want you to. What about your A-levels? University? What about me?'

'I'd probably fail my A-levels anyway,' he said.

'No you wouldn't.'

'I might.'

'That's typical of you,' I said, annoyed that he'd completely ignored the 'what about me' bit. 'Anything you might possibly have to try at, anything there's the teeniest possibility you might fail at, you're just not prepared to risk it, are you?'

'You're clever,' he said. 'You don't understand what it's like for normal people.'

'Are you saying I'm abnormal?'

'Too bloody right. Anyway, listen, come and stay when your exams are finished,' he said. 'We can celebrate.'

And then I hadn't heard from him again. I tried not to mind. I knew the mobile network was pretty dodgy where he was and he'd given me the address, so in the end I'd just decided to go. *It's the kind of thing he'd do*, I thought.

The journey took for ever. A train, then another train, then a bus. I'd walked the last bit. Looking at the map I'd seen I could take a short cut by taking a footpath across some fields near to Reuben's house. I'd imagined arriving all fresh-faced and sparkling-eyed but the weather was both warm and showery so I'd got there bedraggled and lightly poached inside my coat. He'd laughed when he saw me standing on the doorstep.

'I knew you'd come,' he said.

The house was not what I'd imagined. Reuben had always made it sound like a ramshackle old place but it seemed incredibly grand to me. It's true some of the rooms smelt a bit of damp and the garden was a bit overgrown. Everything looked as though it could do with a lick of paint. But still. There was no flat-pack furniture. Everything was an antique. There were valuable-looking but ugly oil paintings on the walls and Persian rugs on the floor. Part of the garden was an orchard and beyond that, Reuben told me, was a tennis court.

I looked around, wide-eyed. 'Your parents really are minted, aren't they?'

'Yep. They really are.' He laughed, bitterly. 'If anyone ever needed proof that money doesn't buy you happiness, my parents are it.'

He took a gulp out of a rather dusty bottle of what looked like expensive wine – was there an actual wine cellar? – and then picked up the paper and stared at it.

'Oh sorry,' I said. 'Am I boring you?'

He looked up, surprised. 'What?'

'Well, I haven't seen you for three weeks. And now I've made all the effort to get here and you just sit here reading the bloody newspaper.'

'Oh, right,' he said. 'I was just trying to do the crossword.'

'You could offer me a drink? Ask me how my exams went? Say "Thanks, Hattie, for travelling what felt like a billion miles across the fens and decoding mysterious bus timetables and actually striding across cowpat-riddled fields just to come and see me"?'

'Can we just imagine I've done all that?'

I sigh and sit down.

'Since when did you do crosswords anyway?'

'Since last week. I decided I want to be the sort of person who can do cryptic crosswords.'

'Okaaay,' I said. 'Any particular reason?'

'I liked the idea of being cryptic. I thought it would make me more like Sherlock Holmes.'

He stared at the crossword a while longer. '"Quaker on board vessel finds fellow-feeling."'

He stared at it a while longer. 'Quaker? Vessel?'

I shrug. 'No idea.'

'Bollocks.' He threw the newspaper across the room, where it landed next to a very beautiful stained-glass lamp.

'I'm no crossword expert but I'm pretty sure that's not right,' I said.

'You're not funny.'

'Sherlock Holmes was a coke addict anyway, wasn't he?' I said, consolingly.

'True,' he said, as if considering the possibility that this might be where he's been going wrong.

'*No*, Reuben. That wasn't a suggestion. That was me explaining why it's good that you're not like Sherlock Holmes. I'm not sure he even did crosswords, did he?'

'I didn't say he did. I just wanted to do something that would give the impression that I was that sort of person. You know, clever and a bit weird. And I thought it would be easier than solving loads of mysteries that had thwarted Scotland Yard. And quicker than learning the violin. Just something so that people would say, "Oh, yeah, Reuben, he may be a twat but that's just because he's a Flawed Genius."' He took another drink from the bottle. 'It's the genius bit that's important really. Without that you're just flawed, like everyone else.'

'You do flawed fantastically well though, to be fair,' I said, grabbing the bottle off him and taking a gulp.

He sighed heavily.

'What's the matter with you, Reuben?

'I don't know,' he said. 'I don't know.' He was silent for a while, thinking. 'Do you ever feel like you don't know who you're supposed to be?'

I laughed. 'God, Reuben, you're the living embodiment of *ennui*.'

'What's *ennui*?'

'It is *you*, Reuben. Bored. Stagnating.'

'Oh,' he said and looked at me, smirking.

I stuck my tongue out at him. He laughed and then just as suddenly stopped and sighed again.

'You haven't got back together with William, have you?' he said, suspicious.

'No, Reuben, I haven't and never will get back together with William.'

Reuben pulled the hideous face that he always refers to as 'William's sex face'. I hit him and he laughed. Then he stopped laughing and sank into gloom again.

'Melody said she thinks I'm cold. Do you think I'm cold?'

'No,' I said, honestly. 'I don't think you're cold. But I think sometimes you act in a way that makes people think you're cold.'

'Yes. That's it. Trust you to know,' he said, gloomily.

'Is this what it's all about? Melody?'

'No. She's a symptom, not a cause.'

'Reuben, what's the matter with you? Really?'

'Nothing. Everything. I dunno.'

I look at him.

'I'm the matter with me,' he said.

'Meaning . . . ?'

'Do you ever feel like you don't know who you really are?'

'Ummm . . .'

He smiled. 'No, of course you don't. That's what's so brilliant about you, Hats. You know exactly who you are. And you don't care what anyone else thinks.'

'What's that supposed to mean? That everyone else thinks I'm a loser?' The whole accountant thing came flooding back.

'No!' he said. 'That's not what I meant. I just meant, you're confident in who you are.'

'I do care what people think, actually. Of course I do. Everyone does.'

'But you don't change yourself to try to fit in or stand out or get attention, do you?'

I thought about this. 'I guess not.'

'But I do. I feel like I've been putting on the Reuben Wilde show for so long I don't know what would happen if I stopped. And it's exhausting. And boring. The thing is, how I feel inside doesn't always match what people see on the outside. I don't always like myself very much, Hats.'

'We all feel like that sometimes, Reuben.'

'I just feel a bit . . . lost. Like I've spent all these years defining myself by being what other people don't want me

232

to be. My parents. School. And now . . . well, now it's getting to the point where no one cares what I am any more.'

He took another swig out of the wine bottle.

'Oh, Reuben. How long have you been sat indoors drinking your dad's hugely expensive wine and watching westerns and forgetting to change your pants? Days? Weeks?'

He shrugged. 'Sometimes I play on the X-Box.'

'Let's go for a walk,' I said, taking his hand and pulling him up off the sofa. 'I want to build a sandcastle. You've got a bucket and spade, right?'

He brightened.

'Yes,' he said. 'Somewhere. Left over from when I was a kid.'

'We could take a picnic.'

The picnic turned out to be another bottle of Reuben's dad's wine, a box of Pop-Tarts that went off in December the year before last, and a multipack of Frazzles.

It was hot on the beach, even though was late afternoon. We scrambled barefoot up the rough grass of the dunes and down onto the soft sand, the sea spread before us. We built a sandcastle, with towers and turrets and we decorated it with shells and we filled the moat with seawater. We swam, the water biting and cold for the first breathless seconds, then cool and refreshing and perfect.

Then we lay on sandy towels, passing the bottle of wine between us, our skin hot and tight with drying salt, drinking straight from the bottle. I read and then dozed and then I sat and buried my feet in the warm sand and Reuben sat next to me and we drank some more.

'Thank you,' he said.

I looked up at him, surprised. Gratitude isn't generally one of Reuben's strong points.

'Write that down for me, will you?' I said, shielding my eyes from the sun to look at him. 'No wait, I'll do it. Fetch my diary. The day Reuben said thank you. We can celebrate it every year with some kind of official ceremony. Perhaps we could erect a small memorial, right here. What are you thanking me for, by the way?'

'Oh, you know. Just . . . everything.'

'Okay,' I said. 'Not sure I can really take credit for absolutely *everything*. Happy to humour you, though, but on the basis that you quite often don't thank me for things you should I'm happy to let you over-thank me this time.'

I went back to reading my book, but out of the corner of my eye I could see Reuben watching me. In the end it was so distracting that I had to put the book down.

'Why are you looking at me like that, Reuben?' I said.

'Like what?'

'Like *that*. Stop it. You're freaking me out. Go and have a swim or find a dog to play with or something.'

I squinted along the beach to where a damp, black Labrador was nosing around in the sand dunes. There were families packing up to go home, games of football and badminton being called to a halt, and toddlers smeared in sunscreen tottering along after their parents. Everyone had that thrill of disbelieving joy about them that only comes from having spent a hot day on a beach in the UK.

'What would I do without you?' Reuben said.

'I dunno,' I said. 'Probably pine completely away. That's my guess. You'd weep uncontrollably most of the time due to the sheer pointlessness of existence without me. You'd gnash your teeth and rip your hair out and rend your clothing, all that kind of stuff. Maybe write some really bad poetry or learn to play guitar and sing terrible croony ballads.

And then eventually you'd just lie down in a darkened room and say, "If this is life, I don't want any part in the meaningless drudgery of it" and then you'd just expire, like this.'

I flopped backwards onto the sand and let out a sad, whispery dying breath and closed my eyes.

Then I looked up at him, shielding my eyes from the orange-pink glow of the setting sun.

'I expect that's how it would be, don't you? Or alternatively you might just do exactly what you do now, except with no one to laugh at your appalling jokes. Pass the wine, will you?'

But he didn't. Instead he leant over and kissed me on the lips. Gently but purposefully, lingering slightly. I felt my eyes open wide in surprise. I looked at him, his face still close to mine as he watched me. His skin was pinky-brown across his nose and cheeks, his hair long and still a bit wet from the sea.

'What was that for?' I said.

He didn't reply, just reached out and pushed a stray strand of hair back from my face. Then he kissed me again, and this time it was different. It wasn't a friends-who-have-drunk-a-bit-too-much-wine-and-are-feeling-very-happy kind of kiss. It was an I-really-want-to-kiss-you kind of kiss. He tasted of wine and salt and cigarettes and something sweet. He tasted familiar and new and right. And I pulled my body towards his until we were intertwined and hot and breathless.

'Let's go home,' he said. 'There are too many people here.'

All the time we were walking I was aware only of the place where our bodies touched, where our fingers intertwined. I was dizzy with the wine and with elation and desire and nervousness and disbelief. I didn't let myself think about it. I couldn't think about anything except the taste of him, the feel of his skin beneath my fingers. The walk was longer than on the way there. I could hardly breathe with the thought of getting home and of his tongue touching mine, the heat of our bodies.

When we got back to the house he led me to his bedroom. We didn't speak. We both knew what was going to happen and we both knew it was what we wanted and what the other wanted. It wasn't what I expected but felt right. The feel of his skin under my fingers, the smell of him, the taste of him. *No*, I remember thinking in the blur of wine and sun and desire. *Nothing could be more right than this*. My whole body shaking as he fiddled with the catch of my bikini top and pushed me gently down onto the bed as I pulled him down towards me.

I woke up during the night parched and already feeling the start of tomorrow's hangover. Reuben was lying next to me in the dark and I could see that his eyes were open.

'Have you been watching me sleep?' I said.

'Yes.'

'Okay,' I said. 'That's a bit weird.'

'No it's not.'

'Was I snoring?'

'No. You were beautiful.'

'Reuben,' I croak. 'Go to sleep.'

'You're not like anyone else,' he said.

'Mmm. Go to sleep.'

'I feel different when I'm with you from how I feel with anyone else. No, I *am* different. You make me different. You make me feel like it's okay to be me. I don't have to pretend to be someone else.'

'It *is* okay to be you, Reuben. You should try it with more people. That way less of them might think you're a wanker. Possibly.'

'You understand me.'

'I really don't, Reuben.'

'Yes, you do.'

I groped around for the bottle of water that was on the floor somewhere by the bed.

'You're a riddle wrapped in a mystery inside an enigma, disguised as an evil genius playing the part of a total bloody idiot. You're a cryptic crossword clue that even you don't know the answer to.'

I took a swig of water and then collapsed back down on the bed.

'And the dangerous lunatic who wrote the crossword is dead.'

'See,' he said, smiling as he pulled me towards him again. 'You do understand me.'

The next time I woke up, bright sunlight was coming in through the window. Reuben was gone. My head was throbbing and my throat sore and dry. I lay there thinking about it all, feeling happy and nervous and wondering where Reuben was. I got up, embarrassed by my nakedness despite the fact that there was no one to see it, quickly pulling clean clothes out of my bag and pulling them on. I went through to the bathroom and brushed my teeth, trying to get rid of the stale morning smell, avoiding my own reflection.

Reuben. I had sex with Reuben. Reuben had sex with me.

I looked at myself at last, and couldn't help noticing that I'd caught the sun on my face, and also that I was smiling.

I took a deep breath and went downstairs.

Reuben wasn't anywhere. I was disappointed and a bit confused. Where could he have gone? Why hadn't he left a note?

There was nothing to eat for breakfast except the remains of the stale Pop-Tarts and Frazzles, which I couldn't really face, so I made myself some tea and hunted for some paracetamol in my bag before taking a shower.

Reuben got back about an hour later. He didn't quite meet my eye.

'Morning,' he said, a bit too brightly. 'Just been to the supermarket to stock up. I've got a load of people arriving today.'

'What?' I said. 'Who?'

'Oh, just friends from my old school. No one you know. Bit of a party. Should be good.'

'Right. You didn't mention this yesterday.'

He shrugged. 'You didn't ask.'

I stared at him.

'It's not a problem,' he said, not meeting my eye. 'There's plenty of space for everyone to doss down. You'll like them.'

I didn't like them, as it turned out. They were loud and arrogant. The girls were too thin and too busy being beautiful to smile much. The boys all seemed to have necks that were too wide for their heads and were soon very, very drunk. They got cigarette burns in the Persian carpets and laughed when they smashed an old photo of Reuben and his parents in a frame on the mantelpiece. I didn't feel like drinking. By the end of the night there were people noisily making use of all the beds. I presumed Reuben was one of them.

If I could have done I'd have left right then. I would have, but all my things were in Reuben's room and there was no way I was going in to get them. In any case, I didn't fancy the walk back across the fields to the village in the dark, and it would be hours before a bus came. I didn't have a taxi number and I couldn't get a signal on my mobile. But I had to get out of the house, at least. The air was thick with cigarette smoke and dope and pretty much everyone who was still conscious was either talking loudly and slurrily about how the death penalty should be brought back in or trying to sing along to terrible music or having sex or vomiting or some unimaginably awful combination of all the above.

I knew there'd be no one else outside – it was cold and there had been a heavy shower earlier. The rain had stopped now, but the ground was still wet, and the air smelt of damp grass and lavender in the darkness. The cool air on my face made me feel calmer. I walked down through the garden, picking my way through shadowy shrubs and spongy lawns towards the tennis courts, wet leaves brushing against my legs, cold drops landing on my face and neck from the trees above as the wind blew them. Eventually I came to a damp, decrepit wooden bench. I sat on it, hugging my knees and shivering as hot tears slipped down my face.

Should I feel angry with Reuben? We hadn't promised anything to each other. It wasn't even like I wanted to go out with him. Not really. I knew that would never work. But it wasn't just about sex. It was about intimacy. People use 'intimacy' as a euphemism for sex, but sex can be less intimate than shaking hands. (I should know, I shagged William, for God's sake.)

I'd felt closer to Reuben that night than ever before. He had finally been the person I'd always known was there, that I'd seen glimpses of, the reason I put up with him when he was a pain in the arse, the Reuben he probably wanted to be more of the time. But today that person was gone again. Not only had he chosen his awful friends over me; he'd chosen the Reuben everyone thought he was over the Reuben he really was.

I'd been stupid. I shouldn't have slept with him. We were friends, that was how it had always been and that was how it should have stayed. I'd wanted our relationship to be special and this would ruin everything. It would reduce us to sex and jealousy and sneaking around and lying to each other and not trusting each other. The thing that was special about our relationship was honesty. We had admitted things to each other that we couldn't to anyone else. I could always tell Reuben what I thought of him in a way that no one else could, and he would listen to it without resentment or feeling like I was getting at him or trying to change him. All of that would be lost now.

So . . .

So the best thing was to pretend it hadn't happened. It had just been one of those things, we'd had too much to drink and . . . well, these things happen. We could be grown-up about it, couldn't we?

And yet still the tears came. I dashed them angrily away. I was just tired. That was all. I had a thumping headache from Reuben's bloody friends and all their loud braying and waheying and guffawing and terrible music.

I rested my head on my knees and wondered if I could just fall asleep here for a while. Then once everyone was up tomorrow I could sneak in, get my stuff and go. I heard rustling leaves and footsteps on the grass behind me. Great. The last thing I needed was for Reuben's friends to find me out here crying. I sat perfectly still, hoping they wouldn't notice me. The footsteps got closer.

'There you are!' It was Reuben's voice. 'I've been looking for you everywhere.'

'Really?'

'Yeah. It's carnage in there. Bodies everywhere.'

'I know. That's why I'm out here.'

He sat down next to me and got out a packet of cigarettes.

'Did you enjoy the party?'

I watched him as he lit up. He didn't meet my eye.

'No, Reuben, I didn't enjoy the party.'

'Oh.'

He looked at me then. 'You're crying,' he said, reaching up to wipe away a tear. I flinched away at his touch.

'No, I'm not.'

'You are. Hattie—'

'Can you go and get my stuff for me? It's in your room and I don't want to go back in.'

He stared.

'What stuff?'

'My rucksack. I'm going home.'

'What? No! You can't.'

'Yes, I can.'

I shivered. The cool air that had seemed so welcoming when I first came out was now starting to nip.

'It's the middle of the night,' Reuben said.

'I know what time it is, Reuben.'

'But there won't be a bus for ages.'

'I'll wait. I'd rather be on my own at the bus stop than here.'

'Why? You don't need to go, Hats.' He put his hand on my arm. 'Just stay. We can all have breakfast and maybe we'll all go to the beach later—'

241

'I don't want to. I came to see you, not your friends.'

'Well, then I'll tell them to go.' He stood up as if about to go and do it right then and there. I didn't fancy his chances. 'I don't care about them. They're all wankers anyway.'

I half smiled. 'No kidding.'

'I care about you. I want you to stay.'

'Why?'

He sat back down. 'Is this about . . . about what happened?'

'Not like you think. It's just . . .' I had to say it. 'Was it all an act? All that stuff about me understanding you? Are you like that with every girl you sleep with? Do you convince everyone they understand you like no one else does? Or do you actually mean it?'

He looked away from me and took a long drag on his cigarette. 'Look, Hats,' he said. 'The thing is—'

'Fine,' I said. 'That answers my question.'

Once he realized I wasn't going to change my mind about leaving he went in and got my stuff, carrying it down through the garden to the road for me.

'Bye then,' I said. The sky was starting to get lighter and all I wanted was to be away from there, away from Reuben. He stood there in the half-light, looking dejected and uncertain.

'Hattie, about . . . everything—'

'Let's just pretend it never happened, okay?'

He looked surprised.

'Is that really what you want?' he said.

'Yes. It really is.' I forced a smile. 'We're friends, right? Nothing's going to mess that up.'

Then I walked out into the fresh early-morning air and walked away from the house as fast as I could, desperate to leave it behind me.

242

I'd expected him to call me the next day, but he didn't. I waited a couple of days, then gave in and phoned him, only to be greeted by a chirpy answerphone message of Reuben putting on a fake French accent, saying he was off to St Tropez and leaving his phone behind. He'd taken up his dad's offer and gone without saying a word.

Once Gloria has finished jotting in her red book, she looks up at me. 'If you don't mind me saying,' Gloria says, in a voice that I know means she actually couldn't care less whether I mind or not, 'your Reuben sounds like a bit of an arse.'

I think about this. I want to protest. I want to say she's wrong, that she doesn't understand. Reuben's screwed up and he acts the part but I know inside there's a good person trying to get out. And he's funny. And sometimes he's unexpectedly kind, like when he used his Ransomes staff discount to get some special pens for Ollie, and when he decked the bloke who called me and Kat ugly lesbians at school (well, okay, that wasn't kind exactly, but we appreciated the thought) and the time I was ill and he brought me round a load of magazines and made hot lemon and ginger for me. And how he understands how I feel about Dad in a way that nobody else does because he's one of the only people I can open up to. But I can't say it. Because however true all of that is, Gloria does understand.

'You're wrong,' I say at last. 'He's not "my Reuben".'

Gloria heads up to bed soon after.

'So,' I say, trying to sound casual. 'What are we doing tomorrow? Boat trip?'

'I'd like to go St Monica's.'

243

I wake up early the next morning, my mind full of the day ahead, of St Monica's and what it will be like for Gloria to go back there. It's where she had her baby, where she spent the only few weeks of her life she shared with them. What will it feel like to go back there? It's also where she gave her baby up. Even if she didn't want to keep it that can't have been easy, especially knowing she didn't have any choice in the matter. Does she know what happened to him afterwards?

I think again about Whitby. I'm sure I'm right, that *must* be why we're going to Whitby, mustn't it? He must be there. Gloria has made it clear she doesn't want to tell me why we're going till we get there, but what else could it be? This journey has been all about Gloria and Sam and the baby she had to give up. That has to be what she meant by the end of the story.

The bed is comfortable and I could happily have stayed there, but as usual I'm starving so I head downstairs to the kitchen and make myself some toast. As I eat it I decide, guiltily, that since I can't pick up phone messages I'd better check my email, just in case Mum's been trying to get in touch.

She hasn't, but Alice has.

From: aliceisright@starmail.com
To: hattiedlockwood@starmail.com
Subject: HATTIE IS CRUEL AND ALSO SMELLS


WE HAVE COME HOME FROM AUNTY BECKY'S ERLY BECAUSE
MUM TOLD CARL SHE DOESNT WANT TO GET MARRYD. WHY
HAVE YOU GONE AWAY? MUM IS GOING MENTAL BECAUSE
SHE'S GOT NOT CAR AND IN A REELLY BAD MOOD ALL THE
TIME AND IT IS ALL YOUR FORLT BECAUSE SHE IS WORRYD
ABOUT YOU AND ALSO ANGRY WITH YOU AND TAKING IT
OUT ON US BECAUSE WE ARE HERE AND YOU ARE NOT
WHICH IS NOT FARE. CARL IS ALL QUIET AND SAD AND HE
KEEPS COOKING AND CLEENING AND BYING MUM FLOWERS
SO SHE WILL THINK WHAT A GOOD HUSBAND HE WILL BE
BUT ITS ACHALLY REELY ANOYING.

*What?* Mum and Carl aren't getting married? I *knew* she
was getting cold feet. But I didn't think she'd actually call it
off. Poor Carl. I feel so sorry for him that I hardly even feel
happy at all about the fact that I'm off the hook on the
bridesmaid-dress-of-horror front. I should call home. But
then if Carl answers he might cry and I don't think I can
take that. Or worse, Mum will answer and just yell at me for
taking the car and tell me I've got to come home RIGHT
NOW THIS VERY MINUTE and I'll tell her I can't, which
will just make everything worse for everyone. Mum can be
pretty scary when she's angry. Maybe it's best just to wait
till I get back. She might have calmed down a bit by then.
The wedding might even be back on by the time my trip
with Gloria is done. Anyway, I can always just pretend I
didn't know. I could tell them I didn't get Alice's email . . .

BECAUSE YOUR NOT HERE CARL IS LOOKING AFTER US AND
INSTED OF LETTING US WATCH LOOSE WOMEN AND TOM
AND JERRY AND DOCUMENTRYS ABOUT PREDATORS AND
SPYS HE IS MAKING US DO STUFF LIKE WRTING A STORY
ABOUT THE ENVIROMENT AND MAKING MODELS OUT OF
RECYCLED RUBBISH AND SINGING OLD BEETELS SONGS
WHILE HE PLAYS HIS GITAR. HE IS MAKING US HELP HIM
COOK NUTRISHUS FOOD. IT IS ALL TOO HORRIBLE HATTIE. IT
IS WORSE THAN SCHOOL IF THAT IS EVEN LIKE POSSIBLE.
AND IT IS ALL YOUR FORLT.

IS IT REALY TRUE THAT YOU'VE KIDNAPPED AN OLD LADY?
THAT'S WHAT RUEBEN SAID—

Reuben? When did she speak to Reuben? Why has he
phoned home and not my mobile when he knows I'm not
there? I suppose I've been out of range since we got here . . .
I'm not sure how I feel about the fact he wants to speak to
me. Pleased? Grudgingly, yes. But also irritated. Resentful,
even. Does he assume I'm just sitting around waiting for
him to get in touch while he parties his way round Europe?
Probably.

I turn back to Alice's email.

—BUT CARL SAYS RUEBEN IS FULL OF IT. ATCHALLY HE SAID
A SWARE WORD BUT I AM NOT GOING TO WRITE IT
INCASE THIS EMAIL IS BEING MONITERED BY GCHQ.

I wonder, briefly, what Alice thinks GCHQ would do if she
swore, and have a fleeting but intense moment of love for
Carl. I hope Mum changes her mind. I'm sure it must just
be pre-wedding jitters.

ANYWAY I DON'T CARE ABOUT ALL THAT. IT IS UNRELAVANT. WHAT I CARE ABOUT IS THAT YOU ARE NOT HERE. YOU HAVE ABANDONED US HATTIE AND I WILL NOT EVER FORGIVE YOU EVEN IF I LIVE TO BE 200 AND EVEN IF YOU CRAWL TO ME EVERY DAY FOR THAT 200 YERS BEGGING FOR MERSEY. OLLIE IS WORKING OUT ON HIS CALCULATOR HOW MANY DAYS THAT IS BUT I CAN TELL YOU IT IS SO MANY THAT YOUR KNEES WILL HAVE WORN RIGHT AWAY AND YOU WILL HAVE TO SLITHER ON YOUR FAT TUMMY LIKE A SLUGG.

I WOULD RATHER HAVE A SACK OF POTATOS FOR A SISTER THAN YOU. AT LEAST WITH POTATOS I COULD MAKE CHIPS AND FRY THEM TILL THEY WERE CRISPY AND EAT THEM WITHOUT GOING TO PRISON. ALTHOGH CARL WOULD PROBABLY THROW THEM IN THE BIN AND MAKE ME A BLOODY ORGANIC SALUD INSTEAD (SORRY GCHQ IF YOUR READING THIS BUT I DONT THINK BLOODY IS TECNICLY A REAL SWARE WORD)

I AM GOING TO FIND OUT ABOTU WEATHER ITIS POSIBLE TO DIVORCE YOUR SISTER. IF IT IS THEN YOU WILL BE HERRING FROM MY SOLISITTER SOON.

ALICE PERSEPHONE LOCKWOOD

PS OLLIE SAYS IT IS 72975 DAYS BY THE WAY.

PPS OR MAYBE 72974 DEPENDING ON WHEN THE LEAP YEARS ARE.

I make myself another round of toast, layering it thickly with marmalade this time. Apparently I'm not just eating for two but for an entire football team. I panic briefly at the thought that I could be carrying sextuplets.

But realistically I'm probably just greedy.

Then I sit down again, trying not to get smeary butter and crumbs on the keyboard, and type:

From: hattiedlockwood@starmail.com
To: aliceisright@starmail.com
Subject: Re: HATTIE IS CRUEL AND ALSO SMELLS

Als, what is going on with mum and Carl? when did you speak to Reuben? What did he say? Has he been trying to get hold of me? My mobile isn't working. (You can tell Carl that from me too.) Is Reuben ok?

I'm sorry about all the singing and nutritious food. That sounds awful. I'll be home soon I promise. I'm just doing something nice for an old lady who is our great-aunt. Her name is Gloria. She's not very well and a bit sad. I think you'd like her. She is quite rude and likes doing things she thinks people don't want her to. Sometimes she reminds me a little bit of you.

Love you lots and Ols too.

Hattiexxxx

Alice's reply is almost instantaneous, which makes me suspect she's got up early to sneak in some computer games before Carl gets up and starts another day of educational and 'fun' activities. It is short and to the point.

HE WAS TRYING HERE BECAUSE NO ONE CAN GET HOLD
OF YOU ON YOUR MOBILE. YOU MUST HAVE LIKE 5
GAZILLION VOICEMAIL MESSAGES IF YOU CAN BE
BOTHERD TO LISTEN TO THEM BUT I WOUDNT BOTHER
COZ MOST OF THEM ARE MUM YELLING OR ME SWARING.

Surely GCHQ could be tapping the phone, I think. Who
knows how Alice's mind works.

IF U WANT TO NO WHAT ELSE RUEBEN SAID YOULL HAVE
TO COME HOME WONT YOU. IM NOT TELLING U TIL THEN.

*　　*　　*

St Monica's is about a ten-mile drive away, along winding,
damp roads. It's not called St Monica's any more. I looked
it up on the internet and found that it hasn't been a Mother
and Baby Home since the sixties. I suppose once unmarried and pregnant girls stopped being something that had
to be hidden away, once they were allowed to keep their
babies if they wanted to, there was no need for places like
that.

Now there are signs up saying it's been bought by a
company planning to turn it into a luxury country house
hotel. What a strange thought, that if Gloria and I came
back in a couple of years' time she'd be able to stay in the
place she had her baby. But by then . . . I try not to think it
but the thought comes anyway. Maybe she won't even
remember by then that she had a baby . . . I look over at
Gloria, her face almost hidden under her fedora and

unnecessary sunglasses. There's no sun; it's a grey, gloomy day, much more like the Lake District I remember. At first I think it's just vanity, but watching her sit, pale and tense, in the passenger seat, I realize that they form a barrier between her and the outside world. I can understand why she feels the need for protection, considering the place we're going to visit. If it was me . . . I can't imagine it. It feels hard enough making the choice I have to make. But if I had no choice at all, and then got to know my baby for three months before it was taken away, all the while being treated like a shameful secret, an outcast from society, something sinful and wicked . . . No, I can't imagine it. But Gloria doesn't have to imagine it. She lived it.

'You okay?' I say, trying to sound reassuring and casual, as if we're off on a day trip to one of those National Trust places Mum drags us all round on Sundays when she's trying to be improving. ('We don't NEED improving,' Alice says and generally finds a way of making Mum wish she'd left us in our natural, unimproved state in front of the TV, by falling in lakes or breaking historical artefacts or setting off fire alarms.) 'Does any of this look familiar?'

She doesn't respond. We drive through a small village – more of a hamlet, really – and then turn along a narrow road.

I park at the side of the road nearby and we walk up the little lane towards the building that had been St Monica's.

It's a huge Victorian house set in lawned grounds, screened from the road by dripping trees, which we have to peer through to get a good view of it. It's very grand-looking, grey brick, dark against the green that surrounds it. It looks a bit like a haunted house from a kids' book. Even from here I can see that bits of it are boarded up. Obviously empty.

Gloria just stares at it from where we stand at the end of the drive.

'Do you want to go closer?' I say tentatively. 'We might even be able to get inside. Or at least look in through a window.'

She shudders.

'No. This is close enough.' She stands looking at it, her face fixed.

As we stand there looking, it starts to rain again, water pattering on the leaves of the trees around us, splashing in puddles on the lane.

'Did you have the baby here?' I say at last.

She shakes her head.

'I'd like to go now,' she says.

The pain is the worst I've ever felt. It begins in the middle of the night – the clock on the dorm wall says it's ten past one when I open my eyes in the darkness, waking from a restless dream, crying out with the sudden shock of it.

It doesn't start, as Edie had said it would, with the gripey twinges and heavy backache of the Curse. The thought had comforted me when I'd lain awake at night worrying about the mystery of labour, about what it might be like and whether I could bear it: that perhaps it could be eased with sweet tea and a hot-water bottle to the small of the back, like Mum used to give me for my Monthlies.

No. It's not like that. It is instant agony: sudden, shocking, starting from a place so deep inside me I didn't know it was there, and it radiates out until it fills me up, until I am nothing but pain and fear.

'Gloria?' It's Edie's sleepy voice from across the dorm. 'What is it? You all right?'

I try to speak to her, to say *'It hurts'*, and *'Help me'*, and *'I'm afraid'*, but it all comes out as a wordless, gasping shriek.

'Katie, get Sister Annunciata, will you?' Edie says, awake now. 'Quick. Tell her it looks like Gloria's baby's on its way.'

She pads over in her bare feet as I sit rocking back and forth on the bed, hugging the covers to me, trying to make the pain less.

She takes my hand and strokes it, puts her other arm round my shoulders.

'Shhh,' she says, like she does when she's settling baby Ted, trying to soothe him to sleep. 'Shhh, now. I know it hurts like bloody buggery but it'll pass. It will, I promise.' She tries to smile at me. 'Just think, Glo. You'll be able to give your baby a cuddle before the day's out.'

'No,' I say, and I whisper it because if I don't I will cry out, I try not to, but I am not in control of my voice any more than I am of the rest of me, and it squeaks and wavers and rises, louder and higher, 'Something's wrong. Something's wrong.'

'Nothing's wrong,' Sister Annunciata says, striding into the room, bringing a cold draught with her. 'Your baby's coming, that's all.' She turns. 'Pack her hospital bag for her, will you, Edie? You know what she'll need.'

I know already that it will never end, this pain. Sister tells me not to be so silly, that it is a contraction, that it will be over soon enough. And it is true that there are gaps in the pain, moments, blurred minutes of numbness when I can lie, limp, and wait for the pain to fill me once again. But still, she is wrong, and I am right. The pain starts then, that night at ten past one and it never ends.

I try to catch my breath, to breathe deeply; if I could breathe deep and slow that would help, I know it would make it better, but my lungs are all squashed up by the baby and the pain and I can't get the air in—

'Can you stand up?' Sister Annunciata says, pulling back the bedclothes. When we look down, the sheets, smooth and neat with their razor-sharp hospital corners, are stained dark red. The lower half of my nightdress is covered in it too, clinging stickily to my legs.

'Oh,' I say. 'There's blood. I didn't know there'd be blood. You didn't tell me, Edie.' I wonder vaguely if it is my blood or the baby's.

'It's okay, Gloria,' Edie says, stroking my hair. Then, softly, 'Why is she bleeding?' And she sounds scared.

'It happens sometimes,' Sister Annunciata says. She turns away. 'We must get her to hospital,' I hear her say to somebody else who is in the room, one of the nurses. 'Call an ambulance. Now.'

'I can't come with you,' Sister Theresa, a younger nun who has helped me into the ambulance, says, holding my hands as the ambulance man wraps a blanket round me. 'There's not enough of us here to keep the girls and the babies safe. I'm sorry.' And I can see that she is, but I still want her to come with me because I'm scared on my own and I cling to her hands, I won't let her go.

'You'll be fine, dear. Strong, stubborn girl like you.' The nuns usually leave us in no doubt that we are paying for our sins, but for a fleeting moment I think perhaps she is actually a kinder person than she lets on. I wonder, dizzily, whether it is because the nuns think it's better for us not to know they care, or because Sister Theresa is afraid to show it. But maybe I'm mistaken. Maybe she is not kind at all.

I travel alone in the ambulance. The siren is loud in the night, making me think of air raids and being carried out in the cold darkness to the shelter, though whether I'm remembering or whether it's just what Mum told me, I couldn't say. I remember how it felt to have my head resting on Mum's shoulder, my face pressed into her neck, the smell of soap on her warm skin. And I cry out for her, for Mum. I want her here. Or Edie. Or Gwen. Anyone. But there is no one. I am alone.

Except I am not alone because the baby is with me. For the first time the thought comforts me. I am not alone. So I talk to the baby, in my head because I still can't trust myself to speak out loud without screaming, and sometimes, when the pain comes on worse, I do scream. But I keep on talking to it in my head because I am its mum and it is inside me; it is part of me still, so perhaps it can hear me even though I'm not saying the words out loud. I also talk to it because I am scared that the blood is the baby's not mine and what if the baby is dying inside me, what if it is dead and that is what is causing the pain . . . ?

*Don't be scared, little one,* I say. And—

*I'm sorry.* And—

*It is not your fault.*

Lights swirl above me, fading now, dimming to grey, and then bright again, so bright they hurt my eyes as they zoom over my head, neon-lit shooting stars in the grey. I am lying down, on something soft, I think; on a bed, yes, but it is rushing along a corridor so maybe it is a dream, maybe all of this is just in my head. In my dream the bed is floating along a river. I remember Sam telling me about the Niagara Falls in America. He'd read about them in a book, and how daredevils and lunatics went over them in barrels and suchlike and I think that maybe that is what will happen, we will reach the end of the river and be carried over the edge in a violent thunder of spray and rainbows. And the pain is so overwhelming now that all I can think is I will die soon and it will be over. *It is coming,* I think, *the end of the river is coming, it is here* and, yes, I feel the bed begin to lurch and tip . . .

The lights swim and fade again and as they go out I wonder if the baby can still hear me and in case it can and I don't get to say it again I think into the darkness *Goodbye*.

And last of all, because I am dying, I think: *I love you*.

I wake, but I am too weak to open my eyes to see where I am, in a place that is too loud. There are women crying out in pain and another shouting. Really shouting, swearing at someone. They are a long way away, I think, but still too loud. The sound hurts my head. I don't open my eyes. I am too weak. Just being awake feels like an effort. My insides feel hollowed out.

At last I force my eyes open. Everything is blurred and too bright. I close them again, sink into the dark.

When I wake next I know where I am. I know I am alive. I know I am in hospital. I look around trying to work out what has happened. How long have I been here? Have I had the baby? I look down and I can see from the shape of the bedclothes over my middle that the baby is no longer there.

It is dead. I know this at once. I try to say this to the doctor, to say, 'It's dead, isn't it? My baby is dead?' but as I try to speak my throat closes and tears are spilling down my face and I think, *How strange*, because in my head there are words thrumming round and round and the words are: *It is for the best; it is meant to be. The baby was never supposed to exist and now it doesn't. That is what everyone wanted, it is what I wanted and now I have what I want. My baby is cold and dead.* But still the tears come, unbidden.

The doctor clears his throat disapprovingly; at my tears I think, tears wasted on a dead bastard baby.

'Mrs Harper,' he says, and my heart leaps because Mum is here, and I look round for her because she is the only person I want to see, the only person who can make this better. But no, she is not here. I am alone. It takes me a while to realize he's talking to me.

'No,' I manage to say. 'I'm Miss—'

'*Mrs Harper*,' he says again, firmly, and I remember now that Edie had told me how they had all called her 'Mrs' in hospital. A nurse had even given her a wedding ring to wear while she was on the ward; they had a little tin of them in the Matron's drawer. 'They still all gave me dirty looks, though,' she'd said. 'Made me feel like I was something they'd scraped off their shoe.'

'My baby,' I say as he leaves, forcing the words from my dry, swollen throat. I have to ask. To know at least whether it was a boy or a girl. But I cannot bring myself to ask.

'He's a little on the small side, of course. But otherwise fine. The nurse will bring him to you later,' he says. 'Assuming we are satisfied with his progress.'

I press my hands over my mouth but a silent sob escapes. Dr Silverman turns away, unimpressed, perhaps, by this display of emotion for my baby. After all, he will not be mine for long.

## Chapter twenty-two

I'd spotted a pub on the way, so we stop off there as we head back to the cottage.

'How do you feel now?' I say to Gloria.

'Better now we're away from that place,' she says, adding tonic water to her gin.

'You don't regret going back, do you?' I've been worrying all the way that I talked her into doing something she didn't really want to.

'No!' she says, indignant. 'Certainly not. It was . . . strange. But it made me see that place for what it is. It's just bricks and mortar. Smaller than I remember it, too. It doesn't have any power over me. The nuns who were there when I was, they'll all be long dead now.'

'Good,' I say, relieved. 'Not about the nuns, I mean. It's just, I was worried it would bring back painful memories . . .'

'Well, it did,' she says. 'Literally in this case. Agonizing, in fact.'

'Is it always that painful?' I ask nervously. 'Giving birth, I mean?'

She stares at me. 'Why do you want to know? You're not planning to, are you?'

'No.'

'You haven't changed your mind? You're not planning to keep the baby, isn't that what you said?'

I shake my head.

'Then can I ask you something?'

'Of course.' I try to look calm and relaxed, but inside my heart is thumping.

'If you're so certain you want to terminate the pregnancy, why haven't you just gone ahead and done it? You've known you're pregnant for . . . how many weeks is it now?' She fishes out the red book. 'Well, you're almost eleven weeks. Is that right?'

I had, in fact, got a text from Kat as we passed fleetingly through somewhere that had a mobile-phone signal that said: **Hats, I tried to call u earlier. I looked up the 11 weeks page and it's all about scans. Not being funny but if u haven't already you need to decide what you're doing and get on with it coz ur running out of time. Sorry. I'll try and call u again if I can. Hugs xxx**

I'd remembered Mum coming back with her fuzzy black-and-white scan pictures of the twins again – that was at twelve weeks, wasn't it? – and had a second of sheer panic. And then I'd switched my phone off. I couldn't face that conversation with Kat.

'Something like that,' I say, as if it's unimportant.

'Well then, why haven't you? Why hang around if you're so sure you want to terminate the pregnancy? You've had plenty of time. I know I would have done if I'd had that choice.'

'Would you?'

'Yes, absolutely. I almost did, even though I knew it was dangerous. Louise took me over to east London to some-where she'd heard about.'

'You mean a backstreet abortion?'

'We got right to the door. And then I thought about what Dr Gilbert had said and I couldn't do it. You haven't got any of that to worry about. So why haven't you done it?'

'I don't know.' I feel my cheeks flush. 'Putting off the inevitable, I suppose,' I say lamely.

'But it's not inevitable, is it?' Gloria says.

I take a sip of my coffee, which is too hot and scalds the roof of my mouth. 'What do you mean?'

'Well,' she says, patiently, 'there is a choice, isn't there? There is an alternative?'

'What, you mean having a baby? It's not really a possibility, is it?'

'Well, obviously it's a possibility. Biologically, I mean. If you don't have an abortion, you *will* have a baby. What I don't understand is why, if you're so desperate to avoid having a baby, you haven't already done something about it?'

I'm silent. I don't know and I don't want to think about it. Every time I start to, everything gets so muddled. I want to keep it simple. I want everything to be how it was, for the future to be the one I'd planned. University. Travelling. Career. Reuben. Not as a couple (probably). As a friend. All of these things seemed impossible with a baby.

'What would *he* say? If he knew you were pregnant?'

'Who, Reuben?'

She nods.

'He'd be horrified! He'd be . . .' I try to imagine it. What would he be? 'Terrified. He'd run for the hills.'

'Is that why you don't want to tell him?'

I shrug. 'I suppose it is,' I admit.

'Is that why you want an abortion?'

I stop. I realize I don't know. *Is* that why I want an abortion? Just so that I don't have to tell Reuben I'm pregnant? Just so that it won't change things between us?

'I want to go to university,' I say. 'I want to travel. I want to see China and India and Laos and Vietnam. I want to get on the Trans-Siberian railway at Vladivostok and I want to go to Thailand and I want to drink Manhattans in Manhattan.' I run mentally through my checklist of ambitions. 'I want to visit Pompeii and Crete and—'

'The Maldives.'

'Yes, *exactly*. The Maldives. And I want to be the first-ever internationally acclaimed film director who's also an archaeologist and international human rights barrister.'

'Is that all?'

'Oh and tap dancer. And chess champion.'

'Can you tap-dance?'

'In my head.'

'Can you play chess?'

'I play with Alice sometimes.' She looks at me, questioning. 'My little sister,' I remind her.

'Who wins?'

'Alice does.'

We sit there for a while then go to the picnic benches outside so that Gloria can smoke.

'So all of that . . .' She waves a hand to signify education, parties, travel, Oscar-winning, a role on Broadway, chess-playing, injustice-fighting and the digging up and dusting off of old bones. 'That's why you want an abortion?'

I think about it, about each of my treasured dreams and hopes, and I want to say to her, *that's who I am, it's who I always thought I'd be.* Okay, not the tap dancing perhaps, not really. Or the chess. And I guess being an archaeologist

261

is less like being Indiana Jones than you might hope. And at some point I'd probably have to decide whether to be Atticus Finch or Ridley Scott, rather than aiming to be both at the same time. But uni, a job that wasn't remotely pancake-related but was actually something I really felt excited about, something I cared about, something I was good at and made some kind of difference, even if it wasn't glamorous or going to earn me loads of cash – that was the me I'd always thought I'd grow into one day. Sure, that me might have a baby or two, in some unimaginable future time and place, after she'd got all the high-powered jet-setting tap dancing and all that out of her system. And now that me was threatened. She was flickering and fading. If I had a baby, I'd have to let her go.

'People do go to university with babies, you know,' Gloria says. 'There are lawyers and archaeologists with children, I believe. You could stick a baby in one of those – what do they call them? – papoose things and merrily tap-dance your way along the Great Wall of China. If you really wanted to.'

'I'd be responsible. For another human being. I can't do that. I'm not ready.'

She smiles.

'So, don't. Make the appointment and that'll be that.'

'Will it?' I so want her to be right.

'If you let it.'

'It's not that simple, though, is it? Some people think abortion is murder. Some people think it's just an operation.'

'It doesn't matter what other people think. It matters what *you* think.'

I look out across the pub car park and the fields to the hills, dark against the silver-grey sky.

'I just want to make a decision I know I won't regret.'

She smiles, a bit sadly.

'No one can do that.'

'What, you think regret is inevitable? That's a pretty gloomy way of looking at things.'

'That's not what I said. I said you can't know whether you'll regret a decision or not when you make it. That's the whole point. That's the joy of being alive, isn't it? The not knowing.'

'Is it?'

'Yes.'

I try to decide whether I find this any less depressing.

'Although,' she says gently, 'in this particular instance I think you may regret whichever decision you make.'

'Great,' I say. 'Brilliant.'

'I don't mean you'll necessarily wish you'd made a different decision. Regret doesn't have to mean wishing everything had been different. But taking one path means not taking another. It's only human to think sometimes about the other path, the life we would have led if we'd have done things differently, perhaps even to grieve a little for the person we would have become, who disappeared when we made our choice. You can't be scared of regret. All you can do is make the choice that seems right at the time.'

My head feels a bit spinny. I've not seen this side of Gloria before: reflective, thoughtful. I'd always thought of her as a To Hell With The Consequences sort of person. But thinking about her past, about the baby she had and never knew, I suppose she's had a lot of time to think about this stuff.

'Did you ever regret giving up your baby?' I ask.

'That was different.'

'How?'

263

'It just was.' She takes my hand. 'Don't be guided by fear of getting it wrong, that's all I'm saying. Make a positive choice and know that whatever you choose it is the thing that seemed right at the time. You can't worry about whether in the future you'll see things differently. You can't know. And who cares? That's what I think.' She blows out smoke through her nose. 'Mind you, you'd be mad to take advice from me. I'm not exactly a shining example of how to live your life.'

'Have you been happy?' I say, curious suddenly about Gloria's life.

'Yes, very. And sad too. Which is how lives are. Even happy lives. No one's happy all the time, are they? And if they were, they'd be incredibly irritating. I loved acting.'

'What sort of acting did you do?'

'All sorts. I was in West End musicals and gloomy Russian plays. Shakespeare. You name it, I've done it.'

'That's amazing! I had no idea.'

I look at Gloria thinking about all the stuff she's done, all those memories stored in her head that she'll lose one by one.

'Tell me about your husbands.'

Gloria makes a snorting sort of noise.

'Oh, come on,' I say. 'They can't have been that bad. What did they do?'

'Well, there was Russell. He was a penniless artist. I was his muse and I'd always had the idea that I really ought to be someone's muse at some point. I thought we'd live a creative life together wearing black polo necks and smoking marijuana and French cigarettes. It was the late sixties, after all.'

'So what went wrong?'

'Well, for a start, being penniless and living in a freezing garret isn't as romantic as it sounds. In fact, it's deeply

264

tedious. Also Russell was a terrible artist. He blamed his lack of success on me, as his muse. Thought I must be insufficiently inspiring, because obviously it couldn't have anything to do with his *complete lack of talent*—'

She stubs out her cigarillo rather violently.

'Then there was Gordon. He was unbelievably rich. A tycoon. I was attracted to the idea of luxury after that garret. He thought he was much more interesting than he really was. That lasted about three years but only because we were living in different countries for most of it.'

'Right.'

'And then there was Gianni. Italian. Very easy on the eye. He was much later. He was twenty years younger than me.'

'A toyboy?'

'Mmm.' She drifts off into a happy reverie.

'You never really told me why it didn't work out with any of them?' I try to imagine Gloria with a husband and find I can't.

'Because they were all, in their different ways, completely unsuitable.' She thinks. 'And because I was me, I suppose.'

'Do you think that it was because they didn't live up to your idea of how things would have been with Sam?'

'I don't suppose Sam would have lived up to my idea of how things would have been with Sam.'

'Do you know what happened to him?' I ask. 'Did you ever track him down, make contact?'

'No,' she says. 'Some things are best left behind. I don't suppose he'd have been too pleased to hear from me, do you? The past is best left behind.'

'But you had a child together—'

'It's starting to rain,' she says. 'Let's go.'

\*     \*     \*

265

Before I start the car I decide that as I've got a mobile signal I should probably check my voicemail. There are, as promised, plenty with Mum yelling and Alice swearing. There are a couple where the person just hangs up – Reuben, perhaps? And finally there is one that only arrived this morning, from Carl.

There's a long pause, so long that I think maybe his phone's cut out or something, and then I think, Oh God, what if he and Mum have actually split up? What if it's really over between them and he's phoning to say a tearful and emotional goodbye? My stomach flips at the thought. I don't want Carl to say goodbye. For all his general annoyingness, I'd really miss him.

*'It's about ... Well. Something properly important. Something ... about you, Hattie. That I think we need to discuss. I found something, under your bed. I wasn't prying, honest, I was just hoovering—'* I remember with a sinking heart Alice's comment about Carl trying to win back Mum's heart through obsessive housework—*'and I found ... something else. Do you know what I'm saying, Hattie? I haven't told anyone about this, love—'* Carl NEVER calls me 'love'—*'and I don't want you to worry or anything because I'm not going to give you a hard time or anything like that, I just ... I'm worried about you, Hats, and I think we need to talk about this. Or, you know, if you don't want to talk to me you definitely need to talk to someone. Your mum would be a good person to start with. But I'm here any time, Hats. If you need me. Any time. Please call.'*

Oh, shit. Oh, Jesus. Oh ... I sit down on the bed, my palms prickling cold with sweat, my insides in a tight little ball.

That's it. He knows. Carl knows. He must have found the tests I stashed under the bed. Why didn't I throw them away? *Why?* If Carl knows, everything's changed. The reality of it all comes hurtling towards me. All my looking in the other direction and pretending everything's okay and distracting myself with things that happened fifty years ago (yes, I realize in a blink, Gloria was right that is exactly what I've been doing) . . . All of that is over.

Even if Carl hasn't told Mum yet, it can only be a matter of time. I guess he's waiting to see if I'll tell her myself, but I know he could never keep a secret like that from her for long.

And when I tell Mum . . . It's time to face up to things. Time to tell Reuben. But how can I? He's in . . . I don't even know where. Mykonos? Santorini? What am I supposed to do, just drop it in an email saying: *Hope you and Camille are still enjoying your summer of island-hopping and amazing sex. All well here. Weather uncharacteristically good. Oh btw I'm pregnant.*

'Everything okay?' Gloria asks, jolting me from my panic.

'No,' I say.

'Was it him? On the phone? Whatsisname?' She consults the red book. '*Reuben.*'

I glance over her shoulder and note that she's written quite a few notes under his name, but I only glimpse Hattie, pregnancy, and Arrogant Narcissist? before she snaps it shut.

'No,' I say. 'It was Carl. You know, Mum's fiancé-not-fiancé. Mint-green sweaters. Bingo Wings Buster. Obsessive wedding-planning disorder.'

'Ah, yes. And that was enough to make you go white as a sheet?'

'Well,' I say, with a limp smile. 'The jumpers are pretty offensive. But no. It wasn't that. Just hormones probably.'

She watches me.

'Come on,' she says. 'I wasn't born yesterday. What's up?'

'He knows,' I say flatly. 'Carl knows I'm pregnant. He must have found the pregnancy tests. I was going to throw them away and then . . . I dunno. I never got round to it.'

'Was he angry?'

'No,' I say. 'He's just worried. But that's it. Now he knows, it's real, isn't it?'

That night, I can't sleep. I try more pillows and then get rid of them all. I take off the heavy patchwork quilt and then put it back on again. I wriggle and toss and turn until the sheets are all tangled up and eventually I give up and tiptoe down the creaking stairs to the kitchen. It's warm because of the Aga, and I sit down at the heavy wooden table. I know why I can't sleep. Gloria and Kat are right. Carl's message only confirms it. I have to do what I haven't done so far: I have to face up to the fact that I'm pregnant. I've been saying this journey would be a chance to think it all through properly but really I've just been running away. That's the truth. And now I can't run any more. In two days we'll be in Whitby, the end of the journey.

And then we go home and everything will be real again.

I think about my conversation with Gloria. Is it true? Will I regret whatever decision I make? I imagine those regrets: an older me regretting the child I could have had, and another older me, longing for the freedom and adventures I missed out on. But Gloria's right. Neither of those is real. The only one that's real is the present me, the one with big dreams and her whole glorious, unknown, life ahead of her. The one who has a cluster of cells growing inside her that would, left to their own devices, eventually grow into a person who would be part Reuben and part

Hattie and entirely someone completely new. The whole thing is mind-bogglingly terrifying.

'What would you do if you were me?' I'd said to Gloria as we drove back to the cottage.

She'd tutted impatiently. 'I don't know,' she said. 'If I were *me* in *your* situation I would choose not to have the baby. But that's utterly irrelevant. I am not you. Only you can make your choice, I'm afraid.'

What if I had the baby?

I haven't let myself think about it, but now my mind races ahead. Would it really be so bad? I know having a baby is hard but it's wonderful too, isn't it? I loved the twins so much when they were tiny. I remember Ollie holding my finger when they were first born, and how they used to lie in the garden watching the branches of the trees sway in the wind. I remember how they used to chat to one another in their own language and how adorable they used to look in their little sleepsuits.

I remember Ollie taking his first wobbly steps, and Alice's little face when she said her first word ('NO'). I've never seen a look of such undiluted triumph and satisfaction on anyone's face EVER. And Ollie wouldn't say anything; he let Alice do all the talking but he'd sit there and watch everything so carefully and we'd all wonder what he was thinking. And everyone would always think Alice was the confident one but if Ollie wasn't there she'd howl and cling to your leg and wouldn't stop until he came back again.

What sort of person would my baby be, if I let it become a baby? Mine and Reuben's baby . . . Who would it look like? I try to imagine it, a real person, with a real face. My eyes. Reuben's chin. And of course it wouldn't be an *it*, would it? It would be a he. Or a she. What if I did it? What if I had the baby?

For a split second I can picture us, the three of us: me, Reuben and our baby. We're in a park somewhere and Reuben's pushing our baby on the swing and she's chuckling and waving her arms just like Alice used to. She's rosy-cheeked and has adorable dimples and long, dark eyelashes . . . 'Dada,' she's saying, as he pushes her higher. 'Not too high,' I'm saying, and Reuben's saying, 'It's not too high; she loves it!' and we're all laughing.

And now we're in an airy apartment somewhere and it's a lazy Sunday morning and we're drinking coffee and eating freshly baked bread, and Reuben's got the baby on his lap and he's reading her one of those cloth books like the mums at the pub in Clapham had.

And now he's got her in one of those carrier things on his front and we're walking back through the park together (is it Regent's Park or Central Park? Hard to be sure) and I'm pushing the empty buggy with one hand – it's one of those really fancy ones like you see celebrities' babies in on the covers of magazines – holding something that I expect is a decaf skinny chai latte in the other. A dog is trotting at my side. An Irish Setter. I've always wanted an Irish Setter. And, of course, we're all laughing. A laughing, happy family.

And now, oh look! It's my university graduation. And Reuben's there, of course, with our adorable daughter on his shoulders and they're waving proudly at me as I walk along in my gown and mortarboard. 'I knew you'd do it,' Reuben says, as I make my way over to them and he gives me a kiss. 'But even I didn't think you'd get a first. Your mum's a genius, you know, Demelza.' And we're all laughing. Again. What a lot of laughing we do, even when nothing particularly funny is happening. We're just that sort of family.

It's as if something lifts from me as I imagine all this, a weight that I hadn't realized was there. I look down at my middle and for the first time I let myself imagine myself looking pregnant. I imagine feeling a baby kicking, imagine saying to Reuben, 'Quick, put your hand there and you'll feel it,' just like Mum used to with me when she was pregnant. I put my hands over the place where the beginnings of what could be the baby I'm imagining are growing, and my heart beats faster. Could I do it? Could *we* do it, together, me and Reuben?

How will I ever know, if I don't tell him? I have to give him a chance.

Can I?

Maybe I can after all. Maybe I'll do it right now. Yes! I'll just email him and tell him . . . I imagine typing the words and pressing Send. No. I imagine Reuben picking up the message with Camille there dressed only in alluring French underwear . . .

The thought of Camille and her lingerie makes me stop. The dizzy warmth I'd felt of my imaginary happy, laughing family cools a bit. I examine them a little more closely and this time I can't help noticing a few suspicious details. For a start, Reuben's wearing clothes like a menswear catalogue, kind of a bit cool but also wholesome and quite alarmingly brightly coloured. It strikes me that this isn't likely, nor the fact that he doesn't smell of hangover or cigarettes but instead of something manly and outdoorsy. He looks like he's been working out a bit too. Also I seem to have been Photoshopped. I'm quite a lot taller and slimmer than I currently am and, after scrutinizing this Me for a while, I see that this is due to the fact that I appear to have borrowed the legs of a super-model, along with her very expensive-looking skinny jeans. And my hair, far from being lank and prone to frizz, is lustrous and falling in coppery blonde ringlets down my back. I also can't help noticing that our chilled Sunday morning seems to be taking place in a very light and airy apartment in somewhere that I imagine to be Hoxton or possibly even Manhattan. How did we come to be there? I wonder. And the homebaked bread . . . Who baked it? I'm pretty sure it wasn't me. I'm even more sure it wasn't Reuben. And although our baby would, I'm sure, prove to be talented in all sorts of unexpected ways, it seems unlikely that she was responsible . . . And then there's the dog. Reuben hates dogs. I'm allergic to them. They make my eyes swell up and my nose go bright red and my entire head fill with mucus.

Hmmmm. I try to ignore these descrepancies, but I can't help feeling uneasy.

No. I can't tell him in an email.

But maybe I could say I've got something important to tell him. Something that I need to speak to him about urgently. Maybe I could even hint at what it is so that it doesn't come as a complete shock . . . *There's something important I've got to tell you. Something that affects us both . . .* Or, *I've got some surprising news that you need to hear . . .*

I'm going to do it. I get out my laptop from my backpack and open my email. As I do so, I realize there's a message waiting for me from Reuben. He's only just sent it. I can't help smiling. It's as if he knew! He's been thinking of me, just as I've been thinking of him. I know Kat's right about Reuben and I know Gloria was right and he acted like an idiot in Norfolk. But the fact is we've got some kind of connection. Perhaps he's missing me. I know he's got Camille and everything, but it's like he said. I understand him in a way other people don't. My heart flutters a tiny bit as I open the email.

From: wilde_one666@starmail.com
To: hattiedlockwood@starmail.com
Subject:

th4qddc vccn?Kk;l

I stare at the screen, trying to work out if there's some mysterious coded message, scrolling down to check that I haven't missed something, that there isn't any more to read. As I do so, another email arrives. It says:

From: wilde_one666@starmail.com
To: hattiedlockwood@starmail.com
Subject: oops

Soz babe didnt mean to sned that!!!! Was trying to email a mate on my phone and been drinkin
ps hop u r ok

I close the laptop and I sit for a long time in silence. As I do, I examine the happy, laughing family a bit more closely.

As I watch them, the image wobbles a bit and becomes blurry. I blink hard to see them more clearly, and when they come back into focus they look a little different. They're not airbrushed in the park any more, or in our mysteriously acquired Manhattan apartment. We're in a small, damp-smelling flat, and the people next door are playing death metal *really* loud. The baby, while still probably very sweet, is red-faced and yelling, so it's quite hard to tell. Reuben, who is now wearing his own clothes, is saying, 'Why the hell won't she just sleep? Can't you feed her or something?' and I (who am still looking just a tiny bit taller

273

than usual) am saying, 'But I've just fed her; it can't be that,' and Reuben says, 'Well, I can't stand this noise any longer. I'm going out.' And I say, 'What do you mean? Out where?' and he says, 'There's no point me being here, is there? I can't do anything to help. She just cries whenever I hold her. I'm going for a cigarette.' And he goes, leaving me sitting in the dingy flat with the drumbeat from next door still banging through the wall and the baby scream-ing. And I have no idea whether he's ever coming back, or whether I want him to.

I look at the screen again.

hop u r ok

Really? Is that it?

hop u r ok?

SERIOUSLY?

I stare at the words, and in that moment everything falls away: every excuse I've ever made for him, any doubt I've ever given him the benefit of. I'm so angry my hands are shaking as I type.

From: hattiedlockwood@starmail.com
To: wilde_one666@starmail.com
Subject: Re: Oops

Fuck off, Reuben, and never contact me again.

And this time, I send it.

# Chapter twenty-three

The next day I sleep in late. When I wake up I feel as though things have sorted themselves out in my head while I've been asleep. I feel very certain of three things: one, everything has changed. I have to forget about Reuben and focus on me. Two, I have to work out whether I want to have an abortion or have a baby. I have a few days to make that decision. I feel surprisingly calm as I think this. Three, we only have two more days in the Lake District and I want to enjoy that time. I'm determined we're going to go on the boat trip I missed out on last time, and Gloria, surprisingly, makes no objections.

It's a beautiful day when we get down to the lake, sunlight splintering and glittering on the dark water, and I'm strangely elated. It feels significant, somehow, making this trip. It's something I didn't do with Dad, and I feel as though in some way I'm doing it in his memory. I try to explain this to Gloria as we clamber onto the boat along with the other tourists, elderly couples in walking gear, students, parents with chattering children.

'You've been to the Lake District before?' she says, surprised.

'Yes!' I say. 'Don't you remember? I told you I came with my dad? With Dominic, your nephew? '

'No, you didn't,' she says.

'I did! Look it up in the book.'

She does.

'Hmmph,' she says, which I translate as, '*Yes, you're right, I'm sorry*.'

'Did you get on well with your dad?' she says suddenly.

'Yes.'

'He must have been away a lot,' she says, reading something she's written down in the notebook, presumably the stuff I told her before about his job and how he was always off in some war zone or another.

'Yeah, he was,' I say.

'I remember how strange it was when my father came home from the war. I'd never met him before. I was conceived just before he was conscripted and four years old when he got home. Everything changed when he came home. Everyone acted differently around him. Mum and Gwen. He was a stranger to me, but everyone expected me to be pleased to see him. I wished he'd go away again. Once I told Gwen I wished he'd been killed in the war. She slapped me round the face.'

I stare at Gloria and for a moment I can't speak because what she's saying has reminded me of something I'd forgotten, something I'd locked away.

I can remember how I'd feel when Dad first arrived home from his trips. I'd drive Mum mad beforehand, chattering, drawing pictures for Dad and asking again and again when he'd be back. And when he first came home I'd be more excited than about anything and he'd treat me differently from how Mum did; he'd take me out and buy me things

276

Mum never let me have, perfume and big sparkly earrings, and let me stay up late and watch films that were way too old for me and eat chocolate for breakfast, and I wished he was there all the time. That's the bit I've always remembered, that I've told Ollie about. But after a few days of him being home it would feel difficult and strange and different. I'd hear them arguing sometimes when I'd gone up to bed. I could never hear what they were saying, just their angry voices, accusing, and doors slamming. Mum would be different too when he was around. She was harder, not as gentle, less smiling and attentive to me, and sometimes she'd cry. That's the bit I'd forgotten. I'd forgotten that I'd end up hoping he'd be gone again soon, which he always was ... and then, once he'd gone, I'd cry, but I never knew why because really everything was much easier when he wasn't there.

'I felt like that too,' I say, quietly, looking out over the black and silver water. 'Not that I wished he'd die. Just that he'd go away. I always thought that maybe it was my fault he wasn't happy when he came back.'

It's funny, I hadn't realized before I said it that he *wasn't* happy when he was at home, with us, but now I've said it it's obvious. He wasn't.

'I always thought next time would be better. But it never was. And then he didn't come back.'

Gloria watches me.

'I'd forgotten,' I say. 'I'd forgotten it was like that. I was just a kid, I suppose. I didn't really understand it at the time.'

Gloria closes the book and puts it in her bag. Then she takes my hand in hers.

'Memories,' she says. 'Some are real, some are made up. Most are a bit of both.'

\*　　\*　　\*

277

That night as she goes off to bed, Gloria says, in an offhand voice, 'Oh, by the way, there's someone I want us to visit tomorrow.'

I stare at her.

Someone she wants to visit? Has she been planning this all along? Has she been keeping it a secret or has she just forgotten to tell me? Or perhaps she's confused and thinks we're back in London.

'Who?' I say.

'I'll explain tomorrow,' she says.

'Do you know where they live?' I ask, cautious.

'Of course I know,' she snaps. 'I've got it written down.'

'Okay,' I say. 'Is it near here.'

'Not too far. Whatsername checked. The busybody.'

'Peggy?'

'Yes. She checked. She said we could drive there and back in a day.'

'Why didn't you mention this before?'

'I wasn't sure,' she says. 'I wasn't sure I'd be brave enough to go.'

'Why?' I say. 'Who is it?'

'Tomorrow,' she says. 'I'm too tired now. Anyway, if I think about it too much I might lose my nerve.'

I sit there after she's gone up and wonder who it could be. I don't think it's her son. He's in Whitby, I'm sure of it. It's the only thing that makes sense: *the end of the story*. So who is here? Could my first idea, that it was a romantic reunion with Sam be right? I can't help hoping so.

But, really, is it likely? She and Sam haven't seen each other since they were teenagers, the same age as I am now, and they can hardly have parted on good terms. Gloria told him she was pregnant and he bailed out on her. Maybe she

278

wants to see him so she can confront him, after all this time? Or forgive him?

But the way she talks about Sam seems final somehow, as though he's not someone she ever expects to see again. So who else could it be? Trust Gloria to make a mystery of it; she can't resist a bit of drama. I smile to myself. I feel as though I'm really starting to understand her.

But my smile fades almost instantly, and all I can feel is how sad it is, how unfair, that I'm getting know her when her illness means we can have so little time to share. If only I'd found her sooner. If only she hadn't been kept a secret. It seems hard to believe that the family could have disowned her just because she had an illegitimate baby. Even Nan, her own sister. Or perhaps it wasn't like that. Perhaps it was Gloria's choice not to have anything to do with her family after the way they'd treated her all those years ago.

I wish we had a bit longer together. The end of our journey isn't far away. Not long till Whitby and then what? How long will it be before she forgets we ever came on this trip?

I force myself not to think about. We are here now. I must make the most of the time we have.

Funny how it bring things back, being here. It's like being taken back in time, feeling everything I felt then, the fear, the anger. For a moment I can remember clear as anything the smell of the hospital. I can feel how I felt then, sore and out of place, lonely.

They make no secret of the fact you aren't like the other mothers on the ward. Visiting time is the worst. The smiling husbands carrying bunches of flowers, the proud mothers clip-clopping in and clucking over the babies, the carefully wrapped presents, the excitement and chatter and the laughing. And there are children, too, carried in their fathers' arms or older ones, with their grazed knees and freckles, peering curiously into the cots containing their new siblings. I cannot watch them.

The first time it catches me unawares and I have to lie there in the middle of it all, in my narrow, unvisited bed, see the sneaked sideways glances in my direction, and try not to let on that I care. I close my eyes and in my head I start the lines for the part of Titania, which I'd been learning for the school play. I wonder who got my part instead. Whoever it was, they won't have played it as well as I would have.

'Hello,' says a child's voice.

I open my eyes and see a little boy, about seven maybe. Fed up with the adulation being showered on his new baby brother, he has sneaked off from his own noisy group and sidled up to my bed. He is the only person in the ward to get close enough to me to notice the tear that has sneaked from the corner of my eye and trickled irritatingly down to my ear.

He watches me for a while, then looks into the cot, then back at me.

'Don't you like your baby?' he says.

'No,' I say. 'Not much.'

He looks pleased. 'I don't know why everyone makes such a fuss about them. Everyone says babies are beautiful, don't they? But really they're rather ugly, aren't they?'

'Yes.'

He looks at me some more as if waiting for me to say something.

'Want a wine gum?' he says at last, taking a rather grubby-looking paper bag from his pocket, along with an even grubbier piece of string and a marble.

I'm about to tell him that's the nicest thing anyone has said to me since I got to hospital and that he's going to make a splendid big brother, when his father spots him from across the ward.

'Eric!' He marches over and hauls him away. He doesn't acknowledge me.

After they've gone, Eric's mother, who hasn't spoken to me since she arrived on the ward yesterday, says, '*Miss* Harper? I don't want the likes of you talking to my son. It's bad enough that we have to put up with you on the same ward as us.'

The next time, I pull the curtains round my bed at visiting time and I pretend to be asleep. I lie with my eyes stubbornly closed, ignoring the noise and chatter all around me, the coos and the clucking, the laughter.

'Mrs Harper,' says a voice.

I don't open my eyes.

'What?'

'There's a visitor here for you.'

My eyes open involuntarily and I see a nurse standing there by the bed.

'No,' I say. 'You've made a mistake. There's no visitor for me.'

And then Gwen's head appears round the curtain. She hands me a bunch of yellow roses and stands, as if she's unsure what to do or say.

'You came all this way,' I say, disbelieving.

'I had to make sure you were all right,' she says. 'But I can't stay long. I'm going straight back on the train after this. Vinnie doesn't know I'm here. I told him Mum was ill and I had to go and stay with her overnight. He won't be happy if he finds out.'

*Thank you.* I say it in my head because I can't get the words out.

'Where's your baby?' Gwen says.

I just lie there, not looking at her, picking petals off the roses Gwen brought, pressing my fingertips into the smoothness of them, rolling them against my thumb.

'They've taken him off somewhere,' I say. 'To weigh him or something.'

'This is Gloria's baby,' says the nurse, bustling in carrying him in her arms. It's the nice nurse, Patsy. She's the only one who hasn't treated me like muck in this place, apart from the cleaner. She hands the baby to Gwen 'Isn't he a handsome little fellow?'

That night I lie awake in the hospital ward thinking of Sam, remembering him so clearly it makes my chest ache. I have a perfect, clear memory of that day in Cambridge after the boy called us names.

*'People think being brave means not being scared of anything. But that's wrong, Gloria. How can you be brave if you're not scared? Feeling afraid and not letting it stop you. That's being brave.'*

I will not cry. All the girls at the Home cry at night but I never do. Some like to make a big song and dance of it, snuffling and then wailing until they get the attention of everyone in the dorm, and everyone crowds round to comfort them, to put their arms round them and stroke their hair and tell them everything will be okay. Some try to do it silently so as not to wake anyone, so that no one will know how sad they are. Edie is one of those. Hard to believe, but I can't wait to get back to the Home. I can't wait to see Edie.

## Chapter twenty-four

'You have reached your destination,' says the sat nav.

We're outside a pretty old stone house on the edge of a picture-postcardy kind of village, all roses growing over doorways and village greens and probably a vicar on a bicycle somewhere, although I haven't spotted one yet. It is exactly what people from other countries think England looks like.

'It's so quaint, isn't it? I bet everyone has marrow-growing competitions and keeps chickens and they bake each other cakes and stuff like that.'

'Ha,' says Gloria. 'Villages. Behind the hanging baskets I bet it's all swingers parties and unmentionable fetishes.'

I switch off the engine and look at her.

'So, are you going to stop all the cloak-and-dagger stuff and tell me who we've come to see?'

She looks at me and I realize suddenly how incredibly nervous she is. Her hands are clenched together in her lap.

'Gloria?'

'Perhaps it was a mistake,' she says, to herself more than me.

'Come on,' I say. 'We've come all this way. Who lives in that house, Gloria?'

She takes a deep breath.

'Edie,' she says. 'Edie lives there.'

'Edie?' I say. 'You kept in touch all these years?'

'No,' Gloria says. 'I haven't seen her for more than fifty years. But we write to each other occasionally and she sends Christmas cards and so I had her address. I don't suppose she expected me to turn up on her doorstep, though. What if she doesn't want to see me?'

Gloria looks almost childlike; I can imagine the frightened girl who Edie took under her wing at St Monica's the first day she arrived.

'Of course she'll want to see you.'

'What if she's not there?'

'Only one way to find out.'

After I've rung the doorbell I begin to panic just a tiny bit. What if she *doesn't* want to see Gloria? What if the time in the Home is something she wants to forget, a secret she's kept from her family. What if Gloria has the wrong address? For all I know this could be where Edie lived twenty years ago and a complete stranger might open the door. But as soon as the door opens and I see the woman standing behind it, I know she's Edie and I know it's all going to be okay. She looks a bit younger than Gloria, even though I know she's the same age, with a kind of healthy glow that makes me think she spends a lot of time outdoors. She has creases round her eyes that show she laughs a lot, silvery hair in a pixie cut, and an open, kind face. She's the sort of person who makes you feel happier as soon as you see her. I picture her as a girl and imagine what a friend she must have been to Gloria. As I do I feel a pang of sadness, thinking of Kat and how much I miss her.

I smile at Edie and then turn to Gloria, waiting for her to introduce herself, but I can see that, for once, she's completely lost for words. She's looking at Edie and her expression is so raw and open that I'm taken aback. She does such a good job of covering up her emotions, Gloria, but here, seeing Edie, she's laid bare.

I turn back to Edie.

'Hello,' I say brightly. 'I'm Hattie, and this is my great-aunt—'

'I know who you are,' Edie says softly, not looking at me. 'You're Gloria.'

Her eyes fill with tears and she throws her arms round Gloria and they laugh and hug each other, Gloria's bony frame against Edie's plump one. Then Edie holds her back so she can look at her. They don't speak for a while and I wonder what memories are going through their minds. 'Look at you,' she says. 'I'd know you anywhere. You always were the stylish one, weren't you?'

'And this is Hattie,' Gloria says. 'She's my nephew Dominic's daughter.' She says it rather forcefully, and I wonder if she doesn't want Edie to guess about her dementia.

'Oh,' Edie says. 'Yes, of course. Lovely to meet you, Hattie.'

'Sorry to arrive unannounced,' Gloria says. 'I hope we haven't caught you at a bad moment?'

'Not at all!' Edie says. 'Come through and we'll go and sit in the garden and have a cup of tea and some cake. My grandchildren are out there, I'm on childminding duty over the summer holidays.'

'Tell me about it,' I say, and we have a chat about Alice and Ollie and Edie's grandchildren, Tariq and Yasmeen, as we go through to the garden.

*   *   *

We sit in the garden in the sunshine and drink tea and eat lemon drizzle cake and I lean back in Edie's comfy garden chairs and shut my eyes and try not to listen too closely to Edie and Gloria's conversation in case there's private stuff they want to discuss, but at the same time I do really want to know EVERYTHING.

I gather from their conversation that Edie married and had children a few years after she and Gloria were in the Mother and Baby Home together.

'Five,' she says.

'Five?' says Gloria, horrified. 'Well, I suppose I shouldn't be surprised. I remember you telling me back at St Monica's you wanted ten.'

Edie laughs. She tells Gloria about how she landed on her feet with her husband Robert, and how he built up his own business from scratch. I get bored and go off to play with the grandchildren, who make me play hide-and-seek and bounce on the trampoline. Suddenly I really miss Alice and Ollie. Not long till I see them, though. One more night in our little cottage and then on to Whitby. And then home.

I turn and watch Gloria and Edie together. I notice that the teacups have been replaced by large glasses of white wine and the two of them are in animated conversation, Gloria throwing her head back and laughing. I've not really seen her like this in the whole time I've known her: relaxed, happy, full of life. That's what friendship does, I suppose, even when you haven't seen each other for decades. Will Kat and I still be friends in fifty years' time? I can't imagine not being friends with her. And seeing Gloria and Edie makes me realize that I'm not going to let Zoe-from-Kettering or anything else get in the way of our friendship.

I get out my phone and try to send Kat a text but then I remember that I've let the battery run out. I tell myself I'll charge it up and send her a message tonight.

I stroll over to where Gloria and Edie are sitting. 'They're lovely kids,' I say to Edie.

'They're my Ian's children from his second marriage,' Edie says. 'Ian was the baby I had at the Home when I first met you, Gloria.'

'But I thought his name was Ted?' I say.

Edie sighs. 'It was. I still think of him as Ted deep down. But Ian's the name his adoptive parents gave him.'

'So you got back in touch with him?' I say.

She nods. 'Eventually. It took a long time.'

I want to ask more, because the more I think about it, the more I wonder whether Gloria going to find her son could be a bad idea. What if he doesn't want to know? What if his adoptive parents never told him he was adopted at all? But I can hardly start interrogating Edie with Gloria sitting there.

'I always knew you would find him,' Gloria says, smiling. 'I told you, didn't I? You loved him too much to let him go for ever.'

Edie rushes down to see her baby every morning. The first feed happens before it's properly light, but she's always up and ready, itching to get down there. I lie in bed, heavy and tired, wishing I could just sleep.

'How can you have so much energy?' I groan.

'I just can't wait to see him,' she says. 'I've not got him for long so I'm going to make the most of every second. Don't you feel like that?'

I sit up in bed and swing my legs out but I don't reply.

She'd looked at me, curious.

'Do you love your baby?'

Her question freezes me. It's the question I'd been dreading, hoping none of the girls would never ask. But I'm a good liar, always have been, so I smiled and I thought I was going to say, 'Course I do.'

But I can't. The words stick. I can't speak. I sit on the narrow, hard bed and I can't move. I can't even breathe.

She reaches up, gently, and wipes away a tear that is somehow on my cheek.

'Thought you'd forgotten how to do that,' she said, taking hold of my hand. It's true: I haven't cried once since the first day

289

I arrived here. 'I think I cry enough for both of us, don't you? In tears every day and twice on Thursdays.' I know she's trying to make me laugh, but I can't.

'I'm not like you, Edie,' I say once I know I can keep my voice steady. 'I'm not the maternal type. I know you're not supposed to feel like that about your own baby but . . .' I shrug. 'Give us a ciggie, will you?'

She hands me one and as I hold the match to the end of it my hand is shaking.

'Sometimes I think I hate him,' I say, and I can't look at her face because I know how shocked she'll be and she won't be able to hide it.

'You're just scared,' she says.

I want to say, 'I'm not scared of anything.' It's what I've always said.

But I can't say it now.

'It's so wonderful to see her after all these years,' Edie says to me. Asma, Ian's wife, has been to pick up the children now and Gloria is dozing next to us. Everything feels so peaceful; I'll be sorry when we have to leave.

'So when did you get back in touch with Ian?'

'Ooh, about twenty years ago now.'

'That must have been amazing,' I say. 'When you hadn't seen him since he was a baby.'

I try to imagine how it must have felt to give up the baby she loved for adoption. Could I do that? It's an option, I suppose. But I don't think I'd be able to do it. Poor Edie didn't have a choice.

'It wasn't easy. Ian didn't want to know at first, he was worried it'd upset his adoptive mother. Which I could understand. She was a lovely woman. She'd brought him up well. I couldn't have wished for a better family for him. He felt she might think it was disloyal of him to get to know me. And it was hard for him to understand that I hadn't wanted to give him up. He couldn't see why I hadn't just said no. But you couldn't. You didn't have a choice. I'd have done anything to keep him.'

'I know,' I say. 'Gloria told me.'

'He felt rejected, and of course I'd gone on to get married and have another family. But when Sheila, his adoptive mother, died, he felt able to get in touch.'

It comes out in a rush. 'Is that why we're going to Whitby? Did Gloria say anything to you? Are we going to meet her son?'

Edie looks at me, with that nervous, guarded look again, as if she's anxious about saying something she shouldn't.

'Are you worried about how he might react?' I guess at last. 'That her son might not want to see her?' This thought hadn't occurred to me. As far as I was concerned it was all going to be happy reunions, hugs and tears and making up for a lifetime of not knowing each other just in the nick of time. And I would have made it happen. But what if it wasn't like that? What if he slammed the door in her face and said he wanted nothing to do with her? What if he blamed her for abandoning him? I remember what Gloria had told me, the sickening fact that back then a baby with a black father wouldn't be adopted, so they'd be put in a children's home. You heard awful stories about what happened in homes back then. What if that's what happened to him and he blamed it all on her?

'What has Gloria told you?' she says.

'About why we're going to Whitby? Nothing,' I say. 'Just that it's "where the story ends". She likes being cryptic.'

I smile at Edie, but she doesn't smile back. She seems worried.

'So Gloria hasn't said anything about . . .' She pauses. 'About what happened in Whitby? What do you know about what happened to her son? About what happened to *her*?'

292

There's something about the way she says it that makes me feel a bit sick. She says it in a way that makes me think whatever it was that happened wasn't anything good.

'No,' I say. 'But if there's something you think I ought to know . . .'

She looks uncertain for a moment. Then she reaches over and takes my hand.

'Gloria will tell you in her own good time,' she says. 'It's not easy for her. These are difficult things to remember for her. Just – don't be shocked. Don't judge her.'

'Of course not,' I say, taking my hand away. 'Why would I?'

She gives me a bright smile. 'No reason,' she says. 'No reason at all. It's just me being silly, love. All these memories being stirred up. It's got me all worked up. Ignore me.'

'I hope you don't mind us coming,' I say. 'I know it must have been a shock after all this time.'

'Mind? I'm delighted. I can't thank you enough, pet. When you go through something like that together it's a real bond.'

'How come you didn't keep in touch? I mean, I know you wrote but did you never meet up?'

'I loved Gloria; I missed her terribly. But none of the girls really kept in touch,' Edie says. 'I never even heard from any of the others after we'd left. It's hard to explain. The Home seemed like another world. It *was* another world really. Different rules applied. In the real world we were sinful, shameful. In there we were just . . . girls. But leaving was so painful. We were encouraged to put it all behind us, pretend it had never happened. Some of the girls had never wanted babies, of course, and it was a relief to be able to put it behind them and get on with their lives. And even for those of us that wanted to keep our babies, it was easier that way. I grieved for my Ted. It was almost as if he'd died. Thinking about him growing up with some other family, another mummy going in to get him in the morning and him smiling and chuckling, his first steps, all of that. I couldn't bear to think about it. Once you were back in your old life it almost seemed as though the Home was a dream. Nobody at home outside the family had known I was expecting. It was easier to pretend it had never happened.'

'So you never saw each other again after you left the Home?'

Edie looks anxious.

'Just the once,' she says, awkward, as though she's not sure whether she should be telling me. 'Anyway, it's wonderful to see her now.'

'She has memory problems, you know.' I've been unsure whether to mention it.

'I had wondered, yes. She repeated herself a couple of times. Is it serious?'

'Not too serious, yet. But yes. I think it's probably Alzheimer's.'

The look on Edie's face makes me feel the full weight of this. In all the story of Gloria's past and worrying about my pregnancy I've got used to Gloria muddling through her forgetfulness. But she can't keep on muddling through. It's going to get worse. *The terminal illness where you get to die twice.*

'I'm so sorry,' Edie says.

'What if we get to Whitby and she forgets it all?'

Edie shakes her head.

'She won't.'

\*     \*     \*

I watch Edie and Gloria as they say goodbye to each other. They just look like two old ladies, one a cosy, grandmotherly type who bakes cakes for the village fête, one thin and glamorous, wearing a bit too much make-up. Just two old ladies saying goodbye to each other. But looking at them I see those two girls and everything they went through together and their friendship still strong after all these years, not wanting to let go of each other, and it makes me so happy and so sad.

'Take care of yourself,' Edie says to Gloria, wiping her eyes. 'Behave yourself.'

'Why break the habit of a lifetime?' Gloria says, and they both laugh. I wonder if they'll see each other again, and if they do whether Gloria will recognize Edie, or remember who she is. Maybe she won't even remember St Monica's or that she had a baby or any of it. Edie's eyes are full of tears and I wonder if she's thinking the same thing.

'Bring her to see me again soon, won't you?' she says to me.

'You think I'd submit myself to her driving again?' says Gloria, trying to make light of their goodbyes. I think again what a brilliant actress she is. I wish I could have seen her on stage.

As Edie looks at Gloria I see her face change as she notices something. 'You've still got the locket. The one I sent you.'

Gloria's hand goes to her neck, touching the heavy silver locket I'd found in her suitcase at the start of our journey. I hadn't noticed she was wearing it. 'Yes,' she says.

As they say their final farewell and we walk back to the car, I look at the locket, intrigued. If Edie sent it to her it must be really old. Whose pictures are inside? Ones of Edie and Gloria perhaps? Did Edie send it all those years ago to remind her of their friendship, of their bond, of their lost babies?

'Can I see the locket?' I say as we do up the seat belts. 'I didn't know you'd had it all that time.'

'No,' Gloria says sharply. 'You may not.'

Gloria doesn't speak as we leave the village. She keeps her mouth clamped shut. I think of everything Edie said.

'What did you name your baby?' I ask at last. It's funny, I've never thought about it until now.

Gloria is silent for a moment.

'I didn't name him,' she says. Her voice warns me not to ask more, much as I want to. Had it been a way of protecting herself, of not becoming attached to him? Or had it simply been because she knew he'd be given another name when he was taken away? Either way it seems sad. What had Gloria felt for her baby? Had she loved him?

We drive on in silence.

'Are you okay?' I say.

'Yes.' It comes out as a strangled croak, and I realize that she's not speaking because if she does she will cry, and she doesn't want to cry. Not in front of me, anyway. So I put the local radio station on and hum along to some eighties pop and have an argument with myself about whether or not it's Bananarama, and I say the name of every village we drive through and make inane comments about the funny names they give places oop north, and about the twinning of obscure villages. What's all that about? (Gloria still hasn't said a word, so I plough on talking to fill the silence.) What does it actually mean if Dol-de-Bretagne in France is your twin? I wonder. Because if it's anything like Ollie and Alice it mainly means that you blame each other when you fart, and make up jokes that no one else in the world finds

296

funny, and find ever more inventive ways of cheating when you play each other at cards, and nick each other's toys because no matter how many times you explain to well-meaning relatives that it's *Ollie* who likes dolls' houses and *Alice* who likes night-vision goggles they can never quite get their heads round it.

All the while there's an uneasy backing track of Edie's questions running round and round in my head on a loop: *What has Gloria told you? About what happened in Whitby? What do you know about what happened to her son? About what happened to* her?

Gloria stares out of the window not hearing any of it.

The overwhelming urge to cry as we drive away from Edie takes me completely by surprise, not just to cry but to weep, to give in to the uncontrollable sobbing that has, it seems, been hiding there inside me. I had thought I was beyond such things as emotional farewells. I haven't seen Edie for so many years. How can it hurt so much to say goodbye again, and to know that the next time I see her I may not know who she is? It shouldn't. I shouldn't let it. But it isn't just me I am crying inside for. It is for the girl who *was* me, who said goodbye to Edie all those years ago, who locked herself in the bathroom at St Monica's so that no one would see her cry. In this moment, somehow, in this little car driving through the hills in the early evening, the lines have become blurred and I am that girl again.

The smell of disinfectant and damp. I am sitting on cold lino-leum, my back against something hard. A cast-iron bathtub. Big old Victorian thing with clawed feet.

I am locked in the bathroom at St Monica's. I am crying so much that I think I will be sick, but silently, because there are people outside the door and I can't let them hear.

'Gloria! Is that you in there?'

'There are girls waiting for the lav out here, you know. Hurry up, will you?'

'Are you okay? Can you hear me, Gloria? Just open the door, there's a good girl.'

None of the voices is Edie's.

She has gone, left this morning with her battered brown suit-case. Perhaps I will never hear her voice again. She said she would write but I wonder. It has been so painful for her, giving up Ted. Perhaps once she is at home with her family she will want to forget it all, put it all behind her, including me.

We went into town the afternoon before they took Ted, just the two of us and our babies. 'Just think, Glo,' she says, rubbing Ted's back to wind him. 'If we had wedding rings on our fingers it'd all be different. We'd be able to meet up in town with our babies and do all the things normal mums do. I've seen my sisters do it. Showing off when one of them takes their first steps or says their first word. We could meet up in the park and push them on the swings in the park or take them to feed the ducks. And then in a few years we'd be watching them go off to school together. That'd be nice, wouldn't it?'

I reached up to her and tried to brush the tears away but there were too many of them.

'Yeah,' I said. 'It would.'

I look at my baby that night as I feed him, and I wish so much that I could love him. I know it would break my heart if I did. Perhaps I should be grateful that I don't. But I feel like a failure, unnatural. How can a mother not love her own baby? It gnaws at my insides, that failure, the numbness I feel when I look at him, it hollows me out. I examine every bit of him. *'Look at his little fingernails,'* Edie says, when she's looking at Ted. *'So perfect.'* Or she'll just breathe in the smell of him when she's holding him, touching her lips to the soft hair on his head. I try it all. I really, really try. But I can't do it. I can't love him.

*Will he know?* I wonder. Even though he won't know me, will he know his mother didn't love him? Will it be inside him somehow, just as Edie's love will be inside Ted? Will my baby feel the absence of it?

Ted is with his new family now. Edie put on her best clothes to go and sign the papers at the Town Hall. Perhaps she hoped that somehow she could persuade them she was worthy of keeping her baby. As if reheeled shoes and new nylons would persuade them when all her love and devotion to Ted had failed to.

'I know it's for the best,' she said, but her voice was empty. It's like she's not a whole person without him.

And now I feel that I am not a whole person without her. She is the only person who understood. I told her things I can never tell anyone else.

A week after Edie left, a little parcel arrived for me with a Whitby postmark. My heart leapt; Whitby was Edie's hometown.

Before we gave up our babies we had to make a box for them. We had to wrap it in pretty paper and fill it with all the things our babies would need. It would go with them to their families. It seemed a peculiarly cruel thing to do for the girls who would have done anything to keep their babies, a reminder of the things they would be missing out on. The girls made so much effort to make them beautiful, neatly folding the tiny clothes someone else would dress their babies in. Edie wept as she made Ted's, consoling herself with the thought that the clothes she had made would be with him, would keep him warm. We were told we could put in a present for the baby, something for when they were older, that they could keep as a memento of us, their birth mothers. Edie had brought her dad's old Brownie camera with her and when she made her box she put in a locket with a picture of her on one side and a picture of Ted on the other. On the back she wrote their names and the date.

'What will your gift be, Gloria?' she'd said.

I shook my head.

'I won't be giving him a gift.'

It was a locket just like hers, but inside there was a picture she'd taken of me and one of my baby.

And now she is gone. And soon my baby will be gone. Sam is gone.

*I have gone too*, I think. *Like Mum*. Always hiding. I do not know where I have hidden. How will I know where to find myself when all this is over?

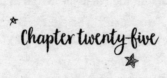

## Chapter twenty-five

Something wakes me that night, after we've been to Edie's. I lie in the dark, disoriented for a moment. What woke me? Was it a dream? I don't think so . . . It was a sound, I think. Was it Gloria? I'm not sure. I clamber, half-awake, out of bed and through the shadows to her room.

Something makes me push the door open a little just to check she's okay.

Her bed is empty.

I stare at it, my mind racing. How long has she been gone? Where might Gloria have gone? Does she even know where she is? She might think she's at home and try to walk to the shops, or she might just have no idea and panic. She may not remember that I'm here with her.

Where should I look? Perhaps the noise that woke me was the front door closing. If so, she can't have gone far. I pull on some trousers and shoes and race downstairs, grabbing the torch from the kitchen before running out into the garden. There's no sign of Gloria. I walk down to the gate and along the path up to a little hill where there's a bench and table. The moon is so bright I don't need the torch and as I get to the top of the slope I see Gloria, sitting at the table with the bottle of brandy I bought at the convenience store and a tumbler, staring up at the sky.

'Thank God,' I say. 'I thought—'

She looks at me and smiles. She doesn't say anything but I know she knows what I thought.

'Look,' she says. 'Come and sit next to me. Can you see? Orion's belt. Sirius, the dog star. And the Pleiades over there. The Seven Sisters.'

'Wow,' I say, sitting down on the bench and looking up into the star-flecked darkness spread wide over the fells. 'It's incredible. Hard to believe it's the same sky as at home. You can see so many stars here.' I'd forgotten. It comes back to me, suddenly, how I'd said the same to Dad when I was a kid.

'Stars,' she says to herself. 'Of course. *Stars*.' She laughs.

I look at her. 'What's funny?'

'I could remember the word "constellation",' she says. 'I could remember that it was Orion I was looking at. I could even remember the myth of Orion. He was the son of Poseidon, who could walk on the sea and hunted with Artemis. I could remember translating Homer at school, with sad Miss Lytton on a rainy day, watching the raindrops trickle down the window and the bedraggled first years out on the hockey pitch, and thinking that one day I should like to travel to Crete.'

I watch her.

'Which I did eventually. With Gordon, unfortunately. Anyway, that's beside the point. The point is, I could remember all of that. But I couldn't for the life of me remember the word for – oh, bugger it, it's gone again. What are they? The little lights. In the sky.'

'Stars?'

'Stars. I couldn't remember the word for stars.'

She takes out a cigarillo and lights it, the flame bright in the darkness, lighting up her face for a moment, with its shadows and secrets.

'Dad loved them,' I say. I remember one holiday, perhaps it was even the one here in the Lake District, though I can't be sure. The twins were in bed. I don't remember where Mum was, probably washing bottles or doing laundry, though I wouldn't have realized at the time. Dad and I played cards for a while, mixing a bit of his beer with my lemonade to make shandy, and I felt very grown-up. Then he lifted me up and took me outside and we looked up at the night sky together. 'I remember him showing me Polaris,' I tell Gloria. 'He said, "All the rest of the stars seem to move in the sky as time passes. But Polaris, the North Star, stays fixed."'

'Did he say that?' Gloria turns to me. 'Did he really?'

'Yes.'

'How wonderful,' she says, taking a sip of brandy.

'There it is,' I say, pointing at a bright star. 'At least I think it is.' Still fixed in its place and Dad long gone. It's a strange thought. Then I remember how the light we see from stars is really thousands of years old and the whole thing seems so mind-boggling I feel a bit dizzy.

'It's beautiful, isn't it? So big. It makes you feel small. Insignificant. I don't usually like to think of myself as insignificant, as you know, but this is different.'

'Yes.' I know what she means.

'How long will it be before it all goes? How long before I forget all of this? Forget everything I've told you on this journey?'

I don't say anything. I know she's not asking me.

'When everything else goes,' she says. 'When language has gone, words, and the names of the stars, and stories. When my story is gone. When I don't remember who you are or who I am, or even what it means that I am and you are ... Do you think I'll still remember how to feel like this? Is feeling something that we learn to do, stored in the memory, or is it something else? Awe and wonder and love ... Do they come from another part of us and bypass the brain?'

'I don't know,' I say, honestly.

'No.'

I think about it. The feeling of sitting here with Gloria, the stars above us, the mountains around us, the darkness and the light of the moon. The feeling in my chest. Surely that wasn't something I'd learned. Surely that would always be there? 'Babies cry and laugh,' I say at last. 'They smile when they see a face or a person they love. It's not something they learn.'

She looks at me sceptically.

'Maybe that's what makes us who we are,' I continue. 'You said it was memories, and without those we're nobody. But maybe that's not right. It's not memories. It's what we feel and what other people feel about us. I mean, if you think about it, it's not the memories themselves that matter, is it? It's what we feel about them, and the people we care about. All the things you've told me about on our journey. Love, sadness, anger, joy. Those are what matter, aren't they? Perhaps happiness and sadness and love are just in us, right from the beginning. Right to the end.'

'Perhaps,' she says. 'Perhaps not. What I need to decide is, is it worth hanging around to find out?'

'What do you mean?'

'You know what I mean.'

Yes, I know what she means. *At a time and in a manner of my own choosing*.

'Yes,' I say. 'Yes, it's worth it.'

I find I'm crying.

'You have to, Gloria. Please. *Please*.'

She's quiet for a long time.

'I have an appointment with the consultant when we get back,' she says, and I remember the letter I saw in her flat. 'Various scans and so on. It will confirm what I already know.'

'I can come with you, if you'd like me to?' She looks at me and she holds my hands, her skin cold against mine.

'I'm scared.' She says it as a statement of fact, her voice quiet but firm. She's never said it to me before, and I don't suppose she ever will again. She isn't asking for my help or asking me to comfort her. I can't comfort her. I can't change how she feels. I can't change what will happen to her. I can only be with her and hope that is enough.

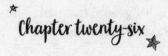
It's a long journey to Whitby. The first bit we spend in traffic jams with cars full of holidaymakers, the sun beating down, the car stuffy and uncomfortable. Gloria dozes, or perhaps pretends to, inscrutable in her sunglasses. She's not in a talkative mood today. She seemed preoccupied as we packed and left, and refused to eat any breakfast.

As we get closer to Whitby the landscape changes. All around us are the sunlit moors, purple with heather, wild and ancient and alive.

'It's beautiful,' I say to Gloria. 'Isn't it so beautiful? I had no idea. I thought it would be . . . bleak. More, I dunno, wuthering.'

Gloria looks out of the window and ignores me. It's as if the last two weeks haven't happened, as if we're back to me being the irritating do-gooder.

'Whatever wuthering is,' I say.

Gloria unwraps another boiled sweet and pops it in her mouth without offering me one.

'Windy,' she says, not looking at me.

'Pardon?'

'Wuthering. Means windy.'

307

'Does it really? '

'Yes. Why would I make it up?'

'I can see why she went for "wuthering". "Windy Heights" doesn't have quite the same ring, really, does it?'

'Haworth is a long way from here anyway,' she says. 'South and over towards Lancashire.'

'Hmm?'

'Haworth. Where Emily Brontë lived.'

'Oh, okay. Maybe we could stop there on the way back. I could get Mum an I-Heart-Heathcliff fridge magnet or something.'

Gloria sighs again, heavily, and fidgets with her hands. She's anxious. This chippiness is just her trying to disguise it. I read that this can be a sign of the disease. Or is it just a normal sign of agitation? This must be what it's like for her. Constantly analyzing her own behaviour, wondering whether something she's lost or forgotten, or someone she doesn't recognize, or some slight eccentricity is just normal, or a sign of the encroaching disease. It must be exhausting. And terrifying. I want to say something to let her know that I understand, but I know it's not the right time; she'll only bite my head off. So I persevere with my inane cheeriness, and it's not even put on. It's all so beautiful you couldn't fail to feel uplifted by it.

'Maybe coming here wasn't such a bad idea after all,' I say. 'Who needs the Maldives when you've got Yorkshire?'

She doesn't reply.

Out of the corner of my eye I can see that Gloria is looking for something, and getting increasingly frantic.

'Where is it?' she says to herself. 'Where can it be?'

'What is it?'

308

She empties out the contents of her bag. All sorts of things tumble out onto her lap, her red book, some make-up, a mirror, sweets, scissors, a pencil, a fork, and various other things that have been put there, intentionally or not it's hard to say, but obviously not what she's looking for.

'What have you done with it?' she says, turning on me. 'You've taken it, haven't you? You're trying to trick me?'

'No,' I say. 'Of course not, Gloria, I would never do that.'

I'm reminded again about mood swings and how people with dementia can get a bit paranoid.

'What is it you've lost?'

'My necklace,' she says. 'My locket.'

'It can't have gone far,' I say. 'You had it yesterday. Don't worry. We'll find it.'

But Gloria gets so agitated I pull over.

'Seriously,' I say. 'It's in here somewhere, I promise. It might be in your suitcase.'

'I don't remember putting it in there.'

'You might have . . . forgotten,' I say gently.

She doesn't reply.

'Are you nervous?' I say to her.

We're coming to the end of our journey. If I'm right about the reason we're here, it's a big deal.

'Nervous?' she says. 'Why would I be nervous?'

'Well,' I say, and in that moment I decide to tell her that I've guessed the reason for our visit. I want to tell her it's going to be all right. I want to help her to make it all right. 'I think I've worked out what we're going to do when we get there.'

'What do you think we're going to do?'

'Well,' I say. 'I'm guessing we're going to go and see someone.'

She ignores me.

'Your son,' I say. 'I think you've found him, haven't you? And you want to go and see him? But now you're getting cold feet. Am I right?'

She ignores me.

'The thing is, Gloria, I think it's a brilliant idea, but have you been in touch with him? Because I think that would definitely be best. I mean, I'm assuming you're not just planning to turn up out of the blue. That'd be a massive shock for him. I'm not saying he won't be pleased to see you or anything, but these things are complicated, aren't they? People can feel . . . rejected. Even though I know there's no reason why he should, you didn't have any choice, it's just—'

'My son is dead.' Her voice is flat, without emotion.

I switch the radio off and stare at her.

'What?'

'He's dead.'

I'm so shocked I can't make sense of what she's saying to me. I *know* he's not dead. I know he lives in Whitby and Gloria's tracked him down and that's why we're here. 'But he can't be,' I say.

'Yes, he can.'

I try to get what she's saying straight in my head.

'How do you know?'

'Because I know,' she says.

'But . . .'

I'm on the brink of tears, angry, disappointed tears. Everything I'd thought this journey was about – a reunion, a resolution . . . I feel tricked, let down.

'Why didn't you tell me? You let me think—'

310

'I didn't let you think anything. You invented a happy ending. If that's what you want, read a fairy tale.'

I think back over everything, and of course she's right. She never said that's what the journey was about. Never even hinted at it. But it seemed so logical. It seemed so neat. Life isn't neat, though, is it? She's right. I wanted to have a happy ending. More than that, I wanted to have been responsible for a happy ending.

I start the engine again and we drive on in silence, as clouds build and are blown across the big sky above us, their shadows dark on the heathery moors.

'Then why did you want to come here?' I say, when I can trust myself to speak. 'You said the answer to a question was here. I thought you meant a person. If it's not a person then, what?'

'This is where it ends.'

'Where what ends?'

'The story. My story.'

'The one you're telling me, you mean?'

She doesn't reply, just keeps on turning the dial of the radio until opera comes blaring out. I grimace instinctively.

'Ah,' she says, satisfied. 'That's proper music. Maria Callas, if I'm not mistaken. That's passion. That's *life*.'

I'm about to protest, but somehow the moors and the sun and the soaring, shimmering, sad music all seem to fit.

Ahead of us on a cliff in the distance the silhouette of Whitby Abbey's ruins appear, dark against the skyline. I shiver. The end of Gloria's story lies ahead of us. Mine too. I must make my decision. Whatever I choose it will be an ending of one kind or another. That is what I must face. Panic grips me, sudden and unexpected. *You invented a happy ending. If that's what you want, read a fairy tale.* She's right. There is no way there can be a happy ending.

I feel small, a tiny speck of life in the middle of the vast, ancient moors, which were here so very long before I was and will be here long after I'm gone.

And inside me is an even tinier speck of life, or of something that could become life.

I feel swallowed up by my smallness and the vastness of the decision I have to make and I feel utterly alone.

'I'm scared too,' I say.

She half smiles. 'How can you be brave if you're not scared?' she says.

I am not alone.

Gloria is with me. We will carry on our journey together to the end, whatever it is.

For some reason, now we are here, I can't stop thinking of Gwen. Dear Gwen. I wish she was here with us. I miss her, even though I didn't see her for so many years.

'Why are you so twitchy?' I say to Gwen. We're in the Lyons Corner House up by Tottenham Court Road and she's jumpy as anything, starting when the waitress asks us what we want, and looking around, anxious, as we wait for our pot of tea and iced cakes.

'You know Vinnie told me he doesn't want me to see you,' she says.

Even the sound of his name makes me angry.

'What right has he got to stop you seeing your own sister?'

'He doesn't mean to be unkind,' Gwen says. 'He's just trying to protect me, my reputation. He just doesn't want me caught up in any unpleasant gossip. You know how people are . . .'

I certainly do.

'It's bad enough that you're not married, but with the baby being coloured as well . . .'

I say nothing. It hurts, that Gwen would judge me in this way. She's hardly been round at all since Mum told her I was

313

expecting. But it's not her, I think. It's him. Vinnie. She'd do anything he told her to.

'You don't have to do what he says, you know.'

'He's my husband, Gloria,' she says. 'I promised to love, honour and obey him, remember?'

I look at her, pale faint lines already round her eyes and mouth. She looks older than she is.

'Why did you marry him, Gwen?'

She smiles a tight smile. 'Because I loved him.'

'Loved?'

'Love.'

I remember when she came back from their honeymoon in Torquay. She seemed different, older, distant, more buttoned-up somehow. She wouldn't take her cardigan off, even though it was a scorching hot day. She'd told us about the hotel and the weather.

'So come on,' I asked her when Mum was out of the room. 'What's it like?'

'What's what like?'

'You know,' I said, giggling. 'On your wedding night.'

'Oh,' Gwen said. She didn't giggle, just pulled her cardigan tighter round her. 'You'll find out when you get married.'

'If I get married,' I said.

It wasn't until a couple of years later, when I'd peeked through the curtains of the changing room in Dickins & Jones while Gwen was trying on a new dress and I'd seen, reflected in the mirror, Gwen's bare arms covered in bruises, that I understood why she never took her cardigan off.

The waitress brings us our tea and cakes, but I find I'm not hungry. My throat is tight suddenly and I feel full and heavy, not just with the baby but with sadness, unexpected and unbearable. I don't know how to tell her what I'm feeling. It's not something I know how to say.

314

'You know I love you, Gwen,' I say at last, blurting it out a bit too loud. She smiles and shakes her head, not even looking at me, pouring herself more tea.

'Daft, you are,' she says, as if I'm a child who's just told a silly joke.

I try not to feel hurt. Showing your feelings isn't done, certainly not in our family. Why would you? What you feel isn't something to dwell on, certainly not something you want other people to know about.

I have to, though. This is important. I have to make her understand.

'I'm not daft,' I say. 'I just want you to know. I love you, Gwen. Nothing can change that.'

She still doesn't look at me, concentrating on topping up her cup and then mine from the jug of boiling water.

'I know.' She says it in the big-sister tone she's always used with me, half amused, half exasperated, but her eyes are full of tears.

I park in the cramped car park round the back of the hotel, hoist the cases out of the boot and start to lug them across the potholed tarmac. Gloria's tetchiness is catching. I'm cursing the wheelie case with a life of its own, which keeps veering off like an over-enthusiastic dog pulling on the lead as I snap it back to heel, and the hold-all with the broken strap, when it strikes me that this is the last time I'll have to do this, and suddenly I feel a great, sad affection for our ramshackle luggage, and the motley collection of places that have been our temporary home on our trip. We're at our last stop. Whatever happens here, whatever secrets are uncovered, memories revisited, ghosts called forth, decisions made, this is it for us. It's the end of my journey with Gloria. I wonder suddenly if that's part of what's bothering her. I've been assuming it's the past, but perhaps it's the present too. And the future of course.

'Booked under the name of Lockwood?' The receptionist smiles brightly at me. The Seaview Hotel is a bit faded at the edges and smells of something that I guess to be yesterday's not-very-delicious dinner, but still, it's a relief to be here and I'm looking forward to making use of the luxurious en-suite bathroom facilities as soon as possible. I curse the weakness of my pregnant bladder.

'Yes,' I say, attempting a tired smile that comes out as a patronizing sort of grimace. 'That's right. Lockwood.'

'There was some confusion about the rooms,' the receptionist says. 'We only had the one twin room under your original booking, but luckily there was a double available due to a cancellation so we're able to fit you all three of you in.'

'All three of us? What do you mean?' I try not to sound impatient, but frankly after all the driving I've got a splitting headache and I'm dying for a wee and could do without having to sort out muddles with the hotel booking.

'Don't worry, Mrs Lockwood. Your husband explained it when he arrived.'

'Wait, what? My *husband*?'

'Yes.' She smiles. 'Mr Lockwood arrived about an hour ago.'

I take a deep breath. 'I think there's been some mistake . . .'

'Yes,' she says, patiently. 'That's what I'm saying. But don't worry. We've sorted it all out. You've got your two rooms, one twin, one double. Must have been a glitch with the online booking app.' She rolls her heavily mascara-laden eyes. 'Technology, eh? It's great when it works, isn't it?'

I just stare at her, trying to make sense of it all.

'Anyway,' she says, flushing slightly and sounding a little out of breath all of a sudden. 'Mr Lockwood was very charming and understanding about it—'

'Was he, indeed?' I say, as the penny finally drops about the identity of my mystery spouse. 'And where is he now, this charming husband of mine?'

'By way of apology we offered him a complimentary beer, wine, or soft beverage at the bar, which I do believe he's enjoying now.'

'Yes, that'd be right,' I say.

'What's she on about?' Gloria says from behind me. 'Did she say "bar"? I could murder a Martini.'

'I'll explain in a minute,' I say.

'The bar's through those double doors there, if you want to go and find him,' the receptionist says.

'Thank you,' I say.

'Oh, no need. Here he is now. They've arrived, Mr Lockwood!' she calls across the lobby, as the double doors open, and through them comes Reuben.

'Why are you sulking?' Reuben says when we're up in the twin room I'm sharing with Gloria. 'I thought you'd be pleased.'

'What the hell are you doing here, Reuben?'

'I'm your young Brad Pitt.'

'We don't need a young Brad bloody Pitt—'

'Speak for yourself, dear,' Gloria interrupts, forcefully.

'Exactly. Thank you, Gloria,' Reuben says, smiling at her and then looking at me in an *I told you so* sort of way. 'Gloria understands.'

'Well, okay. But you're not Young Brad. You're you. So why are you really here?'

He shrugs evasively. 'Wanted to see you.'

'Would you care for a G and T, Brad, dear?' Gloria says, heading for the minibar at speed. 'I fancy a Martini myself, but alas! No olives.'

'No,' I say, flopping down on the bed. 'He's not Brad. He's Reuben, remember?'

'Well, that's tremendously kind of you, Gloria. You don't mind me calling you Gloria, do you? Sorry not to have introduced myself. I'm Reuben. Reuben Wilde, by name and nature.'

'Oh, *please*.' I say.

'Ah, yes,' Gloria says. 'Reuben Wilde. Hattie's *friend*—'

'What about Camille?' I interrupt quickly, before Gloria can say anything that might be incriminating. I'm pretty sure I can trust her not to say anything about the pregnancy, but what if she forgets he doesn't know? What if she just blurts it out? 'And Mykonos?'

Again, the shrug.

I sigh impatiently and snatch the packet of shortbread fingers from him.

He looks me up and down. 'Have you gained weight?'

I stare at him in open-mouthed fury. 'Have you gained *tact*, Reuben?' I snarl. 'Or are you still as much of an offensive arsehole as you always were? Oh, wait. I already know the answer to that one.'

'I didn't mean . . . I mean, it's nice. You're sort of—' he gestures, ill-advisedly, in the region of his chest—'curvy. You know.'

'Quit while you're ahead,' I say. 'Or at least alive.'

'I didn't mean—'

'Shut up.'

'I just—'

'Shut UP.'

'Okay.'

'There's your drink, Brad,' Gloria says, handing him a very full glass and then sitting down in an armchair to drink her own.

'His name's *Reuben*,' I say through gritted teeth.

'I know,' says Gloria. 'I just prefer to think of him as Brad.'

I take a deep breath. 'Reuben. What made you want to swap your lithe, rich Frenchwoman and Greek island for a three-star hotel in Whitby?'

His eyes – stupidly, stupidly blue – open wide in their I'm About To Lie way.

'Don't,' I snap. 'I'll know if you're bullshitting.'

'Will you?' He genuinely sounds a bit surprised.

'Oh, come *on*. You know I will.'

He looks at me, sideways though, so he hopes I won't notice. 'How do you do that?'

'I know you. I know how your tiny little brain works.'

'It wasn't really working out with Camille,' he says.

'You mean she dumped you?'

'It turned out not being able to talk to someone isn't the key to a happy relationship after all.'

'Well, who'd have thought?'

'And I had to come back and see Mum. She'd got herself in a bit of a state.' I look at him questioningly, but he doesn't elaborate. 'I went round to yours while I was home to see if anyone knew what had happened to you. Last thing I heard you were heading for the Lake District and then it all went quiet. I couldn't get you on your mobile. I thought maybe you'd been eaten by wolves or abducted by aliens or something. And then I got an email from you telling me to fuck off.'

'I was annonyed.'

'Yeah, I got that. Alice isn't very happy with you by the way. You might want to get yourself a new identity and flee the country.'

'Still doesn't explain why you're in Whitby, pretending to be my husband.'

'Sorry about the husband thing,' he says. 'I just said it. I thought it'd be funny. It *is* quite funny. Isn't it?'

I say nothing, just stare at him, arms folded.

'And obviously it was mainly the promise of the Seaview's impressive facilities that lured me to Whitby. The selection of teas. Coffee. *Shortbread fingers*.' He holds up a packet in case I don't know what they are. 'You kept quiet about them, didn't you? And slippers. Actual free slippers.'

He gestures to his feet, on which are a pair of said slippers, white towelling and utterly ridiculous with his jeans.

'*That's* mainly why I came.'

Still I say nothing.

'And I missed you,' he says at last.

And because I really do know how his tiny little mind works, I know he's telling the truth.


'Are you sure you don't mind?' I say to Gloria. We're alone in our room now, Gloria lying on the bed flicking through the TV channels, me towelling my hair dry after my shower. Reuben's gone up to his room on the next floor. 'Why don't you come and have dinner with me and Reuben?'

'No,' she says. 'I'd rather be on my own.'

I'm still trying to get my head around the fact that Reuben's here, torn between being excited that he's come all this way to see me, and feeling sick because I can no longer ignore the pregnancy. I either tell him or I don't. I feel rushed and pressured and resentful that he's turned up before I've had the chance to make that decision. Added to which I'm annoyed with him. It's presumptuous of him just to assume I'll be pleased to see him. This was my journey. Mine and Gloria's and he's gate-crashed it. I wanted to talk to her some more about all of it, about why we're here, about the baby who died, and Reuben being here has given her the perfect excuse to avoid it. But maybe that's how she wants it. Maybe she just wanted to come here to satisfy some need that I'll never know about, to relive a memory that she doesn't want to share. It's her decision after all, her story. Perhaps she doesn't want to tell it after all.

'But I don't like leaving you here on your own,' I say. 'And I wanted us to have time to talk. So you could tell me why we're here. You know. The rest of the story.'

She's been very quiet all afternoon, lost in thought. And what if she wanders off again? When she's on her own is when she's most likely to become disorientated, lose track of where she is, especially given that she's had a couple of very large gins now.

'I'm tired,' she says. 'And anyway, you two need some time together. Are you going to tell him?'

'I don't know,' I say. I feel ambushed, on the defensive. Reuben shouldn't be here. That wasn't the plan. This trip was about Gloria, not him. Typical that he'd just assume I'd be happy to see him. But why wouldn't he? I've always been before.

'I wanted to spend the evening with *you*,' I say to Gloria, sounding slightly like a whiny child. 'I wanted to talk about why we're here.'

'That can wait till tomorrow,' she says.

'Is there something particular you want to do?' I say. 'Somewhere you want to visit?'

If this was our final destination there must surely be a specific purpose. Again I feel a flash of worry that she might have forgotten what it is.

'I want to walk up there,' she says, pointing across the harbour to the cliff on the far side.

'To the abbey?' I say. 'It's a long way up. One hundred and ninety-nine steps, apparently. Are you sure?'

'That's the reason we've come all this way,' she says. 'I'm not going to let a few steps stop me.'

'Okay,' I say, wondering why it's so important to her. 'If you want to, that's what we'll do.' Then I add, 'I feel bad leaving you.'

'Well, don't, I'm fine here,' she says, and to be fair she seems happy enough, propped up on her bed with a gin and tonic on the bedside table and the cricket highlights on the widescreen television. 'I do like a chap in cricket whites, don't you?' she says, fondly.

'Okay, I'll see you later then. You can always come down to the bar if you fancy it? We could see you in there?'

'Yes,' she says. 'Maybe I'll do that.'

The hotel restaurant is unexpectedly posh, with starched white napkins folded into elaborate shapes and waiters in waistcoats. I feel horribly self-conscious and out of place, as though everyone's looking at me. Reuben seems completely relaxed, and while I'm staring at the menu he talks and talks about all the fantastic things he's done on his travels, all the friends he's made, how drunk he's got.

'If it was so brilliant why did you come back?' I snap at last.

'No need to be like that,' he says.

'You haven't asked me a single thing about me, about what I've been doing, about how Gloria is, how it's all been.'

'I just . . .'

'What? You just aren't interested in anyone other than you, Reuben. That's the truth of it.'

323

'That's not true!'

'Yes, Reuben, it is.'

We sit in silence, for a while staring at the menu, and I can feel this tightness building and building in my chest, the self-consciousness of being here in this stupid restaurant in a dress I don't really fit into any more, the hurt of Reuben leaving, the anger at his selfishness. Eventually I say, 'You know what, Reuben, this isn't me. I don't want confit of pheasant in a port jus. I don't want smoked venison or kohlrabi or pressed duck-liver terrine. I want to go out and get some fish and chips and I want to sit and eat them out there. You can do what you like.'

I get up from the table and almost mow down a hovering waistcoat-clad waiter as I march out without looking to check whether Reuben's following.

'You're the boss,' I hear Reuben say from behind me, and I think, *Yes, I am*. I never have been, where Reuben's concerned. But I have to be, now.

Outside it is still warm and the streets are full of holiday-makers, kids carrying candy floss and ice cream, dogs sniffing discarded burger boxes, overweight men with bright-red arms and necks and noses.

We head down the hill from the hotel without speaking to each other until we're close to the harbour. We stop at a chippy with a big queue and wait to be served. Then we walk back up to the clifftop and sit on a bench to eat our fish and chips. The abbey is dark across on the other cliff, and the sun is low, turning the sky pink. The sea is spread out below us. The chips are delicious, laden with salt and vinegar and very hot. We eat them in silence.

'Why did you go away without saying goodbye, Reuben?'

I hadn't expected to say it. I'd spent so much time convincing myself and everyone else that I didn't care, I'd almost forgotten that in fact it had hurt more than pretty much anything anyone's ever done to me.

'Apart from the fact that we'd had sex and then you pretended we hadn't and I didn't know what was going on, it was actually just a really hurtful thing to do to someone who's supposed to be your best friend.'

I'm on a roll now.

'I'm always defending you, Reuben. Always saying you're not as bad as everyone thinks. But maybe everyone else was right.'

He's quiet for a long time.

'You know what I said in Norfolk?' he says at last. 'That night. Remember?'

I stiffen and instinctively look away so that he can't see my face.

'Which particular thing?'

He takes a deep breath. 'That you understand me. That you're the only one who does.'

I half smile to myself. 'Yes,' I say. 'Yes, I remember.'

'And you know you asked whether I meant it?'

'And you wouldn't answer?' I say. 'Yes, I do remember that.'

'Well, I did mean it. Of course I did.'

'Then why wouldn't you answer me?'

'Because . . . I dunno. Because I was scared. And because I'm an idiot. But I meant it then and I still mean it. Honestly, Hattie. You are the only person who understands me.'

'Well, why did you go off to France then? Without even saying a proper goodbye, Reuben?' My eyes fill with tears

325

that I don't want him to see so I turn away and start walking towards the cliff edge.

'Hattie,' he says. 'Come back.'

He grabs hold of my arm and turns me round to him.

'I was scared,' he says. 'If we got together, Hattie, I'd screw it up. You know I would. I can't do relationships. I always hurt people. That's why I backed off. I'm sorry. It was stupid of me, I know. It's just, you're too important to me to risk that happening with you. It might sound like bullshit but it's true.'

'Do you honestly think I've been worrying about it?' I snap. 'That I've been sitting around wishing you'd stayed so we could be a couple?'

'Haven't you?'

'God! You're so arrogant. Listen to yourself!'

'Sorry,' he says, putting his head in his hands for a moment and then looking back up at me. 'I'm doing it all wrong. I'm saying it wrong. What I wanted to say is that the real reason I came back is . . . come travelling with me. We'd have the best time, I know we would. We could go anywhere. Just you and me. Italy? Florence, Rome, Capri? Or Prague; we could go to Prague. Or Spain. What about Barcelona?'

I watch him imagine us in all these places and want to let myself imagine it too. But I can't.

'Reuben,' I say. 'I want you to tell me one thing. If Camille hadn't dumped you, would you be here now? Would you have missed me so much that you couldn't bear not to be with me for another day? Or would you have just carried on having a great time and just sent me the occasional email if you could be bothered and didn't have anything more interesting to do?' He looks away from me and fiddles

326

with his lighter, flicking it on and off until it burns his thumb.

'I don't know,' he says.

'Yes.' I take his hands. 'You do. And so do I.'

'Hats—'

'Reuben,' I say. 'I'm pregnant. Eleven weeks pregnant.'

I watch his face change as he realizes what I'm saying, and it would be funny if it weren't for the fact that I know I am watching everything that has ever been between us change, and that it can never change back again.

'Oh,' he says at last.

'Yes,' I say.

'But— What . . . ?'

'I'm just telling you, so that you know.'

He stares at me.

'How long have you known?'

'A while.'

'Are you sure? It couldn't be a mistake?'

'No, Reuben, it couldn't be a mistake.'

He carries on staring at me, mouth slightly open. Probably the first time I've ever seen him lost for words.

'What are you going to do?' he says at last.

'I don't know.'

'You mean you might keep it?'

'I don't know, Reuben. I haven't decided. But I need to. I'm going home when Gloria's done whatever she needs to do here, and then I'm going to talk to Mum about it and make a decision.'

'What do you expect me to do?' he says, not looking at me. 'If you keep it?'

I look at him and I think of Gloria asking me what Reuben would say if he knew I was pregnant. *I know you*, I think.

*I love you*, I think. *But I know what I expect you to do.*

'I can only make my own decision. You'll have to make yours.'

'Hattie,' he says. 'This doesn't need to change anything. We can still go travelling. You can . . . sort this out and then come and join me.'

'I can't, Reuben.'

'Why not?'

I hold his face gently and I kiss him on the cheek.

'I'm going back to see Gloria now,' I say. 'I came here with her and I know she's got stuff she needs to tell me. The whole point of this trip has been to come here. I need to find out why. I said I'd see her in the bar.'

'But you can't,' he says.

'I can,' I say. 'Think about what I've told you and if you want to talk, come and find me later.'

I turn and walk away.

## Chapter twenty-seven

When I get into the hotel, the receptionist is looking flustered.

'Oh,' she says. 'Mrs Lockwood. We tried to call up to your room but there was no answer. It's your aunt. She's in the bar and she's . . . well, she's not very well.'

'What do you mean?' I say, panicking. I knew I shouldn't have left her.

'She's had a bit to drink,' the receptionist says in a loud whisper.

As soon as I get into the bar I can see that Gloria's drunk and not in a good way. She's not going to tell me stories or sing me songs this time.

Her face is fixed and disdainful, and I remember the first time we met. Hard to believe it was only a month ago. I think of how arrogant and cold she seemed. And she was. But I understand now that this means she's scared. Scared and sad. I think of what she said about her father too, about his drinking, about how he didn't laugh when he was drunk. I think of Sister Francis Whatsername saying Gloria was like her father. Maybe she was right. Maybe he was scared and sad too. Gloria's mum said he was different before the war.

'Yes?' she says as I sit down next to her at the table.

'I'm Hattie,' I say, uncertainly.

'I know who you are.'

'Just checking,' I say, cheerily. 'Are you okay?'

'Why wouldn't I be?'

'I don't know,' I say. 'You just seem a bit—'

'What?'

'You don't seem very happy,' I say.

'Of course I'm not happy,' she says. 'Why did you make me come back here, Gwen?'

'Gloria!' I say, trying to hold her arm but she shakes me off. 'Gloria, what are you talking about? It's me, Hattie. I didn't make you come back here. You wanted to come. Look, it's in the book.' I take the red notebook out of Gloria's handbag and try to hold it open on the page about the journey.

'I don't care,' she says. 'It was a mistake. All of it. I want to go home. Take me home.'

'What is it, Gloria? What's upsetting you?' I try to pull everything together in my mind, to work out what I know and whether that gives me a clue about why Gloria's acting like this. But it's like trying to do a jigsaw without all the pieces and not knowing what the final picture is supposed to be. Gloria fell in love with Sam. She had his baby. The baby was taken away. The baby died. And now we're here, in Whitby, to find 'the answer', but I don't know what the question is, and for all I know Gloria's forgotten it. And now she's completely losing the plot.

Reuben was right. It was mad coming here. I press my head into my hands and try to think.

'Is it to do with your son? The fact that he's dead? It must be hard even after all this time.' A thought occurs to me. 'He didn't die *here* did he? Your baby?'

330

'You know nothing about it.'

'Well, how can I? I only know what you've told me. But I understand that it must be very upsetting to remember all of this.'

'I hated my baby.'

'But, Gloria,' I say. 'I know it must have been scary, but you must have loved him.'

'Why?'

'Because he was yours. Yours and Sam's.'

'No,' she says, shaking her head. 'No, he wasn't.'

I stare at her. 'What do you mean?'

She says nothing. But her hands are twisting and knotting together in her lap.

'Gloria,' I say again. 'What do you mean?'

She's shaking her head. 'No,' she mutters. 'No.'

*No.* One little word. I feel a bit dizzy at the possibilities it opens up, off balance suddenly as the firm ground I thought I was standing on starts to give way. In my head I work through the rest of the story that Gloria's told me, trying to make sense of what she's saying. A thought forms in my mind. No . . . it can't be. But I realize I've made assumptions, filled in the gaps in Gloria's history the way I wanted them to be, made everything neat and tidy when in fact, of course, *of course,* it was messier than that. *No, he wasn't.* That's why she never saw Sam again. It all makes sense, even though I don't want it to. Gloria's baby wasn't his.

'It wasn't my fault,' she whispers. 'It wasn't my fault. You mustn't tell Gwen. You mustn't. She can't ever know. It wasn't my fault.'

'What wasn't, Gloria?' I take hold of her hand, scared to hear the answer. But that's nothing compared to the fear in her eyes as she looks into mine.

'I didn't know he'd be there.' Her voice is pleading, desperate. 'I didn't know.'

'Who?'

She shakes her head.

'Who was the father, Gloria? Why mustn't I tell Gwen?'

'I can't,' she says. 'I can't tell you any more.'

'Tell me.' I grip her hand. 'You've got to tell me. Gloria!' I say. 'I can't tell Gwen. She's dead.'

'What?' she says. 'What, Gwen? No, no, she can't be. Why are you saying that? Who are you?' She pulls her hand away from mine and walks away.

'Come back,' I say. 'Gloria!'

As I follow her, she stumbles. I run to her and help her to get her balance, and then take her arm, gently this time.

'Let me help you,' I say. 'Please, Gloria.'

She lets me put my arm round her and I lead her to the lift and up to our room.

In silence I help Gloria to get her shoes off and I lie her down on the bed.

All the while my mind is flipping through everything that's happened, making jittery leaps from the present to the past. I think about how strange it is that physical pain leaves you the moment it passes: you can remember it without flinching. And yet emotional pain is with you for ever. Remembering it can make you cry years later. Why is that? My head lolls and then snaps up suddenly. I glance at Gloria and it makes my stomach lurch a bit to see how small and frail she looks. I close my eyes again and as my mind drifts the doctor's words are playing in my head, and I think about how you can't judge by appearances, and about Gwen and her cardigan sleeves in summer, and about

Vinnie. I think about Sam, and about Vivienne and Danny, the imaginary children. I think about how Gloria told her baby she loved him when she thought they were both dying. I think about how the worst wounds are often the ones you can't see.

'I think I know what happened to you,' I say softly.

She says nothing.

'Do you remember what we were talking about, downstairs at the bar?'

Still she's silent, but I know she's listening. I take a deep breath.

'I know, Gloria. I know why you couldn't tell Sam,' I say, trying to keep my voice strong, although it wants to crack. 'Why you couldn't tell anyone.'

She doesn't say anything, or look at me. I reach for her hand, and she lets me take it.

'It's not fair,' I say, and I try to blink away tears because she's spent so many years, almost a whole lifetime, not crying about it. I don't have the right.

I can hardly bear to think about it. Her grip on my hand tightens a little. 'No,' she says at last. 'It's not fair.'

And when I look at her, a single tear has slipped from her eye onto the pillow.

I open the door quietly, even though I know no one will be there. I close it and smile into the quiet of the house. I will go and get changed out of my school uniform and then I'll meet Sam just as I have done for the last three weeks. I can't believe I've got away with skipping school to see him for this long; I was sure someone would have worked out that I'd forged the letter from Mum about the hospital appointments. I knew there'd be hell to pay when Father found out but I didn't care.

I pick up the hand mirror Mum keeps on the hall table and look at myself in it. It's a pretty mirror, gilt with flowers round the edge, and I smile at my reflection in it.

And then, behind me in the mirror, I see feet coming down the stairs out of the shadows. The feet are wearing black brogues, polished so that they shine. They are Vinnie's shoes.

I don't want to meet his eye. He always makes me feel uneasy, as though he's thinking things about me I don't really understand. There's always a little smile playing on his lips when he speaks to me. He makes my skin crawl.

'What are you doing here?' I say, trying not to sound as irritated as I feel.

'I could ask you the same question.' He smirks, as if he knows.

'They let us out early,' I say.

'Really,' he says. 'Well, that's lucky, isn't it? Nice for the two of us to get to spend some time alone together for once.'

It occurs to me that I've always avoided being alone with Vinnie. I'd never really thought about it before. 'Gwen asked me to drop by and pick up something for her.'

He makes no attempt to make it sound as though he's telling the truth.

'Really?' I say. 'What was that?'

'What does it matter?'

'Just curious,' I say.

'Well, I'll tell you what,' he says. 'You don't try to pick holes in my story and I'll do you the same favour. I'm not sure either of them would stand up to scrutiny, are you?'

'What do you mean?' I say.

'It's just Brenda Onions happened to mention to me that she could have sworn she'd seen you come home early last Friday as well. And the Friday before, too. And the one before that. They letting you out early every Friday, are they? Or might you be telling me fibs?'

I try to push past him.

He catches my arm just above the elbow, gripping it tight, and I drop the mirror.

It falls onto the tiled floor and shatters.

'Look what you've done now!' I say.

'Oh dear,' he says. 'Seven years' bad luck, so they say.'

'Let go of me,' I say, trying to struggle free, but he grips my arm tighter.

'Ow!' I look at him, surprised and annoyed. Not scared. 'That hurts.'

He smiles.

'Does it?' His face is close enough to mine that I can see the sweat glisten on his skin, and that he's got something grey caught between his teeth. I can smell stale smoke on his breath, mixed with the sickly sweet smell of hair pomade.

'Yes,' I say, trying to wrench my arm free. 'What are you doing, Vinnie? Let go, will you. It's not funny.'

I'm still feeling more annoyed than scared. I'd been looking forward to this afternoon all week. On the bus on the way here I'd thought about nothing but Sam and meeting him again: the smell of him, the way he listened intently to everything I said as though it was the most interesting and important thing anyone had ever said, the feel of his lips on mine.

Vinnie laughs, but in his eyes I can see that he doesn't really find it funny either, and he tightens his grip on my arm so that now it really hurts. I think of Gwen's cardigan that she'd worn even on that glaring hot day, the bruises underneath that she'd tried to laugh off. I think of Ursula the bear. *Daddy loves Mummy. That's all that matters, isn't it?'* Something twists in my stomach.

'Come on,' he says, pulling me through into the living room. 'I just want a little dance.'

He pulls me towards him and presses my body against him with one hand, still gripping my arm too tightly in the other. Then he lets go of my wrist and presses my head in against his chest and he sings as he moves me from side to side.

'I've always liked you, Gloria, you know that. Always said you'd be a beauty when you grew up, didn't I? And now look at you.' His eyes slide down my body in a way that makes me want to cover myself up more, even though my school uniform covers me almost completely. 'All grown up.'

'I mean it, Vinnie,' I say, trying to twist and wriggle free. 'Don't be a bloody idiot. Why would I want to dance with you?'

336

He puts his hand on the back of my neck.

'You're disgusting!' I say. 'I wish Gwen had never married you.'

And then his face changes. He isn't laughing any more.

It comes from nowhere before I've realized what's happening: a flash of white light and pain through my head and it takes me a few seconds to understand that he's hit me, hard, across the face. I lose my balance and my bearings, stumbling, and when I come to I'm pressed up against the wall and Vinnie's holding me there with his body. I try to push him away but he grabs my wrists and pushes his face close up against mine so that I can feel the moist warmth of his breath on my skin.

'Think you're clever, don't you? Think you're better than the rest of us?'

He shakes his head, and smiles in a way that makes me think he's going to hit me again. 'There's nothing special about you, Gloria,' he says, with such force that flecks of spit fly out and I feel them land on my face.

I think maybe he's going to kiss me and I brace myself for it. He must be drunk, I think. And then I realize he's undoing the buckle of his belt with the hand that isn't pinning my wrists to the wall, and with his leg he forces mine apart, and it's then that I start to understand; it's then that I panic.

'No!' I say, and although I'm scared I'm angry too. Angry that he hit me, angry that he thinks he can touch me, angry that he's laughing at me. 'Get off me!'

I try to twist my arm so that I can elbow him, try to lift my leg and knee him in the private parts but I can't. He's too strong.

'Pretending to put up a fight?' he says, his voice sneering and breathless. 'I like that. But we all know what girls like you mean when they say no.'

I can't move. I'm trapped, and his hand is where it shouldn't be and I gasp with the shock and disgust and intimacy of it and now, only now, do I realize how scared I should be.

I understand, looking into Vinnie's eyes for a moment, that he hates me, and I'd never realized that what he's about to do could be an act of hate. It's not until he's pulling the buttons of my school shirt apart and I feel his hand up under my skirt that I know how powerless I am. He watches me realize; I see the triumph in his eyes and I want to scream, but the fear numbs me so that I can't speak or move.

'Yeah,' he says. 'Just like all the others underneath.'

Even now I don't really know what's about to happen, because for all I act as though I know everything there is to know about men, I've only a very theoretical understanding of what sex involves. Sam and I have never done anything much more than kiss, much as I've wanted to. 'Don't you want to?' I'd asked him. He laughed. 'Of course! But you're special. I love you, Gloria. I want it to be right.'

And this isn't anything like what I'd imagined with Sam, which would have been gentle and loving and thrilling and maybe a little awkward.

'So you'll do it with that darkie but you think you're too good for me, is that it?' Vinnie says as I struggle. And there's so many things in my head I can't get them all out.

*It's not like that*, I want to say.

*I've never.*

*I love Sam.*

*I love Gwen.*

*Why?*

*Please don't.*

*Please stop.*

But all that comes out is a crying sound, and then he shoves his tongue in my mouth and I can't breathe. He's pulling. And then there's pain like I've never felt before, deep inside me, like being ripped apart.

He's not looking at me now. My face is pressed into the shoulder of his suit as he pushes inside me, crushing me again and again into the wall. I stare up at the place on the wall opposite where the wallpaper join doesn't align and focus on that, on nothing else that is happening. I feel myself leave my body, separate off from it. I understand at last why my mother does it. Sometimes it is the only way to escape.

It stops eventually. I sink to the floor, the wall behind me holding me up, and I wonder if I will be sick.

'So you were a virgin,' Vinnie says, looking at me appraisingly as he pulls out a packet of cigarettes from the pocket of his jacket, which is hanging from the back of an armchair. 'Oh well.' He half smiles as he lights one. 'Not any more.'

He winks at me as he goes.

'I won't tell if you don't,' he says, smiling. 'It can be our little secret, eh? After all, we don't want Gwen to know what a little whore her sister is, do we? 'It'd be a bit of a shock for her, and we don't want to give her a shock, do we? Not in her condition.'

I stare at him. *In her condition?* Does he mean a baby?

'That's right,' he says. 'Gwen's expecting. She's so happy, Gloria. It's what she's always wanted. Nice house, nice husband, nice baby. We're going to be a real family at last.'

He says it mockingly, laughing at Gwen's naivety and trust and hope, at her love for him. I feel sick thinking about Gwen, about the fact that she must be doing something right now, while I am here, stockings laddered, the skirting board digging into my back, as Vinnie smokes and laughs at her. Gardening

339

perhaps; she loves her garden. Sweet peas and roses, carrots and runner beans in the vegetable patch. Or baking in that shiny fitted kitchen of hers. Cooking Vinnie's tea most likely, ready for when he gets home.

I feel sick thinking of her happiness as she does it, the secret smile, the hand resting for a moment on the apron that covers her skirt, because of that hidden, tiny, longed-for life that is growing inside her.

I feel sick to think that she is carrying a baby who will be Vinnie's child.

'Well, aren't you going to congratulate me?' he says.

He looks at me, still sprawled where he left me with my back to the wall. I try to do up the buttons of my blouse, to cover myself beneath his gaze, but my hands are shaking so much I can't do it.

He laughs. 'See, Gloria,' he says. 'You're nothing special. You're no different from anyone else.'

I don't move, even when he is gone. I don't think I can, or that I ever will be able to. I sit with my back against the wall, my legs splayed bare in front of me. I want to cover them up but there is nothing within reach and I can't contemplate standing up or even crawling. All of me hurts. I feel fragile, as if moving might break me, limbs snapping off, nails cracking, teeth falling out until I am just a pile of bones.

The room is silent. I stare at the place on the wall where the paper is wrong for a long time. My eye throbs where he hit me, it's closing up and I can't see properly out of it. Everything goes a little out of focus and fades.

Time has passed, I realize. I don't know how much, but the sunlight coming in the window has turned to shadow, the sun has moved. I have to move before anyone gets home. As slowly as I can, I push myself up onto my knees, and I grip onto the back of the wingback armchair to pull myself up. I cling to it to stop myself falling down. Awkwardly I shuffle towards the kitchen, the pain between my legs making it almost impossible to walk without crying out.

When I get to the sink, I drink water straight from it, letting it run down my chin, spitting it out, trying to rid myself of the taste of him. Then I rinse all trace of Vinnie from between my legs with water from the tap. I want to scrub the skin; I would peel it from me to get rid of his touch, to obliterate him completely from my body. But how can I remove him from inside me? It is not possible.

I am bruised and swollen and cut and I have to stop myself from crying out as the water touches me. I splash water onto my face and dab iodine from the tin Mum keeps under the sink onto my closed eyelid, as I have seen her do to her own face countless times, her expression blank. When I have finished, I stand and stare at the plates draining at the side of the sink, my feet bare on the cold lino. All this I do under the gaze of Jesus with his burning, sacred heart. I can feel him there, watching, but I cannot meet his eye. I am shivering. My teeth chatter.

There is no fire burning in me. It has gone out.

When I am done I make my way slowly back into the sitting room to pick up the discarded clothes that lie on the floor and I go upstairs to change them. As I pass through the hall I pick up the hand mirror from the floor. The cracked glass deforms my face, but even so I can clearly see my closed eye red and purple already. My skin and lips are pale. My open eye is empty-looking, Already I am inventing a story about how I jumped from the back of the bus while it was still moving, how I caught my foot on the kerb and fell onto the pavement. I can hear myself telling it, laughing at myself, describing the rather dashing man who picked me up and dusted me down, lent me his handkerchief like a gent to clean my eye. I see Gwen not sure whether to laugh or scold. 'Trust you,' she's saying. I put the mirror face down on the sideboard and, like I used to when I was a child, clamber upstairs on my hands and knees. I collapse onto my bed, but sitting is too painful, so I lie down, my face against the candlewick counterpane, facing the wall with the pink-flowered wallpaper that I have traced with my finger since I was a little girl.

It is only now, when I think about Sam waiting for me at the gates of the park, expectant, waiting and waiting until he realizes I'm not coming, but still waiting just in case, as the shadows lengthen, that I begin to cry.

After she has told me I hold Gloria's hand until her eyes close and her breathing slows. I watch as she sleeps. My head is so full of what she's told me that I can't think straight. Vinnie – my own grandfather – he'd done that to Gloria. He'd done that while Nan was pregnant with dad. I can hardly breathe with the shock of it, with the anger and sadness.

There's a quiet knock on the door and I get up to answer it. It's Reuben.

'Is everything okay?' he says.

'No,' I say. 'Not really.'

'What is it?'

'Gloria,' I say. 'She's pretty upset. It's a long story.'

'You look upset too,' he says.

'Yes.'

He pauses uncertainly.

'Look, about earlier, about what you told me—'

'Reuben, I can't do this now. We can talk in the morning. I'm too tired and I just need to be with Gloria. She's sleeping but I don't want to leave her on her own in case she wakes up.'

'Can I come in anyway?' I look doubtful. 'Come on, Hats. I've come all the way from Greece on an overnight budget airline packed with drunk people and annoying kids to see you—'

'And your mum.'

'Well—'

'And to get away from your ex-girlfriend—' I stop and shut my eyes for a minute. 'Look, I don't want to have an argument.'

Gloria and everything she's been through is raw in my mind; it hurts to think about it. My mind is working on it feverishly, trying to make sense of this thing, this awful thing that she's lived with for so many years that no one knew anything about.

Our journey has ended so differently from how I thought it would. I can't quite get my head around it.

And now I need to think about me, about what I'm going to do. But I can't. Not with Reuben here.

I look at him. Despite the tan he looks rough, with stubble that's too long but not quite a beard, dark shadows under his eyes. I remember, fleetingly, waking up next to him in the house in Norfolk, the early-morning sunlight streaming in through the windows, the curtains we failed to close. I want to reach out and trace his cheekbone with my finger as I did then, to rest my head on his chest so that I can feel the beat of his heart. I realize I am crying. *It's the hormones*, I tell myself. *And it's been a long day and I'm tired.*

But it's not the hormones making me cry.

I'm not crying because I'm tired.

I'm not even crying because I'm pregnant and I don't know what to do about it.

I'm crying because I am *in* love with Reuben.

I have been in love with him since the first time I saw

him. Completely and utterly and with all my heart and I have never admitted it, not even to myself.

And I am crying, too, because he is not in love with me.

'Hattie,' he says, reaching out to me, but I turn away back into the room. He follows me.

I wipe my eyes on the sleeve of my top.

'I need to go out,' I say to him. 'I need to clear my head.'

'I'll come with you.'

'No,' I say. 'Stay with Gloria, to make sure she's safe till I get back. Will you do that for me?'

He hesitates and I lose patience.

'Come on, Reuben. It's all I'm asking of you. Just this one thing.'

'Okay.' he says. 'Course I'll look after her for you.'

I pick up my jacket and purse and car keys and close the door of the room behind me as quietly as I can.

The last sunlight has long gone and the air is cool now. The town is loud with Friday-night noise, shouting and laughing and the beat of music coming from a club somewhere down the road from the hotel. I feel distant from it all, not part of the world around me. I don't know where I'm going. All I know is that I have to get away from here, away from Reuben and Gloria and away from everything. I need quiet and peace and space.

I get in the car, which smells pretty rank, and I drive it out of the car park and I keep on driving in the direction that I think is more or less the way we came into the town and then I keep on driving, into the darkness, out on to the moors.

I don't know where I'm going, I just want to be far away from the world. I don't look at road signs. The grey-shadowed moors roll around me like a stormy sea. I don't put any music on; I just drive in the silence. There are few cars on the road and I'm glad of it. I want to be the only person alive.

I don't know how long I've been driving for. All I know is that it's very late.

Eventually I pull over and switch off the engine.

I'm alone in the middle of the moors. It is completely quiet except for the wind. It is dark and beautiful. Above, the sky is black and cloudless and the stars are bright. I open the door of the car and stare up at them, hugging myself in the cold. There is the North Star, fixed and unmoving. I think of Gloria and of Dad.

'There's so many of them,' I'd said to Dad, that time when we were on holiday. 'Why can't we see them when we're at home? Where do they go?'

He laughed. 'They're always there,' he said. 'You have to be somewhere really dark to see them.'

I stare at them now, as I did then, astonished by the beauty of them, the pure, white, fierce light that has travelled so far through the dark to get to me.

The wind is rushing through the heather around me and I walk into it a little way, not too far because I can't see my feet in the thick darkness, but enough. I'm struck by the fact that running to the moors in the middle of the night seems rather melodramatic, not a very me thing to do at all, but it doesn't feel melodramatic. It feels right. I feel calmer here, freer, able to think more clearly, able to anchor myself in the moment, able to slow the frenzy of everything going on in my head and examine it more closely.

I'm shivering now, so I get back into the car. I sit and think for a while, about Gloria and everything that has happened to her, about how scared she must have been then and how scared she must be now. I think of Reuben and how certain he always seemed and how lost he is. I think about Mum, and Carl, and how concerned and kind he sounded on the phone, and Alice and Ollie singing Beetels songs and eating nutrishus food and I miss them all so forcefully, and unexpectedly, that if I had a phone signal I'd call them just to hear their voices. Although that might not go down all that well, given that it's about two a.m.

As it is, I clamber into the back and find Gloria's heavy ancient fur coat there. I'm grateful for it, despite the slightly musty smell, and I lie down, pulling it over me. Usually I'd be worrying about everything from axe-murderers to wolves to drunk drivers crashing into me. But I don't feel worried at all. I feel calm and peaceful as my eyes close and heavy dark sleep wraps itself round me.

I dream scattered, fragments of dreams – there are feet coming downstairs, feet in black shoes, and then inexplicably I'm on a beach and the sea is coming in fast and I am running to get away from it, scrambling on rocks. I turn round to look at the sea and realize I'm completely cut off, surrounded by water and on a rock. Further out are Ollie and Alice, and I try to call to them to tell them they'll be okay, that help will come, but my voice won't work and when eventually the girl turns round to me she is not Alice but a girl I don't know . . .

I wake in grey light, chilly despite Gloria's coat. My eyes feel gritty – I left my contact lenses in all night, I realize – and my limbs are achy and stiff. I lie for a while longer, watching the dawn gradually lighten the sky. I stretch my neck from side to side, trying to ease out the crick that has come from a night of sleeping in a car. Eventually I lever myself carefully up to a sitting position, pulling my knees

347

up to my chest and wrapping Gloria's coat tightly round me. There's something hard and heavy in the coat, and I reach into the pocket to see what it is, but it's empty. Confused, I press the outline of the thing through the fur of the coat. It's round or oval, and not in the pocket, but right at the bottom of the coat. Sure enough, when I reach into the pocket a second time I can feel a hole and I realize that whatever it is has slipped though the hole into the lining of the coat.

I poke my fingers down through the hole and feel around. Eventually they close round something cold: metal, and a chain. I pull it out carefully and look at it. It's Gloria's silver locket, engraved with a flower pattern. Gently I press the clasp and the two sides of the locket spring open. Inside are two black-and-white photos. On the left is Gloria looking very young, looking into the camera, not smiling, beautiful, half challenging. The right half contains a picture of a baby: Gloria's baby. I look at it for a long time before finally starting the engine and heading back to the hotel.

As I drive, my thoughts crystallize in my mind. I feel sad and a bit scared, but I also feel calm because I know now. I know what I need to say to Reuben and I know what I need to do.

After I've driven for a while I come to a small town. I park the car and walk along the high street to a café that's brightly painted with a smell of breakfast wafting from it.

Inside it's warm and cosy, all primrose-coloured paint and pine, and pretty prints on the wall that are for sale. I feel grey and crumpled after my night of strange dreams curled up in the back seat of the car. I order a tea and a bacon sandwich and sit down at the table. When I check my phone there are a couple of bars of reception and I see that I've got a message. I panic, thinking it might be the hotel to say something has happened to Gloria. A little bit of me hopes it will be Reuben, to check that I'm okay.

The message is from Ollie. I listen to his clear, high voice, thinking how grown-up he sounds, how he changes every day without me noticing and how it has been nearly two weeks since I last saw him and how desperate I am to see him now.

He says: *'Hi, Hattie, it's Ollie here. I expect you're still asleep but I woke up really early and I wanted to call you because I had a really weird dream that you were in and I wanted to check that you were okay because you weren't okay in the dream and it made me worried about you. Alice said I was silly; it was only a dream and dreams are just your brain getting rid of all the stuff it doesn't need and she said it was probably just because we had cheese toasties for tea because it was Carl's Hips, Bums 'n' Tums night and Mum did tea. But Mum said I should phone because you might reply to me and she's worried about you too. Anyway, Hattie, I love you and so does Alice. We all do and you have to come home soon. Me and Alice want pancakes and no one else can do them. Carl made us have fruit salad for breakfast today even though it's Saturday. Alice told him she was going to call Childline and Carl told her she was ungrateful and had no idea how lucky she was and there was a big row and Alice buried his favourite trainers in the garden. I hope the old lady is okay. She was in my dream too. Love you more than the whole entire world, Hattie. Bye.'*

'You all right, love?'

The woman from behind the counter, who is pretty with grey-streaked hair swept back into a loose knot and green glass earrings, puts down a steaming cup of tea and a bacon sandwich in front of me, then hesitates and sits down in the other chair at my table and leans over to me.

'You look upset. Anything I can do?'

I wipe my eyes and shake my head.

'Not bad news?'

'No, nothing like that.'

'A boy then, is it?'

'No. Well, yes and no.'

She nods.

'Shame,' she says. 'Lovely girl like you.'

'It's just . . . I'm missing my family. Just feeling a bit homesick.'

'Where are you from?'

'London.'

She grimaces. 'Not my cup of tea, love. But of course, wherever your loved ones are, that's where home is, isn't it?'

I nod.

'You sure you're okay? You look awfully pale.'

'I didn't get much sleep,' I say.

'Worrying about this boy of yours?'

'Partly.'

'Well, you take your time, love. I'll bring you over another pot of tea on the house.'

Once I've eaten the sandwich and drunk the tea I feel better. I scan the newspaper that someone's left on the table, which is all about a heatwave – why is the weather always news? – and then I look out of the window and watch the Saturday-morning activity around me: men in waxed jackets walking beefy yellow Labradors, families pushing buggies, toddlers waddling along in wellies, an old lady with a shopping trolley, people stopping to talk to each other and catch up on the gossip. What would it be like to live somewhere like this? I try to imagine me and Reuben with jobs and a mortgage, saving up for holidays and a trampoline in the garden. I almost smile it's so ridiculous. We'd last about five minutes. It's not what he wants. I know that. It's not what I want either. Not now. Maybe not ever. But what do I want?

So much of my thinking about the pregnancy has been centred around Reuben. I couldn't go ahead with it because of Reuben. Reuben couldn't be a dad so therefore I couldn't have the baby. I'd have an abortion without anyone knowing and then things could carry on just the same as they always had been with Reuben.

But it's not about Reuben. This is my decision. I have to make it. That is my responsibility and it is also my right. Gloria was right. I can't know I'm making the right choice, but it is *my* choice. I wish I didn't have to make it, but I'm glad I can. It's a choice Gloria and all those girls like her never had.

I take the locket out of my pocket and look at it again. Gloria's young, beautiful face, the baby's wide eyes. It all seems so unbearably sad. So unfair. She didn't have a choice. Not about any of it. I think of Edie too, of what she suffered handing her baby over. The cruelty of it, the power- lessness those girls must have felt. It was so kind of her to send this locket to Gloria, to care for her and her baby enough to know that it was an important thing to do. And, whatever Gloria's conflicting emotions are, Edie was right. It was important. That much is clear from the fact that Gloria has kept the locket all this time. I wonder again when he died, how Gloria knows. Does she really know or does she just feel that she knows: an instinctive feeling? I want to ask her about it, but I can't. Not now. It isn't fair. If she wants to tell me, she will. It is not a story, a mystery for me to solve. It is her life.

I have to get back to Whitby, to make sure she's all right. I need to be there for her. I'll let her tell me what she needs to. And then I'll take her home.

I feel strangely calm as I get back to the car, calmer than I have done since I found out I was pregnant. I know I will make the right decision for myself. I'm not scared any more. As I reach the car I look round one last time at the moors spreading all around me into the distance, to where they meet the sky and I tip my head back to the sun and think of Gloria spinning on the Common, the joy of being alive. I feel it inside me. It is a wonderful, miraculous thing to be alive.

When I get back to the car I look at myself in the mirror. I look pretty awful, tired and wrung out and hair more prone to frizz than ever before. But I don't care. I rummage around under my seat and sure enough a lipstick that fell out of my bag a few days ago is lurking there, along with a few stray sweets, a random conker and one of Alice's socks. Bit of lippy. Bit of mascara. Could be better. Could be a lot better. Could also be worse. I'll have a hot shower when I get back, wrap myself in a lovely fluffy, white hotel towel and it will all be okay. Everything will be okay.

I start the engine and put on the radio. As I drive out through the moors I think again how beautiful they are and how lucky I am to be alive, and I look around at the sky and I can see storms on the horizon, dark clouds and bands of rain darkening the sky and then blue sky and sunshine; it is all there and all so big and I think of how the stars are always there even when we can't see them, and again I feel tiny, a tiny speck on the surface of a spinning rock, but instead of feeling scared by it and overwhelmed by it I feel glad; I feel miraculous and impossibly lucky to be alive and to be here, now. And, as I think this, I realize that the song on the radio is 'Here Comes the Sun' and I laugh to myself about Alice's fury about the Beetels and I turn it up loud and I put my foot down because the road is empty and I speed my way through the moors—

A rabbit runs out into the road just in front of me as I'm taking a corner – a little baby rabbit—

I think of Fiver and Ollie—

I try to veer out of the way but I'm too late and the car is out of control and there's a stone wall right in front of me and I can't turn the steering wheel fast enough—

I hear myself scream and the wall is in front of the windscreen and there's a *SMASH*—

and as it goes dark I think

*ReubenOllieAliceMumGloriaCarlKat*

and I think

*I can't die yet because—*

## Chapter twenty-eight

In the dark there are voices.

Mostly the voices say things that don't make a whole lot of sense about blood pressure and other stuff I don't understand.

I want to ask them for a drink because I'm unbelievably thirsty.

I want to ask them if I'm dead but then if I was dead I wouldn't be thirsty. Or would I? Who knows? Well, no one, obviously . . .

Sometimes I can't hear what the voices are saying. Sometimes I think I know the voices but they drift in and out and sometimes they aren't real voices at all but people in my dreams.

Alice is there. She says, *'You've got to wake up, Hattie. I've brought you Jaffa Cakes.'*

Ollie reads his favourite bit of *Watership Down*.

Reuben is crying. He says, *'I'm really sorry. I've got to go.'*

Kat says, *'Jeeeezus, I turn my back for FIVE MINUTES and this is what happens. Just as well I'm coming back home. You need keeping an eye on.'*

Mum says, *'Don't worry, we're waiting for you, Hattie. Don't worry about anything.'*

Carl says, *'I know I'm not your dad, Hats, but if anything happened to you I don't know what I'd do.'*

Gloria doesn't say anything. I know she's there because she smells of perfume and smoke. I wish she would speak. If I'm going to die I want her to tell me why we came, why she brought me here. I want to know what the answer is.

I open my eyes slowly. I feel tired in the way that you do when you've slept too long: heavy and headachy. The room seems very bright.

'Hattie?' It's Mum. 'Oh my God, Carl, she's waking up. Hattie, it's me, Mum.'

'I know,' I croak. 'I can see that. Can I have a drink?'

'Of course, sweetheart. Oh thank God. Call the nurse, Carl, tell her Hattie's awake.'

Carl stands up, tears trickling down his cheeks. 'Thank God,' he says, bending down to kiss me on the forehead. 'Welcome back, Hats.' Then he hurries off.

I try and piece together everything that happened.

'I was driving . . .' I say.

'You crashed. That was four days ago.'

'Gloria?'

'She's fine,' Mum says. 'One of the people at the hotel was very helpful, put us in touch with a friend of hers who rents out holiday cottages. We've all been staying together. Kat too. She'd been calling your mobile so Carl let her know what had happened and she came straight away.'

'Reuben?' I croak.

Mum's face closes up. 'He had to go, I'm afraid. He had a flight booked.'

'Mum,' I say, and I try carefully to think of the words, a way of saying it that won't make her disappointed or angry. 'I'm . . . I was pregnant.'

'Oh, sweetheart,' she says, and her voice is a bit wobbly. 'I know. When they called us to say you'd had an accident, Carl told me. Don't be angry with him. He had to.'

'Yeah,' I say. 'I suppose.'

'I wish you'd told me.'

'Am I still?'

The moment before she answers seems to stretch and warp and I feel light-headed. I can feel my heartbeat, and I can't work out whether I'm scared of her saying I am or scared of her saying I'm not.

'Yes,' she says. 'You're still pregnant.'

'I think I'm going to be sick,' I say and Mum scrambles for a container, eventually tipping bottles of water, Mars bars and a banana out of a carrier bag and holding it in front of me just in time.

When I stop being sick she hands me a bottle of water and kisses the top of my head while I gulp at it. Then she disappears off to dispose of the bag and find a nurse, and I lie back on the pillow, weak. Too weak to think. I only have enough energy to feel.

And I feel relieved. I don't want to. But in that instant, inescapably, it is how I feel. My only just conscious brain is relieved that I am alive.

Relieved that Mum knows.

Relieved that Reuben is gone. Heartbroken, but relieved. Devastated even. But still relieved. I was right: I do know him. And the fact that he's left me now means that I'm not just waiting for him to do it later.

And, most of all, I find that I'm relieved that I am still pregnant.

'Hattie, why didn't you tell me?' Mum says, and I can tell she's trying not to cry. 'All the time you've been unconscious I've been sitting here watching you and I've been going over and over it. Why did she not tell me? Am I such a bad mother that my own daughter can't turn to me when she needs me? Is she scared of me? Please tell me you're not scared of me, Hattie. Did you think I'd be angry?'

'No—' I try to interrupt, but she's on a roll.

'You're my baby, Hattie. I can't bear that you felt you couldn't share this with me.'

She's crying now, properly. And seeing her tears makes me cry too.

'I thought you might not wake up,' she says. 'When we got the phone call to say you'd had an accident. And then when we got here and you just looked so pale and lifeless and . . . small. And Carl had told me on the way up, he'd told me you were pregnant. He'd found the tests you'd hidden under the bed. And I thought I might never be able to tell you how much I love you and that I'll always be there for you and—'

'*Mum*,' I say. 'Shut up a minute, will you? I know all that. I didn't feel scared of you. I felt . . . stupid. I felt embarrassed. I was sort of in denial about it.'

'You told Gloria,' she says.

'I didn't mean to. I was angry. I only said it to shut her up.'

'Yes, well that I can quite believe. We've been getting to know each other this week.'

I smile. 'How's that been going?'

357

Mum rolls her eyes but in a funny way rather than a genuinely annoyed way. I'm relieved. I can tell she likes Gloria. I don't know why it matters, but it does. 'Carl's good with her,' Mum says. 'You know he's got a bit of a way with the older ladies. And she likes me as long as I keep her supplied with large gin and tonics. She's been worried about you.'

'Where is she now?'

'At the pub across the road with Alice.'

I laugh, which makes my head and chest hurt. 'Jesus,' I say. 'What could possibly go wrong? I hope you've got all emergency services on standby.'

'Don't worry,' Mum says. 'We've got to know the landlady rather well over the last few days. She'll keep an eye on them.'

'I hope she's got good insurance cover.'

'Where's Ollie?'

'He's here. With Kat.'

'Kat's here?'

'Yes. I called her when we were driving up to let her know what'd happened. She came straight away. She'll be so relieved.'

I feel a flood of happiness.

'You told her too. About being pregnant.'

'She's my friend.'

'I'm your *mum*.'

'Exactly! I didn't want to upset you. Or disappoint you. That's all. I didn't want you to be worried. I would have told you. I just needed to get my head round it.'

'Oh, Hattie. I'm not disappointed in you,' she says. 'Although, you know. *Contraception?*'

'I know, Mum.'

'I know. I'm sorry.' She sighs and takes my hand. 'I just wish you didn't have to deal with this.'

I lie back.

'Do you know what you're going to do?' she says, and I can tell from the way she says it that she's scared to ask, scared of the answer I'll give. I don't know whether it's because she knows the answer she hopes I'll give, and she's worried it's not the one I'm going to give her. Or maybe it's just because of what Gloria said: that there's no choice that won't be hard, that won't hurt, that I won't regret.

I pause. 'I think so.'

She stops and looks at me, pushes the hair back from my face.

'I had an abortion, you know,' she says quietly.

I stare at her. 'When?'

'When the twins were about a year old. Things weren't good between me and your dad at the time. We tried, but I think we both knew the marriage wasn't going to last. I could barely cope with the twins as it was.'

I think about how it must have been for Mum.

'I knew an abortion was the right thing. I've never felt guilty about it.'

'Why did things go wrong with you and Dad?'

She sighs and smooths the bed sheet. 'Lots of reasons,' she says. 'We should never have got married. He didn't want a domestic life. I thought we were in love, but really I think I found your dad exciting and a bit dangerous. Now I've got Carl I know what love is.'

I look at her doubtfully and she laughs.

'I know you think Carl's a bit dim and superficial.'

'No!' I say. She looks at me, eyebrows raised. 'Well, not exactly,' I concede. 'Dim *and* superficial. That's a bit harsh.'

'You think he's all about six-packs and biceps and stuff that you don't think is important. But he's not shallow. It's not all vanity. You know, the reason all the old ladies want him to do their personal training sessions is because he listens to them, he takes them seriously, he treats them with respect. He wants them to feel good about themselves. He understands people.'

I think of the times Carl has somehow managed to know what I'm feeling without me telling him. Why have I never given him credit for that? I always found it irritating more than anything, but why?

'I suppose it's just he's so different from Dad and I kind of . . .'

I can't think of the right way to explain it. My head is throbbing and my mouth is dry. Everything feels like an effort.

'You resent him for that?'

'No! I don't resent Carl,' I say. But as I say it I'm suddenly not sure. 'I suppose I just always felt like maybe he wasn't really good enough for you.'

'Or good enough to take your dad's place?'

I think about it. 'Maybe.' I'd never thought of it like that but maybe Carl had always suffered because I'd inevitably compared him with Dad. Not even with Dad, really, but with the dashing, heroic father I'd created by filling in the gaps left by his absence, even before he died, with what I wanted to be true. Not very fair, comparing someone with a fairy tale.

'There are different ways of being brave, Hattie,' Mum says, taking my hand. 'Putting yourself in physical danger isn't the only way.'

'I know that, Mum,' I say. 'I'm not a little kid.'

'Don't be annoyed,' she says, soothing. 'I wasn't having a dig at your dad. He was brave. He really was. Put him in front of a man with a gun or stand him in a marketplace where a bomb's just gone off and he was fearless. But you know there was stuff he couldn't face too. Boredom. The claustrophobia of family, responsibility. Of love even. Being needed. That stuff scared him.'

I think about what she's saying. 'Do you mean he didn't love us?'

'No,' she says. 'Not at all. he did. Very much. I'm just saying that facing up to the realities of life, accepting the truth about yourself and other people, accepting responsibility, that's hard. It's brave in a different way. And on that score, no one will ever beat Carl, Hattie. He loves me. And you. He's been beside himself while you've been in here.'

'So why did you call the wedding off?'

She looks away.

'I got married before, Hattie, and it was a mistake.'

'But he really loves you.'

'And I really love him. That's not what this is about.'

'What is it about then?'

'Love and marriage aren't the same thing.'

'So you're scared it'll go wrong like last time?'

'It's not as simple as that. It's not just me who'll get hurt if it doesn't work out. It's Carl too. I just don't see why we can't carry on like we are. What I feel for Carl – it's not about a big dress and flowers and themed tables and co-ordinating wedding favours, whatever they are. I never did listen properly while he was trying to explain it to me. I never wanted the big showy thing with the ice sculptures and the bubbles and the bloody doves—'

'Doves?'

She sighs. 'Don't ask.'

'Okay. Well, I get that. I wasn't wild about the whole peach-bridesmaid thing as you know—'

'Exactly! I thought you'd be with me on this one.'

'But just because you don't want all that doesn't mean you can't get married, does it? If you said to Carl that you wanted to make it a quiet thing he might be a bit disappointed but he wouldn't really care as long as he got to marry you. You know he would. I reckon you're just using that as an excuse. I think you're just scared.'

'Maybe I am!' Mum says, her voice louder. 'And maybe I'm allowed to be. That's exactly what I'm trying to say to you, love, about *your* decision.'

'Don't try to change the subject—'

'I'm not! This is exactly what I mean. It's okay to say "I'm not ready and I don't want to make a choice that will hurt me and risk hurting another person" – a person who doesn't even exist yet – and I mean *really* hurting them, Hattie, because nothing could be more hurtful than growing up feeling resented, unwanted. Imagine how that would feel.'

I think of Reuben, and how growing up unloved has made him feel. I think of it clearly and dispassionately, not as an excuse but as a fact.

'You can be brave by saying I can't do that, saying I'm not going to attempt something that's impossible for me, something that I will regret or resent. Facing up to that reality . . . I think that would be an incredibly brave thing to do. If you knew deep down it was the right choice.'

I look her in the eye. 'But you don't know what you'll feel later.' I think again of Gloria's words: *You can't be scared of regret.* 'And don't you think it's also brave to trust other people to know what's right for them. Even if you hate the choice they're making? Even if you think it's a terrible mistake?'

As I say this, I wonder if I'm being hypocritical. When Gloria had suggested she wanted to end her life I'd argued with her. If she made the choice that her life wasn't worth living, that death at the time and in the manner of her choosing was what she wanted, would I try to stop her, save her? I'd want to. But what right do I have really, to make that decision for her? It's her life.

I feel exhausted suddenly, overwhelmed. My body hurts and my head aches so much it feels as though it's bursting. I want to sleep again, to switch everything off for a while. Hot tears trickle down my cheeks. I feel exactly like the little kid I've just told Mum I'm not.

'I know what I want to do, Mum, I just don't know if I can. I'm not brave.'

She takes my hand.

'Oh, love,' she says. 'Inside nobody is.'


I must have been sleeping, because when I open my eyes Kat's sitting there on the seat next to me engrossed in a book, her long blue-streaked hair falling over her face.

'Hello, stranger,' I croak. 'I like the new hair.'

'Oh my God, Hattie! You're awake!' She gives me a careful hug, making sure not to hurt me or pull out any of my wires. 'I came as soon as your mum called and said—' her voice wobbles—'you'd had an accident. You scared the life out of us.'

'Sorry about that. I can't believe you came all the way from Edinburgh,' I say, unable to stop smiling. 'It feels like years. It's so good to see you.'

'Of course I came,' she says.

'What about Zoe?' I bet she wasn't best pleased. Probably thought I'd engineered the whole thing just to get Kat's attention. 'Did she come too?'

Kat shakes her head and her forehead creases. 'She went mad. Said if I came to see you it was over between me and her.' She smiles. 'I told her if she was making me choose between her and my best friend there was no contest.'

'Oh, Kat,' I say. 'I'm sorry.'

'Don't be,' she says. 'I really liked her and at first it was kind of flattering that she was so jealous and wanted me all to herself.'

I nod, just a little bit because my head is still sore. I don't think anyone's ever wanted me all to themselves. I can see the appeal of it.

'But the longer it went on the more I knew it wasn't right,' Kat says. 'Zoe was so controlling. I started to act like someone else when I was with her. I didn't feel like I could be myself. If I went anywhere without her she'd give me the third degree afterwards or sulk. If I spoke to anyone else for more than two minutes when we were out she'd start yelling at me afterwards. She started going through my messages on my phone. It was horrible.'

'God, Kat, that's awful. You should have said.'

'The thing is, it happened gradually. I didn't even realize, and she made it feel as though it was my fault, like I was being unreasonable. Anyway, alarm bells really started ringing when I found out she'd been checking my voicemail and texts but I figured you had enough going on what with crazy great-aunts and pregnancy and all. And then just when I was thinking I'd have to tell you, you had the accident. After those weeks in the flat with her up in

Edinburgh I started to feel as though I was forgetting how to be myself. I know that sounds stupid.'

'It doesn't sound stupid at all.'

She shudders. 'It wasn't a nice feeling.'

'Well, it's her loss,' I say.

I give her hand a squeeze. 'Why is it so easy to know that someone else has fallen in love with a dangerous lunatic and so hard to tell when it's you?'

'Yeah,' she laughs. 'We haven't exactly got the best track record, have we?'

'No.'

We're silent for a moment. The beep of the monitor thingy I'm attached to sounds loud.

'Reuben's gone then?' she says quietly.

'Yep.' I look at my hands. 'I knew he would, once I told him.'

'He's such a selfish—'

'Yeah.'

'Are you going to keep the baby?' Kat says.

'I think so,' I say. 'Yes.'

Even saying it makes me scared. Can I really do it? I don't know. I'm going to try.

'Blimey,' Kat says. 'Do you think I can be Aunty Kat?'

'Fine by me,' I say. 'But you'd probably better run it past Alice.'

'Jesus.' Kat laughs. 'Can you imagine Alice being your aunt?'

I smile. 'Have you met Gloria yet?' I ask.

'Oh, yeah. We're old mates now. Got to know each other while you've been in here.'

Weird to think of everyone carrying on while I've just been lying here unconscious.

'Is she okay?' I feel guilty about leaving Gloria, just driving off like that. And now I've ruined the end of our journey. I might never even find out what it was she wanted to come here for. I'm determined to make sure we go up to the abbey before we leave, just like she planned. Will she tell me the end of the story? I guess that's up to her.

'I think so. Worried about you. Keeps calling me Beryl. Fancies Carl. Other than that all fine.'

'She was . . . upset last time I saw her. And then I left and told Reuben to look after her. And then the next thing I had the accident.'

'Don't worry,' she says. 'Carl's been looking after her. She's very keen on him. Why was she upset?'

'Long story,' I say. 'It's to do with what happened to her in the past, all the stuff she'd been telling me on the journey.'

# Chapter twenty-nine

There are so many steps up to the abbey I wonder whether I'm going to make it to the top, let alone Gloria. I'm still weak from my stay in hospital. We take it slow, stopping often. But we will make it to the top, because this is why we came. This is the end of the journey.

When we get to the top I follow Gloria through the graveyard to the edge of the cliff and we stare out over the sea. When at last we've caught our breath I turn to Gloria.

'So,' I say. 'Why here? Why is this end of the story?'

She pauses, looking into the distance.

'I came here, back then. With the baby.'

'With the baby? When?'

'It was his first birthday.'

'But I thought they wouldn't let you see him? I thought once he was adopted that was it?'

'I tricked them.'

'But why here?'

'This was where Edie lived. I knew her address from the letter she'd sent me after she left. I took the baby and then I panicked. I had nowhere to go. Edie was the only person I could think of who would understand. So I came here.'

\*  \*  \*

367

It's so clear, still. Edie's face as she sees me standing on her doorstep, clutching the baby. He's screaming; he's hungry and he wants his mum. His mum is not me.

Her face lights up on seeing me, but I see her look at the baby and the smile disappear. She hugs me tight.

'Oh, Gloria,' she says. 'What have you done?'

'I don't know,' I say. 'I don't know.'

'Come in,' she says. 'You look perished. Let me take the little one and you get warm by the fire.'

'His mum will be worrying about him,' Edie says. 'You know she will. It'll be breaking her heart. You've got to let her know where he is, Gloria.'

I know she is right. I let her make the phone call. But I cannot sleep that night, and when it starts to get light I know what I must do.

I step into the long grass and yellow flowering weeds and thistles that grow wild on the other side at the cliff edge, the baby clutched to me, warm, heavy with sleep. I'm breathless, and my heart is beating hard against him from the exertion of climbing the steps. Strange to think that it's the same heart that beat for him, that kept him alive, that he knew from all those months hidden away inside me, under the elasticated school skirt, beneath the duffel coat. Do I feel familiar to him? Do I smell right to him? Animals know their families by their scent. Perhaps it is the same for babies.

Perhaps it is the same for mothers.

There is something – I cannot describe it – a physical feeling that I have when I see him, when I hold him. Is it love? It can't be. I can't love him. I know I never can.

I want to. I should.

I never will.

And yet he is mine. My body can feel it. It carried him. He was part of it. All these thoughts bubble in my mind as I stand there, at the cliff edge, the cold dawn air biting at me, the sea spread grey and silver below me, out, out to the horizon. It is beautiful.

A few steps forward, just a few steps, a breath in and out, eyes closed, a drop through darkness like in a dream, and we will be part of it. We will be together, without the world, without the thinking and the guilt, without the memory. The weight of all that is too much. It is too heavy. It will drag us down quickly beneath the waves into the silver and the grey. It won't take long to fill us up and make us part of it. Yes. That is what I want. It is what I need. To be free of everything. To be rid of this body that was his body too. To be light and free . . .

I am spinning in the park, head thrown back to the sun, the world a blur around me, floating off into the sky . . .

But I'm not. I can never be her again, the girl who threw her head back to the sky and pirouetted on the Common, who said I am not afraid. She has gone. She is lost. I can never find her. Can I?

A few steps forward and I will disappear. A breath in and out and then—

Gone.

And yet—

She stops and stares silently out at the sea and sky, her eyes grey as the rain-heavy clouds.

'Oh, Gloria,' I say, my voice choked. 'God, Gloria, I'm so sorry.'

She doesn't hear me, though. She is there. In this moment she is the girl, not much older than me, who had wanted to die and take her baby with her. The thought of her desperation, her fear, her despair, and worse, the thought of her reliving it now, is unbearable.

'Why did you want to come here?' I ask, and my heart thuds. 'Gloria, did your baby die here? Did you . . . ?'

I can't say the words. Could it be that in her traumatized state something terrible had happened, some unthinkable accident or . . . or something that wasn't an accident? Surely not. And still the questions race through my mind. How did she find her baby? She'd said that a baby with a black father would have been put in a home, but I realize that a baby with a white father would have had families queuing up for him, never mind that his mother had been raped. I feel so angry thinking about it, about the prejudice and ugly injustice of it, about the poor, innocent baby at the centre of it all, and about what Gloria had been through. She'd still been a girl really, suffering in a way no one understood, not even herself. What could it have pushed her to?

I watch Gloria's face, looking for some clue, something that will tell me that what I'm imagining isn't what happened. She doesn't seem to hear me, just stares out to sea. And I remember what she said about her mother, watching the same memories unfold again and again, with no control over which ones they were, some happy, some heartbreaking, some terrifying, replaying in her mind again and again like a film on a loop, but worse because she believed them to be real. Is this what Gloria dreads, being trapped in this place, haunted by the memory she is now reliving as her disease progresses? Wouldn't anything be better than that? Wouldn't death be better? I look at her, standing frail but strong against the wind at the edge of the cliff. No. That can't be why we're here, can it? Is that what she meant by the end of the story?

'Gloria, the cliff,' I say. 'You didn't come here to . . .'

She hears me now, and looks round at me but doesn't speak.

'You don't want to do now what you didn't do then?'

She smiles.

'Die?'

'Yes.'

'I thought perhaps I did,' she says. 'I still think perhaps I do. But no. Not yet. You don't need to worry. I'm not going to jump. That's not why I came.'

'Why then?'

She pauses.

'I came to remember why I didn't,' she says at last.

The grass is wet with overnight rain and my brown shoes are stained dark with it at the toes. I'm reminded, incongruously, of Louise's red satin shoes, the ones she wore the night I met Sam. They were ruined in the slush, just as her mum had said they would be, and Louise's feet were stained bright red for days. Dear Lou. She's in Canada now, her and Johnny, expecting a baby in March. Mum will write to tell her, I suppose, about me. But she won't know for weeks. All that time I'll be at the bottom of the sea and she won't know. What would she say if she knew that I was thinking of her shoes just before I stepped off a cliff? *She'd be delighted*, I think. She loved those shoes. The thought of it almost makes me smile. The thought of my own feet, crushed into black patent. The thought of Sam. It is painful to think of him and yet the memory of how I felt when I was with him, the joy of it, the knowledge that I loved him and he loved me – the fact of being capable of love. Isn't that a reason enough to live?

'I came here then because I couldn't face the future,' Gloria says. 'I was more scared and lonely than I had ever been in my life. I didn't know how I could go on. That's how I felt when you came to visit me, that first time.'

'And what did stop you, then?'

'Edie. Mum. Gwen. The fact that there were people who cared about me. The realization that if I didn't let myself hide, if I allowed myself to feel, if I didn't disappear, then perhaps I could live my life after all. There was something else I realized too, standing here, all those years ago. I did love my baby. I knew I couldn't care for him. I knew I couldn't be a mother to him. But I did love him. I never got to tell him that. And so . . .' She stops, uncertain for a moment. 'And so I'm telling you. While I remember. It's important that *you* know.'

'Why me?'

She looks at me, silently, as if working out how to say something important. I wonder if a vital word or fact has escaped her, but it's not that. She's nervous.

'What is it, Gloria?'

'I came here – with you – because you are the end of the story.'

'What do you mean?'

'Have you still got the locket?' she says at last.

'Yes.' They'd found it on me when I crashed the car and Gloria had told me to keep it.

'Open it,' she says.

I open the locket.

'Take the photos out,' she says. 'Look at what's written on the back.'

Carefully I ease out the photo of Gloria and turn it over. On the back is written in faded brown ink:

*Gloria, St Monica's, 1959*

I slip it carefully back into the locket and then, my hands shaking a little, I gently slide out the picture of her baby and turn that over.

'My baby didn't die here, Hattie,' Gloria says. 'He didn't die until many years after. He lived a full life and had a family of his own.'

On the back, in the same neat handwriting, is written:
*Dominic, St Monica's, 1959*

I look up at her, disbelieving.

'Dad,' I say. 'Your baby was Dominic. He was my dad.'

'Yes.'

'It was Nan – Gwen – who adopted him?'

She doesn't speak. She can't. She just nods, silent.


In the hospital. Still sore and empty and sick from the exertion of birth. 'Handsome little fellow, isn't he?' Patsy, the nice nurse, says. Gwen holding my pale, blue-eyed baby, staring at him and then at me in confusion.

'I thought he'd be coloured. I thought – can that happen? If the father is coloured?' she says.

I say nothing, and Patsy coughs, busying herself with straightening the cotsheets and pretending not to hear.

'Gloria,' she says. 'Look at him. He's perfect.'

*He'd have been perfect if he'd been Sam's baby*, I think.

And now Gwen is looking at me with that urgent look on her face that I haven't recognized yet. Me, trying not to show anything on my face, picking petals off the roses Gwen brought, pressing my fingertips into the smoothness of them, rolling them against my thumb, and Patsy, the kind nurse, chatting cheerfully in the background.

'I suggested James for a name. After James Dean. I fancy him something rotten,' she's saying. Gwen's not listening. She's staring at the baby and then back at me.

'Want to hold him, Mrs Lockwood?' Patsy says. She's given up trying to get me to hold him, except to feed him when I can't very well not.

Gwen nods slowly, her eyes still fixed on me.

'Don't let Matron see you, though,' Patsy laughs. 'She doesn't like to see babies being cuddled when it's supposed to be nap time. Can't go without saying hello to your handsome nephew, though, can you?'

The baby starts to fuss as she lifts him out of the cot and I think he's going to start screaming; I brace myself for it because I can't bear the sound of it. But when she places him gently into Gwen's arms he is soothed. She rocks him gently and whispers to him and he looks up at her, calm.

'Oh, you're a natural, Mrs Lockwood. He's usually a fretful little chap but look at him now, happy as you like. You've babies of your own, no doubt?'

There's a pause.

'No,' Gwen says. 'I've hoped many times, but I just can't seem to hang on to them, I'm afraid.' She tries to sound matter-of-fact about it, but her voice is strained. 'I should have given birth just three months ago. But I lost the baby.'

'Oh, I'm so sorry,' Patsy says, her cheeks turning a blotchy pink. 'That must be very hard.'

'Yes,' Gwen says.

Patsy puts her hand on Gwen's arm and gives it a squeeze. 'I'm sure one day you'll have a baby of your own.'

Gwen bends her head over the baby, looking down at his bright blue eyes and hair the colour of copper and his pale, purple-veined skin.

'If I'd had a boy I was going to call him Dominic,' she says, and tears fall from her eyes onto the cheeks of my baby.

'Dominic,' Patsy says, smiling at me. 'There you go, that's perfect.'

It isn't until weeks have passed that I understand the look on Gwen's face as she held my baby. She comes to see me at St

374

Monica's. She pleads. Surely it is better than giving him to a stranger. She would love him more than anyone else could because he is mine. Her baby died before it could be born. Mine lived. Surely I must see that it is meant to be, it is God's plan.

'I don't believe in God,' I say.

'Fate, then. Call it fate. Call it love. Do this for me.'

She squeezes my hands so tight it hurts.

'But Vinnie . . .' I say. But I cannot say more. Not to Gwen. Not to anyone. I cannot even think of what happened. Not ever.

'Vinnie will love him as if he was his own son,' she says. 'I know he has it in him to be a good father.'

I turn away from her and look out of the window. There is blossom on the apple trees in the garden. *It is spring*, I think with a shock. Those trees were bare when I arrived. Time is passing. It will keep passing. It is relentless. And we change with it, I suppose. I'm not the girl I was a year ago, spinning on the Common in the first sunshine of spring.

'We've already spoken to the authorities about it,' she says at last, softly. 'They are happy for the adoption to go ahead. But I want to do it with your blessing, Gloria. I want you to see that this is the best thing for all of us.'

I know what she is telling me. She is saying that I have no choice. And I do want to help Gwen, to make her happy. I do.

There is no other way. I will hand the baby over and he will be theirs and I will pretend none of it ever happened.

I will forget.


'So . . .' My mind whirls dizzily, and I shiver in the breeze as I try to take it all in. 'I'm your granddaughter.'

She turns away from the edge of the cliff and the sea that stretches silver-grey away from us, out to places we cannot see. She turns towards me.

375

'That is the end of the story,' she says.

I nod, understanding at last. The journey and what it was about. Not just about remembering. Not just about the past. About the present, too. Our journey together to this place, this moment: the two of us here, together, connected by a son and a father neither of us ever really got to know. And our journey together beyond it, into whatever lies ahead.

I take her hand. It is cold and thin, and it grips mine hard.

'Perhaps not,' I say. 'Perhaps it's the beginning of the story.'

'But I still don't understand,' I say when we have come down from the abbey and are sitting in a café. 'Why didn't you tell them? About Vinnie?'

'I was ashamed. And no one would have believed me. They'd have believed him. He was a respectable man, wasn't he? He had money, a nice wife he bought flowers and pretty clothes for, a new house in the suburbs with a fitted kitchen and a lovely big garden. I was a girl. I didn't do as I was told. What could you expect from someone like me? I'd already proved I had no moral character by going out with Sam. A "coloured man"! I might as well have had "slut" written on my forehead as far as most people were concerned. They'd have said I was lying or that it was my fault. Even *I* believed it was my fault.'

I shake my head.

'But after what he did to you ... He raped you. How could you think that?'

She smiles.

'I'd been told all my life that eventually I'd get what was coming to me, like all bad girls do. By my father. By Sister Mary Francis. I thought they'd been proved right.'

'But it was him!' I say, furious. 'It was all him and he got away with it and you had to suffer! Why weren't you angry?'

'I'd stopped feeling anything,' Gloria says. 'I'd learned how to disappear, remember? Just like my mother. If you aren't really there, you can't really feel.'

'Do you think Nan knew?' I ask. 'Did Gwen know? About Vinnie?'

I think about the Nan I had known, quiet, tidy, and wonder at the fact that she was hiding this secret, that she had this drama and no one knew.

Gloria doesn't answer. She folds the paper serviette.

'Surely she can't have,' I say. 'She couldn't have known that her husband raped you and just pretended it didn't happen. She couldn't have taken that child—'

'We didn't talk about it.'

'Not ever?'

She unfolds and refolds the serviette. 'It took me a long time to understand how terrified Gwen was of Vinnie. I thought it was love. I think perhaps she did too. But it wasn't. It was paralysing, abject fear. He detached her from us bit by bit, from her family, her friends, the people who loved her. He detached her from herself, from the person she had been. He told her she was worthless. He was violent. Not like Father. Not in drunken rage. The marks I saw on her arms that day: some of them were fresh and raw, some of them were old, old scars. They had been inflicted methodically where no one would see them. He probably raped her.'

She takes a sip of her tea and I sit staring at her, not knowing what to say.

'I don't think she realized at first that Dominic was his

son. He looked more like me than anyone when he was born. But as he grew a little and began to look more like Vinnie . . . Who knows? There are secrets we keep, even from ourselves. But I know now that Gwen did what she did out of love and kindness. She did it for herself, because she was desperate for a child, but she did it for Dominic too and for me. She knew I didn't want a baby and she knew she could give him more care and love than I ever could. I understand this now. I didn't fully understand it then.'

I shudder. 'He was my grandfather.'

I think about it, about his blood running in my veins. Have I inherited anything from him? Did Dad? Gloria watches me.

'Who we are isn't decided before we're born. It's decided in the choices we make, the people we choose to be.'

I remember what she said, about how she wasn't like her father.

'If Vinnie hadn't . . . I mean—' I stop. I don't know how to say it. 'If it hadn't been for what he did to you, I wouldn't be here. I wouldn't exist.'

It's a horrible thought, one I don't really know what to do with.

'Which just goes to show,' she says. 'Sometimes good can come from bad.'

At least he died before Dad could know him, before he could play a part in his life. I'd always thought that was sad before. Now it seems like a blessing.

'What about after Vinnie died?' Couldn't you and Nan – Gwen – couldn't you have found a way of sorting things out? So that you could have got to know Dad at least?'

'No.' She says it quietly but firmly. 'Things were better as they were. He was gone and it seemed best that all the pain he'd inflicted went with him. We both wanted to forget everything that had happened, put it behind us. Seeing each other made it impossible to do that. Dominic was with a mother who loved him. She *was* his mother. It was better that way.'

'So he never knew?'

'No.'

'But what about Sam?' I try to piece it together. 'Did you tell him you were pregnant?'

She shakes her head. 'How could I? I couldn't tell him what had happened to me. I couldn't tell anyone. I didn't even have a word for what Vinnie had done to me. After it happened, for a long time I think, I was in shock. I thought it must have been my fault. When I found out I was pregnant I knew the only thing I could do was end things with Sam.'

'That was what you went to tell Sam that day you met him in the park. Not that you were pregnant. That you were ending it?'

She nods.

'But you loved him.' Tears at the unfairness of it spring to my eyes.

'I did. But it was a long, long time ago.'

I look round and see Alice pulling faces at me through the window. Mum, Carl, Ollie and Kat are making their way through the door of the café.

'Don't look now,' says Gloria. 'But there's an extremely attractive man coming towards our table.'

'It's Carl,' I say. 'Mum's fiancé. I mean, partner. Boyfriend. I dunno.'

'Have I met him before?'

'You've been living with him for the last week.'

'Have I?' She looks disconcerted. Then she smiles. 'Well, lucky me. He's rather easy on the eye, isn't he? Buff, isn't that what people say these days? Nice bottom.'

Carl, who's caught sight of himself in the mirrors on the café wall, seems to be thinking exactly the same thing. I sigh, in a way that may or may not be affectionate. What is it with Carl and older ladies? He must emit some phero-mone that can only be detected by women in possession of a free bus pass.

'Oh, *please*,' I say to Gloria. 'Just don't let him hear you say that. We'll never hear the end of it.'

'And how are my two favourite ladies?' asks Carl.

'Oi,' says Mum.

'Oh yes,' Carl says, winking at us. 'I was forgetting Alice.'

Alice kicks him. 'I'm not a lady.'

'And of course,' he says, putting his arm round Mum, who's grinning at him in that alarming My Heathcliff kind of a way, 'My beautiful wife-to-be.'

'What?' I say.

'Yeah, we've got a little announcement,' Carl says. 'We're getting married.'

'Jesus.' I put my head in my hands. 'What is the matter with you people?'

'Aww,' says the café owner, who happens to be within earshot. 'Did you hear that everyone? They're getting married.'

There's an impromptu but mortifying cheer and round of applause. Alice crawls under the table.

'But not yet,' says Mum, hastily. 'Just . . . one day.'

'Maybe next year,' says Carl.

'Or the year after,' says Mum. 'And not with any fancy stuff. No big dress or castle or wedding favours that match the flowers—'

'Or peach bridesmaids' dresses?' I say. 'Thank you, GOD.'

'Oh, no,' says Carl. 'We're definitely having the peach bridesmaids' dresses. Great big puffy ones with bows – OW!' Alice has kicked him again from under the table.

'Maybe by the sea,' says Mum.

'Wait,' I say, as we walk down towards the cottage. 'I just need to post this.'

I take out of my bag a postcard that Gloria and I wrote together in the café. It says:

Dear Edie, just to let you know we reached the end of our journey and are now starting on a new one. I have the locket you sent to Gloria all those years ago. I will treasure it always. Gloria says thank you for everything, then and now. We both hope we'll see you again soon. Love to Tariq and Yasmeen too. Love, Hattie and Gloria xxx

I watch the girl, Hattie, as she runs off down the street. It is freeing, knowing that she knows. My granddaughter. I will forget the things I have told her, but she will not forget them now. She knows it all. After all, no one ever knows the whole story. There are always secrets. Secrets we keep from others, secrets we keep from ourselves. There are things I have held back without realizing I'm doing it, I'm sure. Our memories are both real and made up. And of course there will be other things that I have left out by mistake, because I've forgotten them or got confused. But there is only one secret that I have chosen to keep, to be washed away when the tide comes in.

It is better that way. It is not my secret to tell.


'I should have done it sooner.' Gwen says, standing at the door of my flat in Battersea, late at night. I haven't seen her for more than a year. We'd agreed then it was better that way.

'Come in,' I say, still half asleep, confused by her being here, by her words. She looks pale, thinner than I remember.

She shakes her head. 'I should have done it sooner.'

'Done what? Gwen, what's up? You're shaking.'

Even now my thoughts flash to him, to my boy who is now Gwen's boy, and I have to work to quell the panic. No, if something had happened to him Gwen wouldn't be pale and shaking on my doorstep, smelling faintly of – can it be whisky I can smell on her breath? Gwen never drinks ... But no, if anything had happened to the boy, *her* boy, she would be hysterical, inconsolable. She would be with him, I know that. She would never leave him.

'Gloria, I know what you wanted to tell me that day,' she says. 'I know now. Perhaps ...' Her voice falters. 'Perhaps I knew it then. I don't know. I don't know.'

She is so agitated that I take her hand to try to calm her.

'What day? Gwen what are you talking about?'

'Do you remember? We were in Lyons. You said, "I love you Gwen. Nothing can ever change that".'

'Yes,' I say. I remember that day. The baby still inside me and hers no longer inside her, the unfairness of it clear to both of us.

'I love you too.'

She turns to go.

'Gwen!' I call after her.

She looks up at me from the shadow of the stairs so that her face is lit by the bulb on the landing.

'I'm sorry, Gloria. I should have done it sooner.'

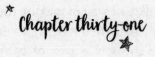

Back at the cottage, while we're all packing I can hear Mum and Carl talking in the room next door to mine. It's so hot that all the windows are open and their words drift out into the sunny late afternoon.

'If I could get my hands on that toe-rag Reuben I'd wring his bloody neck. Running out on her like that,' Carl says.

'I know,' I hear Mum reply. 'But if he can't handle it, maybe it's better that Hattie knows that now.

'Maybe. But he's broken Hattie's heart and that's enough to make me want to throttle him.'

There's a pause.

'Oh, come on, honey. Don't cry. She'll be okay,' I hear Carl say.

'But she's my baby, how can she possibly have a baby of her own? She hasn't got any idea what she's taking on. I just wish I could make her see. All the responsibility. All the things she'll miss out on. And I think she's doing it out of a misguided sense of love for Reuben. Do you suppose she'd have kept the baby if it had been Adrian's? Because I don't.'

I close my eyes. Is she right? 'People have babies for all sorts of crap reasons,' Carl's saying. 'They have 'em to save their marriage, or because everyone else has already had one and keep putting cute photos of them on Facebook, or because they want to live their life through someone else, or because they suddenly realize they're going to die one day and they think it's a way of making themselves immortal, or because they hate their job. My sister's mate Kayleigh had one because she saw a pair of baby UGG boots in Selfridge's and she couldn't resist buying them and then she thought she needed a baby to wear them. She's not the brightest, Kayleigh. But that said, as it turns out she's a great mum and her little 'un, Kai, he's a lovely lad. People make decisions for bad reasons all the time. Doesn't always make them bad decisions.'

'But this is Hattie we're talking about,' Mum says. 'Is she really going to be able to handle going to university with a baby? Is she always going to be waiting for Reuben to come back? What's she going to do when he finally grows up and gets married to someone else and has a family?'

Carl sighs. 'I don't know the answer to that, babe, and I don't suppose Hattie does either. But it's her decision. You've said your piece and now you've got to trust her. I know you're worried for her. So am I. But she'll be all right because she's smart and she's kind and she's got you, hasn't she? She's got us.'

I carry on packing my case, with tears trickling down my face and off the end of my nose and landing on my clothes and washbag and Gloria's hen-night deely boppers, thinking about the fact that this is the end of the journey for me and Gloria, remembering the places we've been together. I cry because of all the things Gloria went through, and because I love her and she is losing her memory and she is scared and maybe it won't be long before she won't even know who I am. I cry because I am pregnant. I cry because Reuben is gone and because I knew he would be. I cry because things will never be the same between us again, and because he is sad and I can't help him. I cry because I love him.

Then, when I've stopped crying, I type this:

From: hattiedlockwood@starmail.com
To: wilde_one666@starmail.com
Subject: How Not To Disappear

So, I was talking to Gloria the other day – and I realized something really important.

I didn't say it very well and I probably won't explain it right now, either, but the thing I realized is this: you can't be lost – you can't disappear – however lost you may feel, however far away – if you are loved.

Love is an anchor and that can be a bad thing because sometimes we want to float off and drift away and it weighs us down, it's heavy and it keeps us in a place we don't want to be.

But it is a good thing too, Reuben, because it means when someone's feeling lost or when we don't know who we are and even when we hide ourselves away – we can't disappear. However distant or lost we feel, love means that we can't disappear because it places us and knows us and is inside us whether we like it or not, and love is bigger than us – outlasting us like landfill or nuclear waste, except in a good way.

So anyway, that's it really. I said it to Gloria, because I know her and I think I understand her a bit and I know she is scared and I love her and that means that even when she is lost she can't disappear.

And that is also why I'm saying it to you.

Just so you know.

Hattie xx

But of course I don't send it.

# Chapter thirty-two

We all travel back together in Carl's boss's people carrier that has *Pec's Appeal – the gym 4 u!* emblazoned on the side.

'Could you not at least have said something about the apostrophe, Carl?' I say.

'Well, NO actually, Hats,' he says. 'Seeing as my BOSS had very GENEROUSLY just given me free use of his nice shiny people carrier because my almost-stepdaughter had totalled my almost-wife's car after taking it to YORKSHIRE without asking, I thought it probably wasn't the best moment for grammar pedantry.'

'Still, though,' I say.

'Walk then,' he says, and then smiles at Gloria, holding out a hand to help her into her seat.

'And who are you?' she says, smiling at him, like the queen.

'I'm Carl,' he says.

'Ah yes, Carl. I think Hattie's mentioned you,' she says. 'I thought you said he was an annoying idiot, Hattie,' she calls back over her shoulder. 'He seems quite delightful to me.'

Bloody Gloria. Never forgets the stuff you want her to.

'I said *at times* he was an annoying idiot. Other times he's really quite bearable.' I smile at Carl. "'Delightful' is definitely pushing it, though.'

'Nice bottom too,' Gloria adds appreciatively as she settles herself into her seat.

'Easy, tiger,' says Carl, looking pleased. 'Still got it,' he says to me as I push past.

'Only cos no one else wants it,' I say. He laughs and then he squeezes my shoulder. We both know the banter is because he feels sorry for me.

'Look, Hattie,' he says in a low voice, so the others won't hear. 'I know I'm not your dad but I really do—'

'I know, Carl. So do I.' I give him a kiss on the cheek. 'Now just drive, will you?'

Mum and Carl sit in the front and Carl makes us listen to terrible Dad Rock all the way, despite the howls of protest from everyone else.

'Are you all right, love?' Mum calls back to me every five minutes. 'Not dizzy, are you, Hattie? You know the doctor said you've got to tell us if you are,' or 'How's your head?' or 'Let us know if you feel car sick. I couldn't get in a car without projectile vomiting when I was pregnant with the twins.' At which Carl gives me a look that says he might just dump me at the next lay-by.

Alice and Ollie play card games and Kat teaches them new ways to cheat while trying to avoid questions from Alice about how lesbians do sex and why.

'Now's really not the time, Al,' Mum calls back.

'Hmmm, I dunno,' says Carl hopefully.

'Shut up, Carl,' we all chorus.

'Pervert,' Alice adds, for good measure.

I sit at the very back with Gloria.

'Like being in the back row at the flicks,' says Gloria. 'Except without the You Know.'

'Definitely without that,' I say.

I watch the world flash by outside: hills, fields of sheep, vast cooling towers, villages and cities. There's so much of it. Eventually I feel myself dozing. I look at Gloria and see she's watching me.

'I didn't think it would end like this,' I say to her as I begin to drift off.

She half smiles.

'No one ever does,' she says.

## ⋆ Epilogue
### Four years later

Mum throws her bouquet over her shoulder and it soars through the air. I keep well away from it. Carl's sister Estelle runs across the sand, impressive given she's wearing platform sandals, elbowing people out of the way. Alice's natural competitiveness kicks in and she launches herself in front of Estelle like a goalkeeper making a save and manages to get there first. She looks triumphant until Carl's mum explains to her that this means she'll be the next to get married, and she drops it, appalled.

Mum laughs. She looks so happy. It only took her four years to get round to actually marrying Carl – just a few friends at the registry office near his mum's house in Cornwall and then a barbecue on the tiny sheltered beach nearby to celebrate. No co-ordinating wedding favours. No peach bridesmaids' dresses. Just paddling in the sea for those brave enough, and sausages and champagne.

It's a perfect early autumn day, the sky blue above the rocky cove, the wind strong but not cold, carrying the shouts and laughter of the children scrambling in the rock pools and the smoke from the barbecue Carl and his mates have set up. The beach is deserted except for us. The coppery light of the late-afternoon sun and the heady fizz of the champagne making everything look a little bit magical.

Gloria sits on the deckchair that Carl set up for her, sipping her glass of champagne and watching it all happily, though how much she understands of what's going on I don't know. Not much of the detail, exactly who is who, or why we're here. But she knows everyone's having a good time, knows it's a party, and she's still in her element at a party.

I try not to feel sad as I watch her. So much of who she was when I first met her is gone. There are things I never got to talk to her about, that I never asked her about while I could and now I never can.

When I helped clear out Gloria's flat after she moved to the home I found all sorts of things. One of them was a letter from Nan dated a couple of months before she died.

*Dear Gloria,*

*I know it will be a bit of a shock for you to get this letter. I do hope that you will read it, after all this time.*

*I am dying, Gloria. I'm not writing to ask for pity, I don't mind. Since Dominic passed away I have been waiting to die. The nuns used to tell us we would be reunited with our loved ones in heaven, didn't they? I stopped believing in such things a long time ago, but I tell myself perhaps they were right after all. He was my life, Gloria, and I have you to thank for him. I can never thank you enough for the gift you gave me. The gift of a son, the gift of my beloved boy. I can't imagine what my life*

393

would have been without him, and I owe that to you, Gloria. At the time I told myself it was simple, it was for the best. And I still believe it was for the best, but it was certainly not simple. I know the pain it must have caused you and I am so very sorry for it. I hope you can forgive me. I was young and I was desperate, for a child, for love, for something to prove to me that I was worthy of being alive. (My husband, as I think you know, had done a very good job of convincing me I was not.) I believe I was a good mother, as good as anyone could have been. I was devoted to Dominic and I believe he loved me as much as any son could love his mother.

I just wish, now, that I had allowed you to be part of his life too, if you had chosen. Perhaps you didn't want to be. The fact is, I never gave you the chance.

I enclose the address and phone number for his family. He had a daughter, Hattie, who is now ten and baby twins, Alice and Ollie. If you should wish to contact them, I am sure they would be very pleased. And if, at some point, you choose to tell them the truth of what happened, do it with my blessing but not until after I am gone, if I can ask that of you.

With love and gratitude,
Your sister, Gwen

There was another letter in the same box. It was creased, as though it had been screwed up into a ball and then smoothed out again later. This letter said:

*Dear Harriet,*

*You don't know me but I know you. Sorry, that isn't quite what I meant. It makes me sound like a deranged stalker, which I'm not. (Not a stalker at least; there have always been those who have said I am deranged). All I mean is I know a bit about you. You are Dominic Lockwood's daughter, and he is someone I cared very greatly about and so, by default, I care about you. He didn't really know me either. I am a relative of his but*

(There is a bit of an ink blot here and a rather fierce crossing out,)

*I'm not doing this at all well so I think the best thing would be if you came and saw me, don't you? I can explain it better then. I'm not very well you see and while I can I ~~would like to explain would like to tell you~~ would like to get to know you*

*damn*

*I would like to*
*I would like for you to*
*I would like*

*a gin and tonic*

At which point it stops and was, I presume, scrunched up and thrown aside.

I asked Peggy about it and it turned out she had found the letter and quizzed Gloria about it. Gloria had told her everything. She told her that Nan had got in touch with Gloria when she was ill, and talked to her about Dad, about me and Alice and Ollie, and said that if she wanted, Gloria could tell us after Nan was dead that she was really our grandmother. At the time Gloria hadn't known whether or not she wanted to, but as her memory started to get worse she decided she would. They had agreed that Peggy would contact me. But then Gloria bottled out at the last minute and decided it was all a mistake. Luckily Peggy had decided it wasn't. The letter had been tied up with a pile of newspaper cuttings. Articles that Dad had written, right back to his student days, and his earliest stories about school fêtes and retiring dinner ladies and obituaries. Gloria had followed his career every step of the way.

It was quite an eye-opener, clearing out Gloria's flat. I found all sorts that she'd hoarded over the years. Reviews of her performances as Hedda Gabler and Ophelia and a whole load of other roles. There was a picture of Gianni (he really was very easy on the eye), a truly awful painting of someone I assume is supposed to be a young Gloria looking out of a window by RG (who must be Russell) and nothing whatsoever to show she was ever married to Gordon, except for the divorce papers.

There was also an article cut from a broadsheet, an interview with a scientist, Professor Danielle Carter, with a full-page photo of her, striking, about Mum's age, maybe a bit older, laughing. I recognized her vaguely from the TV; the article said she'd been 'credited with making science cool'. The bit of the interview that was underlined was the bit where she talked about her inspiration. Her father, Samuel, she said, who had arrived at Tilbury Docks in 1948 on the *Empire Windrush*, had become a teacher and a local councillor, and who had taught her to work hard and believe in yourself. He'd died four years before and she missed him every day. It took me a moment to make the connection. Sam. Gloria's Sam.

What would have happened, if Gloria hadn't gone back home that day, if Vinnie hadn't been waiting? Would she and Sam have got married and had their children, Danny and Vivienne? Or would their relationship have ended anyway? Gloria never was the settling-down type after all . . . What does it matter now, anyway? Sam lived a happy life and I'm glad of it, as Gloria must have been.

She is talking to Ollie now. They have a special bond, those two. Alice grows impatient of Gloria's constant repetition of things, of her forgetting what has just been said and who anyone is. She tries not to but she always ends up rolling her eyes and then Gloria gets snappish with her, though they always make it up. I wonder if that's how it always would have been with the two of them. They're too like each other. But Ollie seems to understand what she is feeling and what she is trying to say. She's always calm when he's around. She is gentler now. Sometimes I hate the gentleness. It is a sign that Gloria is disappearing. But she hasn't disappeared. She is still with us. And if I ask her to tell me about the time she cut one of Brenda Onions' pigtails off, she's just like her old self again.

Kat's brilliant with Gloria. She dropped out of art college and decided to become a doctor instead. That summer with Zoe-f-K changed her. 'You've got to see things how they really are, not how you want them to be,' she said, 'And I want to be good at art but I'm not. I'm crap at it.'

'Not crap,' I said. 'Just . . . mediocre.'

'*Thanks*,' she said. 'There is such a thing as being too honest, you know, Hats.' She's two years into her medical training and wants to become a neurologist. ('So am I your homework?' Gloria used to say, but she doesn't understand what a neurologist is any more.)

So, I know what you're thinking. What about Reuben? Don't pretend you're not. Everyone always wants to know what happened to Reuben, even if it's just because they hope it's something very painful. (Everyone except Kat, who, in her own words, *couldn't give a monkey's, frankly. Knob.* One of the many, many reasons I love Kat.)

Did he see the error of his ways and come running back to me and Dylan?

Come off it. Of course he bloody didn't. And if he had, I'd have sent him packing. Don't look at me like that. I totally would have.

Rumours still circulate among the old Mayfield Comp crowd. He's found God and is a missionary. He's in prison in Mexico. He's a male escort in Vienna. He's in witness protection. He's been recruited by MI6. He lost a leg in a shark attack off the coast of South Africa. He contracted bubonic plague. (I like to think this last was a tribute to Ms Horace.) He's married to the daughter of a wealthy American businessman. Actually this last one turned out to be true, though not for long.

And then one day, about six months ago, I got an email from him. There was a photo attached, of the sun setting over a landscape that looked like Africa. It said:

Hey Hats,

See if you can work this one out: Initially saw short vehicle in sad state.

xR

No *'How are you?'* or *'What have you been up to for the last four years?'* Probably didn't even occur to him that I might have been doing anything at all. Certainly not dashing from university lectures to the nursery to shifts at the Happy Diner. (Melanie turned out to be a rock in my hour of need. *'I knew you were up the spout,'* she'd said, *'soon as you started crying in the loos and going green when you were anywhere near the deep-fat fryer. And your face went all puffed up like a balloon but kind of more flabby, you know.'* Thanks, Mel. She gave me unwanted but well-meaning advice about stretch marks and she now lets me do whatever shifts I can fit in. She calls me into her office for coffee on a regular basis.) There hasn't been quite as much tap dancing along the Great Wall of China as I'd wish for, but I live in hope. Once I've finished my degree, who knows?

Despite all of that, I reread the message a hundred times after it pinged into my inbox. I finally worked out it was supposed to be an attempt at a cryptic crossword clue. It meant (I think) 'sorry'. I didn't reply. I have let him go. If you keep on running, if you don't let people love you, eventually they will let you go.

Reuben Wilde. Most Likely To: Disappear.

Dylan.

He has Reuben's chaotic hair and his casual disregard for authority, although perhaps that's to be expected from a three-year-old. He has eyes like mine and Dad's and Gloria's. He is gentle like his Uncle Ollie and spirited like his Aunty Alice. He is adored by us all, especially his Grandad Carl.

Has it been as hard as I thought it would be, having a kid? No. It's been harder than I ever imagined, even with everyone's help. It's been lonely and exhausting and boring and heartbreaking. I don't fit in with the other students who are my age, and I don't fit in with the mature students with grown-up kids. Kat's been there for me, of course, and I know she always will be. But she's away studying now, and she's got her own life.

People make assumptions about me, about my character, my ambitions, my intelligence, my motives, my selfishness. Most people don't do it maliciously, though some do. Things may have changed since Gloria was forced to give up her baby, but a young unmarried girl with a baby is still not treated the same as a married woman with a baby. Not by everyone anyway. That's the truth of it.

I've cried for the lives I did not choose. And then I've cried with guilt, because I love Dylan more than anything, more fiercely than I have ever felt anything before, and in spite of everything I would not be without him, or change a single thing about him.

He stands now with his back to me, up to his ankles in the ice-cold waves that lick the shore, throwing stone after stone into the sea that crashes and foams in front of him, dark, wild, powerful. I can see him breathing it in, the salt spray and the noise and the power, the danger, the vastness. I know he is feeling the thrill and the thunder of it shake his tiny ribcage, that his heart is full and pounding inside it.

He throws in another stone, and another, transfixed. As each one disappears he crouches to pick up another. I call to him but he doesn't hear. His face is alight and fixed and alive with the power of the sea. And still he throws the stones as if he cannot stop.

I am overwhelmed, suddenly, with love for him, for Dylan, and with fear for how small and helpless and fragile he is, and with pride at his fearlessness and with joy at his joy.

'What's he doing?' asks Becky, Carl's still-very-annoying sister. 'Always has been a funny little thing, hasn't he?'

And I'm so bursting with all the love and fear and pride and joy that I just smile sweetly at her and don't point out that her own child is a spoilt pain in the arse.

'Oh, look, Alice seems to have your Bertie in a headlock again,' I say, trying not to sound pleased. 'He really should know by now not to try and pick a fight with her. He always comes off worse.'

She curses under her breath and sprints off down the sand in the direction of the screaming.

And then I turn my face to the wind and walk down to my boy. I put my hand on his shoulder and we stand there together. He doesn't notice me. In one cold hand he clutches the stones and with the other he hurls them, one by one, silently into the waves.

I watch him. It's as if he is taunting the sea, defying it. He is saying to it, with his stones, *I am here. You are bigger than me. I cannot stop you. But I am here.*

The sea crashes on, cold and oblivious and inevitable, as powerful as time.

It is all we can do. I close my eyes and lean into the wind.

I let myself feel the warmth where my hand touches Dylan's shoulder, the heat that passes between us, that connects us and that I will feel even when he is far away from me.

Then I crouch and pick up the biggest stone and I send it into the deep dark of the sea. In time it will be ground down until it is sand. But for now it makes a splash, it makes a sound and I see its mark; I see the light flash, I see the rainbow it leaves for a split second before it disappears, as if it never was there at all.

I am here. You are bigger than me. I cannot stop you. But I am here.

I live. I love. I remember. I forget.

But still I live. And still I love.

Still I am.

They fly through the air, the – what are they called again? You know. With the petals, from the garden. There was a jam jar of them on the kitchen table. The girl who catches them doesn't look very pleased. *I know her*, I think, but I don't know who she is. She looks like trouble. She's thrown them away now. *Flowers*, that's it. She has thrown the flowers away.

I can see the ones on the kitchen table. They are pretty but there is something sad about them. I can't remember what. They make me scared but I can't remember why. There is blood dripping. The thorns, perhaps. 'Be careful, Gloria, they are sharp,' Mum is saying. 'Don't hurt yourself.' Always worrying about everything, Mum. I wonder where she's got to. It's not like her to be late.

There is a fair girl paddling in the sea. She is young and the thing when you aren't sad. What is it when you smile? Happy, the boy, Ollie, says. Yes. She is happy. *She is my mother*, I think. She isn't scared yet. She isn't sad yet. She is beautiful. *Il faut souffrir pour être belle, Gloria*.

My eyes close, and when they open again I can't help crying out at the noise, the darkness in front of me, coming towards me . . . What is the word for it? It is big and cold and unforgiving and terrifying.

'What is it, Gloria?' the boy says.

I point. 'The dark,' I say. 'The big dark.'

'It's just the sea, Gloria.' It makes me shiver and the boy knows I am scared and he holds my hand. Ah, yes. *The sea*. It is beautiful and big and loud and deep and dark. It would welcome you into it and make you part of it, if you let it. I feel the warmth of the boy's hand. It is comforting, yet when I look at my hand it doesn't look like mine. It has liver spots and ugly veins. It is old. His hand is young.

'I'm not afraid.' I say it as clearly and firmly as I can, because if I say it enough perhaps I can make it true.

I close my eyes again. I feel very tired, though I can't think why, when all I've done today is – well, you know. This and that.

'What have we been doing today?' I say to the boy.

'The wedding,' he says. 'Remember?'

'Hmmm,' I say, because I'm too tired to tell him that he's wrong. I close my eyes.

Further out is another girl. *She is Vivienne*, I think. *She is my daughter*, I think. Is that right? It seems right and not right. She is too far out, a long, long way out. She is just a tiny dot, but I don't feel worried. *No harm can come to her*, I think, and that thought makes me not sad. What is it when you smile? Oh well. The word doesn't matter. It is the smiling that matters.

When I open my eyes the boy has gone and I am sad for a moment but then I see him coming towards me with a glass. He gives it to me and I drink. The drink tickles when I drink it.

'It's the bubbles,' Ollie says, smiling.

'Did you see her?' I say to the boy. 'Vivienne, the little dark girl. Do you see her swimming? I'm sure I saw her.'

He smiles. 'Yes, I saw her.'

I can't remember why this makes me cry. It is the not-sad crying. It is because I love this boy, although I can't remember who he is. I can't even remember who I am really. Perhaps that makes loving easier. I have a feeling I was never much good at it before; it felt difficult. It is simple now. This boy is here and he is holding my hand and that is good.

'I had a son, I think,' I say to Ollie. 'You're not him, are you?'

'I'm Ollie,' he says. 'I'm your grandson, Gloria.'

'You're pulling my leg,' I say, because I am far too young to have grandchildren. But then I think time has become strange; it doesn't behave as it used to. It stretches like elastic and then snaps back, unravelling, so that you don't know where you are with it. It brings ghosts and dreams and sometimes you don't know which are real.

'No, really,' he says. 'In true life, Gloria.'

'Are you sure?'

He nods. 'And Alice and Hattie are your granddaughters.'

'Yes.' I smile. 'Hattie.' She is special, though I can't remember why. Sometimes who she is disappears when I reach for it. But that doesn't matter. I always know that she is special and what more do you need to know about a person than that?

'And Dylan is your great-grandson.'

I giggle. Perhaps I drank a little too much of the – you know what I mean. With the tickly bubbles, that makes you giggle.

'Now you're just being silly,' I say. 'Where's Gwen got to anyway? Is she with Mum? They should be here by now.'

I don't know where Father is either, but I don't bother asking. We always know where he is when he's not where he's supposed to be. At the Rose and Crown, that's where, drinking all his wages away. I just hope Mum doesn't send me down to get him.

'Don't worry,' the boy says. 'They're fine.'

He bends down and kisses me on the cheek. He smells of – what makes you clean. Soup? Not soup.

'Soap,' Ollie says. 'Look, here comes Hattie.'

The special girl who was by the sea comes up and hugs me and her cheek against mine makes me feel – I reach for the word but it floats away and I let it. It's the word for the feeling inside that is like the sun on my skin. Light. Shining. Warm. Those words are all wrong, but they are all right too.

'Hattie,' I say and I smile at her, and I don't want her name to slip away, so I say it again. 'Hattie.'

'Would you like some more champagne?' the boy says. 'I think the barbecue is nearly done too. Shall I get you a hot dog?'

A hot dog? I nod anyway.

'You were drinking champagne the first time I met you,' she says. 'Do you remember?'

'Yes!' I say, though I don't. 'I've always been fond of a drop of champagne.'

Have I? It sounds right.

'You told me off for drinking tea. You said that you didn't know why anyone would drink tea when there was perfectly good Bollinger on offer.'

We laugh, the special girl and me. It is a such a feeling to laugh and for someone else to laugh too, at the same time, about the same thing, so your laugh is one laugh. Such a *big* feeling. It is inside me but it is so big that it is outside me too. It is all around me. Not-sad.

'Let's go for a walk,' I say to the girl. 'Let's go and see . . .'

I point to the boy at the edge of the sea.

'Dominic,' I say. Of course! How could I forget his name?

'Dylan,' she says and I don't put her right. 'He's getting big, isn't he? Are you sure you'll be okay walking on the sand?'

I look at my feet and see that they are wearing the wrong shoes. They are those ugly shoes for old people, grey and comfortable.

'Whose shoes are these?' I say to the girl. 'These are not my shoes at all. I don't wear shoes like this!'

The girl looks at me and laughs but her face is – what is that thing? Watery. Sad and not-sad.

'No,' says Hattie. 'You don't. Shall we take them off?'

'Yes,' I say. So she takes them off and I stand up. The tickly bubbles have made everything a bit wobbly.

'Give me your hand,' I say to the girl. The stones are cold and hurt under my feet but it is better than the shoes that are not *my* shoes. They are shoes for someone else, and I am not someone else. Not at all. I am me.

I close my eyes and turn my face up to the sky to the warmth and light and it fills me up and I want to spin, round and round. I can feel how it would feel, the world whirling, my hair flying. 'Stop,' Mum says, but I never will, I will keep on for ever.

When I open my eyes, Mum has disappeared, although I know she can't be far away, and there is a girl there instead. She is special, though I can't remember why.

'I thought you were Mum,' I say. 'We were on the Common. I was dancing. She wanted me to stop.'

'I'm Hattie,' she says. 'I don't want you to stop.'

'Oh yes,' I say. 'Hattie.'

I lean on the girl, and she is strong.

'Come on,' she says. 'It's all right, I've got you.'

And slowly we walk down towards the deep, terrifying darkness, my old hand in her young one, together.

# Acknowledgements

Heartfelt thanks to my mum, who made the writing of this book possible in so many ways, from proofreading and advising on historical detail to childminding and generally being incredibly supportive. Thanks also to my dad, and of course to the rest of my family, David, Marianne, Joe and Ewan, for their support and patience.

Thank you to my editor, Jane Griffiths, for all her hard work and for getting me over the bumps in the road on this journey. I'm also very grateful to Laura Hough, Elisa Offord, Jade Westwood, Becky Peacock and the rest of the team at Simon and Schuster, and to Catherine Ward.

Thank you to Ingrid Selberg for believing in my writing.

Thank you to all the friends who have supported me while I've been writing this book.

Thank you to Deborah and Bob at Retreats for You for providing the flapjacks, wine and space I needed to get this book written.

Thank you to Faye Talbott for your generosity to Authors for Nepal.

Finally, enormous thanks to Catherine Clarke, who I feel incredibly lucky to have as my agent.